THE ANTHOLOGY OF ITALIAN-CANADIAN WRITING

Prose Series 52

The Anthology of Italian-Canadian Writing

Edited by Joseph Pivato

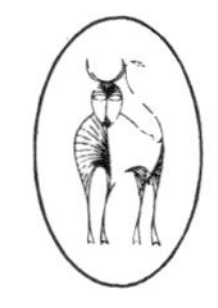

Guernica
Toronto·Buffalo·Lancaster (U.K.)
1998

Joseph Pivato, guest editor.
Guernica Editions Inc.
P.O. Box 117, Station P, Toronto (ON), Canada M5S 2S6
2250 Military Rd., Tonawanda, N.Y. 14150-6000 U.S.A.
Gazelle, Falcon House, Queen Square, Lancaster LR1 1RN U.K.

The Publisher gratefully acknowledges the financial support of The Canada Council and the Department of Canadian Heritage (Multiculturalism).
Typeset by Selina, Toronto.
Printed in Canada.

Legal Deposit — Fourth Quarter.
National Library of Canada
Library of Congress Card Number: 98-73309

Canadian Cataloguing in Publication Data
The anthology of Italian-Canadian writing
(Prose series ; 52)
ISBN 1-55071-069-9
1. Canadian literature (English) – Italian-Canadian authors.
I. Pivato, Joseph. II. Series.
PS8235.I8A58 1998 C810.8'0851 C98-900810-X
PR9194.5.I82A58 1998

Contents

Section Three: Ironies of Identity

Introduction

Joseph Pivato

Before the Beginning

When did Italian-Canadian writing begin? The first Italians to reach the shores of what is now Canada were explorers. Giovanni Caboto landed here in 1497 and was the first to write about what he saw. His capitain's log may have read something like this,"Today we found a new land. When we went ashore to claim our discovery we found great forests, some wild animals, but no people, though we did see smoke rising in the distance. Tomorrow we will explore inland and see if we can find the inhabitants of this country . . ." But since Caboto, later called John Cabot, was sailing for the king of England, Henry VII, he probably wrote these words in Latin, rather than in Italian, or English.

In 1524 another Italian explorer, Giovanni Da Verrazzano sailed for King Francis I of France and charted the east coast of North America, naming part of it Nuova Gallia and Nouvelle France. Da Verrazzano was probably the first to write down the words New France, thus naming the new territories of Canada in terms of European geography. Da Verrazzano wrote a long report in Latin on his voyage of discovery for King Francis I, *Codex de Cellere*, which still exists in libraries in the Vatican, Florence and New York. Da Verrazzano was killed by hostile Natives on his voyage in 1528; one of his crew members was Jacques Cartier who continued these French explorations on his own later voyages.

When we use the term Italian for these centuries of European history we must remember that the people living on the Italian penninsula were not a unified nation as France, England or Spain were at this time, but a collection of city states, principalities, papal states and territories often occupied by foreign powers like Spain, France and the Germans of the Holy Roman Emperor. Giovanni Caboto was a Venetian navigator. Venice had been an independent republic for several hundred years. Caboto was born in Genova like Colombo, but his family moved to Venice. Giovanni Da Verrazzano was from Florence like Amerigo Vespucci.

The first Italian visitor to Canada who wrote about his experiences in Italian for an Italian audience was Francesco Giuseppe Bressani, a Jesuit missionary who worked in New France.

Brief sections of his long work, *Breve Relatione* (1653), are included in this anthology and demonstrate Bressani's conscious effort to look at Canada and its Native people from an Italian perspective and with terms of reference that are Italian rather than French.

There were many Italian explorers and soldiers with the French in North America. In 1682 Enrico Tonti assisted Robert de La Salle to explore the Mississippi. In 1759 Francesco Carlo Burlamacchi was a general in the army of Montcalm during the battle of Quebec. There were Italian soldiers in the de Meuron Regiment and the Watteville Regiment who settled in Canada in 1816. Did any of these people write back to relatives and friends in Italy about their experiences in Canada? Descendants of these soldiers included Monsignor Paolo Bruchesi, Bishop of Montreal (1897-1939), and Quebec historian, Jean Bruchesi.

There were many Italian writers and many books by Italians living in Canada, but they did not constitute a conscious literature. Most were individual works produced by isolated writers who did not see themselves as creators of a new literature but as Italian writers in exile, or travellers or as writers in Canada who adopted the new language. Writers like A.A. Nobile and Anna Moroni were vistors to Canada, as was the inventor Marconi. Most of the poetry of Liborio Lattoni and Francesco Gualtieri has disappeared. In 1959 Mario Duliani wrote a book review of Elena Albani's Italian novel, *Canada, mia seconda patria*. This is the only extant evidence that there was a spark of an Italian writing community in Montreal. In the 1950s Italian language papers did flourish in both Toronto and Montreal, but there was little literary activity in these weekly periodicals. When Antonio Spada published his social history, *The Italians in Canada* (1969), he included a few pages on writers. Among the authors he described briefly are Mario Duliani, Elena Albani, John Robert Colombo, Jean Bruchesi, Guglielmo Vangelisti and a few birds of passage like Giose Rimanelli.

In the 1960s and 1970s the sons and daughters of the great post-war immigration from Italy started to attend univesities in Canada. This is also the period of the great awakening in Canadian nationalism reflected in English Canadian literature. Young Italian-Canadian writers were influenced by this spirit promoting cultural identity and diversity in Canada. In Quebec the 1960s is the time of the

Quiet Revolution and here too Italians become conscious of the search for cultural identity. For the first time a large group of university-educated young people provided the critical mass to create a community of writers, artists, filmmakers, musicians and academics.

This was also the time when historian, Robert Harney, began to publish his articles on the immigration of Italians to Canada and thus fostered more research in the social history of ethnicity. Harney's pioneering work encouraged a whole generation of young scholars to study the history of Italian settlement in Canada. These researchers included Franc Sturino, Bruno Ramirez, John Zucchi, Roberto Perin, Gabriele Scardellato and Franca Iacovetta; people who often worked with writers on conferences and publications devoted to the study of the Italian-Canadian community. One such historic event was an international conference on "Writing About the Italian Immigrant Experience in Canada" held in Rome in May, 1984, at the Canadian Academic Centre in Italy. The conference organizers, Roberto Perin and Franc Sturino later, edited a collection of papers from this meeting, *Arrangiarsi: The Italian Immigration Experience in Canada* (1989).

The Beginning of Italian-Canadian Literature

Italian-Canadian literature began with Pier Giorgio Di Cicco in about 1975. This writer was the first person to realize that the possibility for a distinct body of literature did exist in Canada. As an editor for the Ontario literary magazine, *Books in Canada*, Pier Giorgio became aware of a number of young writers of Italian background who were just then beginning to publish in literary magazines and with small presses. On November 5, 1976 Pier Giorgio Di Cicco wrote to me from Toronto: *I am preparing an anthology of Italo-Canadian poets . . . I'd be very pleased to consider a selection of your poetry for inclusion . . .*

I sent him some of my poems as did fifeen other writers from across Canada, and in the summer of 1978 *Roman Candles* was published. The experience was both exciting and shocking. We were happy with the reception of this first anthology of Italian-Canadian poetry, but we were shocked as well by the realization that we had discovered a literature about ourselves, and the great responsibility which this entailed. This is where Italian-Canadian literature begins: with a self-conscious realization about our writing. Di Cicco clearly articulates this self-awareness in the introduction to *Roman Candles*:

> In searching for contributors, I found isolated gestures by isolated poets, isolated mainly by the condition of nationalism prevalent in Canada in the last ten years. However pluralistic the landscape seemed to be to sociologists, the sheer force of Canadianism had been enough to intimidate all but the older "unofficial-language" writers. Some of the contributors I had already been aware of through their publishing efforts, but most came as a surprise; and finally, all involved were surprised by the anthology itself. It put a stop to the aforementioned isolationism (9).

A mere six years later Caroline Morgan Di Giovanni edited *Italian Canadian Voices* (1984), the first anthology of this writing, which tried to represent it as a body of literature. There were other anthologies which collected works from groups of writers: *La poesia italiana nel Quebec* (1983), edited by Tonino Caticchio, *Quetes: Textes d'auteurs italo-quebecois* (1983), edited by Caccia and D'Alfonso, and Dore Michelut's *A Furlan Harvest* (1993). The anthology you are now reading is in this tradition of service to the diverse communities of Canada: the English, the French, the Italian-Canadian and others. In this context of service we must also mention the founding of Guernica Editions by Antonio D'Alfonso which has published writers working in English, French and Italian, and has promoted translations among these languages.

These previous anthologies are evidence of the growth of groups of writers who became aware of their ethnic identity. In 1986 one group of writers in Vancouver, Dino Minni, Genni Gunn and Anna Foschi, organized the first national conference of Italian-Canadian writers. By the end of this historic meeting the Association of Italian-Canadian Writers was founded to promote the work of these writers and continue to foster a sense of community across the country.

This anthology is different from the previous ones in many ways. This volume is more inclusive than any previous collection as we will explain below. We include here two winners of Governor General Awards, Nino Ricci for English Fiction with *Lives of the Saints* (1990) and Fulvio Caccia for French poetry with *Aknos* (1994). Several of the other contributors have also won literary awards: Mary di Michele, Marco Micone and Antonino Mazza. This anthology tries to place all this writing in an historical context and tries to be sensitive to the linguistic diversity of the writers both to their Italian regional languages and to the languages of Canada.

Selecting the Texts for this Anthology

There are more than 120 writers of Italian background in Canada. Most publish in English, but a number use Italian or French, and a few use one of the other Italian languages such as Friulan. This anthology is meant to represent this growing body of literature and so I have limited my selections to writers who have previously been published, and primarily to those who have one or more books in print. In this way the anthology serves as a sample of their work and readers can be directed to seek out the other books by the authors. The selections were difficult to make among these many authors and even within the oeuvre of an individual artist: How do we choose from among the seven English novels of Frank Paci or the four Italian novels of Maria Ardizzi?

For many writers I have only selected a small sample of work, a mere taste, in the hopes that readers will want to read more.

I must also explain that while there are chapters from recently published novels like *Surface Tension* (1994) and *Infertility Rites* (1991), approximately 50% of the texts included here are not available in print or have never been published.

This anthology tries to be inclusive of a wide variety of writers and literary forms: there are authors from across Canada and who represent many regions of Italy. There is a writer who lives in the U.S.A., another in France and another who has returned to live in Italy. There is work by some historical figures such as Bressani, Lattoni, Duliani, Albani (Randaccio) and Grohovaz.

There is a great mixture of genres included here: various forms of poetry from narrative to haiku, short stories, prose poems, sketches, diaries, literary essays, scenes from plays, film scripts, scenes from novels, life-writing, a folktale and a political essay.

I must confess that as much as I tried to be inclusive I also had to make the difficult decision to leave out many, many writers. I am confident that these writers will be part of a future anthology of Italian-Canadian literature. In any case I mention many other writers and the titles of their works in notes, commentaries and the bibliography at the end of this volume.

This is an English language anthology. Most of the texts were originally written in English. Some of the works were originally written in French or Italian and are included here in English translation. All translations are identified with the name of the translator immeditely following the English text. Many of the texts have never been published before in English translation.

Many of these writers who were once invisible or forgotten are now the subjects of literary studies and theses in universities in Canada and Italy. There are now many critical articles on some of these writers in literary journals. It may be useful to mention some books which are devoted to the work of these writers: *Contrasts: Comparative Essays on Italian-Canadian Writing* (1985 and 1990), edited by Joseph Pivato, *Echo: Essays on Other Literatures* (1994) by Joseph Pivato, *Social Pluralism and Literary History* (1996), edited by Francesco Loriggio, *In Italics* (1996), by Antonio D'Alfonso, *The Power of Allegiances* (1997), by Marino Tuzi and *Devils in Paradise* (1997) by Pasquale Verdicchio.

The exercise of selecting also involves personal preferences. I tried to keep in mind what I thought readers might find interesting or stimulating to read. I also tried to be aware of what would move younger readers — in contrast to much popular entertainment saturated with the special effects of mass media. What stories and poems represent authentic experiences of real people in the Italian communities of Canada? In the end I hope that this anthology is a collection of good reading and an example of good taste.

Most of all I hope that you enjoy reading the selections in this anthology.

Edmonton, May, 1997

Editor's Note

I would like to thank all the many writers who send me material for this anthology. I would like to thank the writers, and their publishers, who gave me permission to use the selected texts. In some cases we were not able to locate the copyright holder of a given text. We would be happy to acknowledge these persons in future reprintings of this anthology. Previously published material is identified in the brief biography of each author at the end of this anthology.

I would like to thank the Multiculturalism program, Department of Canadian Heritage, for the grant in support of this project. I would like to recognize the support of Athabasca University for my work in ethnic minority writing. And finally I would like to thank Emma Pivato for her faith in my many endeavours. I am also grateful to the publisher, Antonio D'Alfonso, for his support and help.

Writers from Our Past

1653 to 1953

Much less has been said of emigration's impact on the people's morale, and the reasons for this are significant. First, having seen the harm done by racists and restrictionists and, later, by a few insensitive social scientists, the historian is disinclined to emphasize the disruptive and pathological aspects of sojourning. It is far safer to describe it as simply the first step in the journey to assimilation or as an orderly advance by means of which families and villages adjust traditions in order to maintain their commonwealth. However, not since the turn-of-the-century debate on emigration in Italy . . . has the Italian migrant himself been at the centre of study.

Robert F. Harney,
Men Without Women

FRANCESCO GIUSEPPE BRESSANI

Proemio

I successi funesti e gloriosi insieme delle Missioni della Nuova Francia, paese dell'Amercia . . .

The sad and glorious events of the Missions in New France, a country in North America, have up to now been known only within the confines of old France since every year they have been recorded only in the French language. On the other hand they deserve to be known everywhere and merit being communicated in a language that might be understood where French is not current.

This has been, and is, the wish of many people, full of holy zeal and curiosity to learn about the progress of the Faith in these new lands. And to please them . . . I allowed myself to be convinced . . . to make a sketch, or rather to present an essay with as much simplicity and brevity as possible. I do not pretend to tell about everything, but only to give a rough notion, particularly of the Missions among the Hurons . . .

ᔕᔕ

The Location and Founding of New France

It is a part of the great land of North America about three thousand miles distant from Europe in a direct line as we have observed by various stars. It is located in a temperate zone but has a climate of great extremes: a winter of severe cold, deep snow and hard ice and a summer no less hot than Italy *[l'estate caldi non minori di quelli dell'Italia]*.

The first French who lived here thought the cause for such extreme cold (for nearly four months every liquid freezes, which among other things, makes it impossible to write, unless you hold your pen very close to the fire) was the very vast forests which cover the whole land.

ʚɞ

From experience, I can say, that the scarcity of rain and the dry air are very healthy. During the sixteen and more years in which the Huron Missions have lasted, where we have seen as many as sixty Europeans, many of whom were of weak constitution, not one has died of natural causes.

And this despite the great inconveniences and suffering as we shall see. In Europe, on the other hand few are the years in which some one does not die in our Colleges if their members are numerous. So as the Latin saying goes, "Humidity is always corrupting and on the contrary dryness is healthy." It is because of this, perhaps, besides the change of diet, that the Natives find it difficult to get used to the damp air of Europe . . . The very cold winds come from the nearby mountains, which cross the whole country as the Apennines do Italy.

ʚɞ

Some believe that these lands were previously discovered by the Spaniards from whom they got the name Canada, as if they meant to say *ha nada*, there is nothing but forests.

But we are certain that the French took possession of this territory for the first time in 1504. From them it got the name New France, without losing the name Canada, which some like to apply to the more northern parts.

ꙮ

Kebec is 120 miles further inland and is a fortress of the French which commands the River Saint Lawrence. It is constructed on its bank upon a mountain at the narrowest point in the river which is about a mile wide. Here there is a French colony, and recently a Huron settlement, and the Native group called Algonquins spend several months a year here before going on their hunt.

ꙮ

The Country of the Hurons

The Country of the Hurons is part of New France . . . In the direction of the western sunset there is a lake of 1200 miles in circumference, which we call "the fresh water sea" . . . It has innumerable islands and among them one 200 miles in circumference inhabited by a tribe of Natives they call Ondatauauat. To the west along the shores of this lake was a nation which we called "Tobacco," because the plant grew there in abundance.

ꙮ

There is a lake about 600 miles in circumference called Herie, formed by the fresh water sea which flows into it, and then by way of a very high falls it flows into a third lake, greater and more beautiful, called Ontario or Beautiful Lake, but we wanted to call it Lake St. Louis.

ʚɞ

But the Hurons and the other peoples far from the sea who are settled hunt only for recreation, or for extraordinary reasons. They have no bread, no wine, no salt, no meat, no vegetables nor other foods common in Europe. They are content with Turkish corn cooked in pure water, or when possible, flavoured with some fish or fresh meat, or smoked, without salt or other seasoning. They sow this corn in the fields which they cultivate. They also planted some fava beans and small beans after our arrival. The clothing of the men is free and light. With the exception of a certain tribe of Algonquins, all cover that which decency requires. The women are more covered; the Huron women, even at home, cover from the waist to the knee. The Algonquin women are covered more than very religious women in Europe. This clothing is usually made of various animal skins sewen together in pieces five or six hands square. At night they serve as blankets.

ʚɞ

The women wear their hair tied in a single braid and let it fall behind their shoulders. The men wear their hair in various ways: some shave half the head, others shave it all leaving here and there some tufts of hair. The most common style is to leave the hair very long. Others leave it straight as bristles in the middle or on the forehead. From this hair the first Frenchmen gave our Natives the name of Hurons, from the *hure,* the straight tufts of hair like the bristle of the boar which they wore on their head; this is what hure means in French. As a common rule they all have black hair, and hate curls which are very rare among them, if they exist at all.

ꙮ

The Goverment of the Hurons

These people have neither King nor absolute Prince. Rather they have certain ones, like the heads of a Republic whom we call Captains, different though from those in a war. These commonly hold office by succession on the side of their mothers, or sometimes by election. They take office on the death of their predecessor (whom they say they reincarnate). These Chiefs have no force of will over their people. Even fathers do not exercise force over their sons in order to correct them since they use only words. Thus, the more the sons get older the more they love and respect their fathers. Therefore the former and the latter obtain everything by means of entreaties, exhortations and eloquence . . .

Indeed there were some virtues so common among them they did not value them as such. One of these was a great hospitality. They welcomed every vistor to their house, never driving him away, instead serving and giving him food like any family member, without asking for any payment. They also demonstrate an invincible patience in trials; a fortitude in accepting the worst news such as the death of a loved one. They have an imperturbable tranquility when injured by countrymen, even in the case of personal loss . . .

1653

Translation by Joseph Pivato

Note

In the 1880s there is evidence of Italian visitors to Canada who write about their experiences. The earliest English account by traveller Antonio Gallenga, *Episodes of My Second Life* (1884), includes a chapter on his teaching year in Windsor, Nova Scotia. In Toronto A.A. Nobile published *An Anonymous Letter, Una lettera anonima* (1885), a bilingual novel with English and Italian on facing pages. Anna Moroni Parken produced *Emmigranti: Quattro anni al Canada* (1896). One of the most interesting books is by Francesco Mario Gualtieri, a brief social history of Italians in Canada, *We Italians: A Study in Italian Immigration in Canada,* published in Toronto in 1928 by the Italian World War Veterans' Association.

Liborio Lattoni

Winter Night

Outdoors, the howling wind is sibilant,
Shaking the trees like gallows-skeletons
That rattle sinisterly
With desperate, low moanings

And in the squalid silence of my room
The melancholy winter night descends.
I sit beside the fire,
Staring in meditation.

This heavy shadow that enfolds my heart
And shrouds the inmost powers of my being,
Gnawing my spirit's vitals —
Ah, will it never vanish?

This bitter midnight of the stricken soul,
Freezing the spirit as the frost the body,
Who will dispel it from me?
When will the sun return?

Outdoors, the howling wind is sibilant,
Shaking the trees; the squalid night of winter
Presses with cold relentless —
Yet do I trust in summer!

1935

Mario Duliani

The City Without Women

The train travels at full speed through the first light of dawn.

I think of the imminent return of millions and millions of men, who were like us separated from their families for months, for years! How will they find their homes? Their wives? Their loved ones?

This will be tomorrow's drama.

The train travels full speed under the burning rays of the midday sun.

I think that events and the human species repeat themselves in an eternal beginning.

If we could accelerate time, as in the movies, speed up the centuries into seconds, we might be surprised to see the same men reappearing over and over on the screen, performing the exact same feats throughout time!

I think of the Germans who have allowed themselves to be perverted by bad philosophers, and who four centuries after the cataclysmic Reformation, have repeated an experience as radical and as profound as the first — no longer on the religious question this time, but on the matter of race. And with identical and indomitable will to rule.

The train travels at full speed.

I open the notes that I have made in this journal over the past forty months and read at random what I've written.

I begin to deny everything I have written. Usually, when we reread what we've written, at a certain distance, we realize that we no longer think the same thoughts. Still, this doesn't mean that we did not think them once.

The interest of a personal journal may consist precisely in that it shows a sequence of successive truths. Journals of this kind are like a series of instant photographs. Here the image resembles us, there it does not. Or, if this photograph no longer resembles us, it once did resemble us.

Perhaps because we are an evolving series of different people.

The train speeds into the dusk that gathers over the Quebec countryside. Eagerly, I watch from the window this land that now becomes familiar once more, to whose features my sensibility adapts easily.

Night returns.

The train, with deafening sound, pas ses through tiny towns illuminated by electric bulbs in front of which people's shadows appear like Chinese lanterns. They are small localities whose names ring in my ear with supple intimacy.

Finally the train enters a majestic station spilling over with cries, with incessant movement, with comings and goings.

Montreal!

I step on the ground. The fatigue of thirty-six hours without sleep has miraculously vanished, dispelled by the joy of mixing together with women, with children, with other men, who have unconstrained lives. It is consoling to find oneself among secure friendships. Freedom is an inebriating joy!

While the automobile races through the streets of the metropolis I see myself again as I was two nights ago, down there in my barrack.

Two days! The passage from Life to Death would not have been so long. But here it is my return from Death to Life.

Translated by Antonino Mazza

Elena Maccaferri Randaccio

Ricordo bene quella sera

I remember very well that night. I had just put the children to bed and was finishing up in the kitchen when I heard a knock on the door. When I opened it I found two policemen. They asked if Beppe was home.

"Yes." Beppe answered and came to the door.

They said Beppe had to go with them. I told them that he could go tomorrow. No, right away they insisted. And so they brought him away, and I remained alone in the house for the first night since we got married. I could not sleep, I was cold and had a strange fear. Then for days I tried to find out where he was and what they wanted with him. When I was able to talk to an official he told me that Beppe had carried the banner during a Fascist rally in Montreal. They wanted to hold him for security reasons. And so he was sent to an internment camp. So was his cousin, Ciccio and many, many other men who were Fascist supporters. We did not know when they would be coming back.

I found myself alone and I understood that with two children, the cows, the chickens, the pigs and the fields I could never run the farm on my own. The farm produced well in those days, and for a few days I tried desperately to manage on my own. The neighbours came to give me a hand.

Someone cared for the children, someone else milked the cows, another collected the eggs. But it was like trying to empty a lake with a glass. It was easier to rent the farm out. I didn't want to sell it even for a good price. In fact I wanted Beppe to find everything as he had left it. I was born a country girl and knew that the land would never let me down. And I had two children to inherit the land.

With a lump in my throat, a fist full of dollars and a lot of good will we left for the city of Montreal. Because of the children I could not go out to work. So I rented two rooms and tried to do work from home. I tried various jobs from seamstress to hairdresser, to sewing on uniform insignia. I was able to save a little money.

Ciccio came home after a year and convinced me to put the kids in the daycare run by the nuns, and he found me work in a restaurant. I got good tips and after a few months I was promoted to the cash register. Many months went by . . .

I was thirty-eight years old, Rosa seven and Dino six. They went to school nearby. I learned that Beppe would soon be coming home. We now owned a farm and a motel. But I was not really at peace. Maybe for this reason I always worked so hard; I had seen many sunrises and worked 'til the stars came out. If I stopped working a long pain would grab my heart, a pain which came from many problems and from nothing. Then I felt I was a stranger to myself, to my children and to the place where I lived. And I was not satisfied with my life. And when I learned that Beppe would return I no longer understood why, after having waited for him so long, I felt so full of anxiety.

One morning Ciccio asked me, "Are you coming to Montreal with me to pick him up?"

"No," I answered, "I'll wait for him at home."

"I'll bring him home to you," Ciccio assured me.

And Beppe arrived home with all of Ciccio's family.

I had dressed up the kids in their good clothes. I had put on my best outfit. I had prepared tortellini and chicken for everyone. And we had spumante.

Beppe looked well. He had put on some weight. In the camp he had worked as a lumberjack and had built up an appetite. He had callused hands and a face burned by sun and wind. In fact, he had changed little from the time he had left. Instead, I had changed a lot, he said to me after we first embraced.

"You have the bearing of a real lady . . . I recognized the kids from their pictures, but you I did not recognize."

"You will get to know me again," I tried to reassure him.

Translated by Joseph Pivato

Note

These scenes are from *Diario di une emigrante* which appeared under the pen-name E. MacRan.

Gianni Grohovaz

Quando me meto a scriver queste robe

Quando me meto a scriver queste robe
Non lassario mai piu'
Cascar la pena,
Eco perche' difizile xe ciuder
Quest' umile pensiero a Fiume mia . . .

Ritornaremo ancora nel Quarnero?
Non xe soltanto una speranza magra
Ma la certeza de chi crede sempre
Che tuto quel che noi butemo in aria
Deve tornar per forza su la tera.

When I begin to write these things

When I begin to write these things
I can no longer
Put down the pen
That is why it is difficult to end
This humble thought about my Fiume . . .

Will we return again to Quarnero?
It's not just a meager hope
But a certainty of those who believe always
That all that we throw up into the air
Must come back down to earth.

Translated by Joseph Pivato

More Italian Language Writers in Canada

There are many more Italian language writers in Canada, both past and present, than I can include in this anthology. Rather than attempt and fail to do justice to them through the inclusion of a few more representative excerpts I have chosen to chronicle the work of as many as possible in the following pages. I do not pretend to include all of them here since there are some who have never come to my attention or whose work has gone lost such as the poetry books of Francesco Gualtieri. I would not include in such a list the book, *Biglietto di terza* (1958), by Giose Rimanelli since he only stayed in Canada a short time.

One of the senior writers is Camillo Menchini in Montreal who produced many books of history including: *Giovanni Caboto, scopritore del Canada* (1974), *Giovanni da Verrazzano e la Nuova Francia* (1977) and *Francesco Giuseppe Bressani, primo missionario italiano in Canada* (1980). The first attempt at a complete history of Italians in Canada is Guglielmo Vangelisti's *Gli Italiani in Canada* (1956). In Toronto historian Luigi Pautasso published *Il Santo cappuccino di Toronto* in 1990.

One of the most common genre's is the memoir or personal history of the immigrant experience. Giuseppe Ricci's *L'orfano di padre* (1981) is a personal account of his life beginning in 1907, his immigration to Canada in 1927 to 1944. Another autobiography is *La dottoressa di Cappadocia* (1982) by Toronto doctor, Matilde Torres. In Ottawa Anello Castrucci put his life story in a novel-like narrative with *I miei lontani pascoli* (1984). In Montreal, Aldo Gioseffini produced, *L'amarezza della sconfitta,* a mixture of personal memoir and political commentary.

Jos Mingarelli helped Andrea Masci publish his *Diario di un povero soldato* (1996).

In the narrative by Dino Fruchi, *Il prezzo del benessere* (1988), we have real life experiences disguised in a novel form. In this tradition of realism and social criticism we have the novels of Giuseppe Ierfino, *L'orfano di Cassino* (1990) and *Il cammino dell'emigrante* (1992). In Montreal Ermanno La Riccia brought out a collection of short stories about the experiences of immigrants caught between Italy and Canada, *Terra mia* (1984). Guelph's Gianni Bartocci has produced a number of books which deal with his years in exotic New Zealand; however his North American short stories are in a literary collection *La riabilitazione di Galileo* (1980). Another world traveller is Camillo Carli who wrote the novel *La giornata di Fabio* (1984). The editor of *Vice Versa* magazine, Lamberto Tassinari produced *Durante la partenza* (1985). In the genre of childrens' fiction we have Elettra Bedon *Ma l'estate verra ancora* (1985).

The other genre which is chosen by Italian writers in Canada is social commentary. One of the earliest, *Non dateci lenticchie* (1962), by Ottorino Bressan makes pointed criticism of social conditions in Canada. This tradition of social critique was practiced by Gianni Grohovaz as a journalist. Benito Framarin examines personal morality with *I cattivi pensieri di Don Smarto* (1986). The trials and tribulations of working at a private Italian school in Toronto are captured in Giuseppe Ranieri's book, *Intervista Professore* (1996).

The books of Italian poetry are too numerous to list; however, I will mention a few which have struck me as interesting. One of the earliest is *Tristezza* (1961) by Baldassare Savona who returned to Italy. Typical of his poems is this one called "In Canada":

> Furon quattro anni,
> quattr'anni di gran pene.
> quattr'anni lunghi penosi e tormentosi,
> in questo selvo Canada e la gente,
> s'ignorante, incolta e materiale,
> pesava sempre piu su le mie spalle:
> con quello, loro fare si barbarico,
> e con l'ipocrisia loro maetra.
>
> It has been four years
> Four years of hard labour
> Four long years of trouble and torment
> In this wild Canada and the people
> So ignorant, uncultured and materialistic
> Weighed more and more on my shoulders
> With their very barbaric ways,
> And with hypocrisy their teacher.
>
> *Translated by Joseph Pivato*

It is not clear here if Savona is criticising English Canadians, Italian immigrants in Canada, or both. The poem also captures in an unvarnished way the snobbery and sense of superiority sometimes found among the better educated immigrants from Europe.

In contrast to Savona's negative attitude are the many books of poems which try to explore the simple feelings of newcomers to the New World. Montreal has the most active group of writers beginning with Tonino Caticchio who wrote poems in Roman dialect, *Rugantino* (1982), *La storia de Roma* (1981), *La scoperta der Canada* (1980), and edited the bilingual anthology, *La poesia italiana nel Quebec* (1983). Among the younger writers included in this Quebec anthology is Giovanni di Lullo who produced *Il fuoco della pira* (1976) and the trilingual Filippo Salvatore with *Tufo e gramigna* (1977). Lisa Carducci also writes in French, but one of her best books is her Italian work, *L'ultima fede* (1990). One of the senior poets of the Montreal group is Corrado Mastropasqua who collected his Neopolitan poems in *Ibrido: poesie 1949-1986* (1988).

Toronto has a variety of writers. The modest little collection by the ninety-year old Vito Papa, *Poesie del carpentiere* (1976), includes a poem in Calabrian dialect. Antonio Filippo Corea's first collection, *I passi* (1981), is all in Italian but his second book, *Per non finire* (1986) includes many Calabrian poems. Using the pen-name Bepo Frangel, Father Ermanno Bulfon published *Un friul vivut in Canada* (1977), a collection of his poems in the Friulan language. In Montreal Doris Vorano published the unique *Puisis e riflessions* (1983). The work of five Friulan women was collected in *A Furlan Harvest* (1993), edited by Dore Michelut and featuring the Friulan poems of Rina Del Nin Cralli. In Ernesto Carbonelli's *Fieno secco* (1990), each poem has an Italian commentary.

In Burlington Anthony M. Buzzelli produced *The Immigrant's Prayer* (1994), a bilingual collection of short poems. Windsor's Maria Agnese Letizia in D'Agnillo published 172 poems in *Cento poesie molisane . . . plus* (1992). In Hamilton, Ontario, Franco De Santis produced *Sotto Vento* (1990) and *L'impronto del tempo* (1991). In Sarnia Anthony Barbato published his bilingial collection of poems, *Acque chiare, Clear Waters* (1989).

We do not often think of Western Canada as a space for Italian language writing. For decades the paper, *L'Eco d'Italia*, has appeared in Vancouver and has promoted Italian writers and artists. One of these prolific authors is Romano Perticarini who has three books of poetry, all with the English translation on facing pages: *Quelli della fionda* (1981), *Il mio quaderno di Novembre* (1983) and *Via Diaz* (1989). Carlo Toselli produced two trilingual collections of his Italian poetry by including both English and French translations: *Lo specchio di peltro* (1993) and *La fanciulla di terracotta* (1996). Stories of Italian pioneers in British Columbia were collected by Giovanni Bitelli and Anna Foschi in *Emigrante* (1985). In Edmonton Silvano Zamaro wrote, *Autostrada per la luna* (1987). In Winnipeg Carmine Coppola published *Poesie per Giulia* (1996).

One of the early pioneers of Western Canada was Giorgio Pocaterra who arrived in Alberta in 1904 and began to establish the Buffalo Head Ranch in the Kananaskis Valley near the mountains west of Calgary. The Rocky Mountains reminded George of the Italian Alps near his birth place of Rocchette. Though fluent in Italian and some Indian languages George chose to write in English, always inspired by the landscape of Kananskis country:

Kananaskis Lakes
Carry me back
To Kananaskis shores
Its magic waters
And its changing moods
Majestic mountains
And foaming waterfalls
Enfolded softly
By mystic moods!

Writers for Our Time

Within the patriarchal framework of the family, Italian women performed demanding roles as immigrants, workers, wives and mothers. Their active commitment to the family helped bridge the move from Old World to New as women's labour, both paid and unpaid, continued to help ensure the survival and material well-being of their families. The transition from *contadina* (peasant) to worker did not require a funadmental break in the values of women long accustomed to conributing many hours of hard labour to the family. As workers, though, they confronted new forms of economic exploitation . . .

Franca Iacovetta
"From *Contadina* to Worker"

Caterina Edwards

(Back) Water

On the first day of his journey, Nino awakens to the sound of his mother's voice. The bedroom door is closed, but her voice and its hysterical tone carries from the kitchen. "No way. There's no way to reach Venice." And then, in a different, almost satisfied tone: "He'll miss his train. *È un segno*, a sign that he should not go."

Nino pulls his pillow up around his ears. He tenses, stretches. Already the heat is cloying, the heavy linen sheet damp with his sweat. "Goodbye," he thinks, "*Via, via, via.*"

"A country of possibilities," said the official in Rome. "Canada is wide open. For the right man, well, the sky is the limit." He spoke by rote, his face tight. "Space in every sense."

Flipping on his back, he finds himself cocooned by the indestructible sheets that were part of his mother's dowry. He is thrashing his way out when his mother, after one perfunctory knock, enters the room. "The vaporetti went off this morning. *Sciopero*, another strike. You can't count on anything these days." She flips open the shutters. "No way to Venice. All that money. You'll miss the plane. I knew. I knew this trip was a bad idea. It's an omen." She lays the tray on his knees.

"Last time."

"Who else will look after you like your mother? Who? And you have to run off to the other side of the world. Try that jam. Your sister discovered it at the Standa. Can you get a refund? All that money. And no way."

"Mamma, there are lots of ways."

The cheapest involves his brother-in-law, Gianni, and Gianni's boat, a dilapidated vessel with a small outboard motor. This way to Venice has an added appeal; it is impossible for his friends, girl or mother to accompany him. He will be spared an extended lachrymose scene at the station.

On the banks of the narrow canal that runs behind the apartment building, the goodbyes are less urgent, looser. His mother fusses over the positioning of the suitcases in the boat, periodically ordering Gianni to rearrange them. His sister talks and talks. A neighbour hangs out of a third floor window. *"Buona fortuna!"*

A couple of friends, who have already drank a multitude of toasts to his journey, wander by. "*Bravo, Nino*," says one.

"He'll show them what's what," says the other. Giacomo and Paolo were first his schoolmates, and then his companions at university, following Nino from classroom highjinks to drug lowjinks, from girl tasting to politic making, or as Giacomo liked to say, from stink bombs to sex bombs to the real thing. Although, while they followed Nino to the demonstrations, they did not follow him to platforms, microphones, gestetners or into a splinter group like *Lotta Continua*. So they never got close to what they called 'the real thing,' which is why they aren't leaving and Nino is.

His girl, Daniela, stands a bit apart under one of the willow trees, pouting and pulling the top of her white dress away from her skin. The heat is thick, jamlike. They are all sweating.

"Where's your hat? You must have a hat," his mother says. "With this sun. Luisa run up and find his hat."

"Mamma, look at those clouds coming in."

"*Luisa.* The hat. Nino, it is just for awhile, isn't it? You said . . ."

"A little while. Till I make my fortune. Or until things die down here. Whichever comes first."

He begins the rounds of hugs and kisses. His mother has started to cry. Luisa, settling the hat on his head, is damp-eyed. His girl smiles through her tears. "You bastard. You know you'll regret it later. Realize what you gave up."

"But, I'm not giving you up." He places a kiss behind her ear, then traces a trail down her neck.

"Nino, the time." His mother almost taps him on the shoulder. He moves through the second round quickly.

Space, endless plains, grasses as high as a man and the water: glacial, pure.

He jumps. The engine string is pulled, the boat begins to move. On the bank, they wave and call out, "*Addio.*" His mother wipes her eyes and frowns at Daniela who has already turned and is walking away.

"That was easy," he tells Gianni. "*Ciao, arrivederci.* Done."

The boat clears the narrow canal and begins following the Lido shore. Behind the boat, the Lido narrows into a sand bar, gives way to Malomocco, to Pellestrina where he lived as a child, to Chioggia where he was born and from where his father sailed to fish the Adriatic. To their left, the Armenian monastery and the Islands of Sorrows Ahead, the cypresses on San Francesco nel Deserto, the bone piles of San Michele, and tucked far into a corner of the dead lagoon, Valle del Dragosolo, the fish farm where his father went to work after the fish of the sea grew scarce.

"Like the lagoon." Gianni stares at the horizon as he talks.

"What?"

"*Addio*. Easy, smooth."

"Well, I *am* off." Nino says.

"It's too bad you got caught that time at the university. With your little friends. When you were having your bit of fun." Gianni is still staring at the horizon.

"You understand nothing. It was an occupation, not a bit of fun. It was a political action," Nino says.

"Oh, of course. What else? But they didn't use that word in the paper. Vandalism, I think they said."

"And who owns that paper? Whose interest does it represent? God Almighty, you're a worker. You know how things work in this country. That's what we were trying to change."

"And now you're leaving. Because you didn't do anyone any good, especially not yourself." Gianni still won't look at him. "As you found out when you tried to get a job above that of a hotel clerk."

Nino is tempted to tell Gianni that it was not actions but words that caused his problems: words written in excitement and bravado, words written when it seemed Italy must and would change. He was encouraged and, now he thinks, confused by certain professors. But what was the use of drawing out the argument? And Gianni was right in saying he hadn't done himself any good. While those professors, they still had their positions. They were still comfortable. "It's my version of going to sea. A family tradition of sorts. And I'll be back," Nino says, believing he will be. "I'm not leaving Venice for good."

"Back with booty? I always liked those Chinese vases your great grandfather brought back. What sort of booty do they have in Canada?"

Slow, easygoing Gianni. "A good man," all the women in the family would say, always ready to help. "A good man." Though Luisa would sport the odd black eye or bracelet of bruises.

"What is it with her?" Nino asked his mother. And the habitual bustle did stop; she hesitated for a long moment.

"Ask her. She might tell you."

But Luisa didn't. "My little brother, whose backside I cleaned, worried." She laughed. "I'm a big girl, remember?"

Gianni's hands on the tiller are thick, blunt. If he grabbed those hands? If he shouted into that round face. "My sister is not clumsy. My sister . . . You . . ." Rock not just this boat. If he could puncture the outer calm, bring forth the anger, expose it. He tries to imagine Gianni's face contorted, the two of them scuffling over the suitcases. Ridiculous. And if the boat tipped? He remains on the middle plank, suppressing a smile, looking ahead.

And there, through the glittering expanse of reflected heat and sun, the city hovers. Retreats. The boat is pulling back.

"Where are we going? We'll be late . . . Gianni, for Christ's sake . . . " He answers only by a slight gesture of the head at a white figure on the landing: Daniela.

She calls out. "Ayyi, sailors. Give a poor girl a ride." Her stance, hands on hip, legs braced and head tilted back, is as studied as her words. When the boat pulls up, she changes tone. "I fooled you, didn't I? You thought you'd seen the end of me."

"There's no room. The boat will sink," Nino tells her. He does not extend her a hand. Gianni does.

"Don't be silly." She settles in beside him. "I'm just a wraith of a thing."

"We should hurry." Nino points up at an approaching mass of cloud. Gianni opens the throttle. The engine backfires, sputters and the boat creeps out in to the canal.

"Did you have a car waiting?"

"I could have walked. I've been waiting ages. In this damned heat. Giacomo gave me a ride in his motor launch."

"You could have offered the launch and solved the problem."

She pushes her left thigh, knee to hip, against his right one. "I know how you feel about my snotty friends." She walks two fingers up his side, pinches his damp shirt and holds it away from his back. The heat has piled up with the clouds, weighing weighing down. She begins to whisper the usual questions in his ear: did he love her? Would he forget her?

(It had taken three solid months before she let him lay his hands on her breast, six more until she fully surrendered. And then he discovered she was experienced, more experienced that he.) "Of course, I do. And I won't." She stretches her mouth and aspirates his whole ear. He pulls away embarrassed at his obvious reaction but Daniela hangs on with her teeth. Gianni smirks.

Space, endless plains, grasses . . .

Goodbye, goodbye, goodbye.

Beside them, close, too close, a snub nosed *bragozzo*, sails of red and burnt orange, decorated in the old way, a black heart split open by a black wedge. The two men standing on the broad stern call out rudely in Chioggioto dialect.

"Daniela, we aren't alone, please," and when she still hangs on, her tongue busy exploring, Nino grabs her arm.

"Ouucch." The men are still gesturing, leaning out over the lagoon and gesturing, but the *bragozzo* is sailing away as quickly and silently as it came. "What are they saying?"

"Guess, *testa di zucca*."

"I could tell you," says Gianni.

"The wind is picking up."

"At last." Daniela spreads out her arms and throws back her head. "A breath of air."

Above, the charcoal grey clouds are about to break. Below, the waves build. The boat rises and falls. The spume first caresses and then needles.

"Can't we go faster?" says Nino.

"I'm getting soaked." Daniela's arms are no longer extended around Nino. She is hugging herself.

"Slow and steady," says Gianni, "gets you there every time."

Venice is veiled in spray and even the *bricole* are blurred. The waves are splashing over the side of the stubby boat. The water sloshes around the suitcases and their feet. "We're too heavy. I knew it," says Nino. And to Daniela, "You and your bright ideas."

"Listen, *stupido*, this is not my fault. Throw in one of your suitcases, if you're so frightened."

There is no other boat to be seen. The lagoon is a grey empty expanse. "You always have to have your way, spoiled little rich girl."

Gianni hands him a child's yellow beach bucket. "Bail." The rain begins, but their clothes are already soaked.

Daniela is huddled at the front of the boat. Her wet dress is almost transparent, outlining her high breasts. "I feel sick."

She manages to hang on, all three of them manage, until they reach Piazza San Marco and enter the shelter of the Canal Grande. There, surrounded by palaces, gondolas, and vegetable boats, there, she vomits into the slimy water. As the boat threads its way up the serpentine canal, the rain thins, then stops. Nino opens a suitcase, exchanging his wet shirt for a dry one. He gives Daniela a sweater, pulling it gently over her head.

"Come, sit beside me." He puts one arm around her shivering shoulder, his other hand caressing her face. (Goodbye.)

She catches his hand, pulls the palm to her lips. "But what will you do there?"

Nino was seven years old when the family left Chioggia. His mother was happy to leave, although she, like his father, had lived there all her life. "I was tired of the stink of fish," she would say. "The very streets were paved with fish scales. And I was more than tired of sitting outside my door, with all the other women, gossiping, mending the nets, waiting for the sea to bring back my husband." When his father started working on the ferryboats, they moved to Pellestrina, but it proved too ramshackle. "Empty of everything but sand," his mother pronounced though they had aunts, uncles and cousins there. "I left Chioggia to get away from Poverty and Ignorance." Her voice capitalized both words. After their father began working in the Valle, they found an apartment on the Lido. It was too far for his father to come home, except on weekends, but they were used to his being away.

Nino was twelve before he visited the *Valle*. (His father died the next year.) And that one visit took several weekends of negotiation. "Don't get it into your head that he's going to follow in your footsteps. I want more for my son," said his mother.

"He could do worse. It's steady. And I don't have to kiss anyone's hand. '*Sì, signore; no, signore.*' *Pah!* That's your move," said his father.

"Don't you go giving yourself airs. You're humble enough. It's not your *valle*."

At first, Nino was to go the long way round, by land — "What can happen on a bus?"— but then his father secured him a ride on the supervisor's motor launch. And such a ride, all noise and waves, heading not straight for the horizon, no, even such a shiny, golden oak wonder of a boat had to respect the shoals and currents of the lagoon, but at least seeming to follow no preordained path, yes, seeming to cut a new way. The supervisor, big-nosed and curly-haired, stood at the wheel pointing to the lost islands as they passed, shouting their names. "Torcello, Saint'Ariano. Used to be cities, Mazzorbo. It comes from *major urbs*, understand? Major centres. And now: ruins, water weeds. That one, over there, when the people moved, they took their houses with them. Now it's a bonehouse. Just lizards and bones."

He continued to lecture Nino when they reached the Valle, though he switched from the historical to the biological: tides, salinity, pollution, plankton and water temperature, and he paused politely, benignly, to acknowledge Nino's father, standing on the small wooden dock. His father repeated many of these facts, as he guided Nino past the ponds of carp, slow, stolid with only the odd gold flash; of sole, the water heaved white then dark; the pools of trout, layer over layer of shuddering silver, a sudden leap, and open jaw and Nino stepped back trembling.

"You scared?" His father's words flowed not smoothly but in clots. "We got control here. Order." Then, "There are worse jobs . . . You're young but you can start thinking . . ."

Years later Nino wished he had asked his father about the routine, the constraints. Did he ever regret taking shelter? Did he long for the open sea? The shifting horizons, the uncertainty, the taste of salt (existence on the tip of the tongue)?

The eel tank was last; his father was sending him home with a trophy. He bent fearlessly over that dark water so full of twisting and toiling life. His hands plunged in and pulled out a fat, slithering specimen. He held it with one hand, the other lifted the blade.

Chop, the head fell, chop, black skin, white flesh, chop, chop, neat, even slices. "Here," he thrust the plastic bag at Nino. "Your mother will be pleased."

Nino was waiting for the bus when the pieces began to seethe; movement in memoriam.

The immigration officer at the Edmonton airport is courteous. Nino's papers are in order. But the smiling customs lady gives him a yellow card instead of a pink one.

Nino is tired; he has not slept since his mother woke him the day before, and he does not know where he will sleep that night. He is disoriented. When he closes his eyes for a second, he sees an endless corridor and, then, stairs leading nowhere. Where is he to go? The lady points, repeating her instructions more loudly. He thanks her in English but swears to himself in Italian. He reminds himself that behind the door, beyond the fluorescent lights of the arrivals hall, beyond the sliding glass door, the space, the plains, the pure water wait for him. "A country of possibilities," the man said. Nino lifts, then unlocks the suitcases. His legs are unsteady, the floor seems to shift under his feet. This official is slow, thorough. "That one too." Nino's still damp sweater is on top of the second suitcase. The stink rises, and the customs man makes a face. Embarrassed, Nino steps back. But the essence of the lagoon has engulfed him, clinging, inescapable.

C.D. Minni

Details from the Canadian Mosaic

Mario dreamed of running barefoot across a beach to tell his grandfather, to tell him they were going to Canada. The old man sat in the lee of a red-brick church that stood half on the paving, half on the shore. He was mending his fishing nets, removing the weakened outer edges. The harbour shone like an oily green mirror; the town shone with whitewash and the bright awnings of shops . . .

He dreamed of baggage piled in the street, green trunks and bulging suitcases fastened with rope. He sat on one of the trunks, waiting. The house was crowded with relatives, friends and neighbours, but they did not miss him until later. "Mario? Where's Mario?" He was embraced, kissed, crushed, tears on his cheeks. It was time to go. The bus to Naples pulled out of the village square, down a street of vine-hung balconies and out along the rocky coast, north. Oleanders flowered blood-red in crags; below, the sea flashed an incredible blue. The bus passed nondescript towns like his own, olive groves, twisted railroad tracks, scars of war . . .

He dreamed of a ship, a Greek liner, and of how passengers in native costumes squatted in a circle on deck, clapping hands rhythmically, yelling, as one of them danced in their center. He was learning new words, passports, emigration, disembarkation . . . But then it seemed that he was, with the shifting quality of dreams, on a train rattling across frozen prairies where snow drifted, and he was celebrating his ninth birthday with his parents in the restaurant car . . .

He dreamed, but he woke to the shrill cry of gulls in a room surrounded by green trunks, and he remembered: the bus, the ship, the train. All of them now unreal as if he had indeed dreamed them. But he was here. Destination: one of his new words. He smelled coffee and heard voices downstairs.

One of the suitcases was open, and he saw that his mother had already laid out clean clothes for him. He dressed: knee trousers with stockings and a blue shirt, for today he was to sign up at school.

He went to the window and pushed up the sash. It was drizzling, and the wind blew from the Ocean. The Pacific, his teacher had called it on the last day. She had suspended the regular lesson and asked the class to take out their geography books and look up where Mario was going. Everyone was awed that he was going so far away.

Now, gulls circled against the grey sky, crying ruefully, sped seaward or alighted on warehouses and men's bunkhouses built on pilings over the shore. There was, he saw, scarcely space for a town on this inlet. The rain-beaten houses climbed the mountainside in haphazard rows up to the forest's edge. Across the inlet was the pulp mill, where his father worked, its chimney belching out smoke. Men, carrying black lunchbuckets, were crossing over the wooden bridge. They reminded him of ants, each burdened with a grain of wheat.

In the street below, his small brother was already exploring the neighbourhood.

Mario went into the bathroom and drew water to wash. His mother came in and made him scrub his ears until they squeaked. She had prepared a big Canadian breakfast; these were their first real home meals, and they had sat down to it when his small brother ran inside in bewilderment.

"Hey, no one knows how to talk in this place!"

He looked so funny standing there that they could not help but laugh — at his turned-up nose, at his child's logic, at their own strangeness.

"Mario is going to school to learn," his father said and fetched their coats.

Only three weeks ago, in his native village, it was spring. Orange trees and roses bloomed in gardens behind stone houses. Now, here, in a yard daffodils pushed bravely through leftover snow, but the wind was cold. Mario turned up his coat collar as he followed his father through unfamiliar streets, past strange wood-frame houses, work of carpenters with hammer and nails.

Up ahead surrounded by a steel fence was the schoolyard. He heard shouting and the whack of a bat, but only weeks later knew the game was called baseball.

In the principal's office he waited, sitting, while registration papers were filled. The principal was a tall man with a polished dome of a head, and he motioned for the boy to follow him. Down a corridor. Up some stairs. Knocked on a door. Room number 6. A teacher with silver hair.

She introduced him to the class, a new student — from Italy. Some giggled, and for the first time he became conscious of his clothes. But he took an empty seat and received workbooks and pencils.

Some subjects he could do even on that first day— arithmetic, art, gym. Others puzzled him. At recess another boy showed him where the washroom was, then left. He was alone until the bell rang. He walked home alone. The teacher began to keep him in after school to learn English. By the time he left, the schoolyard was almost empty, except for a few boys. Usually the same boys.

Three of them came up to him one day, shouting: "Hey, dummy! Cat got your tongue?" When he tried to run, they blocked his way, surrounding him. "Where'd ya get the funny getup, eh?" They began to pull at his clothes, and he heard his blue shirt rip. Then he was pushed, knocked down, kicked. He swore at them. "What say?"

"Aw, leave him alone," one said. He had red hair and blue jeans.

In that moment of distraction Mario stood up. The three were laughing at him as if at a joke, and this hurt him most. He threw his arithmetic book. It caught one of the boys in the face; blood gushed from his nose. The others seized him, one holding back his arms, another raising his fist. Mario saw the arm arch, the fist like a hammer, and before knowing it he had kicked with force, connecting with genitals. There was a yelp of pain as the boy buckled and clutched his pants. Mario, having twisted free, ran, his breath like a hot wire in his throat. When he looked back, they were staring after him.

The next morning they were waiting for him. He brandished his arithmetic book as they surrounded him. One of them had red hair and blue jeans, and his face cracked into a grin as he extended a hand.

"Friends?" he said.

Were they his friends?

But they shook.

"Bruce," he said.

"Mario."

"Friends. OK?"

"OK."

His exploit had won him respect in the schoolyard. But on Saturday his father took him to the Bay store and bought him Canadian clothes, his first blue jeans. He wore them when he danced around the May pole and when he signed up for Little League baseball.

With his friend Bruce he explored the woods above the town, saw a black bear, competed and lost in the marbles championships, and fished off the wharf. He told Bruce that his grandfather was a fisherman.

"Ya? What'd he catch?"

"Everything. Octopus even."

"Really?" — with sudden interest.

"Sure. You eat octopus with bread and olives."

"Yetch!"

He asked Bruce where his grandparents lived.

"In the city," his friend said. "In a home."

"Home?"

"You know, for old folks."

He did not know. In his native village families were large, embracing uncles, cousins and especially grandparents. It puzzled him that there should be no old people in this town.

He had also made other discoveries. One: the pulp mill was the pulse of the town which adjusted to — or complained about — the rhythm of its changing work shifts. Two: his friends seemed to live on hot dogs, potato chips, peanut butter and Cokes. Three: though he was changing, his parents remained foreign. His mother especially needed protection. He became her companion and interpreter — at the store, the post office, the bank, even the church.

The school holidays had begun. The weather turned fine. Bruce asked him if they wanted to be best friends, and together they planned new adventures. They went cycling. They built a tree house where on the wings of imagination anything was possible. They made a raft and sailed it down the Mississippi. They never missed the Saturday twenty-cent matinee where they bought crackerjacks and candy bars, and they collected and traded comics — especially Superman and Batman — with the treasured DC sign.

His coach had told him that he had a good pitching arm, and he spent hours in the schoolyard developing his technique. The Giants were going to win the Little League trophy that year, and he was drawn into the excitement. The fans cheered when he walked to the pitcher's mount. They cheered Mike.

He did not know at what point he had become Mike. One day looking for a suitable translation of his name and finding none, he decided that Mike was closest. By the end of summer, he was Mario at home and Mike in the streets.

It was Mike who pitched a five-hitter for the Giants, Mike who in August watched the salmon run upstream to spawn and Mike who returned to school in September. At Christmas he received his first pair of skates and toque on his head, planned to learn hockey. When he dreamed, it was of Rocket Richard or three-speed bikes or a girl named Gwendolyn who sat behind him in Grade Five . . .

It is by luck that I find a parking place. There is a crowd. Children are running everywhere. Some line up at a truck that is dispensing free ice cream. Dignitaries, from the provincial government, are shaking hands with leaders of the Italian-Canadian community. Speeches are made. Cameras click.

The sun is warm, and the park's sunken gardens are a riot of colours. There is music, accordions and mandolins, and a troupe in gay folk costumes is performing, twirling in a dance, linking arms, breaking and reforming. A kaleidoscope of colours and patterns.

The music, a sea-song, draws me like a hooked fish. It plays on the stereo of my memory. And I — Mike, Mario — am again running barefoot across the beach to the red-brick church where Grandfather is mending his nets.

He hooks his toes into the net, anchoring it to the ground, lifts a section with his left bronzed hand until the edge pulls tight and with his right hand rips away the line of cable and cork floats. Next, he cuts about a foot of the mesh behind the ripped edge, drops the net, lifts his foot, brings up another section of the edge and starts all over again. The strip of discarded mesh settles in a neat pile near his idle foot.

Gianna Patriarca

Stealing Persimmons

Rosa sits by the bay window staring out at the seasons, watching them play like grandchildren. Games played without fear. She watches from dawn till the light dies. Beyond the clump of summer iris, behind the naked crabapple tree. The games of sunshine. The games of snow. She watches time pass quickly and slowly. She understands time. She knows the minutes of the hour, the hours of the day. She is intimate with time.

ಐ

Her body is slight, angular. A Modigliani woman in black. It is a colour she has come to love, the way she loved her skin before recognizing its roughness, its thirst. Rosa is comfortable here, in this chair with the high, strong back. The wool blanket over her knees and the beads between her fingers. They too are black, co-ordinated. Her fingers move quickly. They have resisted well, they defy time. Their energy is outside of her, almost a miracle. Her once soft grey eyes are thick with cataracts. They fog her images. She blinks constantly to focus. The fourth blink, and she is in a field. An open, vast, green pasture surrounded by gentle hills. She traces their shape, their beautiful curves with her finger. Everywhere she runs. She climbs, planting her feet like giant seeds in the warm earth. She is breathing in everything with a lustful appetite. All around her the echo of her laughter, a sweet symphony.

ꕥ

In the distance she sees Tomaso. Torn wool pants and an old stained jacket. Always buttons missing. Tomaso's thick small hands scratching the crop of matted black hair. His voice clear as the Sunday bells. "*Corri, Rosa, corri*. I'll meet you at the walnut tree." He always gets there first. Like two quick lizards they climb the tree. They gather green walnut balls, counting them, throwing them, using them as marbles. And the sweet symphony plays on.

ꕥ

"*Le mucche*. Tomaso, you have to bring the cows back." They march along, pockets full of walnuts, leading the cows home as the sun settles itself over the scattered hills.

ꕥ

The bay window is her world. It is her memory. At this moment she would like to sleep for a while. Her cloudy eyes hurt, they burn but they will not close. It is as if the lids were sewn to her forehead. She sees Tomaso again. He is in the barn. The October air is cool. It makes her dark skin tingle. "Get the pail, Rosa." Tomaso calms the cows. He is gentle and Rosa is always amazed by this. Tomaso's stalky, rough body, his tattered clothes and reckless hair are so unlike his tender manner. He pulls the stool over to sit beneath the heavy teats of the cows and with his small hands begins to pull at their long pink mass. The milk hits the pail like small stones. Like hail on tin rooftops. Rosa leans by the door watching the rhythm of his hands, listening to his whistling as the frothy white foam fills the pail. She turns away, slowly her feet find their way toward the farmhouse.

ꙮ

The clicking of the doorknob and Rosa blinks again. Maria is home. Rosa breathes a small sigh as she watches her daughter throw her bag on the couch and fling her shoes in the corner. "*Ciao, mamma, come stai?*" The response is one Maria knows too well. A frugal smile, a slight bow of the head. Maria understands. She rests her hand on her mother's fingers. A kiss to the forehead and walks away.

ꙮ

Her voice. Why her voice? Rosa thinks. Why not her eyes? She could still see without her eyes. But this cruel, cruel silence.

ꙮ

Tomaso is whistling. The tune is lively, crisp as the autumn leaves flirting outside the window. "*Vieni*, Rosa, let's light the fire before ma and pa come home, it's getting cold." She gathers an armful of hay and loose bits of wood scooped into her apron. She places them carefully in the stone fireplace and strikes a long, wooden match watching the flames ignite and light up the bare, uneven walls. Soon the kitchen is warm. Soft shadows fluttering around them like thin voiceless birds. They sit, knees beneath their chins and their hands stretched towards the blue-tipped flames.

ɷ

"Would you like some soup tonight, mamma?" Maria's voice is young. Her little girl's voice. It has not changed much. Rosa moves her head to face her daughter's face, she nods. Maria understands. It seems they have come to this now. Understanding. No more long conversations. No more stories. No more songs in any language. Just an understanding of needs. Maria has gone to the kitchen.

ɷ

Rosa turns to the bay window. Tomaso is shovelling potatoes deep into the ashes of the fireplace. "We need salt Rosa." She lifts the heavy wooden top of a chest, opens a brown bag and scoops out a spoonful of salt. The potatoes open and smoke while Tomaso sprinkles the coarse granules over them. "*Mangia, Rosa, sono buone*."

ɷ

"I met an old friend of yours at Nicario's store today, Mamma." Maria speaks as she sets the two plates and glasses on the dining room table. "She said she was from Montecalmo. Her name is Teresa Bovina." Rosa's fingers stop. Her head turns away from the bay window. "She told me you stole persimmons together back home in Montecalmo." Maria's eyes smile. She begins to giggle, like a small child. "Not you, mamma, a thief? I wish you could tell me that story, mamma, I'd love to hear that story."

ꕥ

This time Rosa's eyes are moist. It takes more than four blinks, but she is there. There with Teresa. They are young, lean, fresh faced and always hungry. They are playing a game, running, leaping over each other like frogs. "*Uno, due, tre, prima io e dopo te, corri matta.*" They chant silly rhymes as their voices pant with energy. Teresa's is deep like a man's. She is tall and large with a strong, square face. Rosa admires the strength, the confidence in Teresa's laugh. Breathless and laughing they take air in with large gulps, their cheeks bright pink from the rushing blood and the autumn chill. "We've got to jump over the fence, Rosa. Look at the persimmons they are so ripe. Come on." Rosa is always reluctant. He will catch them, Armando will, and he'll chase them with a pitchfork. If he catches them they will feel the stinging leather of his belt. "Come on, Rosa. Don't be so afraid, we'll fill our aprons and run. The old mule is too slow he'll never catch us. *Dai, dai, andiamo . . .* Come on." Teresa is fearless and Rosa wants to know that feeling. A smile, a wink and they are hand in hand like secret sisters. Their long skirts tucked into their waists, lifting their quick strong legs they disappear over the fence.

ꕥ

"Is it true, mamma, did you and Teresa really steal persimmons together?" Maria is back in the room, her tongue tasting a wooden spoon. "She laughed so hard when she told me about it, I understood it must be a special memory." Maria walks toward her mother and sits facing her. "Are you all right, mamma? Look at me." Rosa lifts her face and looks at Maria. "Teresa wants to visit you. I told her it would be all right. I thought it might cheer you up to see an old friend. You don't see many anymore." Rosa turns again to the bay window. Maria remembers the soup and runs to the kitchen.

ꕤ

They are sitting beneath the walnut tree. The evening air is biting and Teresa wraps her shawl around her shoulders tucking her body close to Rosa's. They are like two schoolgirls exchanging secrets as the sweet orange flesh of persimmon drips from their open lips making sticky little rivers down their chins. They are beneath an evening sky that is a deep, flat purple. Lights begin to dot the countryside like the first fireflies on a summer night. In the distance Tomaso is loading hay onto the wheelbarrow, fresh bedding for the cows. She must get home. "Why are you always in a hurry?" Teresa complains. "You little scared *ladra*, one more persimmon before you go." They laugh and eat huddled together beneath the walnut tree until the chilly night coughs up a giant moon.

ꕤ

She has not seen Teresa in years. Long before this silence, before the pictures from the bay window. She is not sure she wants to see her again. She does not need to see her.

ꕤ

"It's ready, mamma." Maria walks over wiping her hands onto the cotton apron she always wears when she prepares dinner. "Let me help you." Maria takes the beads from her mother's hands placing them on the couch. She folds the blanket and places it beside the beads. She slips her hand under her mother's elbow and gently lifts her to her feet. Maria wraps her other arm around Rosa's delicate body. The take long, slow steps from the window into the dining room. Seven steps. Rosa counts them each time. They sit facing each other. The long teak table covered by a colourful linen tablecloth. Maria has lit some candles. Rosa likes candlelight, it brings back the shadows. They eat in silence. Rosa's spoonfuls take time to reach her thin, pale lips. "You don't think it's a good idea for Teresa to visit, do you, mamma?" Maria breaks the silence, holding her spoon midway between her mouth and the dish. "I really think you should have visitors. You are always sitting by the window, staring. You don't see anyone until I come home at night, it must be so lonely for you. Please, Mamma, let Teresa come, I know you would enjoy it." Maria is genuinely concerned and Rosa understands this. In her heart she wants to tell her daughter that she is not alone, she is not lonely. She does not need visitors. But she sees the pain in Maria's face. She does not want pain for her daughter. Her whole life she has tried to shelter her children from pain. It had never occurred to her that perhaps one day Maria's life would come to this. The guardian angel with the face of pain. A dutiful daughter, a nurse. There is anger in Rosa's eyes. Anger at growing old, helpless.

ꙮ

Dinner is over, Maria walks her mother back to the chair by the window. "Do you want me to turn on television for a while, Mamma, while I do the dishes?" Rosa shakes her head. She does not need television.

ഗ

The dark comes quickly in late October. The speeding headlights hit the bay window, like shooting stars. Rosa's eyes look up to catch their glowing light. Vito's face is there. His beautiful face. He is standing by the large stone pillar of the church of Santa Anna, under the one light of the piazza and a thousand stars nailed to the clear night sky. Vito's wavy hair is black. A thin mustache, even and neat, beneath a straight strong nose. He is leaning smoking a cigarette, blowing feathery circles that rise like miniature clouds. This beautiful young man in a city suit wearing shoes that shine. How elegant he looks. Rosa thinks. Not at all like her brother Tomaso. Not at all like the other boys of the town. She feels something strange inside her, in her throat, her stomach, between her thighs. She knows she wants to touch him. She wants to run her hand along his beautiful cheeks. But she stands petrified like the saints in the church.

ഗ

"I'll make some espresso, mamma, light, so you can sleep." Maria is calling from the kitchen. Rosa smiles. "No milk for you right, mamma?" Her eyes close. When they open again she is at the dining room table. The children are all there. Marco, Concetta, Mimma the oldest and little

Maria. "We want coffee too, mamma, with milk and lots and lots of sugar." There is always an argument. "You are all too little for coffee, it its not good for you." The children protest. "Yes, it is, mamma, yes, it is." They always win.

ꕥ

"Coffee is ready, mamma. Mamma, were you daydreaming again?" Rosa turns to look at Maria, watching her stir the tiny cup with a tinier spoon. Maria hands Rosa the coffee. They sit in silence. They do not need words. Perhaps everything has already been said. Perhaps words are only an ornament. They sit for a long time, breathing, sipping coffee. They are one large shadow on the living room wall. "I bet you were off stealing persimmons again, hey, mamma?"

ꕥ

"I'm going to take a bath, mamma." Maria stands and walks away. Rosa counts the footsteps up the creaky stairs. All sounds seem sharper now. Once, sounds were something to avoid. The sounds of her loud children growing up. The sounds of the factory machines bouncing from hard walls without windows. The sound of her husband's serious, humourless voice. She had often sheltered herself from sounds. But now all sounds were welcome, all sounds were lost friends.

ꕥ

Her eyes on the bay window and he is there again. Vito was her first love, her only real love.

"You must come with me, Rosa. There is nothing here for you, for us. Nothing for anyone in this town." The sound of Vito's clear voice. His hands firm on her arms. The blood has stopped. He is shaking her, wanting her to understand, to accept his dream. Rosa stares into his huge eyes. She recognizes the passion and the fear. She envies his eyes. "I cannot leave them. I cannot go with you, they need me here." She feels her heart rebel inside her chest, wanting to reach the words escaping from her throat, to choke them. She walks away, watching the night swallow his face, his beautiful face, the sound of his voice, forever.

ꙮ

"The bath was wonderful, mamma. It feels good to be clean." Maria is wrapped in her white robe with the red dots. She comes to sit by Rosa straightening the blanket on her mother's knees. "You know, Teresa, she told me that you almost married another man before you met papa. Oh how I wish you could tell me that story, mamma." They both smile and turn their heads toward the bay window.

ꙮ

There is no real reason for stories now, no real need for them, why trouble Maria with more. At times, Rosa wishes her other children would unburden Maria for a while. But their lives are so full of everyday things. The way her own life had once been. She hopes Maria understands.

ꕤ

"I was thinking, mamma, it might be nice to take a trip to Montecalmo this coming summer. What do you think?" Maria's dark eyes widen with possibilities. She stares at her mother hoping for a resonse. A positive response. "I'd love to see all the places you used to tell us about. The farmhouse you lived in, the hills you and uncle Tomaso climbed, the persimmon trees. I think it would be good for you and for me." Rosa sees the excitement in her daughter's face. She wants to hold her in her arms. She wants to tell her one last story. "No, Maria, those places are not there anymore. Look, Maria. Look out the window. There's Tomaso trying to juggle the walnut balls. He's not very good. Keeps dropping them. Look, Maria. There I am. It has started to rain. I must put the pails out to catch the rainwater. Look at me run, Maria, look how fast I can run." A quick shooting star from the bay window lights up the room. They look at each other, understanding something new. Maria wraps her arms around her mother's shoulders, letting her hands rest on Rosa's beating chest. They are again one large shadow, gently rocking. "You know, mamma, tomorrow when I go by Mr. Nicario's store I'm going to steal a couple of sweet, ripe persimmons for me and you."

Dolce-Amaro

he has learned to bend
the way branches do
under the white weight
of endless Januarys.

this country has taken everything
his health, his language
the respect of his modern children
the love of his angry wife.

in some forgotten lifetime
he was a young, dark-haired man
in a ship packed with young
dark-haired men
floating uncomfortably towards
a dream they didn't want to bury
with the still young bones
of mothers and fathers
among the ruins of a postwar Italy.

for most
the dream
did not come easily
the golden paved North America
wasn't paved at all.

there were years of feeling strange
cold and hot months over multiplying bricks
hands turned leathery and large
needs stored away in cave cellars
deep, with the colour of aging wine.

in the evenings
there was the smell of group sweat
cheap meals seasoned with resentment
by the wives of aspiring landlords.

for my father
the dream ended early
when his knees were crushed
by the weight of steel
along some railroad line
he was thirty-one
there was no insurance then
and little interest
for the benefits of the immigrant man.

he bends easily at fifty-seven
walks with a cane
rarely opens his lifeless eyes

the government sends him
fifty-one dollars a month
in recognition.

College Street, Toronto

I have come back to this street
to begin a new chapter of my inheritance
my Canadian odyssey.

for my father it began in 1956
in the basement of a Euclid Street
rooming house

with five other men
homeless, immigrant dreamers
bordanti
young, dark
handsome and strong
bricklayers
carpenters
gamblers.

they cooked their pasta
by the light of a forty watt bulb
drank bad red wine
as they argued the politics of
the country they left behind
avoiding always the new politics.
late in the evenings they
spent their loose change
in the Gatto Nero, the Bar Italia
pool, espresso
cards and cigarettes.

while in all the towns
from Friuli to Sicily
postponed families waited
for the letters, the dollars
the invitations.

then the exodus
of wives and children
trunks and wine glasses
hand stitched linens in hope chests
floating across the Atlantic

slowly
to Halifax
to Union Station
to College Street.

1960
my sister and I cold and frightened
pushed toward a crowded gate
into the arms
of a strange man
who smelled of tobacco.

Crawford Street
three small rooms
in a three story house
dark and airless
smelling of boiled fish
Rose and Louis Yutzman
lived downstairs
Louis died in the middle
of a frozen January night
Rose's screams were nails
driven hard into my eardrums.

my fearless mother
touched his silent face
held his limp, large hand
as she closed his eyes
while my father and I
barefoot and trembling
hid petrified
behind the door

we learned the language quickly
to everyone's surprise
my mother embraced her new life
in long factory lines
while my father continued his pleasures
in pool halls thick with voices
of other men in exile.

1981
the Italians are almost all gone
to new neighbourhoods
modern towns.

my father is gone
Bar Italia has a new clientele
women come here now
I come here
I drink espresso and smoke cigarettes
from the large window
that swims in sunlight
I think I see my father
leaning on the parking meter
passionately arguing
the soccer scores.

How strange this city
sometimes
it seems so much smaller
than all those towns
we came from.

Anthony M. Buzzelli

The Gift

It was Gregorio's first day in the classroom after his wife's fatal heart attack. He had lost his best friend. His principal advised him to take a few days off but the teacher felt that the distraction of work would set his mind straight. He counted on it. He would mourn his wife later.

His daughters had flown back home with their families after the funeral. He wished they lived closer so that he could see his grandchildren more often. When he had driven back from the airport to the empty house he recalled his eagerness to share with his wife that Cindy had finally lost her baby tooth — the same tooth that made her miserable during the short visit. He also recalled the wave of melancholy which consumed him when he realized that his wife was truly gone.

The mind plays mean tricks on us, he thought. All the more reason why I have to be here today. I have to keep busy. The house has too many memories. I can't stay there all day thinking about what we had. Got to move on.

He craved the antics and the impish energy of his students. He knew that he would be fine when he saw them.

The wounds are still fresh, he thought. That was a phrase thrown around a great deal, but he never appreciated its magnitude until his wife's death. The healing would take time, but he knew it would happen. He prayed for the courage to endure the loss and separation. She would be angry with him if he did not get on with his life. He had to be strong for her.

The students from his first period class were surprised to see him back so early. He smiled at those students who had made the effort to go to the funeral home. The teacher had recognized their discomfort in the inability to find the right words to console a man who had lost his lifetime companion. He loved them for that as he also felt uncomfortable in funeral homes with their lugubrious atmosphere where words always failed him.

The teacher took attendance.

"D'Amore? Anyone seen Alfonso?"

"Not here, Mr. Gregorio," shot back from a helpful student in the back row.

As soon as the teacher began the lesson, Alfonso D'Amore entered and proceeded to his desk. The eighteen year old's appearance betrayed a person much older. The long and matted hair stuck to his acned face. The checkered red and blue viyella shirt with fraying cuffs was wrinkled and torn at the shoulder. With a knapsack slung over his back he dragged his feet across the tiled floor, shoelaces trailing behind his boots. All eyes followed him while the teacher made a correction to the register on his desk.

"Nice of you to join us. Better late than never, eh, Alfonso?"

"Sorry, Sir. Alarm clock didn't go off."

The teacher with clenched jaws looked up from the register, shook his head and scowled.

Robert Gregorio realized shortly after he started discussing the Treaty of Versailles that he wasn't into the lesson. And neither was Alfonso who fell asleep at his desk shortly after he sat down.

The boy dreamed about the *kill floor* at the meat plant where 300 cows and 700 pigs were slaughtered daily.

The smell of the fresh blood and meat mingling with the stench of the feces and burning hair. The squeal of the pigs tied by their hooves to hooks of the moving line. The man with the bloody apron and rubber gloves who pierced their strained necks with his long knife. The veterinarian who examined the internal organs for diseases. The sad, begging, droopy eyes of the calves. The man with the gun who brought the submissive cows to their knees by firing a bullet into their heads.

"Why don't you get into this lesson!" snapped the teacher at Alfonso. "Go home if you want to sleep. This is an insult to me and the rest of the students. How would you feel if I came to your house and fell asleep?"

The boy looked up, grateful to be freed from the recurring dream which troubled his sleep. "Sorry, Sir, I . . ."

"Please, sit up."

Alfonso D'Amore worked at the meat plant after school to help his father pay the bills. His mother had abandoned him when he was three years old, shortly after his twin brothers were born. His father never remarried. He refused to talk about his wife and removed from the house all traces of her brief sojourn there. Rumour had it that she had an affair with his best friend, a transgression Alfonso's father was not able to forgive or to forget.

"Alfonso, how did the Treaty of Versailles contribute to the Second World War?" asked the teacher. He felt bad as soon as he asked the question because he knew the student would not be able to give the answer. For that matter, the rest of the class knew as well that Alfonso would stammer an interminable, "I don't know, Sir." In a generous effort to help both the teacher and Alfonso, their hands, one at a time, slowly pierced the oppressive silence of the classroom.

"How the hell do you expect to pass this or any other course if you don't do the work? How can you waste your bloody time like this?"

Alfonso did not answer. The other students pulled their hands down from the air which vibrated tension and discord; they looked down at their desks. Some shuffled uncomfortably; others doodled in their notebooks. The teacher never used words such as *bloody* or *hell*. It's not like him, they thought.

Maybe I should have taken a few more days off. For my sake and theirs, he thought. He quickly scribbled an assignment on the board. "Any questions?" he asked.

An uneasy silence responded.

"Well, then, make sure you hand it in first thing tomorrow. Do you anticipate a problem with my expectations, Alfonso?"

"No, Sir. I'll have it done," he said apologetically.

"Just make sure you do. That's all. Just make sure you all do!"

The teacher sat down at his desk. His face was flushed. He knew his blood pressure must have shot up as he hurled diatribes at the exhausted young man. Such great talent going to waste, he thought. He just has no time for school. Going to bed at two in the morning can't help his performance any. I'll bet he's been up all night working. Why didn't his father keep him home? In the past when he worked through the night his father lied for him at the office. Hell, why didn't he call in today? The kid's a mess. He's not using his God-given talents to make something of himself. He'll just be another statistic whom we failed to educate.

The teacher did not know if he was more upset with a father who would force his son to jeopardize his education or with a son who blindly obeyed his father's irrational wishes.

Did a good job tearing him down in front of the other kids, he thought. Wouldn't think much of it, if it happened to me. What a demoralizing thing I've put him through. No one should be exposed to that crap.

The teacher continued to sort papers and go through the motions of grading. He was just reading words. Thoughts refused to form.

The period trudged towards its much anticipated conclusion.

He looked up at Alfonso D'Amore whose head was cradled on his left arm outstretched on the desk. The teacher walked over and stood beside the boy and become troubled by the overtired waif with the pallid tensed face masked with the death grimace. A curl of hair had gone completely white as if it had been dipped in a can of paint. The baby finger — on the other hand handling between his legs — twitched. The boy's breathing was deep and irregular.

Robert Gregorio returned quietly to his desk and sat down. He caressed the aquamarine ring on his baby finger which he had given to his wife when he proposed to her in his final year of university. He paid $32.00 — all he could afford in those lean years before securing a teaching position. She never removed it even after he gave her the diamond on their tenth anniversary. He teased her, "That trinket's going to get an inferiority complex next to the big rock. Get rid of it." She rebutted, "It's just a reminder of how much my love has grown for you." Neither one tired of the repartee.

The teacher removed his glasses and buried his face into his praying hands. He looked at the boy who continued to sleep. The other students, who saw the teacher stare vacuously at the collapsed and dishevelled young man, worked busily at their assignment waiting for another reprimand to explode from him.

None came. Only the sound of the bell signalling the end of the class. Alfonso slowly raised his head, and rubbed the fatigue from his eyes. This was followed by an energetic yawning stretch which seemed to sound the very depths of his being. Several of the students patted Alfonso's matted black curly hair and gently slapped his back as they filed past his desk.

"Alfonso, please see me before you leave," asked the teacher.

"Yes, Sir."

The teacher stopped moving the papers when the boy, clutching nervously at his backpack, stood in front of him. His shirt, with several buttons missing, was untucked. There was congealed blood over a tear above the right knee of his threadbare jeans frayed at the cuffs. Several cuts on the leather, stretched taut over the steel toes of his boots, gaped. The wet laces smeared with blood and grease snaked behind.

The teacher rose and leaned on the corner of his desk. "Alfonso, you worked again all night at the factory, didn't you?"

"Yes, Sir. Had to. My father got sick."

"Your old man should be locked up letting you work all those hours."

"We need the money."

"It isn't fair. Did you get any sleep last night?"

"No."

"Have you had anything to eat?"

"Yeah, I had a donut and coffee. I'm okay."

"Sorry I chewed you out in front of the class. I hate to see you fail the course. You're going to fail, you know?"

"Yes, Sir, I know. I'll make it up in Summer School. Mr. Gregorio, you worry too much about me. I'll be al-right."

"Well, someone has to."

"Mr. Gregorio, I'm awfully sorry about your wife. I wanted to go to the funeral home, but I had to work."

"Thanks, I appreciate the thought. Don't worry about it.

"Well, at least, Mrs. Gregorio doesn't have any more pain. She's in heaven."

"Unfortunately, Alfonso, you have to die to get to heaven." The teacher picked up a paper clip on his desk and opened it.

"Yeah."

"Alfonso, I really appreciate your sympathy. Why didn't your father keep you at home today? You're no good to anyone here. Go home, for God's sake, and get some sleep."

The boy turned to the door to make sure no one had entered. Nervously, he reached into his knapsack and pulled out a wrapped bottle and a card.

"I know you like coffee," he stammered. "My father's a big coffee drinker. He likes Tia Maria in it. Here, I hope you enjoy it."

The teacher felt his legs go rubbery and immediately sat down.

"Go ahead, unwrap it," encouraged the boy. "I like to unwrap the gift before I read the card."

The teacher tore at the paper. He looked up at Alfonso who was pushing a dirty finger, with grease under the nail, into the corner of his bloodshot eye.

"Paid for this out of my own pocket. Dad would know if one of his bottles was missing. I've been caught before. He knows his booze."

"Pardon?"

"Oh, Mr. Gregorio, I'm only kidding. Never took any of his booze."

The teacher stood up and squeezed the boy's hand — cold, clammy and calloused. "Alfonso, I'm very . . ."

"Mr. Gregorio, I'd appreciate it if ya didn't say anything about this to anyone. Kids'll think I'm sucking up for marks. I'm not, you know. And, besides, with my marks it's safe. Would have to buy you a whole truckload of booze to even pass this course."

"You're an intelligent boy, Alfonso. You have a lot of talent. A lot to offer the world."

"The envelope has a Mass card for your wife. Hope it helps you get through this."

"It will Alfonso, more than you know. Why don't you go home and get some sleep?"

"I will."

"Alfonso, please, take care of yourself."

Alfonso D'Amore walked to the door, turned the handle and looked back.

"Hey, Sir, it may not be a bad idea for you to take a couple of days off. Maybe drink some of that coffee you like so much."

"It may be a good idea, Alfonso. Thank you."

Fiorella De Luca Calce

A Mimosa in Winter

I push against the massive wooden door. The biting wind follows me into the dim square space lit only by the brave glance of the moon from the window at the top of the stairs. Cautious, I press my hands against the cold stone of the passage for support, I take two steps at a time. My rapid pace is momentarily disrupted as my hand brushes against something soft. I draw back in alarm, then look at my feet.

"Gesu!" I expel my breath, bending to pick up the neatly bound cluster of dry parsley leaves. Why my grandmother persists in hanging her vegetables in the hallway instead of her kitchen is beyond me. Last month it was with reluctance that I refastened the hooks on the ceiling as Nonno had taught me. It hadn't been the same as that lazy autumn afternoon Nonno and I had hung those sausages high above our heads and close enough to the window so that they would be sure to get dry and hard. I remember him standing back, surveying the neat rows of suspended pork. The smile on my grandfather's face matched the smile in his eyes when he spotted my uneven line at the end of the row.

"Bravo ragazzo, Mario," he said in Italian. He was sincere. It was in his eyes. They were brown and soft coloured, like velvet and they never lied.

Inevitably, that familiar pang inside of me moves up and around me, like it always does when I think of him. My stomach feels heavy with emptiness and the heaviness rises up like a claw and curls itself around my heart and it hurts — it always hurts. Maybe I'm being punished. Maybe if I had gone to the funeral I wouldn't be feeling like this. Maybe . . .

I sigh and continue up the stairs, feeling the weight of the dark envelop me like a thick cloak. The door is open wide. The darkness taunts me. Can it know that I dread walking in? Can it smell my fear?

Entering, I turn to stand between the two folding doors of the kitchen. I open them. She is there, huddled on a wooden bench by the fireplace. The black dress and her crudely knitted shawl draped across her shoulders seems to make her shrink in size. Her hands, knotted with age, lie clasped on her lap as if in silent prayer. The flames cast shadows across her worn and weary face, deepening the lines that resemble intricate cobwebs. She is staring into the fire, eyes unfocussed, remembering perhaps for one last time.

Uncomfortable, I shift and stare at my feet then my gaze drifts around the room and I see . . . Nonno is sitting beside me on the little workbench in front of the fireplace, telling me one of his stories that was bound to keep me wide-eyed and awake long after bedtime . . .

The kitchen is cluttered and evenly squared. The walls are decorated with dried clusters of parsley, rosemary, celery and sage. Here and there hangs a bright red pepper like an ornament on a Christmas tress. On the right side of the room stands the tilted table that Nonno and I had tried (though unsuccessfully) to even out. Above it are two cupboards filled with jars of sausages and olives drowned in oil. The gas stove has found a comfortable spot in a corner; a tiny kettle sits on it like a puckered whistle. The fireplace takes up two-thirds of the left wall. Someone, perhaps my mother, has placed a bouquet of mimosa on the mantle.

"It is strange how despite the cold winters the mimosa are not afraid to blossom. They smell as fresh as the cold mountain air and look as warm as the afternoon sun," Nonno would say about his favourite flowers. I, too, loved mimosa. It was easy to love the things he loved. In his eyes, everything was beautiful.

There isn't a thing in this room that belongs to him. Whatever treasured belonging he had, he carried with him; his blue notebook and his gold pocket watch. As a child, the watch with the delicate flecks of gold engraved around the glass fascinated me to no end and often I was allowed to play with it. As for the notebook, Nonno would often pause from whatever he was doing to write notes to himself. It was not his lack of trust in me that prevented Nonno from showing me his book, but rather my ignorance. It wasn't time yet.

Now I wonder if it isn't too late. There isn't a thing of his in this room and yet it is the one that best describes him. It is warm and safe. That is how Nonno used to make me feel. Now no longer. The two-room shack my parents lived in was much too small for a family of five and we were much too poor. At the age of four I was taken to live with my grandparents. I was too young to understand the change and in less than a year I felt I had always lived with them. It was easy to love them. They were kind and patient with my wild manners. I never knew a harsh word. The idea of leaving them never crossed my mind, not even after the earthquake of 1978 when my parents moved into the rent-free apartment funded by the Italian Republic. I was six then. My parents' shack had not survived the small tremor and was not sorely missed. Though my parents suggested that there was more than enough room for me to live with them, I declined. My wishes were respected. They knew that my leaving would have broken my grandparents' hearts . . . and mine.

It hurts now. It hurts knowing that Nonno won't be coming back, knowing that when I go out to feed the animals or go to the fields to gather the tomatoes and lettuce, he won't be there working beside me. And when I sit down to supper it won't be the three of us anymore. Everything has changed. I knew it would be this way. I knew it as soon as my family and my grandmother came back from the funeral. I waited at my parents' apartment instead. The villagers followed soon after. They came to pay their last respects as was the custom. My grandmother sat in the corner by herself. She barely noticed the people that went up to her. And I, being the closest to her, was unable to share her pain.

That same day it was decided that my grandmother and I should stay with my parents. My grandmother quickly made herself clear on that matter.

"Don't you go tell me what to do," she had said in Italian.

"But winter is coming," my mother had argued.

"Of what importance is that? I am old not senile. I still have a roof over my head. My roof. And I will live under it!"

"Mamma, father is gone. Who will look after you? You know he used to take care of everything. How will you keep warm in winter? You think you can go into the woods and cut the wood yourself? Can you see yourself travelling every day to the field to gather the crops and feed the animals? It is absurd!"

"I will manage." My grandmother had stood firm.

"You want to end up like father? One foot in this world and one in the other," my mother had scoffed.

"Mario is here. He will help me like always. *Vero, Mario?"*

I was unable to answer, unable to look up.

"But, Mamma, Mario is going to be sixteen soon. He is not a boy anymore. He will be going to the city to look for work. You don't want him to stay in the village all his life do you? What kind of future would he have?"

My grandmother had forced me to look at her, her watery blue eyes silently repeating the question.

I had turned away, unable to face her. I didn't want to go to Rome. I didn't want to live with her either. How could I explain to her that I couldn't live with her anymore? How could I tell her about the unexplainable fear that seemed to grow within me at the thought of walking into that empty house? I can still hear my grandfather's dying moans echoing through the rooms.

"I see. *Adesso capisco,*" she sighs.

"I was unable to run from the shame.

"You are young. I understand," she continues. "But me, I am old. God knows how much longer I have. And when I go, I want to be in my own house, with my husband...

My grandmother went home without me. I watched her limp down that hill on her bad leg... a dark and lonely figure.

Two months later the marshal had a notice posted in the village. All the houses listed on that single sheet could not survive another earthquake and would have to be torn down. There was one house on that paper that throbbed like a sore thumb. *"Casa Vitale,"* my grandparents' house.

They couldn't have done anything worse to her. Having my grandfather die was bad enough but to have to watch them tear down her home . . .

This is why I'm here in this house tonight. I am saying goodbye.

"So you have come." The voice intrudes on my thoughts. My grandmother is beside me. A trace of a smile plays on her lips. I nod my head sheepishly.

"You are a good boy, Mario. Your grandfather taught you well." Her sigh is heavy.

"I am glad Romi didn't live to see this day. Everything changes. He warned me about this. I never listened. Not even when we talked about you going to Rome."

"Rome? How did you know? I never said anything. I wasn't even sure myself until—"

"My boy, you didn't have to." She stops me with her hand. "We both knew you would go one day. If not this summer, then the next."

"I haven't given it a great deal of thought, until now." I say.

"Your grandfather was alive then. When tragedy strikes, we let go of things that were once familiar to us. Things change you know."

I nod, not knowing what to answer.

"You know what your Nonno said to me before he died? He said, 'Maria, I am glad it is me that is leaving. I don't want to see him go first.' He loved you like you were his own."

The tears well up in her eyes, threatening to spill like the sobs that rise in my throat. That familiar heaviness makes itself known again and I hold my stomach to push it down. "Molto bravi, your grandfather and I. We raised you well." She sighs, turning to look into the fire again. Her eyes take on a glazed expression.

"Yes, you did." I pause, then, "It is getting dark. They will turn out the lights in the piazza soon. We will have trouble getting back," I remind her gently.

She doesn't hear me. "We have raised twelve of them in this house. One more beautiful than the other. *Grazie a Dio.*"

"It is late. *È tardi.*"

"I hear you." She waves her hand. "I am not deaf yet. Come here. I have something for you." She gets up from her seat, moves towards the table in the corner.

I hesitate, wondering why she is stalling.

"Vieni," she beckons. She motions me to come next to her.

"Here," she says, pointing to the crumpled handkerchief on the table. "See what he left you." Her hands tug at the folds of white and I gasp at the objects before me. Lying amidst the lace is my grandfather's blue notebook and gold pocket watch.

"Keep them." She hands them to me reverently. I stare at them, speechless. The gold watch feels hot in my hands, and the book makes me feel like a child, much too important for me to hold.

"He meant for you to have them before you left us. Now is as good a time as any. You will go away this summer."

I stare at her, dumbfounded.

"You didn't have to say anything," she says, answering the question on my face. "But I knew. You don't raise a child without learning a little of what goes on in his head. Rome is a good city. You will learn many things."

"Nonno taught me many things."

"Yes, now Rome will have to do," she smiles.

"I don't know what to say."

"There is nothing to say. He wanted you to have them."

"He has given me so much." My voice breaks.

"No, Mario. You gave us both so much. More than you will ever know."

"I still have you." I kiss her cheek. Her face is cold.

"Come, we must be going," she says, giving me her hand and then, "Wait." She turns to the fireplace, raises her arm over the mantle. She takes the bouquet of Mimosa; drops them into the fire.

"Nonna?"

"The Mimosa will grow long after you and I are gone and they will be loved by many that come after us. But gifts such as these . . . " she touches my grandfather's treasures, "these we keep with us always, *per sempre.*"

I nod. Silently we walk out the door.

Pier Giorgio Di Cicco

October Montreal

Se fa dopo le persone dotte.
(The learned ones will come later.)

Montreal is damp and blue this month.
Artie Gold walks the streets, out of love with his lungs.
The wind is from the oak trees of Mount Royal.
The cross bows towards the river, and the buildings, they
will live forever.

I walk to the childhood at St. Zotique.
On Dante Street is the bust of Dante, stern in the sun,
on a little square. A woman and a child play in the
    October
leaves. The world is evacuated.

Under the church de la Défense the wind turns on itself.
In 1921, the bust went up; "se fa dopo le persone dotte," the
inscription reads.

My father, impressed by nothing but a touch of home
saw Dante Street, perhaps that sign that reads "Toscana
    Furniture,"
heard a familiar sound, and called the rest of us to join him.

Twenty-five years later, I leave him under lilacs near
    New York.

The St. Lawrence still flexes its fingers towards the ice floes.

The wind flaps at my trousers. October Montreal is damp
and blue. Leaves are falling on the woman and child. She is on
hands and knees, in black and wears a scarf. She is whispering

in his ear the handhold of all those who are lost in their own
language; he hears the wind.

I hear "se fa dopo le persone dotte." I walk towards the town,
the sky on three sides of my brain, in between I am learning a new

language, always a new language. Like Artie, I am sick of

my lungs.

Returning to St. Dominic's

(Toronto, 1957)

The playground in the dead of night; old buildings cleared
away; I assume the black-top is the same on which I bled the first kick by an upstart boy;
the old nun, the one who'd throw me out, stands
on the gateway steps, chiding my mother, whose bad
englishes make mincemeat of my will to live.

Angela, Maria, Vincenzo, romances, all my
loves and hates; you've gone to hell, I know it
for giving a rough time to an angel.

Talons at my heels, let's say; but that prime time
was flawless except for you.
I alone exist, small ghost on a black-top, rehearsing blood
flows, embarrassments, the dark sky growing darker
in my chest. On the corner of this street and that

the sadness begins. Remembering the bony toil of seven
years
of childhood, a grown man stands here. Having made
his leap away from Christ, the fool, he chokes those
culprits of a tender age.

The playground echoes with the jeers and holler.
There should be blood stains and the signs of
dreaming gone berserk, instead of footsteps

leading me to a safe bequest, another month, another
home, with all the years like burrs stuck in my side.

The Man Called Beppino

When a man loses his barbershop during the war
as well as an only son, and his wife and
daughter sing the blues of starvation, the man
believes in the great white hope, now the red white
and blue. The man ventures overseas, and lands finally
in Baltimore, Maryland, USA — destined to be the
finest barber at eastpoint shopping plaza.

That man works for nothing, because his english is
less than fine; the customers like him,
and the man is easily duped, he believes in the

honest dollar, and is offered peanuts in return.

This while the general manager runs to Las Vegas
to take porno pictures of himself between
tall whores.

The man who lost his barbershop during the war
loves great white roses at the back of a house beside
a highway. The roses dream with him,
of being understood in clear english, or of a large
Italian sun, or of walking forever on a
Sunday afternoon.

Never mind the new son, the family. It is this man,
    whose
hospital cheques are being spent in Las Vegas,
it is this man whose hair will shine like
olive leaves at noon; it is this man who will sit
on his front lawn, after the fifth hemorrhage, having
his last picture taken,
because he drank too much

It is this man who will sit under his mimosa
by the highway, fifty pounds underweight, with no
hospital, and look

there are great white roses in his eyes.

Donna Italiana

Lady, I cannot help myself in you. There is the
song of three thousand years, of little old men with the
eyes of saints, they walk on the hillsides in the mid-day heat,
ghosts, wishing me well. They are my grandfathers, and
 my great-grandfathers,

and the ancient men that kept my ribs burning at Monte
 Cassino, in the
air above my brother's corpse, in the shelled house in
 Arezzo, in

Rimini, where I sat spread-eagled on the sand; they kept
 the ribs
burning through the cold Montreal nights, and in
 Baltimore, behind the
cold hospital where my father died. The ribs burned all
 the nights of my

life, my gentle men, my grandfathers, ghosts in the hills
 behind
Arezzo, burning their gentle eyes at night. Woman, I
 touch you

and remember everything, you open your mouth and
 laugh and I hear the
wind in trees beside the cathedral, the wind that weeps at
 nothing,

running through my shirt, past the skin I have devised
 for myself,

to the ribs, and the ribs sing, cooling. You are that much

gentleness. Yours is the only laughter that can persuade me.
It was that day upon the hilltop, I looked down over the
parapets
of my town, into the hand of noon; hives of sun over the
rivers,

pathways I imagined over distant slopes, farmyards
kneeling over the fields
of grass, behind me the scent of pine from the public
gardens; at that

precise hour, I heard you, I felt you toss your head back,
and your laugh
persuaded me. Like the country of my youth. I cannot
help myself

in you. Only you persuade me that the hills were white.
Only you
persuade me that the ribs burn less and only when a
woman is

the country that I love.

Marisa De Franceschi

Surface Tension

Chapter One

I can't remember the ocean crossing. I only remember what they have told me about it.

I have heard the stories countless times. If that part of my memory which is sealed in the vault of early childhood could resurrect them, they wouldn't be more vivid.

We sailed just after the second great war. That's what my father used to call it. It was great because it managed to annihilate populations, destroy vast cities, and create havoc all over the world. It was not a topical war. It was all encompassing. It showed no prejudice. A democratic war. "You weren't safe anywhere," my father used to say as if this was a merit. And then there was the bomb. It was a war full of rage and fury, power and force. That's why it was great.

We are on a Turkish cargo ship sailing from Genoa. It has a strange foreign name. All I am able to say of it are the first words: the Mohammed Ali. Some of the men on the ship have their heads wrapped up in cloth. I am sure they were blown up during the war. All they have left is a face. I pray they won't ever take the bandages off. I don't want to see what's underneath.

The men with the bandaged heads serve us our food. I can't eat. Not because I don't want to. I am hungry. I can't eat because I am afraid the heavy looking bandages will fall off and then I will see the insides of their heads.

Mother can't eat either. She doesn't ever come up to the dining room. She stays in our tiny cabin and throws up all the time. Father and cousin Tino bring her green apples. They're supposed to help the vomiting, but they don't.

"I guess I'm not as tough as I thought," she says to my father.

It is cousin Tino who notices I am afraid of the men. He laughs and tells me they are just waiters. They are there to serve us and there is nothing wrong with their heads. Those are "turbans" they are wearing. "Underneath," cousin Tino tells me, "they look just like you and me."

My father finds a friend on board. A Scandinavian blond. People think she is my mother. This makes me very angry. I am also very angry when my father invites her to eat her meals with us since we have an extra place at our table.

I am told all these things by my cousin Tino. He especially likes the part about the Scandinavian blond. My father smiles boastfully when Tino tells the story. My mother will either shake her head or utter a short reprimand to cousin Tino. "A good chaperon you turned out to be. While I lay in bed, sick as a dog."

"Is it my fault you were sick?" my father will say. "What's a man to do for seventeen days?" That's how long the trip took.

In those days it was unusual for a woman to accompany her husband to America. Most of the men from our village came over alone to pave the way for the wife and family. But my mother and father wouldn't have it any other way.

"And let you loose in America?" my mother would say, her big brown eyes fixed on my father.

"*Vedi*, Tino. See that,?" my father used to retaliate with just the hint of a smile on his lips. "That's trust for you."

"Come on, uncle Joe," Tino would joke. "It's not you she doesn't trust; it's all the women over here, *le americane.*"

This becomes a standing joke. What it really means is this: My father was extremely attractive and quite irresistible, which I do not doubt. He was handsome even in old age. My mother is not really angry about his flirtations. On the contrary, she basks in the glow of her husband's frivolous transgressions. After all, it is she who is married to him.

I find this quite confusing. I vow the man I marry will do no such thing to me.

We have the misfortune of bad weather. But then, what sort of weather can one expect when crossing the north Atlantic in December? My father has chosen to leave during one of the coldest months of the year.

A storm comes upon us a few days past Gibraltar. Our insides roll. Our balance is betrayed. You can feel the pull of the ship deep within the gut. Everything is tied, chained, or bolted to the floor. Few people are in the dining room tonight. They are all being sick in their rooms. I know my mother is. I have heard her throw up. I have seen her, pale and limp, climb back onto the bunk, tears in her eyes, her body trembling. But my father and I, cousin Tino and the Scandinavian blond are seated in our usual places trying to eat.

As the storm intensifies, this becomes impossible. It rages all around us. Tables and chairs break loose and smash to one side of the dining room. We are hustled out and told to go up to the glass enclosed area on the bow of the ship where we usually have afternoon tea. Up there, we are just a few steps away from the deck, where life boats hang in case of an emergency.

We are huddled together and my father thinks it would have been better if they had left us in the dining room. "Down there, at least, we wouldn't see what we were up against," he says. Here, the glass windows that protect us from the fierce waves also allow us to see the fury of the ocean.

My father is holding on to me. When he realizes my mother is nowhere to be seen, he wants to go look for her. He tries to hand me over to Tino, but a giant wave hits us and the bow of the ship disappears beneath the water's surface. It comes up again like a gigantic whale surfacing for air. Then it thumps down hard, slapping the waves.

A table crashes on my father and he is pinned beneath it. He loses his grip on me and I am swept away by the roll of the ship.

My father cries out my name. "Margherita," he calls. "Hold on." But there is nothing to hold on to. It's useless. I am torn from him and he is sure I will be crushed. But I am not. A hand grasps my leg.

"She's okay. I've got her." I am saved. Tino saves me.

How I wish I could recall this event. To have so much drama submerged is a pity. But it's no use; it will not come up into my mind's screen. For years I was incensed about this non experience, to have crossed the Atlantic and not have the capacity to remember it. Years later, I made the trip again wanting to savor such a voyage for whatever misery or distraction it would offer me. I wanted to know seasickness first hand, to experience what my mother had felt. I wanted to forget Daniel.

Our destination is Canada. We have relatives there: a great aunt and some cousins. They have been in America since the first great war. This is what I hear my parents say. This is how I learn there have been two great wars.

My parents say our relatives are in the hotel business and they are rich. We are going to be staying with them.

It is here my personal memory begins. I find this quite remarkable. To not be able to squeeze out remembrances of that turbulent voyage but to remember events that followed so soon after. From here on, I do not have to rely on the memory of others. I can now accumulate and store events that will surface later, retrieving bits and pieces whenever there is a catalyst. Some, I will notice, remain dormant for decades. But they exist regardless. They are there. And I begin to wonder, what else will I uncover? And when?

Maria Ardizzi

Among the Hills and Beyond the Sea

The episode narrated here is taken from Maria Ardizzi's novel, *Tra le collone e di la dal mare*, from which it also gets its English title. Anna, an Italian-Canadian teacher, returns to Italy to visit her aging parents and married sister.

The dining room had not changed very much. There were the same pictures on the walls, the same mauve coloured sofa, the chairs with straw-woven seats arranged around the large table. The sewing machine was still in one corner; and on the opposite corner where once they kept the radio, there towered the television set. There were a few new things like the chandelier in place of the bare light bulb and metal shade dish. The curtains with gaudy flowers made me suspect the contribution of my sister, Olga. In the air, mixed with the smell of dried fruit and ragu, I smelled the rich odour of the garden. It is necessary to have lived abroad in order to reconstitute these odours, in order to find in each many little stories, many faces.

My father, after living here for so many years, had become a rural person. He had come here when he married my mother and never moved again. He was from Montorio. I know that he had many opportunities to leave but always found some reason to stay. The years had made his serious features more acute: his look more penetrating, his listening more attentive, his intolerance for small talk more pronounced.

Olga was serving at table and her husband, Sergio, was pouring the wine in each glass. The two children, a boy and girl, sat across from me. I smiled; they stared. She had a pleated skirt and a big bow in her hair. He had a white shirt with cufflinks and a tie. They did not remind me of the children of my youth. I could not imagine them barefoot, running through the corn and spashing in the ditch. Olga speaks quickly and in a loud voice. I soon realize that we do not have memories in common. I think she has never had doubts about what she wanted to be. She has never been afraid. I remember when Filippo called her *mocciosa* "little kid" and she, small as she was, would answer by kicking his legs and running around him without getting caught. I always had the impression that my mother had a softness for her.

"Olga was born by a miracle, *per miracolo,*" she would say. And then would go on to tell the story of that Sunday afternoon in 1944 when some drunken German soldiers had taken the donkey from a farmer returning from his field and had wanted to make him race with his full load. There was a crowd of soldiers on the square in front of the school and on the street. From doors and windows people looked on frightened. My father was on our balcony and my mother came out to watch. As she was going in there was a shot and my father fell back holding his hand to his head. According to the trajectory she should have been hit. She was pregnant with Olga. We learned later that it was the German captain who fired from the square. He had spotted the priest who at that moment was walking under our balcony and had seen black. I had heard this story many times. My mother retold it always in the same way.

"I could have died then," my father would add as if to himself.

My mother would suddenly stop talking.

Sergio is proud to let everyone know that it is due to him that the town school now has a kindergarten and a refectory. His self-satisfaction is all over his shiny, forty-year-old face as he explains how difficult it was, how often he had to protest to get them. I observe his broad shoulders, his greying head on a short neck, his manner of opening and closing his hands on the table as if to reinforce his words. Olga listens to him admiringly. She explains that since she and her husband have been the permanent teachers in town they have done many things to improve the people.

My father throws them a passing glance and observes coldly, "People are getting worse and worse." He gets up and goes to his bedroom. My mother follows him. There is silence.

"See how he has become," complains Olga, *sotto voce.*

Sergio refills his glass of wine and nods to the kids who run to play in the next room. After a while my mother returns and begins to clear the table.

It is dark quickly. The fire is lit in the hearth. We hear the rain against the window panes, a steady and even patter, the only sound from outside. Around the table we continue to talk. I breathe in the acrid odour of smoke, the emotion of distant evenings that I cannot forget.

Sergio wants to know about America, and I ask, "Which America?" He begins to laugh. I tell them that people always get confused: Canada is Canada. Olga, instead, wants to know if its true that women *there* are totally independent. She lights a cigarette and throws her head back.

She says that here too there have been great changes for women. I tell her that there are still many women who are exploited. In a gesture of contradiction she answers: "You can't expect everything to change at once."

After Olga and Sergio have left my mother comes near. She has many questions to ask me: Does my brother Filippo get along with his wife? How are his children? With hesitation she asks about me. I know that these questions weigh heavily on her. Why don't I get married? She regards my forty-two years with regret and pain. I cannot tell her that I don't want to get married. I say instead that I am a contrary person, that it is difficult to get along with me. I tell her about my work as a teacher, and of the satisfaction which I get from helping my students. She does not seem convinced. She shakes her head and mumbles, "*Gli anni passano,* the years pass . . . "

I survey the room at a glance. Everything seems smaller and the new objects seem foreign. In the failing light I make out the entrance to the old post office. It is now only a storage room. At the end of the hall are the stairs to the attic. I think that sooner or later I will go up there to find fragments of my childhood among the abandoned objects.

In the voice of my mother, who is retelling me about events since my last visit, I hear her voice from my youth. "*Finitela lassu!* Stop it up there!" Sometimes a group of us would take an old radio up to the attic to learn to dance. From the window under the eaves we would drop bits of chalk on people in the street below. The swallows flew over our heads. I would often go up there alone to watch the swallows fly, *le rondini.*

My mother complains to me that my father eats little and never goes out. She gets up and adds, "Lets go see if he is asleep."

He is not sleeping but leaning on his pillows and listening to a concert on the radio. My mother says that he could listen to the concert sitting up, but goes to adjust his blankets.

As soon as I am in my room I open the window. A wave of strong country odours hits me, along with the hidden night sounds of crickets and frogs. The rain has stopped. The old street light reflects off the many puddles in the street. The laurel tree rises near my window and I can make out many familiar plants. The hedge marks the end of our garden. It seems to me that the night expands the spaces, that a breath of air, a noise, a voice become a crowd.

Once more I feel the anxiety of when I slept in this room, but a dozing anxiety. Then my anxiety ran on the string of my dreams: the ambitious things that I wanted to do, the good things; the fever that hit me after I had read Tolstoy and Dostoevsky.

In the drawer of the bedside table my father kept books, newspapers, and papers crammed with his subtle, even handwriting. I would borrow the books and read them secretly.

The chest of drawers was full of things my mother was saving: scraps of cloth, buttons, holy pictures which recalled some event. If she was given a gift she saved it wrapped in its original paper. It might have been useful, but for her it was saved as is.

How far away from here, it seems to me, is that sea of lights, the Canadian city which has been my home for many years. Of my own there is nothing anywhere, except in memory. In that sea there are only my attempts, my days of waiting, the sense of an always-more-distant probability. There are innumerable faces, many forgotten in time, others retained in memory like something on the point of becoming . . . There is Riccardo, or Rick, with his optimism, his fury for life. With him I walked, I ran, I laughed. Until I was afraid. There are Filippo and his wife, Kate, caught in their world of parties, business and spending. I have met many people in their home, the ambitious and the cunning; hangers-on to the so-called personalities for a position or a promotion. And there have also been the anonymous ones, who, like me, still believe in the possibility of noble and generous action.

A diffuse light rises beyond the hills, outlining the trees around the garden and the roof-line of nearby houses. I had not noticed that the sky had become dull and that soon a new moon would rise, *la luna nuova.*

Translated by Joseph Pivato

JOSEPH RANALLO

Mythologies

For the older Italian women
Who have outlived two husbands, one in Italy, one in
Canada,
November is the cruelest of all the winter months.

The days are long, repetitive, and monotonous;
The nights, a continuum of intermittent flashbacks and
nightmares.

They drift uneasily in and out of pre-winter mental fogs
Uncertain that the Canadian spring songbirds
Can return in time
Before the northern Iceman, dispassionate and oblivious,
Calls on them.

They find small comfort in their rosary beads
And their self-imposed penitence;
Relish in their aches and pains.

They long for the flicker of the dying flame
Of the votive candle on a cold, frosty night.

Like legions of ancient women before them
They believe that they were born for sorrow.

As the chill of the pre-Christmas season approaches
Slowly, methodically, and more merciless

Than a northern Alberta thunder storm
They begin to disconnect their feeble ties
With the electronic world that has all but forsaken them.

Alone and helpless they forecast their impending
discharge.

Like the suicidal, sacrificial female gray whale on the
Arctic Sea,
Sensing the immanent starvation of Eskimo children,
They approach the icy shore of their subconsciousness;
Park themselves within boat reach:
Await the inevitable harpoon of solitude
To surge into their bowels
Like a psalm.

ANTONINO MAZZA

Echoes in the Garden

So much echo. I can see so much echo.
In the city where I live,
        in October, when I go to her house
— and there is nothing to say —
we drive to the Gatineaus, and we tread on the dry leaves.

There are lakes in the hills. Through the trees
she discovers the trails
        and we follow each other,
and I watch her watching a tree dropping its colours.

There is a crimson sky in the lake. When we reach
the end of a trail
                        she looks for a boulder in the light
and we sit in the sun, at the edge of the water.

And I listen. And she listens.
And she's silent and I'm silent, sitting close
                                to each other with our toes
in the ripples, and her voice is so clear
I still feel all her laughter.

So I see her sometimes. Here, timeless,
the landscape inside borne up
                                    on a thought.
The slow rivers of cars penetrating the night-swell.
The infinite habitat writhing in want.

How natural it is in the metropolis this October 28,
to awake in the future . . .
A homeless genealogy aching in wants —

And memory reassures. And the soul is pure fiction.

Tiziana Beccarelli Saad

Italy: Spring 1920

Teresa is thirty-six years old. She has returned to her homeland. Her *paesani* are looking at her curiously. Why has she come back to the valley? Only to cry on her mother's grave some say. Others think she is here to stay.

Teresa Bianca was fifteen when her parents decided to send her to America to live with her brother. The voyage was very difficult. First the cart, then the boat; the packed and penniless passengers, the remarks of the sailors with their suggestive stares, the lack of water and food, and finally, landfall. Teresa, a shadow of her former self, descended from the boat. She was dirty and ill. Her brother wasn't happy. Why did his parents send him another useless mouth to feed?

"You'll have to get better quickly, little girl," he told her. "You are here to help me, not to get fat."

The passing of time has changed nothing in the village. The old faces look the same. The old family house is locked up. All the wooden shutters are closed tight. Coming into the village, someone gave her the large, heavy key. Her brothers didn't speak to her. She was aware of their displeasure that it was she who bought back the old house. They expressed no joy. Teresa is neither sad nor troubled. She crosses the piazza and pauses in front of her house. She stares at it. It is totally in ruin. Once inside she is shocked. How on earth could the family have been so poor? Some old and ugly wooden furniture, a large stove, and in the bedrooms some plain beds and a single dresser.

Living in America with Madame had indeed altered her memory.

She must have been around fifteen years of age the day she left, but she could not be exactly sure. Her mother had never really been certain of the exact date of birth of her living children, often confusing them with those who had died. Her brother Giuseppe had been gone for some time already. He lived in a terribly distant place; New York. Coming home late one night, her head light from letting herself be kissed a little too much, Teresa found her old lady sitting in a corner by the fireplace crying uncontrollably.

"Mother, hey? Are you not well?"

The old lady never raised her eyes which she wiped with her apron. But she continued to cry and cry. Quietly, softly, with dignity. She continued to cry and the flow seemed never to want to stop as if she held in those tears the unhappiness of all the dead people she prayed for often and all the living whom she cursed even more often.

"Hey, Mother? Are you ill?

Nothing doing. Teresa had become increasingly bothered by her mother's indifference towards her. Somewhere along the way, the old lady had learned to rely only on her sons, her men. She had nothing but scorn for her daughters, which she regarded as lesser creatures. Teresa turned away slowly and headed for the stairs. Upstairs, in her bedroom four girls were already asleep. In this household the girls had to get up early. The men too, for that matter. In the early morning, the house quietly came to life. Teresa was just finishing her bowl of coffee when her old man looked at her and announced: "Teresa, you are leaving next week."

" I am? But where am I going?"

"You're going to America. Your brother needs you there."

Teresa stammered out some words, but nobody paid any attention.

"You're the one that's going. You're old enough and your brother needs you."

She clasped her hands together to disguise her fear. Her fate was sealed and there was nothing she could say or do about it. Thus, she would go to America, where her brother needed her. She was only fifteen and let boys kiss her far too easily. The village folk were talking. One is not allowed to do certain things so openly. One week later the girl knocked on her parents' door. Her mother was braiding her hair while her father fastened his suspenders. It was her last morning in this house. Without pausing her father said: "Your trunk is ready, have someone write sometime."

Teresa did not know how. Giuseppe would write for her. In the village everyone had something to say about Teresa. If she was going, then good riddance. One less slut to worry about.

Now Teresa is a landowner. It is her house! A ruin, maybe, but it is hers. Her pragmatic nature quickly takes hold. This will have to be redone, while that will have to be repaired, she tells herself.

In a little while it will be pleasant.

Sitting in a chair, her eyes closed, Teresa sees Madame's face. She too passed away. Died of cancer. Teresa received a handsome sum in gratitude for her services. When, exactly, did Teresa submit to the notion that in the village she should be treated as an inferior being? Perhaps it was through her mother's influence. While working for Madame she learned new things simply by observing; things what will serve her well here in the village. She will have everyone's respect. No one is going to take advantage of her now! They will have to submit to her wishes. The old lady can rest easy in her grave. Teresa has buried her American dreams, her golden dreams. But new dreams have come to replace the old ones. She will earn the respect of these ignorant and hard-headed sons of men. Since her return her thoughts are invaded by a single-minded quest for happiness of which she had never previously felt capable. When she stopped at her old lady's grave, just before entering the village, she felt for the first time that maybe the old lady had suffered from her condition, and that it might console her to see, if she could, that at least one of her children had succeeded in a way that she might have wanted to succeed. The heavy burden of inherited poverty had died at that very moment in Teresa's mind.

Never! Never again! She repeated to herself. She would be happy with little, but she would be happy. She knew she was condemned to be alone. At thirty-six no one would take her for a wife.

Too old to bear children. She would take care of other people's children. Upon her death this house, which now belongs to her, would be the prettiest it has ever been.

Towards the end of the day, when the light had begun to fade, when the histories of the other generations took on the semblance of truth, floating around things and people as in a dream, and at a time when life seemed less threatening, Teresa shows herself in public. She enters the *osteria* inhabited by people seemingly at peace with themselves. All around her are men playing cards or simply having a drink. She clears her throat and begins to speak: "I need a good carpenter to fix my house. I won't pay much, but with meals, a bed and laundry, it ought to be just fine."

The men seem too surprised to speak, seeing a woman before them at this hour in this place. One, nevertheless came forward.

"I Amedeo, work clean. I accept your offer. I'll take your food and the laundry, but the bed I can do without."

"Good, then. Come to my house tomorrow morning at seven o'clock. There is plenty of work. You won't be disappointed. As for the rest of you men, good night."

While Amedeo is working on the house, Teresa prefers to go on long walks. She cannot, after all, remain there watching him work all day long. She had always believed in the reputation workers have of daydreaming and not giving a damn unless someone is keeping an eye on them. But after a few weeks she had to concede that this man's work would always meet her expectations, even exceed them. This man appears to take no pleasure in talking, and may only be pausing to listen to her stories about America out of courtesy. Ah! what pleasure she feels in recounting her American adventure. Her memory is improving with time. It seems to her sometimes that her mind has stored things she never knew. She recalls images her physical being, it seems, has never actually explored. Some images are harsh, but most are images of freedom, dignity and joy.

The black veil has rested on the closed eyes of her dead brother who did not learn in time how to decipher America. But she, yes she! Knowing what she knows now, what couldn't she do in America!

Translated by Dominic Cusmano

Darlene Madott

Writer and Lawyer

I became a lawyer because of a writer's block and because I had to find a way of living. I thought, if I cannot write let me do something useful, something that will consume hours like fire to human hair, make writing impossible or, at the very least, make me forget about writing.

On good days I think being an advocate makes sense: an advocate is one who pleads for another, who, in effect, tells his story. And there are many stories.

My first matrimonial file taught me about two people whose love was to hate, who when the decree *nisi* was finally pronounced at the end of a bitter trial, seemed to lose their reason for being. Neither one has applied for the decree absolute. Now the husband has been charged with "watching and besetting" the former matrimonial home — like a ghost haunting a familiar place.

My pleadings were recently the subject of a procedural motion to court. They had offended a rule of civil procedure that every pleading shall contain a concise statement of material fact, not the evidence by which these facts are to be proven. They were "embarrassing" within the meaning of the rules. I argued that the facts were in themselves embarrasing: a wealthy entrepreneur who, for twenty years unbeknownst to his wife has been having an affair with a woman he maintains in a lavish residence some ten blocks distance from the matrimonial home. My description of the homes, the live-in servants, the farmer who daily comes to feed the Arabian stallions, were somewhat prolix.

The purpose of pleading, protested my learned friend, "is *not to write a novel,* but to define the issue in dispute."

The irony was inescapable.

Am I a writer disguised as a lawyer, or a lawyer who yearns to write?

Ironic in a deeper sense: If my pleading had broken the rules (the law, in effect), was there not a more profound disobedience? In becoming a lawyer, had I not betrayed myself, breaking faith with that which I had most wanted to become?

Men contradict themselves, just as they break rules. There is also a way in which men obey themselves when they obey law.

The strange freedom we sometimes find in obedience, or the need borne of a writer's loneliness to collaborate with others in something larger than oneself, may have been what in my own nature first impelled me towards law.

Writers and lawyers have much in common. Both work with the same materials — words and human nature. Both are conduits.

As a litigator, I deal every day with human beings in conflict, struggling sometimes not so much to resolve their problems as to vindicate their own view of the truth. I have learned that there is no truth — only multiple points of view. The role of an advocate is to present his client's truth in the best possible light.

"You will be most effective," one experienced counsel told me, "if you remember never to believe your own client.

That way, you may be pleasantly surprised, but never disappointed." Like writers, the best advocates are skillful manipulators of the facts. And the same guilt I sometimes feel as a writer — pilfering, eavesdropping, using other peoples lives — I feel as a lawyer when I perceive myself to be collaborating in a process that preys upon the greed or disappointment or tragedy of others.

And yet the practice of law is deeply engaging. Every file I open is a new book. I am often overworked. I am rarely bored. There are few ways of life about which one can say as much.

Giovanni Costa

Dare ad una foto la vita
e un'illusione;
come strappare la luce al cuore della notte?

The Cart

To give life to a photo
is an illusion;
how to snatch the light from the heart of night?
Tricketti, trackette, tricketti, trackette
trickette, trickette:
wheels of a Sicilian cart
and bitter singsong of the night,
like a sword you enter
my cozy little room
and you break a shadow of memories.
He sings softly, the Iblei Mountain carter,
with a shuffling voice
and while he's going away . . .
the tricketti, trackette, tricketti, trackette
leaves a part of my village in my heart.

Translated by Robert McBryde

Romano Perticarini

Tu vivi nel giardino
della nostra sud-Italia . . .

To My Friend, Nino

You inhabit the garden
— I once had such a garden—
in our southern part of Italy,
cloyed by the morning
that finds you breathing
after a sleepy night.

You leave barefoot the marks
of a light gait on the shore
whitened by salt and dead shells.

In only one breath
you embrace the sun, the sea,
the scent of every colored flower.

Nino, I am next to the hearth,
consuming the last hours
of this cold night
September has brought me.
I dream of shores and seagulls.
And to quiet the fire
in my heart I read
your book of poems.

Translated by Carlo Giacobbe

Anna Foschi Ciampolini

The Scissors

By five o'clock in the morning the little bedroom was already flooded with light which filtered through the brown and blue flowered curtains screening the windows. Angelina tried to shield her eyes and then she turned over impatiently in bed. She would have liked to sleep just a little longer but the glare, although diffused, irritated her. She had noticed right away that the windows in that house did not have shutters but her brother had laughed at her surprise saying, "This way there is no need for an alarm clock in the morning and we won't be late for work." Already she could hear him rattling around in the little kitchen preparing caffè latte, and so with a vague sense of guilt she jumped out of bed.

"Leave it! I will do it," she said to Salvatore, slapping her hand on the corner of the table, her eyes still puffy with sleep.

"But don't you see you are still sleeping standing up. Don't worry about it this morning. Pretend you are still on holiday," said her brother, extending to her a steaming cup of caffè latte.

"Today and tomorrow if you want you can rest and later I will take you around town a bit and then you can begin work. I've already found a good job for you in a factory where they make clothes. You are a seamstress and they will pay you so much a piece. The starting pay is pretty good and then if the boss is pleased with you they will give you a raise. You will like it there. Many women from our part of Italy have worked there."

While saying this Salvatore was filling a small metal box with bread, salami and fruit. Then he went to the bathroom and soon came out dressed in his mechanic's overalls.

"Well I haven't got time to fool around. Its already six and my garage is quite far so I better leave now. You stay here and wait for me. I'm going now. I'll be back home around four. You can eat your breakfast now. If you want to go outside later you can. Do whatever you like." As he said this Salvatore looked around him with an air of pride. He opened the fridge door.

"Here we have everything: meat, cheese, salami, even cookies, milk — everything. Not like our hometown. Don't be shy. Eat what you like. And under here there is everything for washing dishes: here is soap and look, see how the sink spray works. Did you ever see a kitchen like this? Who at home has a kitchen like this?" — and he patted the large refrigerator, the electric stove and the other kitchen marvels. And as he went out the door he continued: "And this is nothing. Now that you are working too, in six months we'll have our own house. You'll see that here we can have whatever we want just by working."

Angelina heard the outside door close and a moment later the suffocating roar of his big American car. Salvatore had come to pick her up at the Vancouver Railway Station only a few days earlier and she remembered how she had been left breathless when they took off together in it. It had taken five days by train to get from Halifax to Vancouver after the long trans-Atlantic voyage on the "Saturnia." The images, the words, the faces, the thoughts and the towns had raced before her eyes leaving her dizzy. She was afraid of everything, of losing her luggage, of not being able to answer the immigration officials, of not getting on the right train. She was comforted a little when she noticed that everybody else was in the same situation as her. They stared wide-eyed trying to guess at things and trying to help each other. "Now they are going to look at our passports. Now they are going to put us on the train," everyone full of the same anxiety and the same dreams. Salvatore had made that trip two years earlier. At first he boarded with other immigrants. Then he found some work as an auto mechanic. He had written home that he was lonely. He didn't want to get married right away because he wanted to save some money first but if his sister would come to stay with him in Canada he would find her work and together they would rent an apartment. She could make lots of money. What was Angelina waiting for? She could save up for a good dowry in a few months.

She visualized the face of her mother. She recalled the words of sisters and friends. Whoever went to America made a fortune. Didn't we see how much money they sent home, the pictures of big houses and big cars? They said there was lots of work, lots of jobs to choose from — not like their town where the men stood in the piazza all day with their hats on wasting away the hours after Don Rosario that morning had picked the laborers who would work that day. Angelina was a good seamstress. At seven years of age she had gone to apprentice with Signora Concetta, who had clients as far away as Palermo. Now, at eighteen, she sewed suits which were a marvel and which in America would have cost a fortune. So she decided to go. Her brother sent her *l'atto di richiamo* and the other necessary immigration documents. The days passed too quickly. She had wanted to slow down those last few days and hours, the evenings of warm sunlight and the colors of spring, talks with her friends and promises to write, the last night in her childhood bed in the room she shared with her sleeping sisters, listening to the sounds of wooden clogs and wagon wheels on the pavement outside.

Angelina passed her hand over the kitchen table and turned towards the window to convince herself that she was really in America. She repeated this to herself over and over in a low voice until the words seemed to break up into a thousand fragments.

Outside the nearby roads seemed silent and virtually deserted. The houses seemed like doll's houses, all painted in bright colors and made of wood, all with a little garden of flowers and a green lawn, bordered with a fence or a green hedge. Every once in a while she heard a dog bark or a child would interrupt his play in the garden to look at her with surprised eyes and without saying a word. There were no stores nearby. She had to go a good distance to reach a large department store. The city centre was so far that you needed a car or a bus to get there. Angelina had not spoken to anyone yet, even though her brother had told her that in the neighbourhood there were many Italians. She was afraid of getting confused again as she had the first day when the apartment manager, an Irish woman with dyed curly hair had persistently pointed out a room at the end of the hall as if she had wanted to take her there by force, until Angelina had run back into the apartment. Later her brother had told her, "She only wanted to show you the laundry room. Here there is one laundry room for all the apartments," he continued. "You'll see. We are not going to stay here very long. We are going to buy a house and then we are going to rent *il basamento*. This way we can pay the morgheggio. And when you get married you will have your share. Then we'll buy another old house and we'll fix it up ourselves and rent it out. Do you know. There are people who arrived here without shoes and now own four or five houses. Now we are going to focus on you. Tomorrow you go to the factory and start work right away. We'll save every dollar for the house.

In order to reach the small clothing factory they had to cross half the city. They crossed broad streets half asleep in the morning sun and full of flowering trees where the birds sang hidden among the branches. In the sky she saw strange large, black birds circling around looking for food and large black and grey gulls that flew very high without stopping. There were gardens that were suffocating under the abundance of flowers. The factory was in the center of town and there were buses that she could take there. Salvatore would only be able to take her in his car the odd time. They arrived in a grey neighbourhood without trees or flowers with a few wooden houses eaten by mold among some cement buildings. Salvatore stopped beside a two-story building. "See, this is the place! Up there you'll find the offices and the women work down here. Come with me. Let me do the talking and do whatever *il bosso* tells you to do."

The owner wasn't there yet but the supervisor, a tall blond woman built like a wardrobe, was told about the new employee. She greeted Angelina coolly and then yelled something at a woman bending over a sewing machine in the big work room. Salvatore explained, "The supervisor says that there is another Italian that works here and she will explain to you what you have to do. See, you didn't have to worry! Just do what *la bossa* tells you to do and, on Saturday, you get paid. It's sixty cents an hour. I have to run off now. I'll see you at home this afternoon." And Salvatore left with a couple of parting words for the blond wardrobe who didn't even look at him.

The Italian woman was called Nancy, short for Annuniziata, and she knew how to speak English because every second word she said was *"occhei, occhei"* and *"datsrait"* to the *bossa.* She took Angelina by the arm and brought her to a sewing machine in the large workroom. "This week you'll sew seams and then we'll see what you can do. Do you have your scissors?"

"Not with me, but..." Nancy did not give her time to respond and seemed to get very agitated. She quickly ran back upstairs to tell the blond woman something who then seemed even colder. Even Nancy was making faces of disapproval.

"Why don't you have your scissors? Don't you know that here you need all your tools? You have to have your scissors, the measuring tape and everything else. If tomorrow you don't have these tools you won't be able to work here."

"I'm sorry but I didn't know. My brother didn't . . . Don't worry, tomorrow I'll bring all my own stuff. For today, can you lend me a pair of scissors?"

"*I* don't have any for you. See if someone else can lend you some."

"And how am I supposed to do that? I don't know how to ask . . . "

"Listen! Here you have to work and I've already lost too much time. You look for a pair of scissors and you sit here and you sew all these pieces that are on the table if you know how."

Angelina opened her mouth to answer when the blond woman yelled something from upstairs. "Did you hear? She said to get back to work. Hurry up, get moving."

"I can't without scissors. Look . . . " But Nancy had already turned away with a frown on her face. Another seamstress, a small Chinese girl, thin as a wren, came forward, asked Nancy something, then returned with a pair of scissors which she gave to Angelina.

"She'll lend you a pair of scissors. She has a second pair. Remember to return them tonight," Nancy said and then she turned to her machine manoeuvering it like a captain steering a rudder.

The hours passed without Angelina noticing them because her attention was absorbed in the pile of garments on her work table and by the new machine that sewed so differently from her own little Singer that she had left at home in Italy, and by the desire to do everything quickly and well. She hadn't even eaten and later she noticed that she was hungry and thirsty. She was about to ask when the lunch break was when she noticed that the large work room was half empty. Four or five seamstresses were still there finishing the odd piece or were cutting out new pieces. "But, is it already time to go?" she thought, and she turned to look for Nancy but Nancy must have already left. She then looked for the little Chinese woman but she, too, was no longer at her place. The last workers were quickly leaving and Angelina looked up to see if the supervisor was still there but it was useless. The only thing she could do was to make her understand through gestures that she had finished work and was leaving too. She put her work table in order and saw the scissors. She remembered that the Chinese girl was working in the place behind her on the fourth table and she went to look for a drawer, a secure place in order to leave the scissors. There was a tin box with needles and the oil for the machine. This was the best place for the scissors.

When Angelina reached the street she noticed it was already getting dark and she felt exhausted. Then she noticed that Salvatore was waiting for her, leaning on his blue Chevrolet overly decorated with chrome.

Almost a week went by. Angelina had quickly prepared her collection of tools. That way she didn't need any favors. She had learned how to travel by bus and to bring her bag of lunch which she often ate as she sewed, sitting at her work table. And she had learned that when *la bossa* walked up and down among the work tables she was always saying the same thing, "Faster, work faster" and "Get back to work," if anyone ever raised their head. Angelina didn't speak to anybody except in gestures. She had tried to strike up a conversation with the dark and stocky Nancy during breaks when they were both washing their hands in the small bathroom. "Where are you from?" Angelina had asked Nancy, and that one had pretended not to hear her. "Where are you from?" she had repeated.

"From near Rome," Nancy had mumbled reluctanly, looking at her unpleasantly.

"Have you been here long?" Angelina continued. "I only arrived here a few days ago but my brother has been here for two years, since 1954. He is a mechanic. It's a good job. Do you have family here? Do you have children?"

"You want to know too many things," Nancy retorted suspiciously. "I mind my own business and do my job and that's it" — and she turned away and walked back to the work room where the machines were making an infernal noise and you couldn't even turn your head without hearing the strident voice: "Faster, faster, faster." The Chinese girl who had loaned her the scissors had been missing for two days. Perhaps she was sick... but then she returned to work. She hadn't spoken to Angelina and so Angelina had no reason to be disturbed, at least until the day that Nancy came looking for her with an indecipherable expression in her dark eyes.

She attacked Angelina right away. "What did you do with the scissors that Amy lent you? She says that she can't find them!"

"I put them in her drawer in a box. I returned them right away."

"But they are not there! You had better return them. Otherwise you will be in trouble."

"But I told you that . . . "

At that moment the blond woman yelled at them to come upstairs and Nancy pushed her towards the office. The owner was also there, a thin man with thinning hair combed over the shiny dome of his head. Amy was standing there with an apologetic expression on her face. The blond woman looked at Nancy. "Well?" she asked her. Angelina didn't understand a word. She saw their mouths move and their faces change expressions like in a silent film. She tried to guess what they were saying. She pulled Nancy by the sleeve in order to give her version. At one point Amy, the Chinese girl, left. The owner said something to Nancy and made a gesture with his hand as if to say, "Go now!"

"Tomorrow morning you come and get your pay cheque. You've been fired. The owner says that he is not going to call the police for a thing like this but he doesn't want to see you here again. Understand?"

"But what are you saying? What did you tell them? I didn't do anything. Nothing!" Angelina was now shouting.

"Zitta! Sta zitta! You stole the scissors. That's what you did, and now you better go home."

But Angelina stood her ground and stopped her.

"It's not true! It's not true! I'm not a thief and you know it and you have to tell them!"

"I know no such thing. We can't find the scissors and the boss says you have to leave. Now leave me alone or I'll have him call the police," and she looked towards the office in a threatening way. Angelina felt like dying. The police! She gathered up her things and left in a haze of tears.

Salvatore walked back and forth across the room with his hands on his hips. "No ! Nobody calls my sister a thief!" Tomorrow I'm going to come and talk to your boss and if there is some trick you can be darned sure they are going to hear about it! Don't worry. Leave it to me. We've always been honest people!"

Angelina felt better with Salvatore's assurances. He was going to defend her. He was going to explain things. She calmed down and prepared dinner. To be treated as a thief and threatened with the police! I won't worry anymore. Tomorrow Salvatore will explain everything.

The next morning they arrived in front of the factory a half an hour before starting time. When the blond supervisor arrived with the keys she led them upstairs to the office. "The owner will arrive in ten minutes," she said. The cheque is already signed.

"I don't want the money," Salvatore answered. "I want to speak to him."

"As you wish," the blond lady said, shrugging her shoulders. At that moment the owner entered.

Salvatore spoke with ardor but with dignity which seemed to make an impression on the man who ran his hand over his thinning hair several times. He sighed and finally called for Nancy and Amy. The Chinese girl came up first in her usual subdued way. She repeated that she couldn't find the scissors but that in the end they weren't that important to her because they were an old pair. She didn't want to get anybody into trouble. Yes, she had looked for them again.

The owner interrupted her. "Are you sure you looked carefully?"

"I can look again," she replied humbly, and she went downstairs. Nancy stood in the doorway listening without saying a word.

"Do you want some coffee?" the owner said to Salvatore, as if to say something.

The Chinese girl came running upstairs with an ecstatic expression. "The scissors, here they are! They were in my drawer in my box!" And suddenly she was embarrassed. "I'm sorry. I'm very, very sorry. But I don't know how . . . "

"Next time, by God, be more attentive," said the blond with an acid tone."

"You caused us all a lot of trouble, you stupid girl!"

"I know, I know. I'm sorry! Tonight I'll work until nine. That way I'll finish all the jackets for order number

45. I'm sorry!" she said one more time, turning towards Angelina.

"Alright, now both of you get back to work!" the boss said. "You are not paid to stand around and talk." And to Angelina, he said, "You get back to your workplace!"

Salvatore smiled at her and gave her a sly wink. She wanted to hug him there in front of everybody!

Bending over the sewing machine she thought, "But how could it happen? How could the scissors not be found yesterday and today they were exactly in the place where I left them?"

At noon the lunchbreak bell rang. Amy remained in her place hanging on to her sewing machine like an anchor. She didn't even take out her lunch. She wanted to make up for the mess she had created. Angelina went straight to Nancy. "Come! I have to talk to you!"

"I have to finish here."

"No, you have to come!"

"What do you want?"

"I want to know what you told the boss yesterday! And I want you to take back the words you said to me. I've *never* been a thief!"

"I didn't say it! And now that's enough! You've got your place back. What more do you want? I have work to do. Leave me alone!"

"No! You said that I stole the scissors. Before saying things like that you have to be sure."

Nancy noticed that the blond lady was looking at them and she turned towards her as if to say, "Well, I can't work like this."

La bossa came near and measured the pile of clothing on Angelina's table that had to be finished. "You're behind in your work!" she said coldly. "This stuff has to be finished today! What are you doing wasting time?"

Angelina began to gesture and to complain about not being understood.

"So! What are you waiting for?" yelled La Bossa. And turning to Nancy she asked, "What does she want now?"

Nancy responded, "I dunno. She called me a liar!"

"Fuck! I don't want to hear any more of this crap! Go back to work!" she yelled and then turned to Angelina. And as she saw her hesitate, a bit dazed, she pushed her with force towards the work table. "Go back to work, you understand, you damned spaghetti bitch!" And she punched her roughly in the back.

ꕤ

The voice of Michael Jackson filled the little sewing room, the stereo at full volume.

Angelina sighed. "These kids are all born deaf! But they're all good kids. My daughter is already working at Gold's. Do you want a coffee, a cappuccino? I can make it for you with the *macchina* bar. You'll see how good it is." She got up and turned on the new espresso bar machine that stood in the corner.

"Well? What happened then?" I asked.

"What? I remained in that factory for another month and then I couldn't take it anymore and I found other work on Robson street. There were lots of factories there then. Not like today with all those elegant shops. It was difficult all over, you know. Then, I got married. I had children . . . my father-in-law. I had lots of work to do. Now I work from home as a seamstress. At least I don't have a boss that pushes me around. "

"So! You never knew what really happened to those scissors?"

"What do you want me to tell you? I thought about it many times. Maybe someone took them by mistake and didn't know where to put them back or somebody took them to get me into trouble?"

"Do you think it was Nancy?"

"Maybe it was. I don't know — and nobody knows for sure."

And now she hands me the cup of cappucino brimming with fragrant foam. I look around at the walls, at the photographs of many clients with the most beautiful outfits sewn by Angelina . . . debutantes, wedding pictures, graduations. "What beautiful outfits! I tell her. What intricate patterns!"

"If you're not skilled you can't make them. And you can't imagine how many people are jealous of you when they see that you are doing well! They are afraid of losing their business!"

"But Angelina! Among Italians we should be helping one another."

"But it is not always like that, you know," Angelina replied. "It is particularly among the Italians that I get into trouble. In fact, the biggest problems come from them. But it happens with others, too, with the Chinese, the East Indians and the Germans. Here only the strong survive. You're always alone and you have to be careful even of your friends, who talk behind your back. They are nice people but they gossip."

"Do you ever think of Italy?"

"Do you know how long it is since I have been there? Almost thirty years. Sometimes I dream about my hometown, when I used to sit in the street and sew with my friends. We used to talk and sing together. We loved each other, you know. No, I never returned. We had to build our house. Then the kids came along. Then I started my own sewing shop. What do you think? Whatever America gives us it takes back double in sacrifices." She finished her coffee and began to arrange the dress fabric at her sewing machine. She looked up thoughtfully.

"You know, there is one thing that I can never forget in all these years. It is that punch in the back, right between my shoulders. Like beating a beast of burden. I can still feel it, my welcome to America."

Translated by Joseph Pivato

MARCO FRATICELLI

After the Wake

(A HAIKU SEQUENCE)

Both with our feet

in this freezing river:

our eyes meet

ꕥ

your name

scraped in window frost

my fingertip . . . so cold

ꕥ

a religious calendar

in the dead woman's room

and maps pinned to the wall

ꕥ

funeral home

a father quiets his child

with Easter eggs

ꕥ

by the graveside

our shadows

grow longer

ꕥ

after the wake

you peel the sunburn

from my back

ꕥ

Epilogue

Lately, I have been having a recurring dream. I am sitting crosslegged in a field.

The trees surrounding me are in autumn colours. In slow motion, thousands of bits of paper and pieces of photographs begin drifting down like snowflakes. I reach out to touch them but they dissolve in my hand like ashes. I stick out my tongue to catch one and its taste is not as bitter as I'd feared.

Dôre Michelut

Coming to Terms with the Mother Tongue

Many writers today are first or second-generation immigrants who live and work in another language, one of Canada's two official languages. Although their mother tongue may still occupy a part of their lives, this part has been relegated to a circumscribed private territory which does not enter easily into relation with either living or writing in the acquired dominant language. For a writer, the problems and paradoxes this poses come constantly to the fore and are so complex that any attempt to use the mother tongue as a vehicle for writing is quickly abandoned. To understand the scope of the problem in the life of an individual writer, it is informative to consider what happens to a language upon immigration.

Most North American immigration up to 1960 was of peasant stock due to an industrialization which progressively developed a modern economy by erasing indigenous feudal cultures and enlarging the middle classes. Writers who are children of this wave of immigration and who would work in their mother tongue find themselves writing within a sensibility that is pregnant with feeling and presence, yet speechless.

Peasant speech occupies a place in a cultural hierarchy: its task is to describe the cultivation of soil and the taming of animals. To do this requires physical presence and sound. Being oral, its standards are upheld by cyclical rituals that involve the earth and the speaking self rather than the thinking self and a body of written law. As language, it is not amenable to forms of communication which occur in a society whose allegiance is to a stable corpus of standardized signs rather than to the signs of the earth in seasonal change. The sensibility of language that develops within a scripted tradition is missing.

Between the acquired language and the mother tongue, how can there be common ground? The two languages have long since staked out their territory within the psyche and the balance that has been achieved is seamless and invisible. For writers who would explore that boundary, there is no recourse but to approach both languages in their oral states as reservoirs. But soon the mother tongue would hold the writer in an earth it can no longer cultivate, and the acquired language would become more abstract to accommodate that "unreal" experience. The relations between reservoirs soon become saturated and static: experience in one is felt as a threat by the other. The mother tongue, judged by the requirements of the activity of writing, turns into a barren, moon-like landscape explored by forms proper to the acquired language. The result is inaccessible both to the acquired language and to the original language that evolved in the homeland.

Yet, if I were to look at the phenomenon which touches me intimately solely from a social perspective, as if my languages were objects to manipulate in view of a written goal, I would be forgetting that at some point in time I gave myself to language and that I have entrusted language with my life. I would be calling my experience in language a body separate from myself and I would be saying that the object has grown alien. If I were to stop at this, not only would I end up abandoning Furlan, my mother tongue, I would also be stating that the sounds I made in Friûl until

I was six stayed there when I left, that Furlan belongs to a place outside of me. But those first six years of my life can't be separated from me. They spread through my time like my child body spreads through my adult body. And how many of those six years that run through me are unspoken or abandoned because I can't find their forms in English?

Furlan, my mother tongue, is a marriage between Celtic and vulgar Latin and is a member of the eighth Romance language group, Ladino. It is spoken in a small province of northern Italy and its dialects vary from town to town due to millennia of invasions and very localized life. Although it is a language, it developed a standardized script only recently.

But most of what I have learned about myself and language through writing did not develop because of a rediscovery of Furlan. The balance that Furlan and English struck within me long ago is so very entrenched it feels saturated and inaccessible. At a certain point, my two acquired languages, Italian and English, were forced to come to terms with each other within me. It was this experience that led me to consider ways of approaching the more remote Furlan. When my family emigrated to Canada, my parents decided that Furlan was such a minority language that it would not be of use to their children in the future. Therefore, in our house, our parents spoke Furlan between themselves and they spoke what Italian they knew with the children. It took only a few years for me to reply to both languages exclusively in English. In my teens, I could understand both Italian and Furlan, but I spoke them badly.

To complicate matters further, after high school I decided to go to university in Florence where the Italian seemed to be another language altogether. A background noise became the foreground. After one year I spoke Italian not badly; after two I spoke it well; after five I started having problems with English. When I came back to live in Toronto after having been absent for eight years, it seemed I spoke English just as everyone spoke English but, as soon as a serious conversation got underway, words flew by each other and did not meet. Cultural references I made became irrelevant, concepts that struck sure resonance in Florence, wafted and waned in Toronto, or were too loud, too soft, abstract, or even impolite. I found myself starting to wobble, unable to detect whether I had hit or missed "something."

I suspected that my English had become insufficient so I went back to university in Toronto searching specifically for courses similar to those I had taken in Italy. Immediately, I became aware that the information I was absorbing was already in me but arranged differently. Concepts that flowed together inevitably in Italy, here stood independently, senselessly. It was as if the languages had been amazingly attracted and yet unable to touch and penetrate. As if *aemulateo*, Foucault's second form of similitude, where recognition perpetuates space without contact, were struggling to become *convenentia*, adjacency of place, where fringes touch and mingle. Feeling their exclusiveness, I could commit myself fully to neither. Translation seemed a puny effort in such a struggle; something always seemed betrayed, and I avoided it.

At first I lived the impossibility of translation as silence. In fact, I became aware of the exclusion of myself from one world and the other to such an extent that I started feeling irrelevant to both. The more attention I gave to the English world here, the less I understood the intense and committed life I had lived for eight years in Florence, and the more it haunted me. Then I started to write, in any language and despite all grammars. It would have been unintelligible to most but, as far as I was concerned, I was producing meaning, and on my own terms. And the view I got of myself from the page was that of two different sets of cards shuffled together, each deck playing its own game with its own rules.

Perhaps because the page is white and gives the illusion of being outside the human body and therefore only mildly related to it through language, I realized that the act of speaking is also the act of being spoken. I saw myself shaping language, but I also saw how the page shaped me. Where a language claimed me, the speaker, it claimed not only what I uttered but also dictated the parameters of which I could possibly utter in given circumstance. At this point, I finally started to understand my relationship to language: it premeditated me and I, to the extent that I allowed it to carry me, determined it.

The so-called betrayal of translation was really irrelevant; all form, including sound as language, betrayed for that matter. The point was to fully determine myself in a given circumstance: I could never change the given, but I could shape it as I engaged it. My fear of betrayal was, in fact, my fear of freedom to choose between forms. It had to be either one or the other at a given point in time; simultaneity was impossible. Like the old profile-vase perception exercise, English just could not assimilate my experience of Italian. It made external, stereotypical conjectures, but it could not incorporate the other sensibility as part of its own manifest reality. What was lived in Italian stayed in Italian, belonged to it completely. And vice versa.

I found that I had no choice but to commit myself fully. Unless I offered my statement wholeheartedly to a language's undertow of ironies, to its inner "ear," the meaning was not "felt" and what was manifest in the statement lost sense and sensibility. Since I seemed to be possessed by the language I experienced, the experience had to reside not in me but in the "ear" of the language itself. In theory, this sounds practical; in practice, as I materialized one ghost, the other would fade. I hated the seeming arbitrary blindness of the two languages. Each left me out while stumbling all over the other invisible entity that occupied the same territory — me. Finally, I thought that if the languages could only "see" each other within me, I would stop feeling haunted and cheated.

Writing, I tracked the sighting of one ghost or the other. The more I wrote, the more I found myself grammatically separating the languages. One poem would become two: one in either language. I would work on them until they seemed to snap apart and become independent entities; each becoming progressively more untranslatable as it progressed in its own direction. What surprised, and then delighted was that each poem came to a stop somewhere inside itself when it knew itself as coherent, whole and complete. At this point, each piece could recognize the other and know its conception from the moment it diverged. It could "see" where the other broke off and how far it continued into itself toward its own satisfaction. Together, both constituted the whole bracket that was the extent of my experience of that poem. Nothing was left out;

all the words were ghostless, full of me and present to themselves.

It was then that I understood that translation incorporates the idea of the insufficiency of the object produced while being intimately involved in and committed to its production. Mine was a process of self-translation: I spanned the languages within my awareness simultaneously while each experienced the other in a "felt" relation. I was generating a dialectical experience that was relative to both languages, and yet, at the same time, I was beyond them both. The event could therefore be remembered and explained. By translating myself into myself, by spinning a fine line in-between states of reality, I transcended the paralysis of being either inside or outside form. It was like transmuting lead to gold and back, solely for the pleasure of knitting their interrelation. I understood that the standardized language mattered only inasmuch as I could experience its translation in writing. Grammar was not written in stone, it was writing in me, and I was the only arbiter of the experience. Since I was both the author and the translator, who else could I consult?

At this point I found I had something to say about the forms of these languages in a way that did not exclude my intimacy with them. My writing was a tool with which I held them so that they would produce me while I communicated within them. I could finally speak of English and Italian not as objects, but as subjects with individual personalities which acted upon me.

English and Italian agree and disagree in interesting places. Anyone who has translated has certainly localized these common linguistic *impassi*. Take the English neuter "it," for instance, Hemingway's "it": a genderless, namely identity. It is raining; it goes without saying; how is it going? In Italian: *piove*; *si capisce*; *come va*? Where in English the vagueness of "it," although undetermined, must be acknowledged for the sentence to make grammatical sense, in Italian naming the 'it' is superfluous and tautological. *Esso va bene* is indeed redundant because the use of "it" is determined by the degree of specificity which governs "its" position in regard to the verb. For example, after deciding whether the "it" is masculine or feminine (*lo*, *la*), Italian then considers whether the object is specific enough to be added to the verb, as is *lo* in the phrase *devi vederlo*, or emphatic enough to act as a subject: *lo devi vedere*. But at this point, if the subject is too universal, the *lo* disappears and is absorbed, as in the verb *piove*. In Italian, only conceivability and therefore specificity allows an object the possibility of independent grammatical action. One can imagine how this world-view limits the influence of the object upon the speaking subject.

English, however, insists on containing the unmentionable in a form which functions to keep the "it" separate from the verb. English has a hard time living with what is not comprehensible and vague and must keep pointing "it" out whenever possible: a counter-spell to keep away the indeterminate spirit of "it is a nice day," or perhaps an attempt to expand "it" into liveable, human space. But by doing this English grants independence to "it," an invisible subject, and that independence is tangible since we can say that the "it" which is a nice is not necessarily just a nice day.

In Italian, this does not occur. In fact, since Italian does not have a concept for the English "it," it hears two "days" in one sentence, one as subject and the other as object, and it comes away from the encounter feeling that English obtusely insists on being redundant. From the English point of view, Italian is full of contorted constructions simply because it must find a multitude of ways to get around the naming of "it."

But Italian also has its peculiarities. Those who have tried to translate English into Italian must have met up with the supreme frustration of not being able to do without the reflexive where one doesn't want it. Let me clarify with a line from one of my poems: "And I imagine your hair holding the wind and curling." It is impossible to translate this line into Italian without the reflexive. *E mi immagino i tuoi capelli che si arricciano per stringere il vento.* To the English ear, *me immagino, si arricciano* imply intentionality of the I and of the hair. In English, there is no reason for the hair to be aware of itself holding or the I to imagine itself imagining. "It" just happens. *Succede.*

Perhaps Italian cannot grammatically contain the unnameable because it does not dare to take the phenomenological god in vain, preferring a grand variety of blasphemy instead. As for English, sexual reference in swearing accounts for most linguistic transgression. This is interesting in view of the fact that this very world-view has stripped the phenomenal world of gender.

I hope and remember, but I want to live the present and write the present. I feel uneasy with language always going only part of the way. I want to speak myself. Yet in English, I say that the line of the poem I have translated is not acceptable: it violates the original voice. In Italian, I insist that if what I say is to be meaningful, action cannot be contemplated unless an actor intends it. And that's that.

But how far back must I travel to be present in Furlan, my mother tongue? I spoke it until I was six, and have spoken it sporadically since. My knowledge of it is limited and my experience knows more about the cultivation of culture than it does about the cultivation of the earth. Not having territorial cues to bring memory into focus, the life I have lived in that language is remote and, for the most part, forgotten. There seems to be nothing to say. The claims of Italian and English were conceptual and therefore easier to locate, but Furlan and English have been keeping an agreement struck so long ago that they take their co-habitation for granted to the point that I don't know where each would claim or contest my experience. Since Furlan is my mother tongue, I know that what Furlan would claim would be outrageous, it would want to be the entire universe, and with no vocabulary to boot. To give myself to its unspoken presence, to its ironies, to its "ear," feels like drowning. But I do know that when I speak Furlan, badly as I speak it, it feels "like me" as nothing I can ever say in English or Italian feels "like me."

It might be fruitful to explain the person I become in these languages in terms of what I can imagine within them. For example, in Furlan, the thought that beyond highway 11 in Ontario there are no other roads going north, only a vast expanse of forest wilderness, makes me panic. I cannot enter into relation with this threatening emptiness unless I think of hewing out a plot of land, building solid shelter and planting a garden for food. I would worry about how to get seeds and nails. Perhaps when things become stable I would tame a wild creature, a bear comes to mind. If I approach the same territory in English, I do not worry about food and shelter, somehow they are granted to me and do not cause anxiety. I would perhaps learn to fly so I could enter into some kind of relation with the immensity before me. It would not occur to me to tame animals, I would rather observe them in their natural state and learn small things about myself through watching them.

Rendering that Furlan which feels "like me" in English is a huge problem. Most of my life I have brought Furlan to English and never assumed that my mother tongue could ask questions of English. But since self-translation required a reciprocal flow, I brought English to Furlan. The first time I inverted the process, I felt the odd and frightening sensation that my mother finally understood everything I was saying. As I translated, I felt the English rushing toward Furlan, being pulled in like a lover and shaped. They had been blind to each other because the alternate reciprocal experience had been missing. As I translated, the English text started to change. There were some words I could use and others I couldn't. Furlan just wouldn't accept certain concepts or sensibilities. I've learned to trust it and bend English to suit its needs. And the English that developed, informed by the Furlan, began to sound more and more "like me."

My goal is not to recover specific memories of my remote childhood, although they tend to materialize unexpectedly, nor is it the manipulation of the formal possibilities of Furlan — this happens incidentally. Rather, my goal is to provide a bridge in which English can happen in the light of Furlan and, when possible, vice versa.

There are areas within each of us that have never met, that don't speak or listen to each other. If these areas are enclosed in languages, those of us who still have an active mother tongue have an interesting and definite area to cultivate, one that we can experience and reshape through translation. Because writing holds words in time, it is possible to return and "tame" their meaning. It is possible to form and repeat those parts of ourselves which are repeatable in order to begin to recognize the sound of the self forming as different world views meet to negotiate experience. I find that when a poem or a story has passed through the sieve, gone from English to Furlan and back, from Furlan to Italian or Italian to English and back, each language still speaks me differently, because it must, but each speaks me more fully.

The Third Voice Gives Birth

I research categories to give voice to the exact bitterness of the persimmon. English goes mad. It mutters. It pushes me towards desolate roads, strung with heads of lovers that never were, or that got lost in the place where thighs never get warm, where swarms of black birds still afflicted with the languors of vespers flutter, prisoners of a de Chirico painting. I can smell the dead dream. *O Susanna tal biel cjastiel di Udin with the tanti pesciolini e i fiori di lillà don't you cry for the deer and the dead buffalo . . .*

"Was it for this you ran away?"

"For this. For what was written. Like Corto Maltese, I changed my fate, with a blade, I cut in another."

"Then we can rest. The persimmon will sweeten."

A Story

I walk in this language of walls wet with a bitterness that seeps into my mouth, that shocks my teeth like icy well water. I shudder as this suffering history greets me with kisses, tells me I've been bad, says: "Where have you been? We'll settle this at home." The church is nearly empty. On the men's side two lovers wearing jeans hold hands. The priest complains that people have forgotten how to pray. The old women are without kerchiefs; their eyes do not condemn anymore. Above, the singing seems to come from a choir of huge voices but we know it's just the caretaker and an old *befana*. From behind the sacristy comes the sound of whirlpools. The river Stèle swallows the tongue and carries it to the world in pieces. And we see each other only when the Stèle floods from the mouth of the storyteller who once upon a time would go from barn to barn and say:

Buligon, buligon
Une piore e un cjastron
Pi sot a lavin
Pi biele a la cjatavin.

Michael Mirolla

Giulio Visits a Friend

Giulio used to think that all deaths were pretty much alike. In one scenario, it's a pleasant late-spring day and a jolly, curly-haired, ruby-faced God (one of my better guises) is standing on a street-corner picking out possible victims at random as they stroll by — a variation on the "I got you, babe" theme. It's most fun to select the ones who consider themselves to be in the best of health — or suntanned and well-dressed, seemingly without a care in the world and with a brilliant, bright, glowing, positively incandescent future. In another, a hand snakes into a cage (office, condo, love nest) and someone says: "Sssh!" and the lights go out. Snap. In a third, the middle of the night grabs you by the throat and won't let go — not even when the alarm clock rings with news of your salvation.

Giulio may have had these very vivid imaginings of death: his own death, his parents' deaths, the deaths of acquaintances and total strangers. But the bodies were always interchangeable — almost superimposed on one another. A blur of faces and hair-lines and mummified smiles too late getting the respect they had so loudly clamoured for while alive. So that didn't help much. Nor did the long-distance deaths announced by misspelt telegrams or crackling phone calls from across the ocean. From "The Old Country."

That's why I decide it's time for him to visit his friend. Much against his will, I must point out. In fact, I practically have to drag him there, kicking and screaming, an invisible hand reaching in and pulling him by the scruff of the neck. He keeps coming up with all kinds of excuses: the neighbourhood makes him queasy with all its marble steps, red Camaros and bird-bath statues; the family hasn't sent him an invitation; his friend doesn't really want to see him; he lost the directions the last time he emptied out his pockets.

And he tries to turn back several times before I finally force him to ring the doorbell — pushing his clenched fist against it after a battle of wills he knows he'll lose. I remember him thinking (having him think): "Jeez, it still sounds the lively tune of a *Tarantella siciliana*. Wouldn't a few notes from a funeral march — Debussy or one of those classical sourpusses — be more appropriate under the circumstances? Even a neutral 'ding-dong' would be acceptable if the re-programming instructions proved too much for the simple peasant mind. On the other hand, perhaps they did change it once and now have changed it back — because things have improved to this extent, at least. Yeah, that's it. Things have definitely improved — and it's going to be Bob Dylan's *A Hard Rain's a Gonna Fall* next, my friend's all time favourite."

Wishful thinking. The moment Giulio steps into the house, he knows nothing has improved, that, if anything, the slide has been greased, that the cusp geometry of the to-be-expected unexpected reigns supreme. A figure draped from head-to-toe in black — his friend's mother — flits by, all hunched over. She turns towards him for a moment, charcoal-eyed, unrecognizable and unrecognizing — and then vanishes into one of the side rooms. There, he can hear her beating her head against the wall: so rhythmically you could, as the expression goes, set your watch by it. In the interior designer kitchen, his friend's father sits, squat and unshaven, in his underwear, one hand on a gallon of homemade red, the other rubbing a glass back and forth across the terrazzo tabletop. (His own workmanship, I should point out.) The latest-model halogen track-lighting aims a violet spotlight directly on the father's balding head, a discoloration that's clownish in its effect. But the man himself isn't laughing and doesn't bother looking up when he hears Giulio walking past. Nor does he make the effort to offer him a glass of the homemade — under normal circumstances an unforgivable discourtesy.

It's his friend's sister who leads him into the invalid's room, a room he hasn't entered in years. But Giulio still has vivid memories of it from their shared childhood, a time when they would use any excuse to sleep over, lying there poking and prodding each other and giggling until the sun itself intruded on their revelry. At first he can't see him and it seems that little has changed, that it's an early summer morning and school's out and the air is heady with lilac scent and the baseball gloves pop with studied languorousness. (In deference to Giulio's pronounced sensibilities, I've arranged for the curtains to be drawn, the lights dimmed, his friend with his face to the wall.) But then, sighing, the friend turns in the bed. Giulio takes one step back — a reaction he can't help even while realizing he's doing it. Though knowing that doesn't lessen his guilt in having done it. Giulio's second reaction is: "This isn't my friend. No way. He's not the happy-go-lucky, full-of-mischief kid I went to high school with. He's not the one with whom I shared so many mortadella and provolone sandwiches, so many wrestling matches, so many hell-bent two-for-one bike rides from the top of the mountain to the dangerous unpatrolled edges of the artificial lake."

And he knows that is even worse than the first reaction. (And he knows that I know.) For there is absolutely no doubt as to the identity of the man lying before him. His friend calls out his name and pats the bed. Giulio goes through numerous calculations (distances? possibilities? projections?) before finally sitting down on the edge. It is then that he notices the luminous quality of his friend's eyes, beautiful, unnaturally large, almost bulbous and bulging like that of a stereotypical friendly alien — in direct contrast to the scarred and sunken cheeks, the open sores about the lips, the purplish splotches across the temple and forehead. Giulio tries not to flinch when his friend takes his hand and gives it a gentle squeeze. It feels as if he were being touched by a butterfly, by one of those nymphs left behind when an insect undergoes metamorphosis (an incomplete metamorphosis, in this case, I hasten to point out to Giulio who isn't really listening).

Then, without ceremony, his friend begins to speak. He tells Giulio everything he doesn't want to hear, the secrets he in no way wants to know: how he will be dead within weeks, how all treatments have been exhausted, how each day he manages less and less, how the parts of his body are shutting down one by one, how the coma awaits him like a final blessing, the end-game called relief. But that's nothing compared to the recital of psychic pain Giulio has to endure. It turns out his friend's parents won't accept — or continually deny in the face of hard evidence — what has been happening. At first, they fixate (that's the friend's word) on the idea he has cancer. Leukemia. Some rare blood disorder. One of those new super-duper hantaviruses or something. All it needs is the proper doctor to conduct the proper diagnosis. Followed by the proper treatment and cure. When they can no longer hold onto that, when he confronts them head on and tells them he is dying from AIDS-related complications, they retreat to a different silence. Now, it's the incalculable perils of living in a big bad city; the awful danger of using communal toilets; the terrible cruelty of their son being picked out randomly for senseless destruction by a cruel, uncaring god. (That's a little unfair. Granted I'm not always so ruby-faced and jolly — but "cruel" and "uncaring"?) And each has shrunk away to their own private world. What will the neighbours say? How can we face up to our relatives? Who'll support us in our old age? Why us? Why us? Why us? He hasn't bothered telling them he is gay. That would be an utter and complete waste of breath. They wouldn't believe him, no matter how many character witnesses and lovers he calls in. He was handsome, athletic, outgoing, a fine catch for any of the signorinas who had, until a few years back, come knocking regularly on their side door. Neither of his parents have approached him since the illness made itself manifest. Nor have they hugged him or offered consolation of any kind. Not that they wouldn't like to they just don't know how. Instead, they do their crying privately, weeping for a son who will never fulfill that early promise, the map they laid out for him as far back as the day they baptized him. And his father has spent a lifetime slaving away for him, hauling bricks up the sides of buildings twelve hours a day, six days a week, so they could afford this ritzy house in this ritzy neighbourhood. He has denied himself everything, the least pleasure. And his mother has abandoned her sacred duties as a housewife to do piecework at a sweat shop, slowly going blind in the dim light, feeling her pricked and bruised fingers creaking to a halt. And for what? Ah, misfortune follows us around; bad luck sticks to us; the *mal'occhio* crossed the ocean with us and has re-doubled its strength in this accursed land, this land where disease can rear up from the nearest toilet bowl.

His friend stops talking and lies back on the pillow, at the same time releasing Giulio's hand. Giulio can now hear the sister sobbing in one of the dark corners of the room. He feels sticky all over. He's about to say something when his friend lifts his head and stops him with his hand: I know. You're going to ask me why I don't go to a hospital or a hospice to die. At least, there I would have professional nurses and care-givers, right? Giulio nods. But you see, this is my family. Asp that I am, I want to die snug in the bosom of my family. They may spurn me but I can't spurn them. I've spent my life trying to win their love. Now, I think I might finally be able to do it.

Giulio feels the cold air as he walks back out through the house, the sweat drying on his body, the steam rising from his scalp. The last thing his friend had asked was that Giulio hug him. Giulio's hands had traced the wasted, bony ridges of his spinal cord, the individual ribs unravelling to leave the chest cavity defenceless. It was then that he'd finally understood the thin membrane that separated them — the brazenly alive and the for-all-practical-purposes dead. Both approximations of some other condition. (But I'm not at liberty to come right out and tell Giulio what that other condition might be. I'll leave that for some later occasion. Or I might leave it for him to figure out.)

Nor do I allow him to look back once he has stepped outside. That's strictly verboten. For, if he were to, he would surely notice the entire family — mother, father, sister, brother — standing at the front window. They are standing at the picture window, arm in arm, smiling. They are standing at the interior design picture window, arm in arm, smiling — and proud of themselves. So very proud of themselves.

And who's that behind them, urging them to take a well-deserved bow for the performance of a lifetime? Why, yours truly, or course. As jolly, curly-haired, and ruby-faced as ever.

Carole David

A Laura Secord Box

Between two business trips, my father would arrive loaded down with gifts: perfumes and clothes for my mother's professional appearances, toys and candy for me. I got just what a child of my age wanted.

I'd be feeding my doll, ironing her clothes, washing my pink refrigerator while Connie and Roberto were arguing. I could hear them from my room; my mother was careful to close the door so their shouts were muffled. I kept on with my little chores, hoping they would make up. It was always the same ritual: as soon as my father came into the house, he would head for the dining room to check the ledger with my mother's bookings. Then he would question her about different people, especially about men. When this was over he would start to drink. He'd drink anything there was. My mother and I had to take refuge in her room or at a neighbour's.

My parents threw a party for my fifth birthday. They invited friends and people I didn't know. The women were coiffed and dressed as though they were spending the evening at the *Faisan doré* or some other nightclub where my mother entertained. I was wearing a red velvet dress and black shiny shoes and went running and yelling from room to room. The festivities were taking place in the double living room all festooned with streamers hanging from the ceiling. Connie put a pile of records on her record player, cha-cha-chas, mambos and paso dobles. I watched the adults as they danced or I helped Angelina — I called her my aunt — as she prepared platters of the green, white and pink sandwiches my mother had bought from a pastry shop on the rue Saint-Denis. Actually, Angelina was my great-aunt, the youngest sister of my grandmother. I should mention she has always taken care of me and she still does, even though she has lost her wits. She had never seen coloured bread and she wanted no part of it. She said it wasn't natural.

I though everyone had forgotten about me because there weren't any children to share my birthday cake, all decorated with Life Savers. There were only adults in the double living room and they ignored me and talked about incomprehensible things. Things that were strangely similar to the conversations Connie and Roberto always had. I heard my name, like a tiny sound in the background. It disappeared in smoke rings that I kept trying to capture by inhaling them.

I had made up my mind that day that I would die. My aunt wouldn't eat the coloured sandwiches with me and my mother totally ignored me.

"Breathe and die," I thought. "They'll soon be punished for not being nice to me on my fifth birthday."

My father vanished for good after the party. Connie would sometimes read aloud to me the postcards he still sent us. She kept them in a Laura Secord box. My father's image gradually blurred in my memory. First his face disappeared. His eyes, mouth and nose vanished as soon as I thought of him. And then he lost his voice. So I substituted another voice for his, a singer's voice of course, Perry Como's or Elvis Presley's. Connie started to imitate him when she'd read the telegrams that gradually took the place of his postcards.

Roberto became a dream and the hero of the stories I'd tell myself every time I was left alone in a hotel room when Connie was busy singing somewhere. How many times have I fallen asleep on her beaver coat? How many times did I repeat stories to myself before drifting off to sleep? Stories about when Roberto used to take us to Lafontaine park or to Cap-Saint-Jacques for a swim. Or it was Connie herself who would drive up in her beige Chevrolet Impala, after weeks of absence, and swear to me she would never leave me alone again at bedtime.

As I grew up, other stories came to be grafted on to the old ones: I was Bambi; I would weep for my mother, shot by an evil hunter; or I was dragged by my father onto the scariest ride at Belmont Park, the Wild Mouse, and then he'd leave me all alone in one of the cars. I would find him but then he'd disappear again, this time in the house of mirrors. And that's the exact spot where I would lose sight of him for good. And then the fat lady of Belmont Park would drag me under the Big Top and put me on display beside the others: Siamese twins, captured, strangled and thrust headfirst into formaldehyde; midget wrestlers; children like me, abandoned by their parents.

Translation by Daniel Sloate

Filippo Salvatore

Poems for Giovanni Caboto

I

Giovanni, I didn't need courage,
like you, I didn't set sail
towards the unknown on an unsafe boat,
I didn't have to fight the might
of the waves, I didn't suffer hunger,
I didn't look into death's eyes.

I traveled comfortably
with a DC 8 Alitalia plane,
flew over the perilous ocean,
closed my eyes,
dozed for a few hours and
arrived in the land of my dreams.

And to make me leave,
several bad crops, a sponsored
call, a visa sufficed.
It didn't take much to raise
my arms; despair let me surmount
my love for the native land
and my last indecisions.

Plenty of bread, and warm water too,
now I have, but the Eldorado
I was searching I didn't discover.
I discovered instead

scornful glances, a hostile
environment, an overwhelming
emptiness in my soul,
I discovered what it means
to be an emigrant.

And it didn't take much,
you know, it took so little!

II

Giovanni, they erected you a monument,
but they changed your name; here
they call you John. And you
look at them from your stony
pedestal with a hardly perceivable
grin on your bronze lips.

Where are you looking to?
Towards the new or the old world?
You don't answer me, of course,
you remain standing at Atwater and
keep on gazing afar.
How many Italians took the boat
with you? Today we are many, so many,
and most of us are young,
young and ambitious, like you,
young and forced to emigrate, like you,
to start a new life abroad, like you.

You were the first to plant
on the barren, wave-struck reef
the Lion of St. Mark beside the Royal Jack.

Today at the top of the sky-scrapers
being built in this icy land
by so many of your fellow countrymen,
the tricolore flies
beside the maple leaf.
Listen: how many of them,
coming out of the Métro warmly
wrapped up speak about dollars
and houses to buy while they wait
for the 79 at the terminal
and rub their noses.
Only a few of them know you
as they see you impassable, with a shiny
ice-mantle on your shoulders,
heedless of the frenzied movement
and the blinding glimmers of this rush-hour.

And I who had stopped at your feet
to talk to you, feel the top of my ears
getting frozen as an old drunkard
gives me a shake and mumbles
in his whisky-stinking mouth, maudit.

My People

People, my people,
people as dear to me
as the early morning sun.

Rough-faced people,
dark-dressed plumpy women,

men with patched-up trousers
and corn-like hard hands,
mixed up youths, livestock
ready for slaughter in the huge
city sweat-shops, you who long to kiss
and grasp another young body on Saturday
nights and are content by easy
pleasures and volatile emotions;
elders, you who gather by small groups
in the park during the warm, sunny
days to play scopa squabbling in dialect
like old urchins, waiting patiently
for death,
women, men, youths, elders,
you are all people, all my people.

I watch you live every day,
as you wipe your sweaty brow or
as you blow on your frozen fingers,
as you go out early in the morning
with coffee-odouring mouths or
as you chat in the evening in the bus
about the good food waiting for you home.

I see you arrive, work,
hate, love, learn our new life,
I listen unnoticed to your complaints
sitting strung-eared beside you
for you speak always in a low voice,
I hate your meanness, admire
your courage, adore your tenacity.

I am touched, like a sentimental fool,
if I hear you got a letter from Italy
which says grandma is still sick
and the wheat is already being reaped,
if I hear a beautiful baby-boy was
just born and see your young father's
eye glimmer, if I hear you love him,
for the first time, much, oh, so much,
and he is a handsome man and hard-working too.

It's our little joys, sufferings,
weaknesses, qualities, I hate and love
so much, people, my people,
people as dear to me
as the early morning sun.

Rosanna Battigelli

Francesca's Ways

Angie absentmindedly moved the handle of the meat grinder a quarter turn.

"I told you I'm not ready yet," her mother exclaimed sharply. "Aren't you listening to me?"

Angie swallowed a retort and watched silently as Francesca fit a pork intestine over the top of the funnel attachment on the meat grinder and tied the end of the casing with string. Occasionally her eyes shifted to the intense face of her mother, noting the shadows and lines, the sagging jowls, the grey, thinning hair.

"Okay, Angela, I'm ready. *Avanti*."

Angie began. With her left hand, she put the coarsely ground pork meat into the machine, turning the handle slowly with her right hand. She pushed the meat in carefully with her fingertips, avoiding the turning blades.

"Push like this," the older woman directed, abruptly moving her daughter's hand aside. "The *salsicce* won't come out good if you don't get all the air out." She pushed down forcefully on the meat in the opening and then returned to her job, pricking the sausage with a needle as it filled the casing, to eliminate trapped air. "Faster, or it will take all day."

"If you wanted a professional sausage maker, you should have hired one," Angie returned, her irritation growing.

"If your father was alive I wouldn't have called you. You never did like this kind of work," came the curt response.

Angie counted to ten silently. It was almost a year since her father had died, and the mention of him could still elicit tears. She squeezed her eyes tightly for a moment, willing herself to keep her emotions under control. "I didn't like it because I could never do it well enough for you," she said, struggling to keep her voice even. "You should try not to be so negative, Mother," she added dryly, well aware that negativity was an intrinsic part of her mother's personality. It was in the genetic make-up of Francesca's side of the family. Hadn't she inherited a gene or two herself?

"Don't start with me," Francesca advised shortly. "Concentrate on what you're supposed to be doing."

Angie surveyed the container holding the ground meat of four pork shoulders. That job had been done the night before: cutting the meat off the bones, chopping it up into pieces, grinding it coarsely, and finally adding the salt, chili peppers and fennel. The sight and smell of all that raw meat had made her come close to considering a vegetarian lifestyle.

This part isn't so bad, she thought, moving her fingers to a silent rhythm, imagining herself in an assembly line. That's it, she encouraged herself. Turn, turn, press, press, press, grab more meat. Turn, turn, press, press, press . . .

Mother and daughter worked silently, methodically, the only sounds being the churning of the meat passing through the machine and the release of air from the needle pricking the casing. On the counter in the spacious basement kitchen, the old alarm clock kept vigil.

"Where are the kids?" Francesca asked suddenly, startling Angie.

"With their father."

"*Vigliacco.*"

"Ma, I told you, there's no need for you to insult him. We settled our differences long ago."

"You broke up the family." The words still held bitterness.

"Ma, I tried to explain this to you a hundred times already. We couldn't live like that anymore. It was the best for everybody." Turn, turn, press, press, grab more meat, keep your cool. Don't lose it. Turn, turn, turn.

"Young people today don't know what's best, or there wouldn't be so many divorces," Francesca spat out, pricking the sausage harder. "*Basta!*" she cried suddenly.

Angie stopped turning and watched as Francesca tied the end of the sausage and placed it with the others already coiled on a nearby table, where later she would tie them further to make individual links. Lifting another pork intestine soaking in a bowl, she positioned it on the funnel spout and with a wave of her free hand, signalled to Angie to continue.

Stubborn woman, Angie thought. Stubborn, stubborn woman. And narrow-minded. Stuck in the old ways. She may have adopted a new country forty years earlier, but she had chosen to remain in the old country emotionally. Sure, she had adapted somewhat, learning the language by watching television and enjoying the conveniences she had never experienced in post World War II Italy, but her heart had remained in the old country , *l'Italia bella,* and so she had continued the traditions and expected her children to keep them alive as well.

Expectations which were often unrealistic, Angie mused. And chauvinistic. It didn't bother her so much these days, but in her adolescent years, she had felt stifled and sometimes angry that there seemed to be one set of rules for her and another for her brother.

"Vincenzo is a man. He can protect himself," Francesca would tell her. "Girls have to be more careful."

Which basically meant that Vinnie could spend the whole night out with his buddies and she couldn't. "Vinnie's younger than I am, for crying out loud, and I can take care of myself. You don't give me enough credit," Angie had protested, mostly in vain. Francesca had always been a force to contend with, and Angie had never been much of a rebel, until her departure from home at eighteen.

Her marriage at twenty hadn't brought any significant changes from the constraining lifestyle of her past. It was her separation and the subsequent soul searching in the year to follow that had made her change, become stronger, independent, and confident enough to stand up for herself and eradicate what she considered the weaknesses of her youth.

Enough reminiscing, Angie decided, glancing at the clock, although what had seemed to be a long time absorbed in her thoughts had in reality only been a couple of minutes.

"I need to talk to you about something, Ma." Better to get it over with.

"You need money?"

"No, Ma, I don't need money," and silently, I need you to listen to me, without judgment or criticism. She cleared her throat.

The needle stopped in midair and Francesca's piercing black eyes met hers. Angie stopped turning the handle, and straightening, her arms crossed in front of her as if to shield herself from the inevitable verbal onslaught, said calmly, "My divorce is final."

"*Che mi dici?* You didn't tell me you were getting a divorce." The words were unusually calm, ominously quiet.

"Ma, I tried to talk to you but you never wanted to listen. Every time I brought up anything about the separation, you'd practically cover your ears. I told you John and I weren't getting back together. Did you think I was going to stay separated forever?" she queried, trying to put herself in her mother's shoes — the old country ones.

"*Povere creature*," Francesca exclaimed, shaking her head dolefully from side to side and pursing her lips in an all too familiar manner.

"They are not poor creatures," Angie shot back, her protective instinct toward her children aroused. "If this wasn't the best thing for them, do you think I'd be doing it?"

"You're doing it for yourselves, not for them," the old woman scoffed, eyes flashing. "If you were thinking about them, you'd keep the family together."

"For better or worse, right, Ma?" Angie's voice was edged with anger. "How can you tell me what's best for them? Did you live with us? Did you see what was happening to all of us?"

"You could give him another chance, for the sake of the children."

Angie's mouth fell open and she gave her mother a long, incredulous stare. "A minute ago you were insulting him; now you want me to give him another chance? He had plenty of chances, Ma. It's over. Accept it." She took a deep, controlled breath. "And I'm not here to get your approval, Ma, or your advice. I *am* an adult. I *can* make my own decisions and deal with the consequences of those decisions."

"You never wanted to take my advice," Francesca said bitterly. "If you had, you wouldn't be in this mess." She began shaking her head again and as Angie's lips parted to respond, Francesca lifted her hand firmly. "*Basta*! Enough! I have work to do." She fitted a new pork intestine over the spout, tied the end and picked up the needle.

There was no point trying to convince Francesca about her divorce. Angie eyed the remaining mounds of ground pork, trying to mentally calculate how much time it would take to finish. Fifteen, twenty minutes. Thank God. The basement was so stifling; Francesca's negativity was getting to her again.

As the mound began to diminish, Angie found herself thinking back to the days when her father and Nonna were both alive. She had never known her Nonno — he had died five years before she was born — but Francesca's mother had lived with them until her death a month after Angie's eighteenth birthday.

Papa would be doing this job, grinding the meat, and Angie would be sitting on her Nonna's knee, munching happily on torrone and listening to tales of the yearly pig slaughter in the old country and the tradition of draining the blood from the slit in the pig's neck, and boiling it with milk, pre-fermented wine, cloves, cinnamon, lemon and orange peel to make blood pudding.

Nonna had been fascinating and very superstitious. Angie remembered innocently taking her Nonna's black kerchief and trying it on, only to have Nonna whip it off her head and then quickly make the sign of the cross, before lecturing Angie about the "*mala fortuna*," the bad luck that would befall her if she wore a black article of clothing, or if she spilled oil, (hadn't Domenico Salvatore's mother dropped dead of a heart attack the morning after he had spilled a half litre of oil?), or if she crossed arms with anybody.

The exchange of peace at Sunday Mass had always amused Angie as she watched her parents and "*paesani*" from the old country dodging arms until it was safe. Why it was considered bad luck to make the sign of the cross with someone else's arms, had always baffled her.

"*Ecco*! It's done!" Francesca's words held satisfaction.

Angie watched as her mother placed the last sausage link on the table. How many years had those hands performed this ritual? Forty, maybe fifty. First with her grandparents and parents, then with her husband. Now, even with the latter gone, Francesca still clung to the traditions. Perhaps they brought her solace, Angie thought, forgetting the criticisms and harsh words uttered earlier and feeling sorry for the lonely, embittered woman across from her.

"I'll tie them and hang them up later," Francesca told her, wiping her hands on her faded apron.

"I'll help you clean up," Angie heard herself offering, despite her desire to leave.

"No," Francesca replied firmly. "*Basta* for now. I'm tired." She headed up the stairs, her shoulders stooped with weariness. "I made some *minestrone* last night, like

Nonna used to make for you. It's in the fridge. You want some? I'll warm it up."

Angie followed slowly, her eyes dropping to the shoes her mother was wearing. Her father's old slippers.

Tears welled in her eyes. She wiped them hastily with her sleeve.

Upstairs, Francesca turned to face her. "Well, are you staying?"

Angie's eyes locked with Francesca's. A moment of indecision passed. Francesca looked away, then started to walk away.

"Sure, Ma. Just a small bowl."

Liliane Welch

His Last Visit

What he sought
in his bride of the northern terrain
was a Goddess. When she left,
he dreamed her return.
Nights back home she heard —
"It's better
to have a corpse in your house
than a man from the Marche
outside your door,"
and she paced the wall
of their separation,
the mutations of passion
and love: Fights
come to a head, moans
unseeded, bitterness
sowing the wounds
of mutual blame, till one day
he faced her on the by-road
where he dug his knife into her,
the face opening
as a scarlet ridge.
At the edge of his origins
she saw Aeneas leave Dido
and watched Rinaldo,
two legs fleeing,
driven through the briars
by his southern rage.

Migrations

Grandfather I heard you
in the flock of Canada
geese last night
when their honk came peeling
from the wind, through clouds,
past rooftops into my bed, that pure
lonely, soaring call
lifted me out of my dreams
to the confines of your migrations
to earth's ends. You were bereft of voice
when the northern law willed
a separation from table and bed, when
the wives of two sons changed your
Italian name to flattened French. *René*
Bravy covered once and for all Rinaldo's
yearly southern sins.
But I suspected
last night, hearing your great
wing-beats over the house, that you did
come back with a secret each fall,
blooming, renewed. For me you lie
no more in the potter's field.
You fly through the first dusk
the hush of a steady wing. You wanted
to kick the dust, the open land
telling stories, and find the source
of power there. When the North hurt and
your resolute wife was deep in work
you ran for your life, owned the roads,
your face burned with open skies.

I too am driven by your need
for a hundred migrations to come.
I seek you, Rinaldo. Promise of flight.

Pesto

Today, epiphany or spring
so bright, I make a pesto sauce
and compose the lure of our Italian summers.
Snow, loss and age stay in Canada as
we plot escapes to the villa of Catallus, Garda Lake.

Here's a silence set on fire, ruins
of baths, wild flesh: massive. Offerings scattered
or received — rocks alive with lizards, Lesbia.
Stairways, desires between heart and sky.
Old stories and Sardo cheese, stables, pine nuts
sudden rain.

A friend pounds basil leaves
and serves us a pesto pungent and olive green.

Delia De Santis

The Ache Within

When I came home from school my mother was standing by the stove. I could tell something was wrong: there was a gleam of tears in her eyes. For someone who never cried, that told a lot. Mamma always said that her heart wasn't really made of stone, it was just that the war had taught her how to be strong. Silently, I stood by the table and waited for her to tell me what had happened.

With a weak gesture she indicated the letter on the counter.

There were always two or three air mail letters lying around, and when I didn't have anything to do, I would look at the stamps on them. Doing that always took my mind back to the country we had left behind five months before. Sometimes it made me dream of going back. I could see that the stamp on this letter was different. It was larger and rectangular rather than square. On it there was a picture of a ship sailing on the sea. It looked just like the Irpinia, the ship that had brought us to Canada, to the Montreal harbor. I could have reached for the letter on the counter just by stretching my arm — but my arm wouldn't move. I knew what was in the letter. I knew what it said.

"It's from your Zio Norio . . ."

I always read Zio Norio's letters, but I knew I would never be able to read this one. I didn't want to look at the stamps ever again either. Nonna Evelina was dead.

I didn't know if I should sit down or go outside to play with my skipping rope, or if I should go to do my homework. I wished that Mamma would tell me what to do. It was terrible, standing there. Since we'd come to Canada, not a day had gone by without an awkward moment for me. Sometimes I didn't know how to act or how to react to a situation, but I had never felt confused within the walls of our little rented house. Strange as our knew dwelling was to me, it was still home. It was Mamma, Papa, and my brother Leo; it was people with whom I always knew what to say.

But I had not a word to say to Mamma this time. I don't know if she would have heard me if I did anyway. She seemed to be in another world, slowly stirring in clockwise movements, the cornmeal dinner on the stove.

Polenta was one of my favorite meals, rustic and delicious, Mamma would spread the pale yellow mush on special wooden bowls and ladle the most aromatic ragout sauce, with chunks of beef and pork sausages, over it. She always had to give me a second helping, I was so hungry when I came home from school. But this time my hunger was gone. I finally made myself move from that spot. I went to put my books on the dresser.

My father came out of the bathroom. When he came home from work he always took a bath and put on clean clothes. He was a laborer on construction and the mud was always "up to his waist." Mamma got satisfaction from emphasizing that, implying that maybe life for him had been much better in Italy. There he had worked in a "clean" olive oil factory. I saw that he wasn't crying at all, and that was strange, because I'd seen him cry many times when someone had passed away. Nonna Evelina was his mother.

When my brother came home a little later from the shop where he was apprenticing as an appliance repairman, he seemed to know what had happened already. He went straight to the counter and picked up the letter. I envied him for his courage. But he didn't read all the letter... he couldn't. The sides of his mouth began to twitch, then his whole face contorted, making him look like a comedian trying to arrange his features for an impersonation act. He refolded the thin sheet of blue paper and put it back inside the envelope without even looking at what his hands were doing. It seemed strange to me how he could do that, without looking. He was staring blankly out the window.

My father started to clean the strap of his watch. Usually he asked me to do it. Oh, how I hated having to do it. Now I wished he had asked me; I wished that someone would tell me to do something. I could not think of what to do on my own.

When it was time for me to set the table, I forgot. Mamma started doing it herself. Then I rushed to help. Leo did too. He had never helped in the kitchen before. Leo and I tripped over each other.

I ate a portion of everything that was on the table for supper. We all did. All of us eating slowly, chewing even the polenta, which was soft as pudding.

While Mamma was doing the dishes, she kept turning to look at my father. She wanted to say something to him, but each time she couldn't. When she was wiping the inside of his lunch bucket and was ready to make his sandwiches, she had to say it: "Will you go to work tomorrow?"

He was a big man, and his shoulders seemed too heavy to lift into that small a shrug. "What is there to do?"

Just then I recalled my mother gently trying to persuade my father not to emigrate, not to make us leave our country. "We'll leave all the people we love behind. Children will be born and the old will die and we won't be part of it anymore." I had not wanted her to talk like that because I wanted so much to go to Canada, especially since my father repeatedly said, "It's for the children. Life will be better for them there." I couldn't see that life was bad for my brother and me where we were, but somehow there was great excitement in going to a far away country, in crossing the Atlantic, in seeing a new continent. I'd never been past the country school going in one direction, and the village church going the other. I would be fun to see the world.

Now I began to understand what my mother had meant when she had said those words to my father. My grandmother was dead, and except for Mamma's small show of tears, no one was acting bereaved. It seemed we didn't quite know what to do with Nonna's death.

My brother hesitated for a long time, then awkwardly went up to Mamma and told her that he was going to the park to play baseball with the guys. "If it's all right with you . . ." he added in a whisper that didn't make him sound like Leo at all.

My mother, who was always complaining that Leo couldn't stay home one night, nodded and actually seemed relieved that he was going out.

I wished that I could go somewhere too, but there was no place for me to go. So far, I had made only one friend at school, a girl named Gina, who spoke some Italian because her father was Italian. She always translated for me, and she stuck up for me when someone made fun of my shy attempts to speak English. But Gina lived several blocks away and I wouldn't walk to her house; I was afraid of getting lost. That had happened to me once on the way to the Hudson Bay store downtown. Not knowing where I was anymore, I had cried like a child. I eventually found myself in front of our house again, with no idea of how I had got there. My father said that I must have gone in circles. Now I thought of phoning Gina to come over herself, but I didn't think I should; maybe my parents wouldn't want anyone around just now. Gina was a nice girl, but when she started to giggle, she could never stop. Maybe I couldn't have taken her giggling tonight either.

So I went into the bathroom and started cutting my hair with the sewing scissors. My hair was already in a boy's bob, and when I finished, it was an inch from the scalp. I swept up the hair from the floor and waited for Mamma to say, *"Oh, Dio mio!"* or something like that, but she glanced at me only once and didn't even sigh. "Take a dollar from my purse," she said, "and go get your neck shaved at the hairdresser's on the way home from school tomorrow."

My father took his good black leather shoes, the can of polish and the shoeshine brush and went down to the furnace room. He always shined his good shoes the day before going to a funeral. My mother started to go after him, but on the landing she paused and changed her mind.

It was summertime and we always went outside after the dishes were done. There wasn't enough room to put chairs on the porch, so we sat on the steps. Mamma always sat on the bottom step because it was easier for her to cover her legs with her tight skirt. Sometimes my father reproached her for wearing such tight skirts. She never got mad at him, but always put him in his place with a few words. "I might come from a poor country," she told him, "but not from one that has never seen style."

Usually I sat beside her so that I could tell her all about my day at school. She would always shake her head in disbelief when I would tell her how strict the nun-teachers were, and she would laugh softly when I said that the priest who came to see if we knew the catechism had smelled of whiskey again. But this time I just couldn't sit beside her . . . how could I talk to her of everyday things with Nonna dead? I sat one step above her.

Later, Papa came outside, too. He sat down on the top step. Mamma looked up at him. There was a smile in her eyes, but she kept her lips serious. Mamma had pretty eyes. They seemed to go with her tight black skirt. I had never seen my father put his arm around her, but I always felt embarrassed when I caught the love-looks going back and forth between them.

The neighbors on our street seemed nice. No one had introduced himself to us yet, and we held back, too, because of the language barrier. Tonight the man next door said "Hello" to us from his driveway where he was washing his car. The tall lady across the street gave us a friendly nod when she came to put the garbage on the curb. From a large verandah kitty-corner from us, two blue-haired old ladies daintily waved at us. My mother waved back at them, and I did, too. I saw my father start to lift his arm — and then drop it . . .

I wanted to ask my father why back home people never waved at each other in greeting. Waving was a farewell gesture, like waving to people you might never see again. It was something that went with sadness and tears.

Just like when we waved from the deck of the Irpinia to relatives who had come to see us off: my aunt and uncle, my cousins... Nonna Evelina... But I couldn't ask him. I felt I had to keep that silence between us, as if it were a small ritual.

When the mosquitoes got really bad we went inside. My father got up first, and I let Mamma go ahead of me to follow him. For some reason they seemed to belong together more than ever tonight. I stayed right behind. I was glad they were my parents.

Absorbed in their silence, Mamma and Papa went to bed. I had a lot of homework to do, but I couldn't keep my mind on any of it. I took off my shorts and top and lay on the bed on top of the bedspread. It was too hot to get under.

When my maternal grandmother passed away, there had been the customary two days of "sitting with the dead." Everyone cried and the rosary was said over and over again, with intermissions for friendly gossip. Each person who arrived remarked on the good deeds the deceased had done. There were baskets and baskets of food from neighbors and friends, and the offering of a meal to each one who came to pay his respects. On the third day, the Requiem Mass, with the children from the school singing in the choir. Then the burial, followed by everyone coming back to the house to cry and laugh... and to eat up the rest of the food, the adults acting as silly as the children. After that, it was back to normal, with the painful absence of the departed one unnoticeably shifting into comfortable memory...

I closed my eyes and tried to picture my grandmother Evelina dead. I tried to capture the brown, wrinkled face as if made of wax... the small eyes shut on life forever... but she came to me alive instead, laughing or singing her church hymns, as her quick fingers twisted her thin, long, gray hair into tight braids. I saw myself patiently handing her long, steel hairpins. I watched her turning sideways in front of the wardrobe mirror to see if her bun was perfect. "You should always see that things are done well, my little Tina," she winked.

I closed my eyes tighter. But she laughed at me and walked away, in the quick steps she had while hurrying about doing the evening chores on the farm. *You're supposed to be dead. I want to see you dead.*

Suddenly I felt scared. What was I trying to do? Was I going crazy? A girl in my class, in Italy, had gone crazy. Her parents had a lot of money and they took her to the United States to be cured by a famous doctor. When she came back she was just as crazy as when she had left. I stopped trying to picture Nonna Evelina dead.

In the bedroom next to mine, my parents were not asleep. I knew that because my father always snored when he slept and Mamma moved around a lot. Now they were so quiet, as if they weren't there at all.

After a long time I heard Mamma speak. "The letter took thirteen days . . . she's been buried for at least a week."

People always said that Mamma loved Nonna Evelina more than her own mother. I know it was true. Nonna Evelina was never mean to anyone. She loved flowers and trees and everything that grew. She patted rabbits like children do.

I thought I heard my father breathe.

Just then Leo turned the key in the lock. Leo was ten years older than I. We were not self-conscious or shy of each other, but we more or less lived in two different worlds. He had his job and girls; I had school and pre-teen preoccupations. I never worried about him as Mamma did. She had been frantic once when he didn't come home until seven in the morning from having gone out to a movie the night before. I thought it was just ridiculous that he would be "in a ditch bleeding to death," as Mamma said, or "in jail," as Papa muttered, trying to keep anger out of his voice for Mamma's sake.

"He's probably out with a girl," I told them knowledgeably. Didn't they know that? I knew because Gina had told me that her brother always stayed out all night with girls. I couldn't see what the fuss was all about.

But this time I suddenly felt a gladness come over me, in knowing that my brother was home safe and sound. I wanted to call out to him softly, "Leo, is that you?" the way Mamma often did, but hadn't tonight.

I didn't do it. I couldn't. I probably never would. I just knew that his being there with us made a difference. Like an ache that I couldn't stand. I squeezed the ache between the pillow and myself, wanting to keep it... but also wanting it to go away. Oh, so much to go away.

Joe Fiorito

My Old Man

My old man died on the second of June, of a cancer so muscular and aggressive that it seemed to lift him up and throw him down a dozen times a day, as if he were made of rags instead of flesh and blood.

There were hot spots all over his bones. There was a fist of it near his kidneys, an egg-sized lump under his arm and a great thick slab of it sitting on his chest, above his heart. He tried to fight it off with everything he had. He never gave up any more of himself than he had to. He died with his fists clenched, an inch at a time.

Even though the pain was swift enough to stay one step ahead of the morphine, my old man never admitted there was anything much the matter. As if naming the devil might give it power. When his doctor asked him how he was, he'd reply, "Not so bad," and ask, "How about you?" — as if he were making a social call.

He didn't want to frighten anyone with the extent of the disease. He left it to my mother to parse the grammar of his moans at night, so she could tell the doctor what she'd heard when they went together to the clinic in the morning.

My old man was, among other things, a part-time dance-band musician who played spaghetti jobs for nearly sixty years. A spaghetti job is musician's talk in the Lakehead for a dinner dance, even when the food was roast beef and cabbage rolls, and the dance was at the Finn, and not the Italian Hall.

He was a handsome bugger with a banjo on his knee. He was a young man with a slide trombone. Later in life, he leaned against his bass fiddle and caressed it while he sang the blues, and couples on the dance floor held each other close and made love listening to his voice.

I made the mistake one night of taking a date to watch him play. She spent the evening with her elbows propped on the table, her chin resting in her hands, a dreamy expression on her face, staring at my old man, watching him work the slide of the trombone sweetly back and forth. Too Freudian, even for me. I took her home and said goodnight and shook her hand.

I spent the last month with my old man, sleeping in an armchair in his hospital room, listening to him gasp for breath at night.

The first week, he was well enough to tell me stories, although he'd often fall asleep before he finished what he was saying. Not that it mattered. He always told the same stories the same way every time he told them. I know most of them by heart. The time he stole the piano. The dog who followed him home. The time his cousin got drunk and fell asleep and let the still blow up.

One night, my old man opened his eyes and lifted his head and looked at me and asked, "Who brought the charges?" I asked him what he meant. He looked away. He said, "There had to have been charges." He thought he was in jail.

The next night, he woke and looked at me again. He said, "They can't keep my shoes from me, can they?" He thought if he could get his shoes, he could sneak out. No such luck, Pops.

The second week, the questions tapered off and something happened to the stories. He'd get stuck on certain sentences and repeat them until he forgot what he was talking about. Repeat them until he forgot what he was talking about.

As if his needle was stuck in the groove.

My old man was a small-town Fellini who brought a little magic and a little cruelty to nearly everything he did. One night, when I was a kid and he was playing in the circus band, he brought Victor Julian home for supper. Victor Julian was the guy with the dancing dogs. Victor Julian took one look at my little Trixie, she with the patch over her eye and her little dog grin and her whippet's tail.

Victor Julian smiled possessively.

He waited until I went outside after supper, and then he made my dad an offer. A week's wages, at a time when my folks had no money to speak of, and four boys to raise.

When I came in from playing after supper, the room fell silent. Nobody looked at me. My old man told me Trixie would have a good home with all the other circus dogs. She'd get to travel and see the country. Victor Julian said he'd take her with him on the Ed Sullivan Show.

I was ten years old. It hurt me to see Trixie go. I could understand about the money. We were always broke. But I thought the Ed Sullivan business was a bit much. I thought they didn't have to lie.

Trixie grinned over her shoulder at me as she trotted out the door with Victor Julian. The next day, the newspaper carried a photo of my dog, and a story with the headline *Local Pooch Makes Good.*

Six months later, we got a note telling us Trixie was going to be on TV. I didn't want to believe it, in case it wasn't true. I held my breath until Sunday.

During the second half of the show, Ed Sullivan introduced Victor Julian. He stepped on stage in his tux, with his top hat on his head. Following behind him, last in a line of dancing dogs, dressed in a little skirt, with a little hat on her head and a ruffled collar round her neck, grinning ear to ear and wagging her skinny whip of a tail, was my little Trixie.

She jumped through a hoop. She walked up a ladder. She grinned at the other dogs. I forgave my old man instantly. We were still broke, the money was long gone to pay bills, but one of us, even if it was only the dog, had made it to a better life.

Not all of what my old man did ended with a magic turn. In the end there were too many late nights and too many pieces of himself tendered easily to strangers.

It couldn't have been easy to sell my dog. I forgave him, anyway. He worked hard, he loved his sons, and if he promised us more than he could reasonably deliver, in the end he gave us all he had.

The final week of his life, my old man was down to single words, then gestures. The last thing I saw him do, at quarter to nine on the morning of the last day of his life, was raise his fist and shake it.

Antonio D'Alfonso

Babel

Nativo di Montréal
élevé comme Québécois
forced to learn the tongue of power
viví en México como alternativa
figlio del sole e della campagna
par les franc-parleurs aimé
finding thousands like me suffering
me casé y divorcié en tierra fria
nipote di Guglionesi
parlant politique malgré moi
steeled in the school of Old Aquinas
queriendo luchar con mis amigos latinos
Dio where shall I be demain
(trop vif) qué puedo saber yo
spero che la terra be mine

The Loss of a Culture

Not the trip to a land where words are pronounced as you were taught to pronounce them. Not the adage your grandmother serves you at dinner. The language you speak as a child, flushed down the toilet bowl. Your mother-tongue sounds as foreign to you as any language you do not understand. Forgotten as the life-style you once had. Latin engraved on darkened school desks. What do you tell yourself when you find yourself alone at night? The uneaten bread becomes stale. The avoided meeting of a one-night stand, dreadful. Squashed tomato on the floor sinks into the tiles of your perfection. You forget the past but the past will not forget you. You sit on broken chairs and get cramps when you are about to say something intelligent. If you collapse and smash your head on the floor, it will not be from lack of proper diet, it will be your ancestors who will shoot you from behind.

1981

On Writing

1

Writing as memory. Writing also as a means of parring down reality to its essence. Writing which disclaims, whispers, breaks down. A way of speaking even when speaking entails narration. A narration necessitating expansivity, colouration, complexity.

2

Language a thing that contains itself. Not all language contains a priori memory. It may contain nothing at all. Language is overburdened with itself. It is energy propelling the user of language. Whether he likes it or not.

3

Language is never neutral. It expresses propagandistically what meaning a people has filled language with. To write is to remember the voices of your people, the voices of those who came before you. It is also a parameter reminding you of what can and cannot be done to your language.

4

To write is to remember. It is a memorandum of what you do to language physically.

5

No two people use language in the same manner. No two people use the same language in the same manner. These dissimilarities establish nations. The quality of being different is a matter of praise, not discrimination.

6

I can imitate the style of another writer. I can only emulate the stylistics expounded by writers of a certain era or century. In the end, however, I will find myself alone in front of the blankness of language. For language inevitably loses all its memory when it falls into the hands of a writer. Especially when the writer uses a language that is not his own, that is not the language of *his* people. *Difference*.

7

To record what I do to language: the impulse that pushes me to write. I write with the memory of one language in mind and express this memory in another language. It is the marriage of memories. I cannot write disregarding the Italian words I use to describe to myself the dazzling panoramas of man's command of nature seen from the heights of Guglionesi.

8

Even Italian is a learned language for me. Language of the North, it is not the language my thoughts got formed in nor the music I hear in my head at night when I cannot get to sleep. Already a transformation occurs: from Guglionesano, I must translate into Italian. When I write I translate. Sometimes no translation occurs. The words or phrases come directly into English or French. A linkage of differences.

9

A need for *bondage* and not assimilation of memories. A passion. A blind passion. An untempered impulse seeking science to carry it through pleasure. The sexuality of writing. The nonlinearity of the languages I bind together.

Roma

For Maria di Michele

Roma. Rain. Roaming along Lungotevere. Past midnight. Under an umbrella too small for two. Going in circles in front of the Palazzo di Giustizia. The sky, one giant fountain. Trying to make sense of the past stolen from us. Born elsewhere, not from here. Always there, and the need to be here. Neither here nor there imagined as ideal. Our Utopia, the choice to be here and there. *Passim*. Roma. Rain. Roaming about Roman roads. Two Leos born on August 6. Speaking the feminine dialect of the masculine Fretani. History wrings us with its Baroque love. Perversity about being from nowhere. Antipatriotic. Blasphemous for this omnipresence of divinities. But we are not gods, for we have no place of comfort, no home to call our own, no hole to sneak into. We are balancing in midair like a direction sign loose at its hinges. We are dust blown from old furniture falling everywhere, nowhere. In which box to put our X? Roma. Rain. Roaming on Via della Conciliazione. Reconciling ourselves under Bernini's pillars, running on Vittorio Emmanuelle II's Ponte and Corso, stumbling into the Pink Bar where a gay Sardinian buys us a Scotch-on-ice for being from the Abruzzi. Two passports. Two persons in one. Lovers we never know who to kiss first. Who to speak to? What part to boast about? We suffer from insomnia. Who can we blame? "I wouldn't want to be in your shoes," repeats our friend, whose eyes jump from one body to another until they find the right bed to sleep in. "You'll end up looking like a portrait by Picasso." *Passim.* Roma. Rain. Roaming to the Piazza della Rotonda. Soaking wet with pleasure and schizophrenia, and what others call our *Ars poetica.* Will we ever quench our thirst? This grace with a modern air to it? At last Vicolo del Divino Amore, drying ourselves to sleep in the folds of our measures.

10 giugno 1984

Pasquale Verdicchio

Letter

A blue envelope stained by foreign fingers;
in one corner a far land's pride.
The wind has carried you far
and your feet
have touched many soils.
And when your memory permits,
pen in one hand
and all you have gathered
tight in the other,
you send me
what your sun-dark hands have held.

Another place name fallen
to the page, its letters broken
to mean a thousand words.
Rain will wash the blue letter tiles
to white in time;
time will change the blue words
to yellow . . . on this page.

You have sold yourself.
The bones, in the sun
they so much desired,
pass time to white and dust;
these I will use
to make more names of places
which may not even be.

Mexico

1

A carnation lights the way
to words we once thought spoken.
They are scattered as old petals
seeking recollection of the shape.
Fire crown of heliotropic transfer;
a warm face staring up in self-proclamation.

2

The wash on the roof sways back and forth
remembering the movements of bodies.
Night listens for the last door to close
and footsteps to climb the stair.
In a dark room a bright star moves
to invisible lips belonging to a man
who continually listens for daybreak.

3

A glass of wax:
offering to unknown faces
that hold secrets we would like to glimpse.
Wax, hard and cold;
fingers have left their mark
for the gods.
Wax: soul in solid state
rememberance for the forgetful.

4

The tombs of kings
with jade skulls and shell
eyes staring into empty promises.
Only priests knew how to deceive
both men and gods;
their names still repeated
in the steps of pyramids.

5

"An invisible landscape
conditions the visible one."
A thousand wells touch water,
move upward. Where gods are left a choice
they inhabit everything.

Barcelona

The door of Hostel Marmo greets us
with a cracked smile.
The hall
stairs
small and winding
cold
as is the room.
Night follows us in.

Morning reveals early Spanish furniture.
The post office across the way has begun
juggling mail. On the ledge
of the next building, a pigeon,

dying, does not notice a cat
moving in on him.

There is no flamenco echoing in these streets anymore:
the accent is all that is left.
Picasso women, white powdered faces and twisted eyes,
stare and follow their noses up alleys.
Black kerchiefs, dark eyes, *boinas*, and white shirts
run for trains leaving early. At every corner
armed guards protect democracy with their mustaches.

The port is the only way out:
Columbus stands in the square and points the way.
Everyone fixes their eyes on the invisible dreamland.
In the backstreets roams America.
Jeans, tee-shirts, and an occasional O.K. rise up
between buildings out of the exhaust.

Columbus turns around.

Ancestors

1

Because we are the dreams
that ancestors carved in stone
and described in jewels
we are lost and confused
as to whether these lives are our own
or if they will cease with another's waking.

2

The blueness of the sky not as immediate
as the horizon pretends it to be,
whiteness shows through
where the artist overlooked space.
Incomplete mosaic of our lives
betrays the subtle equilibrium.

3

Arms with bracelets of gold wound
around blood of their wrists.
Arms of Etruscan figures
whose loins spawned words gold and silver
from the sperm of mystery that spilled
into rivers and down to the sea.
Only tombs of anagrams are left
telling of freedom in the guise of figurines:
their eyes closed in damp excavations,
arms embracing the memory
we hold of them.

4

Ancestors invented reigns
for their imagination
and promised lands they were
unable to keep; these
we now suffer as beliefs.

Reconsidering the Southern Question

The Southern Question is an elemental component of Italian socio-cultural politics that has retained its import and intensity during the hundred and thirty odd years since the national unification of the peninsula. This moniker, which hints at the problematic relationship between Northern and Southern Italy, has served many politicians, cultural commentators, and other intellectuals interested in analyzing the complexities of nation building and national identity. Indeed, in the late 19th century the Italian Southern Question even became a term of reference and comparison for Americans addressing the North-South dichotomy and disparities in the United States of America. While many writers have addressed the Southern Question within the Italian context, Antonio Gramsci stands as the major contributor to the debate with an unfinished essay that dates back to 1926, the year of his imprisonment at the hands of Mussolini's Fascists in an attempt "to stop his mind from working."

Among a number of important considerations that must be valued when dealing with the Southern Question is the situation that emerged from Italian unification. In short, while the South was liberated from its Bourbon rulers, the Piedmontese liberators did little to alter the feudal situation that persisted in the region. The resulting power structure differed only slightly from what had preceded unification. As a result, the general population saw little benefit from the establishment of the Italian nation state. It is no accident that soon after unification the patterns of Italian emigration changed drastically. While before unification most emigration had been from Northern Italy, the period soon after saw a drop in emigration from the North and an exponential increase of it from the South. Taking into consideration the total history of Italian emigration the impact of unification on the South becomes apparent. In the tally of total numbers, three-quarters of Italian emigrants originated in Southern Italy. It is this fact that leads me to state with confidence that any and all discussions on the Southern Question must include an assessment of that dispersed portion of the population. In other words, the culture of Italians outside of Italy is part and parcel of Italian culture. As such it represents not only an invaluable source for the extention of the concept of Italian culture, but also a potential instrument of critique in the development of the Italian nation since unification.

Today's Southern Question, though no longer easily classifiable in terms of the relationships city/countryside or peasant/industrial worker, nevertheless persists in the conditions that influence civil life, "meaning, the state of public services and administration, the political system" (Bevilacqua, 122). Just over seventy years since Gramsci penned his essay, "Notes on the Southern Problem and on the Attitudes Toward it of Communists, Socialists, and Democrats," many of the questions regarding the North-South articulation remain unresolved. The terms of the equation are in fact complicated today by European unity and Italy's position within it, and the country's transition from a country of emigration to a country of immigration.

In a speech on the Southern Question given in 1971 in Palermo, Sicily, Enrico Berlinguer, then secretary of the Italian Communist Party (PCI), related how "the degradation of the South consists not in that it has been forgotten, but in that it has been utilized so as to guarantee and exalt the economic development of the nation." Berlinguer also noted an interesting appropriation of Gramsci's exhortation to Northern workers to unite with Southern peasants by La Malfa, then secretary of the Italian Republican Party (PRI). La Malfa had extended an invitation "to the workers of the North to show solidarity with Sourthern populations . . ." (Berlinguer, 4). His suggestion, while appearing to mirror Gramsci's call for an alliance, merely implied that Northern workers could, by tightening their belts, allow corporations and industries to increase their earnings, which, in turn, would provide capital for investment in the South. The divisiveness of such a proposal, which works not to the interests of either Northern or Southern populations, "to orient industrial production to useful work that will promote peace between the city and the countryside, between North and South" (3), but for the benefit of industries and corporations, needs no further elucidation.

Even in the 1990s the degradation of Southerners persists in the political discourse of such groups as *the Lega Lombarda* (the Lombard League), a Northern separatist party, much of whose rhetoric is based on positivist constructions of Northern racial superiority and Southern inferiority. According to some commentators, the success of the Lega in the elections of June 1993 was indicative of the fact that Northern hegemony over the South had not really changed since unification (Abse, 18).[1] It might in fact appear that, within the rhetoric of federalism, Umberto Bossi's expressions regarding the North-South relationship reserve the misconceptions of a majority of Northern populations regarding the South. By injecting his view of history with false altruism, Bossi spews his prejudices in statements such as:

> We are tired of being a land of invasion, first from the South and now from the Third World. There is no work, and opening our doors to immigrants to then leave them in miserable conditions is a crime (Brindani, 36).

And:

> In these less than disastrous conditions, we witness day after day the imbalanced conflict between an Italy that aspires to become European with its head held high, creating a modern nation, democratic and civil, and the forces that orbit around the public machinery and are fed by it, the forces whose objectives are to become part of the African peninsula (53).

The developments that enable this attitude call for a reconsideration of Gramscian writings in a contemporary context that not only enables us, but indeed requires us, to envision a potential redrawing of alliances, perhaps even towards an extra-national sphere.

The events of 1994 have come to represent a moment of convergence for the issues addressed by Antonio Gramsci in the pages of *The Southern Question*. The results of the 1994 elections, in which a right-wing alliance came to power, further go to emphasize a North-South division and the exertion of Northern hegemony. The victorious alliance between the newly formed *Forza Italia*, representative of Northern industrialism, the neo-fascist *MSI* (Movimento Sociale Italiano) reborn as *Alleanza Nazionale* (National Alliance), and the *Lega Lombarda* defeated a

Left that not only held its ground but actually gained in the Southern regions. These developments would seem to reflect the situation around the time when Gramsci found it necessary to address the issues contained in the pages of *The Southern Question*. The triumverate of this more contemporary alliance, though now failed due to internal discord, is as threatening as the alliance that formed in the early 1920s and allowed the rise of Fascism. In many terms, the search for national stability by turning emphatically to the right, cannot but point to issues that promise a certain parallelism between Italian unification and European unity.

The Southern Question Beyond Italy

To truly appreciate the breadth and import of *The Southern Question*, I believe that another inextricable, yet neglected, component of the Southern Question must be addressed. I am referring to the Southern Italian emigrant diaspora. Given the extensive emigration from the South to foreign lands, I think that it is possible to recuperate various aspects of Gramsci's critique of the Italian nation-state by viewing emigrants as a decontextualized expression of the contradictory process of Italian state formation. The inclusion of those externalized histories into the equation of both country of origin and receptor country enables us to rethink concepts of nation, race and ethnicity, their role in the construction of Italian unification and their influence on international relations (Verdicchio, 1997).

Individuals of various Italian expatriate generations are renewing contact with their cultural background, which necessitates a critical encounter with the history of

Italian emigration on terms that have never before been approached, that is, from the perspective of the e/immigrants themselves. Only as that decontextualized component of the South grows in its awareness of its background and history, and with a re-assessment of the national conditions that engendered emigration, can a fully operable critique of the Italian nation and all its myths truly be undertaken.

The elaboration and historicization of the Italian immigrant experience will invariably bring to light the commonalities that tie Italians to minority and immigrant groups that are marginal to the official power structure of various nations. While over the decades the history that Italian immigrants have shared with other ethnic and minority groups in North America has been greatly voided by pressures and attempts to assimilate to dominant cultural norms, a potential realignment with non-dominant (subaltern) groups may still be possible. *The Southern Question* should be taken as a work that emphasizes and extends the spirit of alliance to groups that are today living the history that the Italiam immigrant community seems to have long denied. In addition, it is a work through which Italian immigrants to all parts of the globe might find a path by which to revive and acknowledge a neglected history. In a certain way, that the topic can be discussed in the context of an anthology such as this represents in itself a coming to full circle for the importance of Gramsci's *Southern Question* and the maturation of certain attitudes and historical perspectives within Italian immigrant communities.

While *The Southern Question* deals particularly with the North-South relationship in Italy, its usefulness as a tool of analysis should not be limited to the Italian context.

Antonio Gramsci's concerns are to promote a "national popular" culture which would reflect the peculiarities of Italian cultural diversity and to enable different social strata in the North and South to form new alliances, ones that would defy the cultural hegemony consolidated at the time of Italy's unification.[2] Gramsci's concept of new alliances has also been influential for a number of movements and intellectuals, such as those associated with the Birmingham Cultural Studies Collective. Stuart Hall, in his "Gramsci's Relevance for the Study of Race and Ethnicity," as elsewhere, offers useful examples of Gramscian application to contemporary situations concerning issues of race, ethnicity, and colonialism.[3] Renate Holub, in her *Antonio Gramsci: Beyond Marxism and Postmodernism* (Routledge, 1992), outlines lines of resistance made available to feminist thought through Gramscian elaborations. Lucia Chiavola Birnbaum has analyzed sites of resistance to cultural officialdom through long-standing popular rituals and "spiritual" representations in *Black Madonnas: Feminism, Religion and Politics in Italy* (Northeastern University Press, 1993). And Cornell West, Gramscian by self-definition, is adamant on the importance of Gramsci's concepts for African Americans, and as aids in a transition toward inclusive and collaborative politics and human relations.

In conclusion, I do not suggest that Gramscian concepts can or should be simply overlayed on separately evolved historical situations. The *Southern Question* is merely one view of national struggle as it is carried out by non-dominant groups within the boundaries of a specific national situation that may illuminate parallel patterns in varying contexts. It is only logical that the Gramscian concept of alliances should become relevant now to Italian Americans who, as they slowly acknowledge their historically dysfunctional relationship to so-called "white" America, are following the lead of Latino and Latina, Asian and African Americans and others in their reflections on cultural specificity.

The circumstances that condition the relationship between industrial and non-industrial societies, or First and Third-World societies, as well as the inequities extant between populations within the First-World, are consistently comparable, even in their differences, with the North-South relationship in Italy. Much as it functioned, and to some extent continues to function, in the North-South binarism, oppositions such as First World/Third World, Black/White, are similarly limited in scope because they are based upon, and therefore tend to validate conditions predicated by the backwardness of one of the elements vis-à-vis the superiority of the other. Gramsci's relevance resides in the concrete possibilities opened by his theories; always breaking down bipolar representations of the North-South relation into more complex views of social stratification, Gramsci provides more constructive designations which unveil new and pertinent grounds for activist strategies and alliances.[4]

Notes

1 Abse, Tobias, "The Triumph of the Leopard," *New left review,* no. 199 (1993):18. This is a telling statement as far as Abse is concerned. In fact, the belief of a corrupt South continues to predominate in the minds of most non-southerners, Italian or foreign. While this is a view undoubtably conditioned by the presence of the Mafia, 'ndrangheta, and camorra, it retains elements of that positivist view that tends to generalize in its references to Southerners, be they involved in criminal activity or not.

Another article that further illustrates the staying power of positivist depictions of the South is Frank Viviano's article on the Lombard League, "The Fall of Rome," *Mother Jones,* September/October (1993):36-40. The Italian elections of June 20th, 1993, during which the stronghold of the Christian Democrats and their Socialist cronies was undone, provides a picture of the "two Italies" that in some respects has remained unchanged since the unification of the country. During the course of these elections, the result of an electoral reform referendum that took place in April 1993, the Lombard League swept the North, and the South redefined itself on the Left not within the scope of larger parties but in smaller parties of localized concerns and presence, many of which were created in response and opposition to the influence of organized criminality.

2 A bipolar and simple dichotomy would be inadequate to describe the situation. In *The Southern Question* for example, Gramsci himself envisioned the South as three politically homogeneous regions on the social and class levels but nevertheless different by civil and cultural traditions. Furthermore, in the notes for the project that will be his *Prison Notebooks*, Gramsci notes, as the title for "argument 9": "La quistione meridionale e la quistione delle isole." In addition, there are considerations of three distinct "Southern Questions" addressed in paragraph 47 of notebook 14, and paragraph 26 of notebook 19 (Giuseppe Fiori, *Gramsci Togliatti Stalin,* Bari: Laterza, 1991) 193).

3 I would briefly like to note that, while many have recognized Gramsci's importance for the study of race and ethnicity, a certain distance remains in relation to his work when it comes to recognizing that his analysis of the North-South situation was also a critique of constructions of race and ethnic differences as found in the work of positivist anthropologists, followers of Lombroso's systems of categorization. I would add that a recognition of such subtleties within what is referred to as "white" might in fact be a useful way to undermine that category from within. The failure to acknowledge this aspect of Gramsci's writings may indeed be related to a perceived necessity to maintain, at least on a subliminal level and within situations such as the U.S., an image of Italy as a homogeneous nation without racial or ethnic difference. This, however, precludes the possibility of understanding the racial foundation of Italian nationhood, the very basis from which Gramscian thought emerged.

4 This is a partially rewritten excerpt from the introduction to my translation of Antonio Gramsci's *The Southern Question* (Bordighera, 1995): 1-13.

Bibliography

Abse, Tobia. "The Triumph of the Leopard," in *New Left Review,* No. 199 (1993).

Berlinguer, Enrico. Introduction to Antonio Gramsci, *The Southern Question.* Gift with the weekly Avvenimenti (June 1993).

Bevilacqua, Piero. *Breve storia dell'Italia meridionale dall'Ottocento a oggi. Storia e scienze sociale* (Roma: Donazelli, 1993): 122.

Brindani, Umberto and Daniele Vimercati, eds. *Il pensiero Bossi: 1979-1993. La prima raccolta di scritti e discorsi per capire chi è e che cosa vuole davvero l'uomo più temuto d'Italia.* Panorma documenti, 1993.

Chiavola-Birnbaum, Lucia. *Black Madonnas: Feminism, Religion and Politics in Italy* (Northeastern University Press, 1993).

Hall, Stuart. "Gramsci's relevance for the study of race and ethnicity," in *Journal of Communication Inquiry*, 10, 2 (1986): 5-27.

Verdicchio, Pasquale. *Bound by Distance: Rethinking Nationalism through the Italian Disapora* (Madison: Fairleigh Dickison University Press, 1997).

Nino Ricci

Fountain

For the Centennial, the Italians were building a fountain. John Street had been rerouted — not to accommodate the Italians, of course, but for traffic reasons — and a triangle of green had opened up in front of the public library. Tony himself had had the idea one grey Sunday in July when he was hurrying through a fine drizzle to return a book. He was thinking of some design changes he had to make to the front foyer of a hotel complex his father was building for some of the local business men when he suddenly noticed, as if for the first time, this tapering green space wedged between the library and the street, the lines still showing between the squares of sod that had been laid there in the spring, and the grass glistening now in the wet.

"It's a waste," Tony thought, stopping to survey the space with an architect's eye. But his mind wouldn't yield up any novel images; all he could think of filling the space up with were the standard park benches, flagstone paths, and flower gardens. He continued staring until he noticed, under an umbrella across the street, a dark-haired girl he didn't recognize peering at him through the drizzle, and smiling. Embarrassed, and realizing that the rain was beginning to seep through his clothes and swell the book in his hand, he turned towards the library.

Before he dropped the book in the after-hours return slot, Tony, protected now by a canopy, glanced down at the cover. The book was an Italian novel his sister Rita had taken out for his mother; it looked like an Italian version of a Harlequin Romance. *Incontro al Paradiso*, the title read, and underneath, "*la tragica storia d'un amore appassionato ma condannato a fallire.*" Why was his mother reading this crap? And why was his sister feeding it to her? The bottom half of the cover showed two young lovers gazing into each other's eyes, the man rugged and intense, the woman with eyelids drooping and lips formed into a sinister smile. A white, three-tiered fountain gushed in the background, its outlines obscured by a haze of spray.

Tony looked up from the book to the wedge of green, from the green back to the book. But finally he shook his head. It's just the kind of thing, he thought, that people would expect from Italians. And still shaking his head he dropped the book into the return slot and hurried back through the drizzle to his car.

But over the next few days Tony couldn't get the idea out of his head. Next year was Mersea's centennial, and though it was still only July the town had already been gearing up for it for some time: a book was being compiled, festivities and parades were being planned, hats and buttons made up, posters printed. The Italians, too, were looking for a contribution, something commensurate with their own sense of importance: in a town of twelve thousand residents almost two thousand were Italian, many among the town's most prosperous citizens.

Every time he passed the library now, Tony would park his car to survey the little strip of land there, his mind making little calculations, his inner eye, despite himself, visualizing what form the thing might take. Once he went out and made some rough measurements, jotting the figures down in his notebook. In his office at his parents' house (where, at age twenty-eight, he still lived, though as a trained architect he could easily have supported himself, had his own place, his own office), his mind wandered from the plans he was working on for his father, and he found himself doodling little open-winged angels on his drafting sheets. But when he thought about the idea carefully he couldn't see how a fountain would reflect the cultural heritage of Mersea's Italians: the only culture they'd known, past and present, was *agri*culture, and fountains were no more a part of their lives than they were for the *inglese*. Tony himself had been born in Italy, and the only fountain he remembered, apart from the village tap where the women used to go to fill their water jugs, was one he had glimpsed fleetingly in a square in Naples when a bus had been taking him and his mother to the port to board a boat for Canada. For a long time Tony sat at his desk trying to visualize that fountain, but all he got were the stereotypical little angels spurting water from their lips and naked nymphs spurting water from their nipples — images, he figured, he'd probably picked up from movies and postcards. He'd never been back to Italy since he'd left it at age six.

Finally, though, about two weeks after the original inspiration, Tony went to the library to look up some models. A general members' meeting was coming up at the Roma Club the following Sunday (most of Mersea's Italians were members of the Club, and all events of a communal nature — festivals, community projects, Italian classes — were organized through it), and the Mersea Centennial would be a prime item on the agenda. Tony hadn't mentioned his idea to anyone yet, not even his father, who was very busy these days with the hotel project, also planned to be ready for the Centennial, and already running into serious design and budget problems (problems which Tony refused to hold himself responsible for — he'd warned the building's backers when he'd drawn up the original plans, but they'd refused to give in to his suggestions for greater simplicity). But Tony decided that if he was going to put the idea forward at all, he should do it with conviction, and with something solid to show. The more authoritative you sounded, Tony knew from his past dealings with the Club, the less likely anyone would be brave enough to contradict you; but as soon as you showed the least amount of doubt, everyone would be ready to pipe in with their own two lire.

In the cool, sterile hush of the library, Tony sorted awkwardly through catalogues and shelves — he hadn't been in here in years — till he came out with a few books on Italian art and architecture and some tourist books on Rome and Naples and Florence. Back home, Tony almost fell over his mother, who was scrubbing the kitchen floor on hands and knees — Tony never got over seeing this thick-set peasant woman in the gleaming chrome and formica of their modern kitchen, and as he passed by her now he had a sudden image of her stopping to shove twigs and branches under a blackened pot in a fireplace — but he greeted her without breaking his stride, and hurried up to his office.

"*Ma che, te ne vai a l'Italia?*" his mother called after him, but Tony closed the door of his room without responding. She must have seen the covers of one of the books he had under his arm; but when Tony set the books on his desk he saw that the cover which had been showing — the plastic-clad jacket back of one of the art books — had print too small for his mother to have made anything out of it while he passed by her. What his mother must have recognized was the picture on the cover's bottom half, a black and white reproduction of the Mona Lisa. It struck him that his semi-literate mother, who after twenty-two years in Canada spoke almost no English, and who had enough problems getting through a cheap hundred-page Italian novel, could still have made an immediate connection between that enigmatic face and her native country.

Under the fluorescent glare of his desk lamp, Tony began to leaf through the books he'd brought back with him. He looked first through the book on Naples, hoping to find the lost fountain of his youth; but none of the fountains he came across sparked any glimmer of recognition. With this initial disappointment, he began to go through the books more perfunctorily, as if he were going through suppliers' catalogues; sometimes he noted down a page reference for some fountain in a piazza or some frieze or sculpture in a church that might offer a useful image. But it wasn't long before his brain grew numb; everything began to look the same, the swirls and the piping angels and the colonnades, and Tony felt that he must be missing something, that for some reason these much-praised beauties refused to yield up their mysteries to him. He knew little about Italian history and culture — some Roman stuff from high school, some big names like Columbus and Michelangelo and Machiavelli, maybe a few more specialized ones like Garibaldi and Vittorio Emanuele — but even that little he did know had come down to him mainly through the general haze of hybrid North American culture, and so seemed to have little connection to his Italian roots. The Italy he remembered — and even these scattered memories came to him like dim objects emerging out of a fog — was a village of crude, rock-hewn peasant houses; a ragged, sloping countryside where he tended the sheep and cut the wheat; a crumbling church with a garishly painted plaster madonna whose smiling face showed no knowledge of the fact that the paint on her nose was peeling. His mother, he figured, had probably seen the Mona Lisa on television, which she spent a lot of time watching, though it didn't seem to improve her English much. It was probably fitting, at any rate, that da Vinci's masterpiece was housed, as one of the art books told him, not in Italy but in Paris.

It was only as Tony began to make a few rough sketches, half-heartedly at first but then with growing absorption, that the mist which had settled around his brain began to lift. Now, caught up in his own creation, he began to go back to the pages he had noted and to see the images there in a new light, not as part of some distant culture but as material for his own imagination, to be reworked and remoulded into something personal and unique. When he had a few sketches that satisfied him, he began to make phone calls. A call to Mayor Sterling — whose patronizing good will Tony disliked, but who was a friend of his father's, and one of the backers of the hotel project: yes, the mayor said, if the Italians had some ideas for that strip of land he was sure he could get them access to it (through Tony refused to tell the mayor what his idea was). Then a call to Public Works, about water supply and electricity for the pump, and finally some long distance calls to suppliers, inquiries about marble, about figurines, about other suppliers. By supper time Tony had a pretty good idea of what was possible, as well as a rough estimate of what it would cost.

Tony's father was absent again from the supper table; he often stayed out at the work site now past dark. Meals were getting quieter and quieter these days, Tony had noticed, even though his brother Jimmy was home for the summer from university, and Rita came home every day from her job at the corner store for lunch. What was all this hype about Italian families being so close: Tony couldn't remember the last time he'd hugged his mother, or the last time he'd talked anything but business with his father. More and more it seemed to him like everyone in his family moved in a separate world. At least Rita and his mother had the soap operas in common, his mother keeping Rita informed while Rita's summer job kept her away from the television in the afternoons (though it was a running joke that his mother's plot summaries were more often the product of her imagination than of accurate understanding); and Rita, partly because she had taken lesson through the club, could at least manage a passable Italian. Maybe, Tony thought, there was some kind of renaissance going on with the younger generation, now that it was respectable to be Italian. But Jimmy: Jimmy was another story. Jimmy, who used the house, it seemed to Tony, only to eat, shit, and sleep, could hardly speak to his mother. Even though most of his friends were Italian, Jimmy had more or less forgotten what little Abruzzese he'd learned as a child, and whenever he spoke to his mother he did so, to Tony's continual irritation, in a fast English that left her helpless and confused. As Tony watched Jimmy wolfing down his supper now, he felt all the resentments of an eldest son rising up in him again: Jimmy, who had it so easy, born in Canada, no problem with language at school, none of the stigma of being a dago or a wop, no black eyes, no bloody lips, by his time Italians had become almost a majority; who'd dressed in blue jeans and sneakers, like all the other kids, worn his hair as long as he'd wanted, played football after school, hadn't had to come home to work for his father or be hired out to some other Italian, to bring in a few extra dollars; who'd got to keep all the money he'd earned on his summer jobs, every cent of it, had always had pocket money for movies and cigarettes and pinball; who'd been allowed to go away to school instead of living at home and commuting. To top it off, and to complete the town's stereotype for the spoiled children of *nouveau rich*e Italians, Tony's father had bought Jimmy a new Camaro when he'd gone off to university the previous year. Tony, still driving the battered hand-me-down Ford which had been the only legacy *he'd* received from his father, had said nothing; but inside he had burned with rage.

Still bringing a last forkful of salad to his mouth, Jimmy stood now and pulled his windbreaker off his chair.

"Where are you going?" Tony said roughly.

"Out," Jimmy said, and a minute later Tony heard Jimmy's engine revving up in the drive, then his tires squealing slightly as he drove off down the street.

On Sunday, before the meeting, Tony took a drive along the lakeshore. He was having second thoughts about the fountain idea again, and the drive was his way of trying to talk himself out of it completely. There were many stately homes along the lakeshore highway and in the subdivisions leading off of it which Tony had designed and which his father had built. But most of these were not the ones the Italians lived in — Tony's father was probably the only Italian contractor in town who didn't derive a major portion of his income building the one, two, and sometimes three hundred thousand dollar homes which had become the Italians' trademark in Mersea, and which they scrimped and sacrificed a lifetime for. The design of these houses never ceased to infuriate Tony: the sole criterion, it seemed, was excess, with little allowance made for subtlety, efficiency, or, for that matter, originality. The important thing was that the house look just like every other Italian house, only more expensive, and over the years this competitiveness had set off a dizzying spiral of extravagance. Many of these houses had enough floor space for a soccer field, but it was always boxed up in the same unimaginative ways, huge bedrooms that would never be used because all the children had moved out, expensively furnished living and dining rooms intended only for visits by popes and presidents, useless third bathrooms with long mirrors and bidets and three sinks, kitchens crammed with new microwaves and dishwashers and 30-cubic-foot refrigerators. Then, with the main floor fitted out like a palace, the owners would retreat to the basement, where they had arranged the old stove, the old fridge, the comfortable old couch, the old T.V., and the expensive upstairs would become the refuge of ghosts.

But it was always their homes — homes which seldom carried mortgages — that Italians pointed to when they wanted to compare themselves to the *inglese*, to pride themselves on their superior industry and ability for self-sacrifice. For the Italians in Mersea, these homes were the visible symbol of having arrived, proof that they could survive and prosper in someone else's country. And regardless of how they made their money — through greenhouse farming, through construction, even through the daily grind of working in the town's canning factory — there were few who did not see their homes as the culmination of their life's efforts. Tony was glad that his father, at least, had not succumbed to this mentality — about ten years before he had bought a modest older home in the center of town, the only excesses of which now were a gilt-edged madonna over the living room couch and a few knick knacks from Florida on the T.V. and on the coffee table.

The lakeshore, though, offered some of the worst examples of Italian extravagance, sticking out like caricatures among the more quietly affluent houses of the *inglese*. Tony drove slowly down the curving highway, looking from side to side and pulling over once in a while to let a honking car pass. Tony had to admit that some of the houses, the ones anyway which weren't laid out in the standard boring ranch style, might almost have attained a certain level of beauty, if the red-tiled roofs hadn't been so red or the glossy white bricks so glossy. But soon all the old excesses began to grate on his nerves again, the little fountains and statues on the huge circular front lawns, the fake stone work, the elaborately arched and pillared entranceways. What did any of this have to do with the Italy these people had left behind? Did they get their idea of Italy from the same place as Tony, from television and postcards and guidebooks? Or maybe there was some kind of collective memory operating here, one that went back not just to the Risorgimento or the Renaissance but all the way back to ancient Rome. Even the name of their club, the *Roma* Club, its insignia a picture of Romulus and Remus sucking the teats of a wolf. This was not the Roma of the twentieth century — there were no natives of *that* Rome in Mersea — but of the Coliseum and the Roman Forum. But these reflections, though they seemed to bring Tony to the verge of some insight, didn't settle his mind about the fountain.

The Club building sat at the edge of town just off the main highway, flanked on one side by a funeral home and on the other by the Kinsmen Curling Club. It occupied about five acres of land: a huge parking lot, a shaded picnic area, a bocce court out back, and then the building itself, which looked from a distance like a big barn with a few low stables attached along one side. It had been built some twenty years before, when the Italians couldn't afford much ostentation, and since then it had changed little, retaining both inside and out its almost strictly functional design.

Though Tony arrived fifteen minutes late the meeting showed no signs yet of getting under way. Grey-haired men, their stomachs bulging against weathered black belts and white permapress shirts, sat playing *tre sette* and *briscola* in the smoke-filled members' lounge; a slightly younger crowd milled around in the bar, laughing over bottles of Blue or talking prices and marketing boards and local politics. Tony, file folder containing sketches and estimates under one arm, went around exchanging greetings and pleasantries, inquiring after uncles' families, after cousins' business affairs. There was hardly anyone here who hadn't been a part of Tony's life for as long as he could remember: the weddings, the festivals, the evenings he'd spent at the Club playing blackjack for pennies till three in the morning or working in the kitchen or coat room when it was his father's turn for a tour of volunteer duty. The men here — only recently had the women begun to take an active part in the Club's activities, but they were usually shuffled off into societies and committees, and the

Club remained a bastion of Italian patriarchy — the men here treated Tony with the respect and intimacy they accorded a son who had stuck to the fold, with an added deference thrown in because of Tony's university education. Yet more and more Tony found himself fighting a feeling of condescension around them — it often amazed him that these men who had moved so dramatically from rags to riches could sometimes be so simple-minded. He remembered having asked his uncle once about a CO_2 system he'd had installed in his greenhouse: his uncle had had no idea about the principle of oxygen exchange by which the system operated, simply turned the system on and off as he'd been told, investing an almost mystical faith in the wonders of modern technology.

The meeting began about forty-five minutes late. Chairs had been set up in the main hall, with a table at the front for the seven members of the board. Some two hundred and fifty members or so were present, not a bad turnout — almost half the total membership, if you included all the sons who automatically became members at age twenty-one, whether they liked it or not. Tony sat at the back, growing bored and listless while the board went through its business: old minutes, budget reports, date for the annual members' party. Then a report from the committee organizing the three-day Grape Festival in September — the Club's biggest annual event, and a popular one in Mersea, not just among the Italians. But Tony, who had missed the last few meetings, had almost forgotten how unnecessarily tedious they could be: the petty objections, the infighting. There were two factions among the members, divided not as one might expect along tribal lines — Abruzzese on one side for example, and Ciociari on the other — but along lines that were more subtle and difficult to trace. One group, headed by a handful of men whose fathers had come over before the war, in the 1920s, had been the first Italians in Mersea. The don of this group was Dino Mancini, a balding, round-faced, round-bellied joker in his early sixties who, having inherited his father's modest pre-war wealth, had done nothing much in his own lifetime to increase it. Dino, despite his slightly pompous attitude towards Italians who had come over after the war, had nonetheless managed, through old loyalties (who had called you over, who had given you your first job) and through a certain easy style of leadership, to attract a fairly large following among the membership. But his main weapon, Tony thought, was laughter: Dino never passed up the chance for a laugh when he had the floor, and in this he seemed to play off a strong Italian need. When Tony thought about the early days in Mersea, when most of the Italians had been united, at least in their poverty, the thing he remembered most was the good cheer, the laughter which bubbled up even when people had no more to celebrate than a shared lunch of bread and wine in the middle of a long day in the fields.

The second faction was headed by a dozen or so members who had come over mainly in the 1950s and early 1960s and who, while they felt a certain loyalty to the founding fathers of Mersea's Italian community, resented Dino's attempts to use that loyalty for personal benefit. This post-war group seemed genuinely committed to the Club's prosperity (and had never, Tony thought, gotten over their resentment of the fact that Dino had managed to take most of the credit for the Club's founding). But their painstaking seriousness and their attempts to keep everyone happy were often translated by the members as vacillation and under-confidence. So even though they got more done than Dino's group ever did, they didn't maintain the same high profile; and it had more than once turned out, as with the Club's founding, that projects which they had worked and sweated to bring to fruition had with the passage of time eventually been credited to Dino.

It almost always happened that the Club's board was heavily stacked one way or the other, as if these matters were arranged beforehand (and indeed they often were — Dino's group especially would be careful to load the audience with loyal supporters on election day if it had some particular reason for wanting to seize power). But whichever group happened to be in, the other always set itself up as a kind of Royal Opposition, so that no matter could be passed until a good deal of sometimes quite useless dispute and digression had been wasted on it, particularly when Dino was the leader of the opposition, a post he seemed to enjoy, and one he often secured for himself by simply not running for the board in a given year. This year the postwar group held power, and Tony could already envisage from the tone of the meeting so far that he would have a long struggle ahead of him if he tried to get his fountain project passed.

Finally the matter of the Centennial came up. The chairman of the Centennial Committee reported on the committee's plans: processions, floats, fireworks, a folk group from Toronto, a day of contests — elaborate enough to spark a few murmurs of approval from the members. But there was nothing new in all of this, Tony thought, it was like a Grape Festival and a Carnival Party and a Festa della Madonna rolled into one. It was Dino, though — Dino gave the impression of being a little stupid, but he could come surprisingly quickly to the point when it was to his advantage — who stood up to voice what Tony was thinking.

"We all appreciate that the Committee has been working very hard," he began in his slow, casual English. "But you have to admit that most of this stuff is old hat." Then, having demonstrated his command of English idiom, he switched into a mixture of English and Abruzzese. "I don't say we shouldn't do all these things, I know *l'ingles,* themselves, tell me that until the Italians came to Mersea no one here knew how to have a good time. The first time they saw a *fisarmonica* they thought it was one of those things you use to blow on a fire, *come si chiama, 'na mantice.* Dino paused to let a ripple of laughter pass through his audience. "But I think the Italians in Mersea have enough money in their pockets to do something really big. Fifty-five years ago, when my father came here, the lakeshore was all English. Now you only have to drive along there to see what Italians have done. I think we should have some kind of project that people will remember, not just these *fissaroie* that they see every year."

Dino sat down and the president of the board, a dark-haired man in his forties who was a second or third cousin of Tony's, cleared his throat.

"I'm sure no one would disagree with what Dino is saying," he started, speaking, as he always did at these meetings, not in his dialect but in perfect Italian. He had a habit, Tony noticed, of clasping his hands together in front of himself as he spoke, as if he were praying. "And at the last meeting some of the members expressed the same feeling. So if anyone has any suggestions to offer, the board would be happy to hear them."

It seemed Dino had been waiting for this invitation, because now almost immediately, before Tony had had the time to decide whether he should raise his hand, Dino started to speak again, this time without standing.

"There's about three hundred and fifty Italian families in this area," he said. "If we could get each of them to give maybe fifty, a hundred dollars apiece, we'd have more than enough for something really special. If we can't raise the money that way, the Club showed a profit last year, which I haven't heard yet what it's going to do with except buy a few new pots for the kitchen." Another ripple of laughter. "What I had in mind was a little monument or something, the way they have in squares in Italy. I was talking to the mayor the other day and he said there's a little strip of land in front of the library —"

That conniving bastard! The mayor must have told Dino about Tony's call, and now Dino, in typical fashion, was using that information to get in on the ground floor of any idea Tony might have come up with. Tony felt himself blushing with anger, and as he listened to Dino go on, in his vague, rambling way, about the possible form of this proposed monument, he was tempted to simply let Dino dig his own grave — Dino's suggestions made Tony think of the picture he'd seen in one of the guidebooks of the great white monstrosity Mussolini had constructed in Rome to Vittorio Emanuele II: the typical Italian extravagance. But what bothered Tony was that this was exactly the kind of thing the members would go for, and he envisioned the little square in front of the library becoming a running joke with the *inglese*: "And you should see their houses," they would say. "At least," Tony thought, hugging the well-formulated plans under his arm, "if I come forward now I might be able to make Dino look like a fool." So when Dino finished speaking, Tony suppressed his anger, raised his hand, and asked for the floor.

He spoke in English, partly because his Italian, particularly when dealing with technical matters, was a little halting, partly because he knew his English, even though it would go over the heads of some of the members, would give him an extra air of authority; though as he spoke he sensed the irony of having to resort to these defensive manoeuvres to convince the members of an idea which was essentially intended for their benefit. And the English made it difficult to expose Dino's ploy: in any language Tony lacked the frame of mind necessary to play Dino's games, and in English he realized as he talked that even his fairly straightforward attempt to set the record straight — he mentioned his own phone call and suggestion to the mayor — would probably be missed by many of the members. So, even though Tony had arrived with detailed plans, Dino, for the simple reason that he had spoken first, would probably be remembered as the initiator. But Tony could see that any more direct confrontation, which was the only sort he was any good at, and even then he tended to lose his temper, would only backfire on him: had Dino, after all, really taken any credit for suggesting the use of that piece of land? The last thing Tony wanted to be seen as was someone out simply for personal grandeur.

When Tony got to the point where he was holding up sketches, the president asked him to come up to the front to show them around. After the board members had looked them over, nodding and murmuring approvingly, Dino, sitting in the third row, asked to see. Tony handed them back and Dino stared at them for a moment, then looked up with an indulgent smile.

"Very nice," he said, in English, "but I don't think the English will go for this kind of thing. It's fine to have naked women and things like that in Italy, people are used to looking at them, with water coming out of *lu sesse* and all that. But the English aren't ready for that sort of thing."

So the disputes started. The drawings were handed around, and now that Dino had inserted the wedge his cronies took their shots at hammering it in. Some objected to the cost (which was no higher than what Dino had suggested for *his* monument); others to the idea of a fountain ("The water will freeze in the winter" — just the kind of trite objection that infuriated Tony, and what infuriated him even more was that he had to hedge a bit when he responded to the objection, because he hadn't yet given any thought to the question of winterizing). Someone even suggested they should put up instead statues of the founding fathers, a suggestion which found a good deal of favour, and maybe, Tony thought, the one which Dino had in mind all along. The post-war contingent, meanwhile, from whom Tony might have counted on for support, was left in a state of confusion: to support the fountain would be, in effect, to support Dino's original proposal for a monument, but to go against it would also play into Dino's hand.

The meeting ended inconclusively, and it was decided that the matter be held over for a special vote in three weeks. Before leaving, Tony felt out the board, and found them generally approving. He also spoke privately with the president, to make sure he'd seen through Dino's subterfuge. He had.

In the parking lot, Tony stopped for a moment to speak with his father, who had come in late. His father was looking more and more worn out these days, his hair beginning to thin, the skin on his cheeks sagging; and though his stomach still strained a bit against his shirt, Tony could tell he'd lost a lot of weight in the past few months.

"You never told me anything about this fountain," his father said, speaking in English.

"I wanted to surprise you."

His father grunted.

"Well, if it goes through you'll have to find someone else to build it . . . I want you to come out and look at that heating system again tomorrow. The way it's set up now the pool in the courtyard will freeze in the winter."

"Look, Dad, I told them a dozen times, you were there, with a glass wall on the north side there's no way you'll be able to keep that courtyard warm in the winter. How many greenhouses do you see in Mersea with glass at the north end? They wanted glass, I gave them glass. They'll have to pay for it.

Tony's father cleared his throat. "Maybe I will too," he said.

"What are you talking about?"

"I put some money into it," his father said heavily.

Tony couldn't believe it.

"What? Are you crazy? How much?"

"A lot."

"How much?"

"Two hundred thousand. So far."

"Jesus Christ, Dad! Didn't I tell you a hundred times that place wouldn't pay for itself? Shit, you've been in the construction business all your life, what got into your head?" Men walking towards their cars were turning their heads, but Tony's temper had gotten the better of him. "Those people are worse than the Italians; at least the Italians don't expect to turn a profit when they throw their money away. I can't believe you'd do something like this without telling me. What do you think I've been breaking my ass for you for the past five years?"

"Calm down, Tony," his father said, his face darkening now. "It's not your money yet."

"Aw, for Christ's sake, Dad, that's not the point."

But now anger and hurt choked him. Inside his car, Tony clenched his fists and pounded them again and again against the steering wheel.

At the next meeting, the fountain project passed, by a narrow margin through not until three hours of discussion had passed, most of it almost verbatim rehash of the objections raised before. Tony had altered the design a little — it had never been his intention, at any rate, to have water shooting out of breasts — but one half-naked figure remained, and she was the subject of heated dispute. Dino himself didn't speak much, but he tried to make it seem — again, by planting an idea here, an idea there, vague enough so he couldn't be pinned down — as if his original idea had been commandeered; but then to allow himself the leeway to fall later on either side, depending on how the matter turned out, he disappeared from the hall, on some pretext, when the time came for a vote.

Tony volunteered himself as coordinator of the project. It was decided that construction would wait till the following spring, to give time to collect funds and get a hold of materials, and to time completion with the official opening of the Centennial celebrations in July. A few weeks later the town council approved the site, and Tony set about making more accurate measurements and plans: he was glad of the distraction; it kept his mind off the hotel. As winter came on, Tony stopped going out to the hotel work site; most of the design problems had been sorted out as best as possible (the glass wall, for instance, had been changed to brick), and now Tony spent his time on some commissions he'd received from other contractors, and on the fountain. The fountain design went through a few more minor changes, quickly approved by the board; and Tony contacted suppliers to have everything ready for spring. But another problem arose when Tony set out to hire a contractor: to be perfectly impartial, Tony accepted bids from all the town's seven construction firms, and — the crowning irony — the lowest bid, undercutting the nearest competition by well over a thousand dollars, came in from a firm run by a German. The board members, unwilling to risk the fallout of hiring a German to build the Italians' fountain, called a general meeting. After a stormy members' session, and then a week of behind-the-scenes negotiating, a consortium made up of the town's three major Italian contractors, Tony's father included, came forward with an offer of free labour; but the whole matter left a bad taste in Tony's mouth.

Finally, in the spring, construction got under way. Pipes and cables were laid, the foundation poured, the recirculating pump installed. A wall of ten-foot high plywood sheets was built up around the work area, ostensibly to protect materials and tools; but Tony guarded access through that wall like a flaming sworded angel, and every evening he came by to put a heavy padlock on the door cut into it. There were more problems, supplies not arriving, marble splitting, intricate cement work crumbling; and the unusually wet spring cut great chunks into available work hours. But all in all work proceeded on schedule and, because of the free labour, well under budget.

Tony himself had refused a fairly generous offer the board had made him for his efforts, but he spent long hours supervising the work. He watched the fountain growing up out of the earth with the spring like something alive, becoming more and more his own, the image in his mind. Sometimes, in the evenings, he stayed long after the workers had gone, carefully inspecting the day's work or running his hand over the contours of freshly hardened concrete like a lover. In the day he often came by to issue instructions or oversee some new addition. He hounded the workers until they began to tease him: "It's not going in your living room," they would say, or, "You're worse than an Italian!" Once, just as one of the workers was putting a finishing cut on a piece of marble, it split in his hands, and Tony lost his temper; but as he railed at the offender Tony noticed the smiles of the other workers and caught himself up, embarrassed suddenly at how personally he had started to take the whole project. Five minutes later, over coffee and cigarettes, they were all laughing together over the incident; but Tony was careful from then on to keep his temper in check. In June the weather cleared up, every day dawning bright and warm; the workers began to put in longer hours, and by the end of the month the bronze head of a smiling young goddess appeared above the ten-foot wall: the crowning touch.

Three days before the unveiling, Tony had the fountain covered with a big canvas tarp. The plywood was taken down, the ground levelled, and sod replaced, and four flagstone paths, one from each side of the triangle and one from the apex, were laid leading up to the fountain. Tony himself looked forward to the unveiling with the excitement of a schoolboy, as if some revelation lay in store for him, too; and when, the night before it, he attended the official opening of his father's hotel (on time but way over budget), he almost found himself taken in by the false optimism of the festivities.

The afternoon of the unveiling threatened rain. But the weather held out through the Centennial Parade, and by three a large crowd had formed around the covered fountain, blocking the traffic coming off of John Street. Tony waited on one of the flagstone paths, making nervous conversation with the photographer from the local paper. There were a lot of faces in the crowd Tony recognized, Italian and otherwise, but also a lot he didn't — a fact which surprised him, since he'd always thought he knew by sight almost everyone in town. Finally the mayor, fresh from his position on the parade's head float and wearing a styrofoam boater with a green, white, and red band, the Centennial's official colours, made his way through the crowd to where Tony was standing — followed, inevitably, by Dino Mancini, who after an unusually vicious election the previous month (too late, Tony thought thankfully, to have affected the fountain) had managed to weasel himself into the Roma Club presidency. They look almost like twins, Tony thought, as each in turn came forward to shake his hand: the same balding round faces, the same benign, indulgent smiles.

After that, under the threat of rain, everything happened very quickly. Mayor Sterling gave a little speech, full of high praise for the Italians; Dino gave a little speech, full of high praise for Mersea — but to Tony the two speeches, rather than building to a crescendo, seemed to cancel each other out, like opposite charges. Then Dino and the mayor, looking in their tight suits like Tweedledee and Tweedledum, each took one end of the canvas tarp and began to pull it back.

"Careful," Tony called out. "Don't let it catch on the statues!"

But in a moment the fountain was revealed: a large round-lipped base of moulded concrete coming up about three feet; then, rising up from a central island, three ascending basins of diminishing size, each of them also moulded out of concrete but lined with white marble. Above the top basin hovered six evenly spaced little bronze angels, wings open, bodies bent forward, and hands holding jugs that were on the point of spilling, waiting only for a source of water. Finally, reigning over all, was the smiling goddess, long hair flowing down her back and a furled toga covering her lower parts but not her breasts. A long round of applause came up from the watching crowd.

But Tony, staring at the fountain as if he too were seeing it for the first time, hardly heard the applause: a horror had suddenly gripped him, and was reaching down now right into his bowels. This was not his fountain, not the one he had fussed and fretted over the past nine months, watched rising up out of the ground. The concrete clashed with the marble, the marble with the bronze: all the extravagances, all the lack of taste — he felt as if some poltergeist had conspired against him and made him build a thing that was the very image of his nightmare.

Maybe the water will help, he thought desperately, and quickly he went around to the little hatch in the fountain's base which hid the filler valve and opened it with his key. He had filled the bottom basin the week before, to test the water system, but after a successful test had drained it again, afraid the water would stagnate before the unveiling. Now, though he felt the tap giving too easily, and didn't hear a familiar whine from the pipe.

"Shit. No water."

Dino and the mayor had come over now, and Tony, blushing red, looked up at them as he played with the tap.

"Problems?" Dino said.

"Water's off. I'm going to call Public Works."

Before Dino or the mayor could respond, Tony had dashed off towards the library to use the phone there. But the door was locked: closed for the day's festivities. Without looking back towards the fountain, Tony made his way through the crowd on the sidewalk; he'd decided to drive the half mile or so to the Public Works office. Fortunately he had parked about a block away and didn't have to drive through the crowd. But when he got to the office, it too was closed: of course — it was Saturday.

As a last ditch effort, Tony decided to drive out to the Public Works warehouse at the edge of town, where the town kept its machinery and maintenance equipment. Maybe there would be somebody there who could help him. Tony's tires squealed as he pulled out of his parking spot; en route he ran a yellow light and a stop sign, pulling the last stretch twenty miles over the speed limit. The warehouse door was locked, but out back in a work shed

Tony found two dirty-overalled men greasing up a small Ford tractor, one an old grey-hair with sagging cheeks and the other a husky, heavily-bearded younger man whose face looked vaguely familiar. Tony explained his problem, and the younger one, collecting up a tool box, agreed to come out and take a look.

A light drizzle had started by the time they got out to the fountain, and much of the crowd had dispersed. Dino and the mayor were nowhere to be seen. The man from Public Works followed Tony to the fountain and tried the tap: still nothing.

"Where's you water come from?" the man asked.

"It's off the library's line."

The bearded man led Tony around the corner of the library to where a metal plate was affixed low down on the library's side wall. Crouching down and hunching his shoulders because of the drizzle, the man pulled an adjustable wrench out of his tool box and began removing the bolts that held the plate. Behind the plate was a large gold valve with a big red handle. The man tried it.

"It's off," he said, the valve groaning as he began to screw it open. Shouldn't be, but it is. Some joker, probably. Must've been last night or this morning, or the library would've been bitching yesterday. Should be a lock on these things."

Some joker. The idea sparked a train of unpleasant associations in Tony, and he suddenly realized why this face had looked familiar.

"You're Doug Vanderhyde," Tony said. "We used to ride the bus together in grade school. Tony Rossi, I lived on the third concession." But Tony felt his voice cracking and his face growing uncontrollably red: the same Doug

Vanderhyde who had made life hell for him during his first years in Mersea, with all the senseless cruelty of childhood — elbows in his ribs, spit-smeared fingers in his eyes, the names, the taunts. Tony felt an old hatred rise inside him like a fire, and had to suppress a sudden urge to bring his knee up hard under Doug's chin.

But Doug, just replacing the last bolt, only looked up and smiled.

"Can't say I remember you," he said. Then, rising, he wiped his hand on his overalls and held it out to Tony. "But glad to meet you again."

Some scattered applause behind Tony's back brought him back to the present with a start, and now he realized he heard, over the drizzle's hiss, the sound of running water. He turned and walked forward until the fountain came into view: the pump must have been on automatic and had kicked in as soon as the bottom basin had started to fill up. A strong, pulsing surge of foamy water was coming up around the feet of the bronze goddess, like laughter, and falling straight down into the second basin; six thick streams were pouring out of the angels' jugs into the second basin; and finally a complete circle of water was falling like curved glass into the third basin. In a moment the third basin would fill and begin spilling its overflow into the fountain's base.

Most of the crowd had gone by now, except for a few who had been wise enought to bring along umbrellas or rain gear. But on the other side of the fountain Tony noticed now, for the first time, his family huddled together on the sidewalk in the drizzle, his mother and his sister stooped shoulder to shoulder under a clear plastic rain poncho, and his father and his brother, one on either side of the women, like guardians, standing with shoulders hunched and arms crossed over their chests. They looked a little pathetic standing there, Tony thought, and the sight both touched and embarrassed him.

"That your fountain?" Tony had momentarily forgotten about Doug, who was standing now at his elbow.

"The Italians built it," Tony said. "I designed it."

"It's beautiful," Doug said. Tony instinctively glanced over at Doug's face to see the sarcasm there, but the face revealed only a pleasant smile.

By now the fountain contained enough water to keep it running smoothly; Tony cut the tap, locked the hatch, then went over to join his family.

"Nice job, Tony," his father said, and Jimmy, speaking in exaggerated Abruzzese: "*Ma ch'è success'*? We've been waiting here almost an hour."

That night, Tony could hardly sleep. Just before he got into bed a sudden whiff of rain-water through his open window brought him to the edge of a memory that seemed at any moment ready to burst into clarity, but which refused to yield itself as he pursued it. For several hours he tossed and turned in his bed, kept at the edge of consciousness by the humming rain and chased by the ghost of his memory. Finally, around four in the morning, he suddenly sat bolt upright in his bed: in his mind he saw his own head sticking out a bus window and getting a whiff of some mist blown off a fountain as the bus passed around it. The fountain in Napoli, Tony thought, but already the image was gone, and the fountain was lost to him again.

As the first light of dawn filtered in through his window, Tony rose and dressed, then crept downstairs and got into his car. The sky had cleared and a rim of orange was showing over the trees that lined his street; a coating like glass covered the trees' leaves and the pavement. As Tony drove down the silent Sunday streets towards the library, though, he began to notice little puffs of white, like fallen pieces of cloud, floating idly over the pavement or stuck up against a tree or fence. The puffs increased, in size and number, as he got closer to the library, until his car was swishing over them as they tried to race away from its currents; they began to thicken now almost into a ground fog, spread out in large patches over the street and sidewalk and bunched up around the corners of buildings. Finally Tony passed the edge of the library and the fountain was in front of him, but all that was showing was the bronze goddess; the rest of the fountain lay buried in a hill of white which had spilled out to cover the triangle of green and was glistening now in the morning's quiet yellow light.

Tony parked his car and sat staring dumbly at the fountain for a long moment. Finally he opened his door and stepped outside. As the white washed around his feet he heard a familiar snap and crackle coming up from it and realized what had happened: someone must have poured a box of laundry soap or something into the fountain, and a night of churning had built up this landscape of foam. Some joker: conspiracy theories began to rise in Tony's head. But then he realized that this train of thought was pointless; the culprits could just as easily have been pranksters like Jimmy and his friends; it was the sort of thing they would do.

Tony leaned against the fender of his car and continued staring, his feet awash in the whispering suds. He could hear the water in the fountain still flowing under the foam, could just see the top of the jet that bubbled up near the fountain's top. The bronze goddess rising up above the whole scene the way she was, sharp and clear against the morning's blushing sky, made Tony think of a story from his grade nine mythology, a story about a goddess' birth. Venus that was it, the goddess of love, rising up from the foam of the sea. From where Tony stood the goddess' face was turned directly towards him, its lips set in their perpetual smile. What was she trying to tell him? But the more Tony stared, the more her smile seemed to recede into the morning's silence.

Ironies of Identity

In the century following Italian Unification, up to the 1970s, almost twenty-six million Italians left their homeland. While a large proportion left only temporarily, this massive migration qualifies as one of the major diasporas of the modern age. Almost half the Italian migrants left for various new world destinations, and today Italians form the fourth-largest ethnic group in Canada, numbering over 800,000. Indeed, in Toronto the Italian population, which totals over 300,000, is equal to that of Venice.

Franc Sturino
Forging the Chain

Carmen Laurenza Ziolkowski

The Life and Fortune of Nicola Masso

Nicola Masso steps into the vineyard. The moon is full riding upwards above the neat rows of grape vines. The pale beams catch clusters of grapes and make each grape a precious stone. Nicola meanders along, letting his eyes feast on the ephemeral hues cast by the blue moon on the grapes and large leaves.

He is happy tonight. In a few days there will be the grape gathering festival. The vintage is abundant this year, and maybe . . . just maybe . . . his wife, her ladyship, will be satisfied. She might, just might, give Nicola a bit of credit. With these thoughts he steps onto the road, and there next to him stands a man. Nicola is startled. He holds his breath, his mouth is getting dry, his hands are out of control. With great effort he steels himself not to run, though fear is creeping through his body. He forces himself to have a good look at the stranger. The pale light of the moon reveals a handsome man in a black suit, impeccably dressed.

"Good evening, Nicola Masso."

"For the love of God how do you know my name? I don't know you, do I?"

"You might not know me, but I know everyone on this planet. I have each name on my list. They should know or think of me from time to time — acknowledge my existence instead of ignoring me and looking at me askance when I approach. As you are doing now. And you're scared stiff too."

Nicola regains a bit of self assurance — after all, the stranger seems to be a gentleman. "Well, whoever you might be, I was on my way to a glass of wine; the vintage will be good this year. Would you like to join me? Hopefully, my wife, the shrew, has gone to bed; you don't have to face her."

"Why not? I came a bit early. We still have a little time."

The house is quiet when they enter; Nicola indicates to his guest the best armchair in his wife's plush parlour. He sets crystal glasses and a bottle of red wine on a silver tray. After opening the bottle he fills the glasses and hands one to his guest.

"Wonderful!" exclaims the stranger. "Nicola Masso you are a perfect host. I've never been treated this well before."

"Sh . . . sh . . . ," admonishes Nicola. "If my wife awakes she'll throw us out."

The stranger laughs. "I haven't heard yet of a man being afraid of his wife."

"You don't know Malva! She's worse than the devil himself. I work my fingers to the bone. There's never praise or gratitude, but the worst is — she keeps telling me I live on her charity. Sometimes I wish I were dead."

At this the stranger has another fit of laughter. From the inner rooms comes the yelling of Nicola's wife. "Angelina, Angelina. My robe! What's that idiot up to now?" An old woman comes into the room followed by her maid. "What the devil are you doing? Making a racket in the middle of the night."

"Please, Malva," tries to soothe Nicola. "We have a guest."

"Who has invited him into my house . . . you tell me that."

"I have invited this gentleman for a glass of wine, and it's not in the middle of the night. It's only a couple of hours since the sun has gone behind Monte Latteo."

"Enough from you Nicola Masso. Get this man out of my house. I will deal with you later." Turning to the maid. "Angela, don't stand there gawking. Get those glasses and bottle out of my parlour." She stalks out, her frilly night cap askew. Before collecting the glasses Angela gives a glance of commiseration to Nicola.

"Let's go to my mansion. I have no wife to bother us."

"Where do you live? Have you just moved to this town?"

"I live everywhere . . . it's hard to explain. Come and you'll see." Nicola follows the stranger. They leave town, going towards a gorge at the foot of the mountain known as Death Valley. Suddenly there is thick fog. Nicola keeps close to the man. Soon a brightly lit tunnel appears. Nicola doesn't know where he is anymore, though he thought he was familiar with all the area around his town. They descend. Nicola sees a myriad of flickering lights. The reflection makes the tunnel's walls like mirrors. The bright light temporarily blinds Nicola. "Where in hell are we?"

"Not far from your house . . . down in the bowels of the earth. This is my kingdom."

"Who are you then?" Nicola is terrified. "Are you the devil . . . do you want my soul?"

"Oh, no! No, I am only Death."

"For the love of God, I never thought that one could actually come face to face with you." Nicola's eyes have become accustomed to the light. Looking around he is astonished at the sea of candles, the flames all mingling together. "What's the meaning of all these tapers?"

"They are the people's souls. When anyone is born a candle is lit here. As soon as the candle burns down I go to get that person. Some burn fast — others burn very slowly."

Nicola inspects the candles, and sees that one is out. "This is on its way out. Whom does it belong to?"

"That one is yours. That's why I came for you."

"Do you mean I am done, my life is over? I am healthy and still young. Take my wife, she's seventy-five . . . I have been waiting for her to go. I want to marry Angela, have children. You see my wife is a rich woman. I worked hard to increase her fortune; we don't have children who will take over."

"How long have you been married?"

"I was only twenty and Malva was forty-five at that time."

"You married her for her money?"

"Well, not really. I had been working for her father as long as I can remember, and when he died she told my mother that if I didn't marry her, my job was finished. She wouldn't have me around the house and have the whole village talking about her. So my mother cried and carried on. I was the only one in the family working, and my two sisters needed the dowry to get married. What was I to do? I gave in and married the woman. But, I tell you, she has driven me to distraction. And here to my early death. I kept telling myself to have patience, hoping she'd go long before me. I wanted a few good years. You seem friendly, why don't you help me?"

"What do you mean by that? What can I do?"

"Well, you could exchange the candles . . . you know, get my wife. How long does she still have?"

"Here it is." Death points. "I'd say that she has about twenty more years to go."

"I'll be satisfied with that. Please help me," begged Nicola.

"A strange request. I have never done this before. Though, I do feel sorry for you, you have had such an awful life. Maybe I'll bend the rule. But, it doesn't mean you'll have all of your wife's time." Death exchanges the tapers and escorts Nicola back to his house.

Next morning when Angela brings coffee to her mistress, she finds her cold, her mouth open as though she had been screaming and terrified. Nicola spares no money for his wife's funeral. He gives her the best money can buy. He makes sure that the statue on her tomb is bigger than anyone else's there. He mourns Malva for six months and then Nicola waits no longer. His desire for Angela is becoming unbearable. He marries her and the next summer they have a son. Finally Nicola's life is fulfilled, he is happy. He tries not to think about "La Morte," Death, but often he feels the presence of the stranger as he refers to it in his mind. But at other times he wonders whether the whole thing had been a dream. Many times Nicola is on the point of asking Angela whether she remembers the stranger who came to the house the night before Malva died.

Time goes by. The boy is growing up nicely. Nicola takes the child around to familiarize him with their land and the people who work for them. The summer of the boy's tenth birthday, Nicola takes him down the valley near the brook to escape the unbearable heat of the early afternoon. Nicola stretches on the silky moss, keeping an eye on his handsome son as he tramps along crushing down ferns with a cruel pleasure. The fragrance of the sap wafts into the warm scented light. But in spite of unbearable heat of the summer day, Nicola feels a shiver as if someone has walked over his grave. The same thing had happened once before — the night the moon shone on his grapes. He hears a whisper, "Nicola Masso, I have come for you." It is definitely the stranger's voice, though Nicola doesn't see him.

"Go away, it's not time yet. Malva's candle had twenty years."

"Papa," says the boy. "Who are you talking to?"

"No one . . . there is no one here. Come on let's go."

"Papa, papa you look white."

Even in his own home Nicola feels terrible. He is frightened; he can't swallow one mouthful of the delicious supper Angela has prepared.

As night falls and the stars show their shining faces, Nicola decides to take a walk. He might meet the stranger and convince him that he needs a little more time to look after the boy. Nicola has not gone far when the stranger appears. "Nicola Masso, are you ready? Your time is up."

Nicola pleads, begs. There are so many reasons and excuses why he needs more time. But the stranger is adamant. Nicola is desperate. He counted on the stranger being his friend. Now there is only one thing he has to outwit — *La Morte.* "If there's nothing you can do, I'll have to go with you. But before we go will you please grant me a last wish."

"If it doesn't take long."

"Promise me that you'll not take me away till I have said my prayers."

"Your wish is granted, and hurry up, there are many more souls I have to get before sun-up."

"Now you can't take me. I'll not say my prayers."

The stranger is defeated and Nicola hurries home, whistling a love song. His happiness has no bounds. If he is careful he could live forever.

A few weeks go by and Nicola's young wife begins nagging at him for not accompanying her and the boy to church. "The whole town is talking about your unusual behaviour."

He takes no notice and abstains from all form of prayers. Then comes his son's name day and Angela organizes a big feast. They all sing and make merry. She makes sure that her husband drinks more wine than usual before starting to say prayers. The wine has clouded Nicola's mind, he's taken off guard. They have no sooner finished praying than the stranger is beside him. "Nicola Masso, come along now."

"I have been so careful," he tells "La Morte." "How has it happened?"

"I enlisted the help of your wife. After all she wants to marry a younger man now. You see Nicola Masso! It was for love you were granted a bit of extra time. It's only fair that you will die for love."

And off they went into the fog of never-ending night.

Paul Tana and Bruno Ramirez

Sarrasine

A Prison Cell.

Ninetta has gone to visit Giuseppe in prison. He wants her to return to Italy with his brother who has come to Canada for his trial and to take her back.

GIUSEPPE

What are you doing here? How come they let you in?

NINETTA

Shrugging her shoulders.

A guard came to get me at home. Maybe because I'm leaving.

Giuseppe looks behind him. The door closes. The couple look at each other in silence for a few moments. Giuseppe is wearing his prisoner's uniform. He takes a few steps toward Ninetta, then stops.

In a murmur.

Giuseppe!

She rushes to take him in her arms, kisses his face and neck.

NINETTA

Hold me tight, Giusé!

Giuseppe hasn't moved. Now, he gently frees himself from her embrace.

NINETTA

Sadly.

Giuseppe, it's me, your Ninetta.

She lays her head on Giuseppe's shoulder . . .

A few minutes later, Ninetta and Giuseppe are sitting face to face. Ninetta strokes Giuseppe's hands.

GIUSEPPE

Have the boarders left?

NINETTA

No, they'll stay with Carmelo till the end of the month.

GIUSEPPE

Have you sold the furniture?

NINETTA

Carmelo's looking after that. He said he'll send the money to me back home.

Later . . .

Ninetta is sitting at the table, toying with her wedding ring. Giuseppe is standing behind her.

GIUSEPPE

Did you take the tickets?

Ninetta turns around, surprised, but doesn't answer.

GIUSEPPE

Do you think my brother's an idiot? Do you realize how you're behaving? Everyone's waiting for you back home. Uncle Saverio has done everything to help you. He's taking you on at his store, a few steps from your mother's home.

Flaring up.

What the hell do you want?

A beat. Giuseppe goes over to Ninetta, and puts his hands on her shoulders.

GIUSEPPE

Nina!

NINETTA

Shaking her head, imploring:

Don't make me leave, Giuseppe!

GIUSEPPE

Tenderly.

Ninetta!

Ninetta stands up abruptly and moves away.

GIUSEPPE

With controlled anger.

You're so stubborn! How many times have I told you there's nothing more for you here!

NINETTA

Sad, but firm.

No! My place is here, near you!

Seizing Ninetta by the shoulders, Giuseppe shakes her, as if this could make her come to here senses.

GIUSEPPE

Here, where? Where? In prison?

NINETTA

Barely audible.

Yes!

GIUSEPPE

As if to himself.

My brother's right, everything in this country's upside-down!

NINETTA

Violently, her eyes gleaming with anger.

Leave your brother out of it!

For a moment Giuseppe can't find words, then he continues, gently.

GIUSEPPE

Nina, I can never be at peace, knowing you're here alone.

NINETTA

Raising her voice, outraged.

Why? Are you afraid I'll end up a whore?

GIUSEPPE

Raising his voice in turn.

Don't raise your voice! No one said anything about whores. It's not that — I have to look after my affairs.

NINETTA

Shouting.

Your affairs? *Our* affairs! Ours!

GIUSEPPE

Nina, I'm still your husband, aren't I? Holy Mary, Mother of God!

Softening, Giuseppe goes over to Ninetta to try to reason with her.

GIUSEPPE

Nina, this country isn't for you.

Taking her hands.

My love, this country is not our blood. So, Nina, if you're really my wife, please . . . I implore you, have the goodness to leave.

Ninetta frees herself from him brusquely. Giuseppe takes Nina's cloak, which she had left on the table, and holds it out to her.

GIUSEPPE

Get out!

Ninetta doesn't move, Giuseppe throws the cloak on the floor, grabs Ninetta by the arm, and roughly pushes her away.

GIUSEPPE

Get out!

NINETTA

Defying him.

The goodness to leave! Goodness! You should thank me! Without me they'd have hung you.

GIUSEPPE

Firmly.

I don't want you to stay here, and that's final!

NINETTA

Shouting.

And you talk to me about goodness?

GIUSEPPE

I won't listen to you any longer.

NINETTA

Shouting, panting.

You have to deal with me, not your brother!

GIUSEPPE

Trying to calm her.

Ninetta, enough!

NINETTA

Shouting and screaming.

Who ruined us? You!

Giuseppe slaps her violently, slamming her against the wall. She collapses, then gets to her feet, sobbing.

NINETTA

In a murmur.

I'm staying, and you can't stop me.

Giuseppe lowers his head.

Translated by Robert Gray

F.G. Paci

Growing Up with the Movies

About a month after Susan's party I was with Rico in the balcony of the Princess Theatre watching *The Alamo.*

Since I helped him so often with his homework over the phone, he sometimes treated me to a movie. It was his way of evening the score, I suppose — though a Saturday matinee didn't cost much. Rico was a John Wayne fan, often imitating his rolling walk and slit-eyed confidence in the face of overwhelming opposition.

That Saturday, however, John Wayne wasn't the only one playing out a drama.

As usual, the theatre was packed that afternoon. The kids were noisy and restless. They draped their feet over the front seats or milled in the aisles, kept up loud conversations, giggled or whooped at the screen, and constantly changed seats with their friends. The young ushers frantically tried to keep order. Every so often an empty popcorn box, squashed flat, was hurled from the balcony like a flying saucer. If it made a direct hit, there was thunderous cheering.

An effort of supreme concentration was needed to follow the movie.

But if you were like me you'd be riveted to the screen, your eyes and ears opened wide to give total access to the mesmerizing world of technicolour, cinemascope, and stereophonic sound. There was something totally entrancing about watching larger-than-life people on a gigantic screen, lit by colours brighter and deeper than real life, with exciting music heightening the drama — the actresses more beautiful and sexy than real life, the actors more daring and handsome and debonair than anyone you'd ever meet in the everyday boredom of the Sault. And even though you went to the theatre with friends and the place was usually full of noisy kids more interested in meeting their friends and socializing, or munching on popcorn all through the movie, the darkness of the theatre still enclosed you, separated you from the rest of them — including the person you came with — so that you always felt alone with the world of the movie. The way I saw it, the darkness made the movie your own, made it part dream, part wishfulfillment, part fantasy, but all a reflection of the deep yearnings in your soul to achieve fame, fortune, and love.

So that it wasn't John Wayne up there with the courage to take on all those Mexicans — it was you. And it wasn't Richard Widmark or Laurence Harvey, or whoever, in those tight breeches of beautifully browned buckskins talking so glibly, filling the screen with their fierce eyes and jut-jawed words. It was you. And it wasn't Charlton Heston turning the eyes of the pharaoh's daughter and parting the Red Sea with all the power of God behind him. Or Gary Cooper, tall and silent in the saddle, resisting the advances of the beautiful Maria Schell because of some secret sorrow in his life. Or the cream-complexioned Pat Boone making eyes at Bernardine or Giget and always getting the girl in the end. Or the dimple-jawed white-haired Jeff Chandler leading a cavalry charge. Or the baby-faced Audie Murphy, small and compact in the saddle, but with more than enough heart and speed in his hands to outdraw those snarling desperadoes. It was me.

There were so many heroes — in Westerns and bible epics and police dramas and war movies and city romances and light comedies.

I'll never forget Burt Lancaster and Kirk Douglas gunning down the Clanton gang in *Gunfight at the O.K.Corral*. And Audie Murphy killing all those Germans in *To Hell and Back*. And Gary Cooper, who for me was the epitome of the strong and silent hero, getting his women in spite of all the barricades of silence and resistance he placed in front of them. And Cary Grant, who had the looks and coy wit. And John Wayne who had that great hulking body and supreme self-confidence. And the lesser known actors like Fess Parker who started the Davey Crockett craze. These and so many more, the heroes on the screen who created the myths that fuelled our drive for fame and fortune and love.

And then there were the women. But the women I remember less for their characters than for their looks and sex appeal. With their breasts as white and soft as whipped cream sticking out from low necklines. And their beautifully coiffed hair and long shapely legs and the look of longing they had for their men. I remember their ruby lips, so thick and pouty and kissable — with so much lipstick you could lose yourself in their mouths. I remember graceful necks and the demure look of interest they gave their men.

Like Sophia Loren in *The Pride and the Passion*. Or Rita Hayworth in *They Came from Cordura* and Marilyn Monroe in *The Seven-Year Itch*. Not to mention Jayne Mansfield, no matter what picture she was in. These and similar women fed my eyes with the wonders of the female body — so ample, so soft, so inviting, and so passionate. All of them such a far cry from the Blessed Virgin in my Missal, her figure covered in loose cloak and her eyes upturned to heaven. Who knows to what extent these holy pictures, along with the immaculate statues of the Blessed Virgin and the Italian saints, distorted my view of women? They could be sexless virginal goddesses on a pedestal one day and sexual tigresses on the prowl the next.

Christ, too, on the cross was sexless. His skin had been so rouged and depilated in an effort to make him appear spiritual that he could be seen as no more than a cosmeticized effeminate male.

Along with sights of true men and women on the screen, the daring deeds and the busty bodies of the film stars, it was the soundtracks that probably, even more than the feasts for the eyes, manipulated our budding emotions. Full symphony orchestras toyed with our hearts as our eyes were diverted by the screen. It seemed, at times, that thousands of violins came out of the pores of the lighted screen, playing pianissimo for the love scenes, thundering like hoof beats or chugging like a locomotive for the action sequences, and smashing to a crescendo of fortisimos for the open breathtaking vistas. The high tension violin could scrape every last bit of feeling out of me, leave me limp and exhausted afterwards, so that it was almost impossible to summon up the requisite emotions in everyday humdrum existence. At times, too, I half expected the violins to wail in the background when I found myself in impossible situations in real life.

A film that affected me greatly in my sexual development was an Italian movie my mother took me to see just that past summer. Contrary to my expectations, television had not improved her English. She watched the pictures and generally understood what was happening. But often, too, she pestered Lianna and me with so many questions on the plot that we became short-tempered with her. *"Che cosa dicono adesso?"* she'd say. *"Dimmi. Che cosa succede?"* The slippers didn't fly anymore if I angered her or was rude. I was too old for that now. But she'd complain and call me an *ingrato* if I didn't help out with the stories.

At any rate, my mother took me because she didn't often get a chance to see an Italian movie — and she wouldn't go alone. My father was working the three-to-eleven shift at the time. The language of the movie I couldn't understand very well. But by aligning the language with the action and images I could get the gist of what was going on. I certainly made it a point not to ask my mother what was happening. Watching something together in relative silence was a welcome relief.

On the surface the movie was a western, but an Italian rendition of the old west and unlike any that I had ever seen. In this western the men were interested more in women as women than as accessories to their heroism. In almost all the other westerns I had seen the women were naturally drawn to the strong silent heroes. But in this movie, whose title I can't recall, something strange happened. The leading lady was very beautiful, very feminine, and wore a tight corset that uplifted her breasts so much I was continually praying for them to pop out. She was interested in two men — one a handsome rugged rancher who typified the Gary Cooper heroic silence I so greatly admired. The other was more loquacious, more of an effeminate buffoon who wore his gun at the side of his stomach like some laughable tenderfoot. The first was strong and silent — full of stoic pride. The second was a foppish weakling, although he had a boyish charm about him. At first, the leading lady wouldn't give him a second look. But he kept pestering her, never taking no for an answer, while the strong silent one had to tend to his heroic duties. It was as if, while the good guy was playing baseball and hockey trying to be a man, the cowardly weakling was always going to dances to flatter his girlfriend.

Finally, when the lady gave in, I couldn't believe it. It felt as if she had betrayed the spirit of every Western I had seen — as if, in fact, she had betrayed every strong and silent hero who had ever walked the dusty streets of a cowardly town to face the evil guns at high noon. How could she fall for such a fop, who spent all his time flattering her? Didn't she see through the smokescreen of his weaselly advances? Didn't she feel faithful to the one who loved her with his silent pride?

And when, in the scene that plays in my memory even now, she made love to this "woman's man," this strutting peacock of a cowboy who wore his guns high at the stomach, I felt utterly devastated. The camera lingered on him kissing her, on those ruby lips, and then further down to her whipped cream breasts — and my rage knew no bounds! I thought surely the strong silent one would burst through the door and pummel him into insensibility. I thought surely at this very last second before she would be violated by this poor excuse for a man, the hero would save her. But no! It didn't happen, of course. For the camera shifted just as the man's head was going even farther down her body, shifted up to the expression of painful torture on the woman's face. There it lingered for a while, capturing her opened mouth and her closed eyes. I thought for a moment she was suffering terrible pain. What was this coward doing to her? I still half expected the hero to come crashing through the door. I was confused by the woman not fighting him off. Until the screen shifted to her outstretched arm on the bedsheet, the hand clutching the sheets harder and harder in the excruciating joy of sexual rapture.

But even then I wasn't sure. It was only afterwards in the movie when the leading lady began to fawn on the cowardly fop like a cat scratching at its master — and completely forgot about her silent suitor — that my worst suspicions were confirmed.

The Alamo, however, wasn't anywhere near that Italian western — that aberration of the myth that only momentarily sidetracked me from the truth of the movies. *The Alamo* was the truth made triumphant. There were no women to sidetrack the men. The men were men — going to their inevitable end with their boots on.

Yet it took ever so long to get to that final attack scene, with so many subplots — with Frankie Avalon as the teenage heart-throb and Richard Boone as Sam Houston and Laurence Harvey as Col. Travis doing his stiff upper lip thing, that many in the theatre began to get bored.

And it was during one of these lulls in the action that Rico and I spotted Perry and Maria down in the orchestra section, his head suspiciously close to hers.

"What the hell is that farmer doing?" Rico spat out.

It was all right to see these little dramas on the screen, with popcorn-smelling actors and actresses in full cinemascope and stereophonic sound, but to actually be a part of one in real life was, to me, very embarrassing. And I would've run away and hidden if Rico hadn't grabbed my arm and dragged me down the aisle, a few rows behind the amorous couple. This just when Santa Ana's army had amassed around the Alamo. When the Americans had settled all their differences and were ready to die with their boots on. Loyal now beyond a shadow of doubt to face the thousands and thousands of Mexican soldiers lined up outside the old church.

At any rate, in a few moments it became quite apparent that Perry and Maria weren't in the least interested in the final confrontation between the Mexicans and Texans. They had resolved their own differences orally. I had to look a second time to be sure they were actually necking.

The sight angered me for reasons I could only untangle afterwards. For one, it was destroying the illusion of the movie, taking away from what the whole blasted thing had taken two hours to build up to. Secondly, Rico had dragged me into something that wasn't my affair at all. And, thirdly, because the sight, curiously enough, seemed as unreal as what was happening on the screen.

Except for Rico, whose eyes were as fierce as Santa Ana wanting his land back, ready to annihilate these foolish interlopers who had dared oppose him.

"Perry!" he shouted above the din of the muskets and screaming Texans.

And all I could do was slink down on my seat, hoping there was a hole six feet deep at the bottom.

"Let's go down. I'll kill that farmer!"

I could've stopped everything right there. If I had acted. If I had done something. Instead of being embarrassed and wanting to hide. I could've perhaps nipped the whole thing in the bud — it was so innocent, so ridiculous also, this playing out the drama of two suitors after the same girl. It looked fine in my mother's photo-romance magazines and on the screen, even acceptable in comic books and novels, but not in real life with people who were still kids. Was this what growing up meant? Playing out all those scenes we had read about or seen on the screen? As if nothing had sunk in? As if all the lessons in the comics and photo-magazines and screens hadn't been learned one iota?

Markie Trecroci had played all the great roles in films and comic books. But when it came the time to play the role of a friend, he was less than successful.

What if I had told Rico to shut up in the Princess, instead of making an ass of himself? What if I had reminded him of our bond—three fingers but one hand? What if I had taken them off to the side and given them pause to think of what they were doing, which was so ludicrous I could've laughed outright, if not for the peculiar look of satisfaction on Maria's face. Because when we all met in the alley at the back of the Princess, the two of them facing each other menacingly, Maria Marino stood to the side only half urging them to stop. The other half of her, which didn't escape my notice, was somehow gloating at what was happening, smiling in a sort of self-satisfied way, as if she were tickled pink that two guys were fighting over her.

But I didn't do anything.

Though part of me was confused by these serious antics more appropriate to adults, another part was as detached as a spectator watching a scene in a movie. For it seemed so obvious that they were playing out the roles that had been assigned to them decades ago when the first fistfight had ever been shot in front of a camera, the same fight that had evolved into mythic proportions in the five renditions of *The Spoilers* — of which I had only seen two: John Wayne against Randolph Scott and Rory Calhoun against

Jeff Chandler. The fight lasting over five minutes, the two leading western stars fighting with their reputations at stake in front of their audiences — and only box office status dictating the final winner. These and many more fist-fights we had witnessed on the screen, the punches always landing with a crashing thud, the combatants getting up as if nothing had happened, the face bloodied but never seriously damaged because the male star always had to look good.

But when Rico's fist hit Perry square in the mouth, there was no crashing sound. Perry simply went down like a rock, a dull moan escaping his lips. And he didn't get up. And the blood was for real.

Rico stood over him panting. Spots of blood were on his knuckles, his face as red as a flame, his eyes a mixture of fear and rage.

"You farmer!" he screamed through clenched teeth. "You dumb farmer! Didn't I warn you about Maria?"

Rico had hit Perry so fast, and without warning, that it took Maria a few seconds to digest the sudden shock of the turnabout. The vain, self-satisfied smile instantly became horrified. Her eyes filled with alarm as she regarded Rico, who made no move to acknowledge her presence whatsoever. His eyes never left Perry, who was writhing with pain on the snow. A mess of blood appeared like a coating of wine. My stomach began to turn with nausea.

Maria and I inched towards the crumpled form of our friend who had folded himself into a foetal position and had become fearfully still.

"What did you do to him?" Maria looked at Rico.

"I didn't hit him that hard," Rico said, his temper now subsiding into fear and remorse as he realized what he had done. He began to inch away.

"How could you?" she said. "How could you?"

"It's his own fault. He wouldn't listen."

"Get outta here," Maria shouted at him. "You spoil everything. We don't want to see your face."

"I couldn't help it. He made me do it. I couldn't help it. It's his own fault."

Rico, shaking his head and walking backwards, finally turned and ran away down the lane that went back to the West End, the flaps of his galoshes thumping against his shins.

In the softly falling snow we watched his black leather jacket receding in the distance. No violins played. No cymbals clashed in resounding victory. There was only a vague sense we were playing out the highlights of our lives in total anonymity.

Fulvio Caccia

1989

Human nature is a labyrinth of corridors which hide secrets, often funny, sometimes disquieting, indeed tragic. Extreme prudence is required to explore its realms. Very early on I understood that I should pay heed to my fears in order to capture what might escape me. This prism filtered out the violence and daily baseness of my work. I thought that I had finally succeeded in overcoming my anguish. I believed this until the 13 of June, 1983, the feast of St. Anthony.

That day — I noted this irony of the calendar in my daybook — I was visited at my office by a young woman of Italian background who was afflicted, I later learned, with a very curious phobia.

Recalling it now makes me smile: this young woman was unable to tolerate eating spaghetti! The very idea of being next to people who ate them produced in her an attack of paranoia. These eposides were followed by lulls during which she would draw strange dragon flies. In each drawing her detail was life-like, her precision astonishing.

Outside these attacks, Lucia Zanzara or Zingaro — her name was spelled differently depending on the documents — was very normal. In fact she had superior intelligence as was confirmed by the teachers and the psychologist at her school. Her family was from Naples and had come to Canada in the early 1960s, but could not explain her behaviour: "She had always eaten her pasta without complaints. She even used to have second helpings." They were quoted in the report.

Her symptoms began at puberty. There were different hypotheses: a bout of anorexia; a schizoid episode released by the first menstruation; a third proposed that the aversion to pasta was related to her Italian origins. According to this hypothesis Lucia's attitude is related to an outburst of temper well understood for an age when one tries to escape the mould of normality.

In twenty years of practice I had never encountered such a peculiar phobia for food. I worked therefore on the elaboration of a model capable of identifying the ethnic genesis of this mental illness found in members of the second generation. We know from the work of Devereaux about the susceptibility of immigrant children to deculturalization, a pernicious illness of the contemporary psyche, but we have not yet found the operational concept needed to explain it in terms of the inner life.

The young Lucia was a welcomed case in my research project. It was because of this research work that they had referred her to me. I had accepted the case, but not without reservation, because on my success depends the fate of the the Centre for Research in Transcultural Behaviour of the Fernando Ortiz Institute, which I have directed for six years.

In this period of budget cut-backs, my situation had become more and more fragile. Proponents of the consensual approach to mental illness increased their attacks on my work. For them I was at best a humbug and my work a simple view of the mind, perfectly inoperational, and one which was getting attention only because of the coincidence of the current discourse on the ideology of integration. The wind could turn if I did not reach some rapid and spectacular results. This was the tacit vow I had made on Lucia's case. I must succeed at all costs. I focused my life solely on my work. I lived alone.

And so on that day I saw her come to the door of my office and walk with assurance to the large leather sofa. My clients usually hesitate to tell me about their problems. Not Lucia. Her self-assurance was that of a woman who was conscious of her own power.

"When do we begin?" she asked coolly. She was all the more intriguing because of her coldness.

Her pale skin contrasted with her feverish look: two pieces of onyx half hidden beneath a head of thick dishevelled hair. Jet black hair.

I learned nothing new from the Rorschach test. She answered all the questions I asked her with serious reflection. Psychological jargon had invaded her speech as if she had wanted to split herself in two and put herself in the doctor's place, and become pure exterior.

I can see her still, lowering her eyes and confessing that Lucia was the given name of her mother's older sister, but which I believed to be the the name of her grandmother whom she never knew. She added with false surprize that her aunt must have died of grief because her mother, upon recalling this event, used to cry without fail. These details led me to ask her what was the correct spelling of her last name. Admininistrative services had mangled her name: Zanzara, Zingaro, Zarara. It was written differently in each report. Even her healthcare card was different. At this tame question I say her quickly change her attitude. She turned red, stammered, searched in her purse and finally explained in a voice not too convincing that she should probably call herself, "Zingaro." Having regained her composure, her facial expressions told me she wanted to end our first interview. I did not keep her longer and made an appointment for the next week.

I was only half satisfied with this first encounter. Certainly her hesitations disturbed the path that my investigation must follow, but something rang false in her confession. A few days later the accented voice of a man on the telephone informed me that his daughter would not be coming to her appointment nor to others. I asked him the reason for this. He answered with a certain prudence that he did not want to unduly trouble his daughter. The voice was weary but firm and definitive. Our conversation was coming to an end. What should I do? My immediate reaction was to go into a long monologue. Perhaps, I said, I need to know the exact cause of death of his late sister-in-law. It is imperative to clarify all this. Failing this, Lucia might risk coming to a similar fate. We are not sure about any of this. All in all, I explained, blowing hot and cold, nothing inexorable has happened yet. If he wished, I was ready to come to his home to explain my therapeutic procedures. At the end of our conversation I made an appointment to see him the next night.

Lucia's family lived in a luxurious apartment at the top of an apartment building in the middle of the city. The Mike Zingaro who opened the door, carried his sixty plus years well with a salt and pepper beard which distinguished him from the typical immigrant worker from southern Italy. I was not surprized when he told me that he made his fortune from building houses in the suburbs and other places he would never want to live. He began by telling me that this highrise was his conception. He took be by the arm and guided me to the bacony: the city below glowed in the evening light. I sensed some anxiety in this gesture. He must not have been home very long because he was looking around for his family.

The balcony was the length of this apartment of a self-made man. Large, overflowing with flowers and potted plants. My feet crunched on the floor-tile. On a closer look I discovered rock salt. There were bits of salt scattered all over the granite floor suggesting the ancient rites of purification. Mike Zingaro smiled at me a little embarrased. My eyes fell on two large knives crossed on a large cast iron grill which led to the next floor by an external staircase.

He explained that his father-in-law had died not long ago. The old man was shy and eccentric, a painter by trade. His studio was up there, and his wife, Rosetta had now forbidden access.

An inky sky filtered a beam of ochre light to illuminate the baclony. Zingaro and I sat together in silence. Up to that point he had been distant. I thought that I had recognized beneath his mask of the nouveau riche a rough and stocky peasant imbued with his patriarchal authority. Instead I found myself before an enigmatic man who was preoccupied with "the strange obsession of his daughter." I barely detected that something rang false in this family. Mike leaned close to me as if he wanted to tell me a secret. He hesitated, took a deep breath and then began to talk:

"Lucia is not my daughter but the natural daughter of my sister-in-law, Maria Lucia, from whom she has her given name. We decided to adopt her at her birth in order to forego the pain of another separation: another baby — a boy — was given up to social services. We raised Lucia as if she were our own daughter. We had forgotten all about the boy. Imagine our surprize when one day he arrived at our door. It was Easter. I can still see him now. He was a good looking young man, thin and with a long face that reminded us of his mother. I say "us" because Rosetta and I had family over for Easter dinner.

"On seeing him my wife retreated to the kitchen crying. I welcomed him like a son. And I took the opportunity to introduce him to the family who were here for dinner. His name was Gabriel and he seemed to take part in these introductions with seriousness and dignity. While he was shaking hands with one relative or hugging another, or joking with the children, I could not help but think of the sad fate of his mother, Maria Lucia Zanzara.

"Those who had know this fragile and passionate woman had felt the same sadness as me. This is what must have registered in the young mind of the little Lucia. In her face I already read her reproaches. But how could I tell a little girl her age that her mother was not the good Rosetta but her aunt Maria Lucia, the family rebel, the misunderstood artist . . . ?"

Mike Zingaro cleared his throat and then continued: "The life of Maria Lucia Zanzara was an uninterruped series of love affairs and deceptions.

Unstable and whimsical — like many other artists — she did not establish stable relationships neither in her work nor in her personal life. I can say that we never met the men who crossed her path. And, to tell the truth, we preferred it that way. For the most part they were a collection of lazy weaklings who abandoned her after having taken advantage of her generosity.

"When she did not hang out at cafes or galleries she'd go home to her father who lived in the suburbs in a building transformed into a studio. She wanted to become a painter like him. Their relationship was stormy, punctuated with violent breaks where she would ransack the studio. Already we saw the mental illness which would overtake her.

"At first Maria Lucia would come every day to see her baby at our house. Then her visits became irregular. In the end her suicide did not surprise anyone. The old man who had been up to that point cantankerous and indifferent to his daughter's fate, entered into a kind of mute rage. We saw that he was taking all on himself the tragedy of what had happened. Then a cerebral embolism tied him to his bed. He never got up again and worked from his bed. When he had to leave the suburbs we welcomed him here, where he died.

"More than once my wife tried to dissuade Maria Lucia from seeing her father. But she would answer with bloodshot eyes that he needed her; without her he was nothing; without him she was nothing. And I must recall that this period of painting was his most productive, to the point that some critics went as far as to suggest that it was the daughter who held the paint brush!"

The man leaned towards me and asked, "Do you want to see one of the works of Maria Lucia?"

He lead me to a maze of rooms covered with canvases full of aggressive colours. Painted in a fauvist style their main source of inspiration seemed to be grimacing masks. In one room Zingaro brought my attention to a small rectagular painting in acrylic which was at the foot of the bed. It was apparently a self-portrait. Green, carmine, indigo and saffron coloured the tremulous features of a woman's face hollow with pain and doubt. I was struck by the curious light deep in the eyes, a light which the artist was successful in reproducing, accentuating, perhaps, the visual signs of her own dementia. But I did not have time to study it for long. Lucia and Rosetta had come home. They gave me some cold greetings. I bid farewell to the family and reminded Lucia that I would see her at our appointment.

In the week that followed I spend most of my time finishing the reports which I had to submit by the end of the month. Each night I got home very late. The answering machine gave me the usual messages. On the night before my next appointment with the young woman, there was an unusually long message. It was from Lucia. The rhythm of her voice was jerky, under great anxiety as if she were committing a forbidden act. She told me that since my visit she has been constantly watched by her uncle, that he had her followed on her way to school each day. That she was forbidden to go out. She added that for a long time now she knew who her mother was, but that a more troubling secret was threatening her. She could not talk about it on the phone.

"I hear a noise . . . They are coming now . . . I will remember you . . . " Those were her concluding words.

I had no more calls from Lucia. At their apartment the maid told me that they had left for Italy, but could not tell me the date of their return. The poor woman also seemed surprised by their sudden departure. The apartment was in shambles as if a hurricane had passed through it.

At school the principal confirmed what I already knew, Zingaro had withdrawn his adopted daughter under the pretext of getting her medical treatment in his home country. I tried to find her whereabouts through colleagues in Italy. All in vain. I ended by putting this case aside. The affairs of the Institute were already requiring all my attention.

The new research council for science and health decided in the end not to renew my application for certification. I sent then an additional report, had a special meeting with the Council and brought what little political pressure I could, all to no avail. I had to resign myself to the fact that the Fernando Ortiz Institute for the Study of Transcultural Behaviour would be no more.

On July 7th we had to move the documents and files. The next day the construction workers came to knock down the office walls. On the 30th, on the very spot where there stood the only research centre in the continent in this field, they opened a new shop to sell newspapers and magazines.

I was disappointed but without bitterness.

This failure gave me a certain liberty. Disengaged from my institutional responsibilities I was able once more to travel for leisure. I began by visiting artistic centres in Europe. Time passed with the rhythm of my teaching terms and my trips abroad. It was during one of these trips that a reminder of the "Zanzara Zingara," as I had come to call her, came to tease my curiosity once more. In the window of a gallary on the rue de Seine in Paris I saw immense canvases half cubist, half fauvist which depicted curious dragonflies in part androids which circled around what resembled a plate of pasta. This seemed to be the central theme of these works. The signature of Lucia Zanzara appeared clearly on each.

Translated by Joseph Pivato

Metamorphosis

I have changed
everything is new
my bearing
my steps on the road
my manner of speaking to you
this very language
you see I no longer resemble you

Occasionally memories filter through
beyond this fragile curtain of words
fleeting shadows of the afternoon
Your familiar accent has now disappeared
the machinery of time is very effective

Nevertheless I still have the strength
to tell you I no longer need
you

Get away from me . . .

I have changed
I no longer recognize myself
in the red mirror of dawn
I become again this other wanderer
with eyes fixed
on the rumbling of the world

Translated by Joseph Pivato

Penny Petrone

Mamma

One winter when I was twelve or thirteen, Mamma must have bought Eaton's entire supply of red, green and white balls of wool. She made the girls tricolour toques, mitts, scarves and dickies. I refused to wear mine. "These are the colours of the Italian flag," she protested. "I am not Italian. I am *Canadese*. I am a Canadian. I am a Canadian," I tried to explain. It was no use. Once I was out of Mamma's sight, I would remove the garments and hide them under the porch steps. I preferred the winter cold to the ridicule of my schoolmates. On another occasion she knitted me a lime green suit of the finest wool with an orange angora Peter Pan collar. The girls at school were not wearing hand-knitted suits, and after one wearing, I refused to wear mine. Alfred, my brother, recalls his embarrassment each time his high school class stood up to sing *God Save the King* because of the patches on the seat of his pants, which he tried to hide with the palms of his hands. Mamma could not understand why we were ashamed of our patches, or our hand made clothes, because, in the Italian mind, they were marks of a woman's management skills.

Mamma's knitting and crocheting always won her prizes at the Canadian Lakehead Exhibition. I recall a rust-coloured suit Mamma knitted for my sister Mary, for which she won second prize. When she wore the suit, I thought she looked like Shirley Temple. Mary had golden hair which Mamma used to put up in rags to make ringlets. I was so proud of her because she did not look Italian.

When I was older, Mamma's finely shaped, capable hands intrigued me. Never still, they moved with quiet skill and speed — darning, sewing, crocheting, knitting, patching, mending, and embroidering. She could knit a pair of mittens overnight. Whether at her whirring Singer treadle sewing machine or sewing by hand, she worked with flair. I can still see her threading her needle. She would wet the thumb and index finger of her right hand with her tongue in order to twist the thread so that it would go through the eye of the needle. Mamma could not sew without the silver thimble she had brought with her from Italy. She used it throughout her life and I have it now. For her, using a thimble was the mark of a good seamstress. I sewed without one, using long strands of thread to finish more quickly, so I thought. Even her Calabrese maxim, *Chine infile l'ago con il filo lungo e vagabonda* (whoever threads the needle with a long thread is lazy) did not deter me. I inherited her jars of buttons and old zippers but not her gifted hands. I never did learn to hold my knitting needles properly or keep my crochet needle at the correct angle. My three youthful productions included a crocheted collar, a knitted dickey and an embroidered tablecloth. But these were botched with frightful errors that were too much for Mamma's patience, and we both gave up.

Sante Arcangelo Viselli

Montpel(l)ier

Montpellier
Un jour de mai
ensolieillé

Montpellier
A day in May
of sun shine
A beautiful multicoloured bird
breaks its neck on the balcony

The sympathetic hearted Patricia weeps
the bird takes flight
In the eternal night
of this beautiful day
of sunshine

Montpelier
A day in May
in North America

A beautiful bird, enigmatic plumes
Lost in a late snow fall
Forgotten in this white day

Without Wings

He dreams of the sun

Oh, poet
Born of the Sun
What are you doing in Newfoundland

Au Manitoba

Le reve fatal
a glaçé tes Aîles
Étrangle ta plume
métisse ton Âme

Tu n'es plus qu'un rocher liquide
Déraisonné par l'Ocean
Un thème de la Plaine

In Manitoba

The fatal dream
has frozen your Wings
Strangled your feathers
cross-bred your Soul

You are nothing but liquid rock
Made delirious by the Ocean
A theme of the Great Plains

Translated by Joseph Pivato

CARMINE COPPOLA

Benvenuta, primavera !
Benvenuta, primavera, come non mai!

Welcome, Spring !

Welcome, Spring, as never before!
Gather my heart reduced to shreds
by the dry cold and icy wind
which violently penetrated within me
and inject it with your blood, blood of life!
Reawaken me! As you do with the medlar tree,
the poplar, the peach tree, with all that is around
which vibrates, beats, awakens and lives.
Shake me! As the April earth,
give me strength, its same vigour.
And let me flow through life,
as the river water on the pebbles
smooth and white, down to the sea.
Immerse me in the scents of May
and release me from the relentless past
that engulfs me and confines me to apathy!
And finally, take me away with you, forever,
there, where you live, in the pastures of life.

Translated by Saveria M. Torquato

Alexandre L. Amprimoz

Roman Afterwar

A warborn spice still nurses the city.
Whatever burns and grows in smoke
Locks the child's eye
And plants a death-taste
In the mouths of longing widows.
The perfumes of ripe soldiers are not kind,
They smell of honour — the scorched blueprints
Of war. We saw the unwed mother cry.
Dark and holding a blond child,
She went to church as she begged for a father.

The tomatoes are back at the market place.
A thousand little children curse the return
Of soldiers. Others learn from living room
Pictures what Daddy was and might have been.
The plastic roses are pregnant with the smell of coffee.
To prove that truth ages and betters in time
Of peace as the best of wines.
So many houses are like the Forum
Open to the winds, to wall grass and to cats.
It is always spring in cemeteries after the war.

The stars are only distant fireflies.
Children, like the foam of the sea,
Are made of vanished flesh, rotten bones and dust;
But they see doves fly over dove-mad roofs
Letting their fingers pass through the angel's chest.

If ghosts of soldiers still fight in the wind
Such a cruel war, and if the morning will reveal
A land covered with scars and wrinkles,
Why, then. should we speak of men?
In the child's mind the smell of garlic equals the idea of
war.

Mary di Michele

Passeggiata di sogno

It's almost light when you stumble off the overnight train, the milkrun from the south, at the Montefalcone station. To drink in the dawn along with a spiced *caffè con latte* is sweet. You find a small cafe where it's easy to catch a fast cab for Duino where you unwind in the stillness of a village holding its breath. Moving into the 21st century, something slow! Something to surprise you with familiarity!

What? Your mecca is a mere suburb, in the brochure described as "a little interlude of past elegance and charm away from the pressures of life today":

— 600 metres from the nearest motorway,

— 20 km from Trieste,

a dormitory of geometric lawns, parallel streets, stucco walls and roses, roses opening reluctantly like eyes after a deep and dreamless sleep, yes, fluttering petals like so many sticky eyelids over no eye.

Cemetery comes from *koimeterion*, the Greek word for sleeping chamber, from *koiman* meaning to put to sleep and this word is related to the Latin word, *cunae*, cradle. The poet here is an archaeologist of language. There are cities built on cities in each word.

To dig is to unearth,
to write is to excavate,
to write is to discover.

Like melody in music there is no meaning in the text without playing the words. Rilke, perpetually entering without arriving, concert tickets in his pockets, attuned

to the instrument he most feared "because a person's life could be ruined if, even in passing, he happened to hear a violin, and that tone deflected his entire will to a denser fate." He preferred, no music, but silence, its notation in the sea gull's cry, in the surge of surf, "you see, I have not arrived at music yet, but I know about sounds."

Such glossy charm! Duino offers you not a Northern Italian village, but a picture postcard for one. Duino, doo — ee — no, your name's a bird's call, doo — weee — know, your name's unanswerable.

Colours, though singularly bold in Italy, here seem demure, horticultural, not of the open field afire with wild poppies, but of plots, of containment. Those neatly fenced and hedged lawns are vivid evidence of how the Latin can so easily be tempered by the Teutonic. The expatriate from Canada empathizes. You too are hybrid — you too are hyphenated.

Longing for a nationalist identity is longing for stereotype! For simplification! How could you hope to find your true name in a flag, in the *tricolore* or the maple leaf! *ou les fleurs de lis du Quebec*? Hybrid yes! Your species comes from the evolution of everything that lives by adding on. Hyphenated no! Hyphenated subtracts both ways, bears the sign of its division at the centre. Such is the insanity of the language of empty sign. Would you buy a carton with EGGS printed on it but with nothing inside! No? But the irony is if you're hungry you will pick it up even if you know that it's empty. It weighs less than nothing, but recalls for you the oily gold of yolk, the sun in a cloud of albumin.

Though you are just thinking of yourself and what you might eat for an American style breakfast, Rilke greets you. You feel rude for having read every one of his letters without writing back.

You think you understand why on his death bed Rilke refused an appointment to the German academy, how born in Bohemia, language failed to make him German enough. Though the angel spoke to him in *Deutsch*, Rilke sometimes wrote in French seeking what was the untranslatable poetic in himself. After all wasn't it the French, Rodin and Cezanne, who taught him how to look at things? Rilke lamented that through words it is too hard to get to the palpable world. In Paris he learned to pray differently. O for a palette thick with paint, O for the molten bronze of casting. Before the French he did not know how to see things although he made do with vision. Before cubism he had to form himself entirely from the inside out.

In a letter to the Princess Maria, Rilke wrote that words were windows, "not to the world, but to infinity," yes to infinity, to the intertextual in the Gutenberg galaxy.

But what of the poetry of no words? Some read the greater mystery in silence, not as when the concert ends though the body continues to vibrate with music, but as when the instrument, buried in its case, can't be touched. In this manner the dead compose most deeply. That recognition took longer than music to arrive. Rilke thought he was waiting to write in the way he could not wait for *La Benvenuta* to respond to his letters.

For every kiss you give me, darling, I'll give you three.

"It has always been my custom to write to you on this paper I normally use for working." But for this stranger, for this most welcome one, for the woman who thanked him as her saviour, who said she knew him as a friend, although he did not know her, for *La Benvenuta* he used a higher element than onionskin. If his reach had not exceeded his grasp he would have skywritten her name with a comet.

Although Magda von Hattingberg knew "The Stories of God," she could not know the thin man in his fortieth year who was estranged from his wife and child. What he read in her letter was more than a reader's gratitude; her script echoed Beethoven's word, the same syllables Rilke imagined hearing from the lips of the Sphinx, *unpronouncable*, "For you love music!"

To love a musician, a pianist, when you're tone deaf and unable to recall the simplest tune is natural if you love absence, if you love silence and the sounds which define it, if you love all those things which you are not. So it was not unnatural for Rilke to choose to court a woman whom he had never met, a woman who was already satisfied with him, who thanked him for a text written by a man he couldn't remember being. Did he hope that she could not be disappointed, she who already had what she wanted from him? And he—he was most happy in the writing to her!

But when writer met reader, he lost artistic control. When reader met writer she found him to be paler than his pages. And sadly the correspondence ended.

In the brochures the Italian, *una passeggiata di sogno* is translated as "a pleasant walk in the Castle gardens with light refreshments." The morning moon is not the dreamer's, the morning moon only shines for those who do not sleep, for those who do not deign to eat. Rilke, this dawning, you are more wan than I ever imagined.

In its setting, the moon seems to pause over the solitary balcony facing out to sea where Rilke would practice listening. In thundering tempest listening, for the angel, for the *sotto voce*.

The cost of maintaining the prince's estate is raised through the sale of tickets for tours of the grounds and selected rooms. The royal secretary guides your group then offers you some tea, included in the price of admission. To think the prince raises his ordinary, if aristocratic, family here. Look, by the fountain, a child as thoughtless as your own has abandoned a golden ball.

In Firenze, during a visit to the Uffizi gallery, you entered a room crowded with other tourists. When Rilke saw the Sphinx, the crush of bodies made the monumental seem commonplace to him. You experienced something similar, something very different. The gallery did not empty suddenly, your eyes did. In the presence of the three graces all else was absence. Such brilliant light radiated from the painting you had to raise your hand to shield your eyes. Blinded by a Botticelli from the fifteenth century more alive than you are today.

The castle has the air of a church filled with invisible presence. "Here is the angel, who doesn't exist, and the devil, who doesn't exist; and the human being, who does exist, stands between them, and (I can't help saying it) their unreality makes him more real to me." More than any devil Rilke dreaded going home. In Clara's well-stocked cupboards, in rugs that needed beating, the visible world stalked. Chores made him feel unreal, ethereal. When a troublesome business letter found the scribe, even within the pristine portals of an Austrian dynasty, he was forced to deal with things, with accounts; his household goods were about to be auctioned off to pay the landlord in Paris. That day the sea clouded over of its own accord, that day he was numbed by numbers to its beauty, the chiaroscuro, a sea silver with storm and light, the north wind raging. "Completely absorbed in the problem of how to answer the letter," he heard the angel of the elegies for the first time. He jotted down the angel's words in his notebook but ran inside to respond to his creditor.

More than Lucifer himself Rilke feared distraction, interruption. Science offers a principle, a thermodynamic law, not a snake, not a woman, not her mate nor the little something they ate as the cause for death on Earth. Entropy curdled Rilke's dinner of fruit and milk. Was the anaemic poet right to desert his family and dedicate himself exclusively to the muse or to make the elegies, his greatest work, the property of Princess Marie von Thurn und Taxis-Hohenlohe, his hostess?

There was no way back from castle to cottage, no way home from royal mistress to wife, no way to hear the angel living with his family, not above the din, not above the quotidian. Or so he thought. While as royalty's guest he could enter the chapel with its invisible smells of incense and embalming fluids and feel more real than in the kitchen where Clara cooked everyday another leek and potato soup.

Rilke's angel was not the guardian kind for children but the terrible mother of death and beauty. His art demanded no family but a sex with fatal edges, a sword, which would shine for him most brightly, but only in the distance, a brilliant blade to be kept sheathed.

In the castello di Duino several sabres, jewelled and ornamental are displayed under glass. Such danger is contained yet on show.

You like best the tower, its staircase, spiral, scalloped. Some trade in their real body for an empty vessel where the sea can sing more fully, more truly; some can only listen from within the conch. At the centre of the vortex you crouch. You are waiting for a sea change. Instead there is a tapping on your shoulder, an official directing you to rejoin the other tourists, all German except for the lone housewife from Trieste, *"Sei, Italiana?"*

Back to the present, back to sensuous delight, gardens filled with roses. You can warm your hands by the red and yellow blooms. But there are other hues which belong more properly to the poet you admire. With the white and ghostly blossoms strumming the trellis, you sense he would be more deeply in tune.

O rose, many-petalled flower, flower feathered as if winged, soaring seraphim of scent, it was you who killed Rilke. By leukaemia, a rare blood disease, a septic infection of the skin starting out from some slight wound. Dying Rilke was comforted that his death was "nobody's disease," that it was his fate to succumb to a scratch from the thorn of a rose tree.

In the mind, memory has the power of smell. From each garden and cottage gate, roses, their fragrance blaring all the way down to the cliffs where the waves, weighty enough to pound huge boulders into pebbles, fail to mute that flower's scent.

Poor Rilke was a poet who learned to mine riches from the unrequited; "Don't think I'm wooing angel/ and if I were, you wouldn't come." You seek to be trained in this art. You have come to Duino to apprentice with even the stones where he sometimes walked.

The elegies became the property of the princess. But his silence may be shared by all, his silence he did not barter away.

Where you stroll along the marine drive, there's a Porsche, there's an Alpha Romeo, there's a chameleon posing as a shrub. A man paints a wrought iron fence dark green. He rests on one knee as if he truly loves, as if he pleads to marry his job. It is not his fence, he's the hired man. Any stranger might guess from his sadly frayed socks. Look where the back of his overalls ride up. This is not your garden, house, or estate for that matter, nor the palace for which you came in search of poetry, in search of his muse.

You discover a wooded path, the Sentiero Rilke, following the cliffs. Below on the beach, below on what must be some private shore, a single white bikini glows. Do you marvel to see the clothes when the woman's invisible?

What's mystery when it's all around you? Not home? Though the sun blazes now in a brilliant blue sky, you're still huddled in a raincoat with the collar rolled up. You ate some milk and fruit for supper almost a century ago. Hunger makes you light-headed.

No, Rilke never waited to write, he waited for dictation. Like a man sitting in the dark whose fingers sadly grope for what withers in his pocket.

"Let such a person go out to his daily work, where/ greatness is lying in ambush." What rooted, what stubborn

Romanticism makes you still believe you won't understand Rilke unless it storms, you won't understand what shook him in the wake of this turquoise and
serene sea. Rilke in storm finding the Real,
Rilke in storm erecting a temple within
the ear.

Life is Theatre

(OR O TO BE ITALIAN IN TORONTO DRINKING CAPPUCCINO ON BLOOR STREET AT BERSANI & CARLEVALE'S)

Back then you couldn't have imagined
yourself openly savouring a cappuccino,
you were too ashamed that your dinners
were in a language you couldn't share
with your friends: their pot roasts,
their turnips, their recipes for Kraft
dinners you glimpsed in TV commercials—
the mysteries of macaroni with marshmallows!
You needed an illustrated dictionary
to translate your meals, looking to the glossary

of vegetables, *melanzane* became eggplant,
African, with the dark sensuality of liver.
But for them even eggplants were exotic
or alien, their purple skins from outer space.

Through the glass oven door
you would watch it bubbling in pyrex,
layered with tomato sauce and cheese,

melanzane alla parmigiana,
the other-worldiness viewed as if
through a microscope
like photosynthesis in a leaf.

ꕤ

Educated in a largely Jewish highschool
you were Catholic. Among doctors' daughters,
the child of a truck driver for la Chiquita banana.
You became known as Miraculous Mary,
announced along with jokes about virgin mothers.

You were as popular as pork on Passover.

You discovered insomnia, migraine headaches,
menstruation, that betrayal of the female
self to the species. You discovered despair.
Only children and the middleaged are consolable.
You were afraid of that millionth part difference
in yourself which might just be character.
What you had was rare and seemed to weigh
you down as if it were composed of plutonium.
What you wanted was to be like everybody else.
What you wanted was to be liked.
You were in love with that Polish boy
with yellow hair everybody thought
looked like Paul Newman.
All the girls wanted to marry him.
There was not much hope for
a fat girl with good grades.

But tonight you are sitting in an Italian cafe
with a man you dated a few times and fondled
fondly until the romance went as flat as the froth
under the domed plastic lid of a cappuccino ordered
to-go. And because you, at least, are committed
to appearing mature as well as urbane
in public you shift easily into the nevertheless doubtful relationship of coffee to conversation.

He insists he remembers you as vividly
as Joan Crawford upstaging Garbo in *Grand Hotel.*
You're so melodramatic, he said, *Marriage*
to you would be like living in an Italian opera!

Being in love with someone who doesn't love you
is like being nominated for an Oscar and losing,
a truly great performance gone to waste.
Still you balanced your espresso expertly
throughout a heated speech without spilling a single
tear into the drink, after which you left him to pay the bill.
For you, Italians! He ran out shouting after you,
life is theatre!

Anna Pia De Luca

Reminiscences and Fairy Tale

Reminiscences and Fairy Tale. That was the title of a short musical piece I used to play on the piano as a child. The sounds of the chords and arpeggios that reverberated through my ears and tingled my fingers always gave me a fascinating sense of lightness as my mind wandered through space. This story begins before I was born in Fruili and long before we came to Canada.

In the orchard at the back of the grey-stoned two story farm house my mother and her two sisters, fondly called *lis frutis*[1] by *none,*[2] were joking and laughing as they picked juicy wild black cherries from the large old tree near the iron gates. The shade of the tree in the last rays of the warm May afternoon sun formed a massive dark block against the stone wall which resembled the rock mountain situated at the end of the chain of the Carnic Pre-Alps surrounding the towns of upper Friuli where I was born. The war had just begun and my mother's brother had been sent off to fight in Albania but news of the horrors had not yet reached the family and though there were many hardships for my widowed grandmother to make ends meet the sisters were still young and their world was luminous and endless.

In those days it was not uncommon to see traveling bands of Cossacks on horseback come to the door to ask for food or shelter. They were a strange and awesome group without a *patria.*[3] During the Russian campaign the Germans had enlisted thousands of Cossacks, victims of

Russian repression, and sent them to our region to suppress the local partisans and confiscate their lands. Their barbaric and primitive ways instilled fear in the hearts of those who had experienced their presence in the towns surrounding Nimis where they were stationed. Stories had reached the lower towns of Friuli of how Tartar hordes had killed the animals in the barns and cooked them over bonfires in the streets while the local people watched helplessly.

On that particular May afternoon a solitary old woman clad in what to the girls seemed exotic garments, stopped near the shaded stone wall and called out to them *"i frutti dei campi sono i doni dei santi."*[4] My grandmother, who had never been to school and spoke no Italian, upon hearing her call thought she was harassing her *frutis* and in a moment of panic ran out from the kitchen and cried out *slontaniti des frutis.*[5] The girls, of course, thought it was a great joke and my mother, warmheartedly grabbed a bunch of cherries to give the poor woman. It was then that the gypsy grabbed her hands and with a deep and dark penetrating glare which transfixed mother's soft blue eyes with fright began telling her to beware, that her future was uncertain, that she would loose sight of her family, cross many oceans, see strange worlds and encounter unbearable hardships. Just the idea of loosing everything she loved plagued my mother's future dreams.

As a child, in Toronto, when we didn't have enough money for a television set and the police used to patrol the streets to make sure that the Italians were not drinking wine or beer on the porch steps after dinner, I used to love listening to this and other stories mother told us before bedtime. My brother, who was a little older than me and already four when we came to Canada, would pipe up that he remembered the orchard, the cherry tree, *none*, the aunts and even the mountains. With resentment that bordered on envy I contradicted him and refused to believe that he could have been part of that world. But by the time I had taken my first trip to Friuli, not much younger than my mother was on that May afternoon, I had already memorized all the landmarks.

That first summer my cousin and I would sit under the shade of the cherry tree in view of those magnificent rock mountains and sew little dresses for our dolls or cook on the tiny tin *spolér*[6] making *polente*[7] and other goodies for those who dared risk eating our concoctions. During later trips to Friuli we would rise at dawn and hike up to the peaks of those Pre-Alps, dizzy with the beauty and vastness of the *Tagliamento Valley* below *Monte Cuarnàn*, mesmerized by the ice blue radiance of *Lago di Cavazzo* below *Monte Simeone*. As we grew older and our mountain skills increased we would reach the alpine refuge on *M. Canin* and risk dangers to look over the peaks into Austria and Slovenia where my father had been stationed with his wireless during the war. After the hikes we would gather around the *fogolâr*[8] roasting chestnuts and drinking *ribolla*[9] while my uncle, then chaplain of a parish church near Udine, but who during the war had not only been an *Alpino*[10] but also one of the founders of a partisan brigade called *Osoppo*, told us tales of his collaboration with the English to help the parachuters in their reconnaissance movements, of the ways in which the English taught young boys the techniques of sabotage, of the German retaliation and the horrors of the *Rastellamento*.[11] But the stories which touched me the most were always related to the cold unshakable courage of the women couriers who cycled through German road blocks and risked their lives and family to smuggle explosives to saboteurs. These same mountains, which now captivate and enfold me with a sense of weightlessness and magic, resounded with the roar of bombings and the whispered strains of women frantic in their attempts at alerting and standing by their men in moments of great danger.

Back in high school in Canada listening to history lessons relating to the Second World War I would find it hard to locate not only my uncle's role, but that of many mountain women, soldiers and partisans of my borderland origins, in helping stop the widespread horrors of a regime which would have annihilated the cultural spirituality and social identity of my ancestors. The history of their battle for freedom has been silenced and ignored though in retrospect I realize that it still exists transformed and idealized in the memory of those who refuse to forget.

Like many Italo-Canadians, my university years in Toronto during the late 1960s and early 1970s were filled with the awareness of my hyphenated identity, of being neither here nor there. I both avoided and was attracted to the circle of friends who, like me, shared a frustrated sense of loss and difference because of a cultural identity not then recognized as an integral part of Canadian life. Even within the Italian community of friends I often missed the inside jokes, the dialect expressions which did not belong to my heritage. I felt like the prisoner encircled by the Italian firing squad depicted on those horrible T-shirts we all used to wear. In moments of depression my mind would be carried off to those visited places where my memory was stored.

It was during my last summer holiday to Italy that I met my husband, a man who in every sense was what the Friulians call *sald onest e lavorador,*[12] and though marriage would mean leaving behind my family, my friends and my Canadian adolescence I plunged into the future with the belief that I could recuperate the past.

My first years of marriage with a protective and caring husband were idyllic and life seemed a continuous holiday. We had bought and refurbished an old stone house with a turret, not far from the large cherry tree where my mother used to spend her afternoons with her sisters, and which my Canadian friends loved to call "the castle." In the late afternoons I would sit in the turret, which had a magnificent view of the Carnic Pre-Alps, with my first child and together we would play and absorb the energy of the last rays of sun before they hid behind the massive rocks. It was, in fact, during one of these pleasurable moments, on a particularly warm day in early May, that the mountains surrounding our valley suddenly cast an awesome shadow. Unexpectedly they began to rumble, come alive and demand attention.

For an indeterminable time my body was swept in air, my movements uncontrollable while I desperately held on tightly to my baby daughter. We were dragged and hurled through a space that heaved and crashed around us. Finally it was over and I was able to get back on my feet and grapple my way down the flight of stairs with my daughter. Night had fallen like a silent and impenetrable fog filled with the stench of debris. All lights were out and a sense of panic overswept me as I frantically tried to locate familiar landmarks now virtually razed to the ground.

Later I realize that we had physically survived an earthquake.

As I staggered along I heard my mother calling to me, *anin a cjase frute,*[13] telling me that it's all right now. I can come out of the dark gorge that has enveloped me. But when I reach the place I heard her calling from she is gone, replaced by an old hag in a long russet dress hidden in the shadows of a wall.

For the first few days after the quake those who had survived moved about like zombies, dazed and bewildered as they tried to dig up the little that remained under the rubble. The school playground had become a morgue where rows upon rows of coffins of every size lay in view of those mountains which in their brightness now seemed to mock any pretense of grief. I remember my uncle saying that earthquakes are worse that war simply because man has no way of controlling nature. The earthquake had devastated or destroyed everything I was attached to in Friuli, and even today any slight vibration still haunts my dreams.

The baby-grand piano that used to sit in our living room in Canada was shipped overseas the week that I was married. In those early years I had acquired enough skills to give occasional concerts or accompany our town choir during their local evening performances. Now it was hanging precariously from the broken wood beams of the turret which had cracked open like a raw egg. For weeks it seemed on the verge of crashing through the lower floors until we were able to find an available crane to hoist it to a safe place. In later years I had the piano fixed, at least the mechanical parts, but I don't really play anymore. The last time was on a makeshift pianola in the school playground.

My daughter, of course, doesn't remember any of this. She had turned two just four days after the earthquake and soon after my son was born. The schools in a radius of forty kilometers were boarded up, my lessons canceled. Our days spent under tents eating from military canteens seemed a long holiday to her. And we tried to rebuild our future from the few scraps that remained of our past, and from the help received from Canada, the land of my forgotten childhood. When my children were still young they demanded stories. I would tell them about Canada. I would take them on rambles through the hills of *Monte Simeone*, the epicenter of my broken yesterdays, now covered with new grown grass. Below, our town took on new shapes.

I have returned to Italy, to Friuli, the land of my birth. It is a long way from the snow-filled ravines of Toronto where we would bob sled as children. It is decades since I skated on a rink in Ontario. I recall the Indian summers when all the neighborhood children raced around on bicycles, or played hide and seek in the red and yellow brightness of autumn leaves. I try to share this, my other life, with my own children, and with my Italian students as I try to teach them about Canadian literature.

As a child part of me was always in Italy; and now part of me will always be in Canada

Notes

1 Friulan term for "the girls."
2 Grandmother.
3 Homeland.
4 The fruits of the fields are the gifts of the saints.
5 Move away from the girls.
6 Firewood stove.

7 Cornmeal.
8 An open hearth located in the centre of the room.
9 A type of white wine that has just been pressed from fresh grapes.
10 A soldier in the Italian mountain corps called Alpini.
11 German armies literally wiped out whole towns in search of partisans.
12 A stable, honest and hard-worker.
13 Come home, daughter.

CARO CANTASANO

My Grandfather Didn't

My grandfather didn't
read Dante
in a rocking chair me
at his feet . . .

Nor did he feel the poet
in his blood an Italian leitmotif
for southern veins . . .

Nonno was a cabinet maker

He could draw, tell stories, intaglio a specialty
but no Dante
just a name
instead he read the draft
for war in Lybia . . .

He came to Canada
he went back — winter in North Bay
he came again a family man
Guelph — New York — Guelph
died in Ontario
he never saw the Western sky
Mediterranean hues.

Grandfathers read Dante
in poems
fake memories mongering
culture . . .

Mine swore
"Cazzu 'mu ti futti!"

Nonno was a man of pierced ears.

Note

This poem on a grandfather is a response to Len Gasparini's poem, "The Photograph of My Grandfather Reading Dante" (*Roman Candles,* 1978).

Concetta Principe

Stained Glass

Yes. I was born yesterday.

Eyes wide open, seeing and not seeing water, hands, my family in the distance, their four hundred eyes, two hundred expectations.

Mouth half open, barely breathing, feeling disembodied till water broke against this face three times. The woman I was drowned. I looked up. Alive. I didn't cry, I wasn't smacked. I bowed my head for the laying on of hands.

My birth into the Catholic Church, April, 1993. The woman who I was is not me. I am a miracle: seed of the Holy Spirit grown in the womb of her consciousness. I would call her mother if she could hear me.

She died and I smiled. She died in ignorance, never knowing it was I, not she, who chose this name. Clara. Pink-ambers of Assisi stone at four o'clock. The little flowers of a saint. I remember. Lilies, iris, mums. I smelled them just as I was born, new to sin, abandoned.

Mother, I am your last miracle: born to believe in water, my family, my name, flowers. Infant that I am, I can't forget.

ꕥ

Nausea swelled through this body, walking home after the ceremony.

I, the newborn, entered this house, as if I had lived here before (*déjà vu*). Just born, I knew the word for dust. I saw it thick on the floorboards, at the corners, on the books someone read. The one who lived dead. You, whose thirty years are in my head.

Around me, lit by streetlight, the mess you left behind.

What I saw as I lay in your bed suffering vertigo, smelling the dead stuff of you: skin, hairs and faith.

ᘓᘐ

"Why Catholic?" the chorus cries when you descend from the alter after each Right of Initiation. And all the world is a stage, and the chorus is composed of believers compelled to keep the sanctity of the church safe from evil and critics trained by cynicism to uphold the tradition that nothing is sacred. Why Catholic?

The question haunts you in your hour of prayer ten days before you shall die giving birth to me.

How did it begin? Twelve months ago that interview with Father Greg asking, "Why?"

You replied, "I believe." He expected more. You continued, stuttering, "In . . . (how to articulate your dreams?) . . . heaven and hell . . . (so that he would not think you're crazy) . . . God, the Holy Spirit and . . . Mother Mary."

When people asked, you said: "Because of Mother Mary." Your mother, her friends, the congregation smiled with joy, silently: a miracle.

Your sister didn't smile, but looked at you with what? Disgust? No. Remember round the eyes, compassion: she could see the suffering in you, an animal dying.

Your father and your sister's friends, however, gaped in disbelief: "Who is Mother Mary but a male figment of he imagination?"

ഌ

"Virgin or unsullied version of a woman, an unsexed notion of motherhood."

"Because Eve was the cause of original sin, forced men from paradise. Men hated women for that. But how could they hate their mother? They deified her and changed her womb into a temple from which they could issue forth, a million little Christs, the true followers of the way of God, and the only leaders of idiots, women, and babies."

"God forbid women should get it in their heads that they can lead us all to heaven." Why Catholic?

Well versed in this discourse, you could not argue. What you felt had nothing to do with argument. You tried to communicate. To a friend of your father's you explained that Mother Mary is not gendered but simply color: a fine blue line through a boundless yellow. He was Catholic. It was the wrong thing to say. Anxious, he asks, "Why Catholic? Why not just paint a picture?" To say that you did would not answer his question; to show him your painting would prove nothing.

Or that day with your father when, exasperated, you blurted: "Like the eighth and forgotten room, flowers still bloom in Assisi. That's why Catholic." He didn't ask you again.

What could he say? The reason was, and perhaps, would always be hermetic. Maybe he was assured that your decision had something to do with the Italian culture he had trained you to respect and love all your life. But others wouldn't let the question drop.

"Because I am half Italian and half Irish."

"Because I believe in God."

"Because I like to watch sunlight through the stained glass windows of the church." Excuses really, because who becomes Catholic in the last decade of the twentieth century? Unless it's a miracle.

Joseph Maviglia

The Old Man End of Things

There's no vision here that says what life is worth
no children warm in rooms with wallpaper cartoons
computer magic fathers tucking in their future.

Here, at the old man end of things, a voice hangs
like sentimental mortar to contaminated buildings.
Here in *Midnight Cowboy* land,
the diners are up for sale
as if the beginning of something is at hand.

But nothing begins. The day drags its shoes
along the streets salting the cuffs of men
bending closer to the streets everyday.

At night sleep waits. Sleep like a hungry wind
un-nourished by the huddles of old men in parks
in cities left behind.

The sun shortens for winter. Ends behind clouds.
Leaves those without without
Holds up a sign to strangers making wrong turns
that somewhere lies a child asleep in comfort.

LINDA HUTCHEON

A Crypto-Ethnic Confession

Though I go by the name of Linda Hutcheon, I was certainly not born a Scot. I was born a Bortolotti. I am, therefore, what I like to think of as a hidden or "crypto-ethnic" — an Italian hidden beneath an Anglo name. The consequences of this silenced marker of Italian heritage are something I share with an entire generation of women "of a certain age" who married at a time when social custom still meant taking their husbands' surnames. For example, there's my friend Cathy N. Davidson, a professor of English at Duke University in the United States. The N. in her name stands for Notari — or, as she prefers, Notari-Fineman-Kotoski. Here, in one small, not quite hidden letter is the sign of a crypto-*multi*-ethnicity: the sign of growing up Italian, Russian and German Jew, and Polish Catholic in working-class Chicago. And then there is Marianna Torgovnick — at least that's what I'd always called her. But, in 1994, she published a book entitled *Crossing Ocean Parkway: Readings by an Italian American Daughter* and, when telling the story of her crossing from Italian to Jewish Brooklyn when she married, she chose to write as Marianna *De Marco* Torgovnick. And then there's the feminist scholar known as Sandra Gilbert, the collaborator (with Susan Gubar) in groundbreaking studies of women's writing, who graduated from highschool as Sandy Mortaro. In other words, beneath the Gilbert, the Torgovnick, the Davidson is an "encrypted" or hidden Mortaro, De Marco, Notari. Of course, there are many male scholars in the field of literary criticism with similar Italian backgrounds: Frank Lentricchia, John Paul Russo, Dominick LaCapra, Joseph Pivato. But for the men, there is no hidden name, no cryptonym.

Beneath the Hutcheon, for me, hides a Bortolotti — something I first wrote about when thinking through the baffling issues surrounding Canadian multiculturalism while editing a book of interviews and short stories called *Other Solitudes.* Inevitably, the name Bortolotti conjures up my father's family from the Friuli, that border region of northeastern Italy prone to earthquakes and invasions. Italian friends tell me that the Friulani are themselves a hybrid ethnic group within Italy, made up of Celtic, Slovenian, Austro-Hungarian and Venetian people. I often wonder whether it was from these Friulani that I inherited some paradoxical desire to blend into the majority Anglo culture while still retaining my ethnic difference. Perhaps they also gave me a taste for incongruities and ironies: those Friulano grandparents homesteaded in Saskatchewan just after the turn of the century, moving from the mountains of Italy to the prairies of Canada. My father was, in fact, born near Viscount, Saskatchewan, in 1914 but the family returned to Italy (with characteristically fine family timing) during the First World War, and re-emigrated in the 1920s. Despite the manifest hardships of life on the prairies, my grandmother recalled her years in the West with great fondness to her dying day at age 103.

But beneath the Bortolotti is another encrypted name: Rossi, the name of my mother's family, who had emigrated from a small hill-town in Tuscany. My mother was the requisite forty days old when the family moved to Toronto — my grandfather having decided that he didn't like the climate of the part of the continent to which his brother had ventured: California. On second thought, maybe the taste for incongruities and ironies came from this side of the family. So, as you can see, though I am Canadian-born, my familial cultural roots are pure Italian. I'm not sure if I'm second- or third-generation, but I have to admit that I don't particularly feel lost in the shifting patterns of migrations and re-emigration like a character in *The Lost Father,* a novel by Marina Warner — another crypto-ethnic critic and writer, this time from the United Kingdom.

What I also share with those other women — the Gilberts, Torgovnicks, and Davidsons — is the fact that we are by profession crypto-ethnic professors of *English.* In other words, we teach and study in university departments structured along the lines of dominant linguistic traditions (English, French, and so on), traditions with intimate connections to the nineteenth-century politics of nation-building. But what does it mean to become an *English* professor when you grow up in an Italian household where "the English" were seen to possess a distinct and different ethnic identity, where roast beef and Yorkshire pudding were considered foreign, but osso buco and polenta were the norm? "The English" were as different, as strange, to us as no doubt we were to them; they too were "ethnic," other, alien — at least from our point of view. This is ethnicity defined as "positionality."

But Sandra, Marianna, and Cathy are all Italian *Americans;* I am Italian *Canadian*. Does this difference in nationality mean different experiences of either ethnicity or cypto-ethnicity? After all the attention given in the world media in the fall of 1995 to the Québec referendum on separation, people in other countries — including the U.S. — may now have an even greater sense of the differences in politics, culture, and national self-image between Canada and the rest of North America as well as between English and French Canada. With no melting pot ideology and no equivalent of even a pluralist "American" national identity to rally around, Canadians — be they of British, Italian, Somali, Chinese or Pakistani origin — have only the paradoxically multiple model of multiculturalism in which to configure their sense of "self-in-nation." This is probably one of the reasons why we Canadians suffer from our infamous and perpetual identity crisis, and why I too have had to think through what my ethnic identity means to me.

It was during the so-called North American "culture wars" that I first realized that the word "multicultural" had very different political associations in Canada and in the United States. Book after book, magazine article after magazine article in the U.S. contained political denunciations of multiculturalism as a social policy destined to "disunite" America. Most often, I found multiculturalism defined as the dominant view on university campuses, contaminated (as they were said to be) by "political correctness." People were said to be worried about what was called the "ethnic cheerleading" implied in some the changes in what was being taught in college courses — as room was made for non-mainstream writers whose inclusion reflected the demographic diversity of the continent more accurately. They expressed concern about potential ethnic chauvinism within the multicultural university. Some raised questions about the possibility that multiculturalism's "politics of difference" might simply be another way of reconfiguring white racial supremacy in America; others voiced fears that the recent interest in ethnic studies would elide the historical realities of race through the use of a European immigrant model for thinking about cultural differences. Despite urgent defenses of minority studies and despite sincere attempts to render more complex the dangerously simplistic views of the new changes in university curricula, the associations of the word, multiculturalism, in the United States often included issues such as gender, sexual choice, and even, occasionally, class.

It was precisely these associations that were so confusing to me as a Canadian, for multiculturalism in Canada is not so much a question of the canon or campus politics but one of national self-definition — and, of course, it is so by law. In Canada, the majority culture's self-understanding is, in part, forcibly defined by its designation as multiple rather than single. The history of the term, multicultural goes back to the part of the 1970 report of the Royal Commission on Bilingualism and Biculturalism that was entitled *The Cultural Contribution of the Other Ethnic Groups* — and here "ethnic" meant all who were not native North American. Out of this came Prime Minister Pierre Elliot Trudeau's 1971 multicultural policy statement and, in 1988, Bill C-93, the Act for the Preservation and Enhancement of Multiculturalism in Canada. The Canadian Charter of Rights and Freedoms also includes within it a commitment to the protection of the multicultural heritage of the nation. Such legal provisions are perhaps typical of Canadian political society, which Charles Taylor has characterized as "more committed to collective provision, over against American society that gives greater weight to individual initiative." In Québec, as in what is really a very polyglot and misnamed "English" Canada, there exists what Taylor calls a "plurality of ways of belonging" or "deep diversity."

It is no accident, however, that it was Pierre Elliot Trudeau, the fierce federalist opponent of Québec separation, who formulated the policy statement about multiculturalism in the early 1970s. Changing Canada's self-image from bicultural to multicultural was not simply a matter of recognizing a demographic reality; it had a political purpose and, in some people's eyes, a political result. On the night of the 1995 separation referendum, Québec Premier Jacques Parizeau lamented that the (French) Québécois chance for independence had been ruined by what he controversially referred to as "money and the ethnic vote." It is no coincidence that multicultural policies were put in place at the same time that Québec was starting to think of itself as independent, as no longer a colony. Today, in some critics' eyes, those policies still function as implicit barriers to the recognition of both Québécois demands for independence and also, of course, of the land claims and demands for self-government of First Nations Peoples.

Yet another worry people have about multiculturalism as a national policy is that ethnicity could become a compulsory and limiting identity label. Smaro Kamboureli fears that "familial genealogies, or biologism" could become the only defining terms of identity. But my reply to this concern would be that, with the inevitable changes that come with displacement, any sense of ethnicity is bound to be configured differently in a new and different place. Human life, as Charles Taylor has argued, is always formed in relation to other people and other customs. In Michael Fischer's terms, "ethnicity is something reinvented and reinterpreted with each generation by each individual . . . Ethnicity is not something that is simply passed on from generation to generation, taught and learned; it is something dynamic, often unsuccessfully repressed or avoided" — even by crypto-ethnics. As the opponents of Canadian multiculturalism policies helpfully remind us, ethnicity should not be something frozen in time; it should never be only the site of nostalgia. Cultures in Canada, as elsewhere, interpenetrate; what's called "transculturation" occurs. Despite the ethnic conflicts raging in various parts of the globe today, the meaning of ethnicity in the late twentieth-century diasporic world should logically no longer mean concepts of purity and authenticity; as Joseph Pivato and others have noted, for many people it is more in the *meeting* of cultures that ethnicity today is actually lived.

I want to resist the urge to find any more precise-sounding image for this *meeting* of cultures that ethnicity means to me. As a model or metaphor, the idea of cultural "hybridity" (in either its positive or negative meanings) seems to depend implicity on an idea of purity, of authenticities brought together. It seems, paradoxically, to be dependent on keeping the very borders it tries to dissolve. I suspect my Friulani ancestors had centuries of this contradictory border experience. But I am a second-generation Italian Canadian and crypto-ethnic, living in multiracial, multiethnic Toronto. I do not really feel caught between what Kamboureli describes as the "experience of loss and of being othered in a web of old and new cultural registers"; for me, ethnicity has much more to do with the process of what Fischer calls "inter-reference between two or more cultural traditions." Marianna De Marco

Torgovnick's image of crossings — between ethnic groups and social classes, between being an insider and an outsider, among the roles of "wife, mother, daughter, mourner, professional woman, critic, and writer"— strikes me as a fruitful one for *many* different situations (as her own long list indeed suggests), but it is not precisely descriptive of my personal sense of what ethnicity means to me.

In a provocative and even prophetic essay written a decade ago and called "A Critique of Pure Pluralism," Werner Sollors urged that the categorization of both writers and critics as members of ethnic groups be understood as "very partial, temporal, and insufficient characterization at best." In arguing instead for a dynamic "transethnic" focus based on the complexities of "polyethnic interaction," he wrote of the dangers of choosing — timidly — to speak with the "authority of ethnic insiders rather than that of readers of texts." When Sollors wrote to American readers that "literature could become recognizable as a productive force that may Americanize *and* ethnicize readers," he implied that you are *what* you read. Perhaps, however, you are also *how* you read (as well as how you are read). This is what Henry Louis Gates, Jr. implied when he argued that, "under the sign of multiculturalism [here used in its broad American sense], literary readings are often guided by the desire to elicit, first and foremost, indices of ethnic particularity, especially those that can be construed as oppositional, transgressive, subversive." The impact of ethnicity — like that of race and gender—on the act of interpretaion is a much debated topic in literary circles. But, like the cultural construction of "nationness" (as Homi Bhabha has argued), the cultural construction of ethnicity may also be a "form of social and textual affiliation"— for readers as for writers, for both are formed (as readers and writers) by being placed in an order of words; both emerge as a function of different and perhaps conflicting encodings.

However, some crypto-Italians — like myself, like Cathy Davidson, Sandra Gilbert, Marianna Torgovnick — end up as *professional* readers and writers, the kind called professors of English. The question is: do "English" professors have to do "English" readings? I received my education in English literary studies in Canada in the 1960s and 1970s, and therefore largely within the normalizing, ethnocentric context of the liberal humanism represented by the work of the British theorist F.R. Leavis: the immigration of "British" professors of "English" to the colonies had guaranteed that Leavis's "great tradition" would be my tradition. In other words, I learned to do what Frances Mulhern calls "English reading." The realization of this particular and particularly insidious form of crypto-ethnicity may well be what drove me into Italian studies and finally into Comparative Literature; it may even have dictated the choice of theory as my scholarly research area. One part of my academic "life-script"—the narrative I use to shape and tell my life as a reader and writer—would have to include my realization that, in the university too, "the English" (as they were known in my family) constituted a specific ethnic group and NOT the voice of the universal. Rather than get rid of foreignness in the name of universal natuarlization, then, maybe we should realize that we are all "foreign" to someone else, while still working toward some kind of "interculturalism" that would make the meeting of ethnicities easier.

In the end, though, I find I cannot resist offering an image of what ethnicity and crypto-ethnicity might mean to me. I borrow it from *In the Skin of a Lion,* a novel by Sri Lankan Canadian writer, Michael Ondaatje. It is a novel about the history of Toronto, the city in which I live and work; the image, however, is one used to describe an Italian Canadian man, evocatively and ironically named David Caravaggio. In prison for theft (he likes to think of himself as a "professional displacer"), Caravaggio learns that his very name is a carrier of ethnicity, a mobile attractor of scorn and abuse: he is called "wop" and "dago." One of his tasks while in prison is to paint the roof of the penitentiary blue. (Caravaggio thus lives up to his famous namesake's profession as painter, even if in a debased and ironic way.) As he goes about his job, he realizes that he is losing all sense of the boundaries between blue sky and blue roof. With this realization comes a sense of liberation and empowerment for the imprisoned man—but not only for the visual illusion of freedom it offers. In an act of cunning self-cryptography, he has his fellow inmates paint him blue, thereby erasing all visible boundaries between himself, the roof and the sky. Caravaggio then escapes.

Crypto-ethnicity is, for me, a fact of life; so too is ethnicity. From these there is no escape. But in the very fact of the "encrypting" there is a potential challenge to purist, imprisoning boundaries, a challenge that (most of the time, at least) I find liberating. I think of blue Caravaggio on the blue roof, and he becomes for me the image not only of crypto-ethnicity but of ethnicity itself — ethnicity as positionality.

Marco Micone

Voiceless People

NANCY
The virgin of Chiuso is packing her bags tonight.

GINO
Excited, after a moment's thought.
You're giving me an idea for the next show. On the stage, we'll put fifty suitcases, no, a hundred, and we'll hand them out to all the women who come to see the show. We won't say a word, like today.

NANCY
You'll do it without me.

GINO
Without you?

NANCY
Yes, without me. I've had enough of being hassled, finding myself in empty theaters or in front of a crowd that's come to see a wrestling match.

GINO
So why are you leaving your family? I thought . . .

NANCY
It's not my parents, I'm leaving. It's Chiuso.

GINO

You can't do that. After all the work we did, it's ridiculous! There are young people counting on us, women counting on you to speak for them.

NANCY

I'm freeing myself from Chiuso. To be able to speak up better for freedom. I feel like... I have the feeling we're going around in circles. That we've been stuck in the same rut for the past two years. I feel exactly like I do on stage, screaming my revolt, without being able to get out of the box I'm in. Today I feel like all the women from Chiuso, set free a few days a year from their kitchens and factories so they can put on a nice show with the kids for the procession. A show none of them ever enjoys, all lined up holding their *bambino*'s hand, all starched, and proudly parading under the searching gaze of their men standing on the sidewalk in a choreography signed by the priest. What did that vulture say today? "My children, you really went too far. We won't be able to trust you anymore." We get crushed on all sides, I've had enough.

GINO

Yes, go ahead and make knots too. Don't let yourself be crushed.

NANCY

Knots?

GINO

Yes, *macramé*.

NANCY

Gino, I teach teenagers who all have Italian names and who have one culture, that of silence. Silence about the peasant origin of their parents. Silence about the manipulation they're victims of. Silence about the country they live in. Silence about the reasons for their silence. Two-thirds of them hardly finish high school and end up with their parents in the same factories. Those youngsters never come to our meetings or our activities. We have to get to them in the classroom.

GINO

We only need a few, we have to push them to do what we are doing for the parents.

NANCY

We can't do anything for the parents. We have to take care of the young people. We have to find the ways the ghetto-keepers haven't used yet. We must replace the culture of silence by immigrant culture, so that the peasant in us stands up, so that the immigrant in us remembers, and so that the Québécois in us can start to live. Write; fine, but in a way that everyone can understand you. Young people must find themselves in texts written by someone who lived like them, who understands and wants to help them. Their being different has to become a reason for them to struggle, and not a cause of complexes and passivity.

GINO

You're really naive, Nancy. If there's no place for us in Chiuso, how do you expect us to find one in a place where people have been gazing at their navels for the past twenty years. They even refused to let us go to their schools back in the Fifties.

NANCY
That's an old story . . .

GINO
We're a minority, and a minority which is beginning to speak up is not well regarded. It becomes dangerous, subversive. The only choice we were given was to unite what we are with what they are, the better to squash us under the weight of their majority. I don't feel like writing a play on the subject of *I Live in Shit, and I'm Staying There*, and see critics and academics short of publications pontificating on fate or other such revolutionary themes.

NANCY
You can't write what you want, but only if you write in the language of the country will our culture get a chance to affirm itself and become part of theirs. It's now or never.

GINO
Ironical.
Sure, let's hurry up. People have never talked about us so much. But the problem is that the more you talk about immigration, the less you talk about immigrants. After having been job-stealers, strangers, Wops, mafiosi, spaghetti, the others and the ethnics, now we're the allophones. Have you ever heard an uglier term? That should be the registered trade mark of some phone! Take advantage of the fashion, Nancy. Get out of Chiuso, and find yourself a real true-blue Québécois.

NANCY

That's your privilege, and you know it. All your friends married Quebec girls, and you'll probably do the same. Girls like me, if they stay in Chiuso, are condemned to marry members of the Sons of Italy, liberal militants and English-speaking. For you and your friends, girls like me are not exciting enough. Not flamboyant enough, not sexy enough. We don't carry integration in our dowry chest, we the well-educated virgins of Chiuso. And you want me to stay here? Unlike you, Gino, I'm twice an immigrant over here: as an Italian in Quebec, and as a woman in Chiuso. Stay, Gino, you're a man.

Suddenly we hear: Balloons, balloons, balloons. *Fly away with red ones, green ones, white ones. Zio appears. The three play with the balloons a few moments. Then the lighting changes.*

ZIO

To Nancy.

Come. Come. Fly away with me. I will show you the voiceless people. I will show you the youngsters of Chiuso, its men and women. We will break the silence, and cross Chiuso's walls so as to join forces with the people who are like us. Fly away with me, Annunziata. Annunziata.

Translation by Maurizia Binda

Addolorata

She takes the guitar and plays a few chords.

LOLITA

I'm learning to play the guitar for Johnny. I'm sure he's going to love that song. It was love at first sight for me anyway.

She sings a verse from "Guantanamera." She plays and sings poorly.

I get shivers all over when I sing that song. I'll sing it to him on our honeymoon. It will keep me busy a bit . . . and it's so romantic!

She sighs.

When I think I practically missed everything because of my name! With a name like Zanni, you're always last in everything. When I went to CEGEP to register for a Spanish class, there was no room left. I couldn't help it, I burst into tears in front of all the teachers. I won them over! They ended up allowing me to take my Spanish class. I think that was the nicest day of my life, nicer still than my first communion. Anyway, when I went to the first class, it was like going to a party: all my friends were there. All Italians, except for one English girl. Fortunately, she left three weeks later. I never heard anyone pronounce so badly. Those people are really not talented with languages. Maybe that's why they've forced so many people to learn theirs.

Pause.

The Spanish teacher was so . . . *hermoso y caloroso.* He made us feel at ease right away by singing "Guantanamera." Ever since then, I sing it at least once a day.

She sings a verse.

If it hadn't been for the Spanish course, I wouldn't have stayed in CEGEP long. But even so, one year is enough. There is so much unemployment, it's no use getting an education. Everyone knows that the educated unemployed are much more unhappy than the uneducated unemployed. I don't want to be unhappy. In September, when I register for night school, I'm going to take two Spanish courses. Then I will know four languages. With four languages I can go ahead and get married without being afraid. If Johnny knew four languages, I'm sure he wouldn't be so afraid of getting married.

Silence.

I learned English and French at bilingual school. At French bilingual school. That's why I speak French naturally. I don't even think when I speak. It's the only French bilingual school in Montreal. But the nuns were so strict, we were hardly allowed to do anything. No speaking in the hall. No leaving the school-yard at lunch. No chewing gum. No staying too long in the washroom: one minute to pee, no more. The nun who watched over the washrooms, we used to call her "poop lady."

She laughs.

I'm the one who thought of that name. This is forbidden . . . that is forbidden . . . No wonder the school was called Notre-Dame-de-la-Défense. In St. Leonard, they already tried setting up English bilingual schools for Italians, but it didn't work out. They realized it was necessary to teach both languages in school because Italians were picking up French in the street. And to pick up French in the street is not worse than learning it in school. It's the same thing for Italian. We don't have to study it: we have it in our blood.

For us Italians, school is practically useless. All my friends dropped out as soon as they could. They considered me the brain of the gang. Johnny didn't even finish grade ten. When you're as smart as he is . . . you always get bored at school. I'm never bored. I'm never bored with my four languages. I can speak English on Monday, French on Tuesday, Italian on Wednesday, Spanish on Thursday, and all four on Friday.

Serious.

On the weekend, I don't talk because my father is home.

Exuberant.

I can also speak English with my friends, French with the neighbours, Italian with the machos, and Spanish with certain customers. With my four languages, I never get bored. With my four languages, I can watch soaps in English, read the French TV Guide, the Italian fotoromanzi, and sing "Guantanamera."

Lighting comes to normal.

When I think that some people get married with only one language and they're happy . . . I can already picture myself married with four languages. That must be something! But the one I prefer is Spanish. I don't know what I would give to be a real Spanish lady. At The Bay, when I have Spanish customers, I introduce myself as Lolita Gomez. It's so much nicer than Addolorata Zanni. Addolorata is so ugly, that most of my cousins changed their name. The one living in Toronto calls herself Laurie. She's the cousin I like least. She's so weird — she studies things that are for men. She wants to be a "lawyer." She only speaks English. She says she also speaks Italian, but when she tries, she speaks half Italian, half English. I don't know where she's going to go with a language and a half. I have another cousin in Argentina. Her name is Dolores. She's the one who sent me the guitar when my uncle came to visit. Dolores is such a beautiful name. My last cousin is almost as horrible as the one in Toronto. She lives in the *villaggio*. She hasn't changed her name. Still calls herself Addolorata. I can't understand why anyone would call herself Addolorata in 1971. She really talks like a man — always about politics. In the small villages in Italy, there are lots of people like that: a bit backward. When I was on vacation there last year, I didn't go out with her more than twice. I preferred going out with my aunt Rosaria, who took me to see the beautiful sanctuaries. We even went to see Padre Pio. Padre Pio is like Brother André here. That day, he worked so many miracles that I almost wished I were a cripple. I don't mean to say that the crippled weren't crippled anymore after having being blessed by him. No, the blind remained blind and those who were limping kept limping. But they smiled, yes, they smiled. For the first time, they were happy to be crippled. Really happy. That's the miracle. I will never forget that sanctuary. It's not far from my *villaggio*. The weather is always beautiful there. It think it's really the best outdoor place to do these things. Compared to that, politics is so boring. In St. Leonard, we elected two Italian deputies just because they're Italian. I remember they came to our house on the eve of the election. They never talked of what they'd do during their term. No. They only talked about wine with my father. After a few glasses, they even sang a few dirty songs with my father.

Laughs shyly.

A real old country scene. They left as soon as they learned my father couldn't vote because he doesn't have Canadian citizenship.

With scorn.

Deputies! Even dogs would have been elected in their place if they could bark in Italian.

Pause, then forcefully.

Even my father could have been elected.

Pause.

My tomato sauce! *Lolita runs off stage back to her kitchen.*

Translated by Maurizia Binda

Bianca Zagolin

November Crossing

I

She had been widowed at thirty-two and was left with three daughters to raise, in a small town where she had little choice but to play the part of the grieving mother, quietly dignified and self-sacrificing to the end.

"After all, your path is clear, Aurora, you've got your children . . . "

This comment was strangely disquieting to her, more troubling than the understandable concerns of a young widow, although she would have been at a loss to say why. With these few words, she was being denied a whole world she could only imagine, one to which she had never had access while she was married. She had been loved, sheltered, and now that she was alone, she wasn't even given the chance to discover it. And yet, Aurora sensed that, beyond the confines of motherhood, countless species of exotic creatures were swarming beneath other skies, in uncharted lands where somehow she belonged, as though she existed potentially somewhere else. And through the strangest paradox, her other self, this unknown Aurora, seemed to have more substance than all of her elusive identities.

Aurora invariably replied with a sigh, which some attributed to grief, others to fatalism. But much as she tried, she could not grasp more clearly the possibilities she was vaguely aware of, nor muster her dormant energy. So she created unnecessary work to make herself useful and thereby justify her existence. After all, she had nothing to worry about: her older brother, in far-off America, looked after her interests kindly but firmly, and she was held accountable to him, as was proper. Aurora had been tamed; the bitterness she could almost taste no longer distressed her, and the idea that she might live any other way barely entered her mind. At most she allowed herself the luxury of mitigated hope in the form of an occasional sentence in the conditional: things would have been different if only her husband hadn't died, if so many obstacles hadn't stood in her way, if she could have leaned on her family. That was it: she needed to be encouraged, pushed a little. If only . . . But she couldn't do anything about it anyway, and besides, who could tell? Maybe her path was clear after all, as everyone kept repeating.

Each day brought its load of clothes to iron, beds to make, floors to scrub, enough chores to set a clear line of action that she could follow unerringly. And, at noon, without fail, Aurora served her daughters a well-prepared meal.

After they had gone off to school, she would set out, with a basket on her arm, and slowly make her way toward the stores on Bonin Boulevard where she did her morning shopping: four escalopes of veal, a kilo of zucchini, a few tomatoes, butter, rolls, peaches and cherries, what she needed for lunch. "Thank you, ma'am, see you tomorrow." Every day, the small villas with pastel stucco walls, forever the same, watched Aurora as she walked home. Only the neighbours' German shepherd, lurking behind the hedge to startle passersby, managed to interrupt her monotonous train of thought on the little problems she would have to deal with shortly. From now on, she would have to keep a closer eye on the gardener who was definitely over-extending his afternoon naps after washing down his sausage with several glassfuls of red wine. She would also ask him to cut firewood, enough for five or six days. The last time she had to do it herself, the axe had slipped and hit her leg. That was in June; the little shed at the bottom of the garden was shrouded in the evening shadows. Blood had gushed out, but Aurora had felt no pain, surprise at most, then something moist and warm trickling down her calf. She had been fascinated to discover this bubbling just below her smooth, cool skin. But she had quickly regained her self-control and called out to her daughter, who had come running, all the while scolding her for being so careless. This was hardly a first; small domestic misfortunes were not unknown to Aurora; she bore the marks of a humdrum existence, yet not without danger: red blotches, scrapes and burns were the scars she acquired on her own little battlefield where the world's greatest heroes wouldn't have lasted a week. But nothing really serious, just trivial occurrences in a life without importance.

That evening, her eldest was to take her sister to a country fair where travelling entertainers set up rides every year at the end of June. For weeks, the child had been dreaming of flying through the air on those giant spiders that shake their fiery legs above the tumultuous crowd. Every year, the town celebrated the arrival of summer on a June night still suffused with the day's delights and amidst cries of joy and the smell of fried foods.

"Don't worry about me; you're not going to let a bit of spilt blood ruin your evening, are you? Now, go and have fun!"

And so they went, with heavy hearts, leaving Aurora behind, a little pale in the fading light, with her leg resting on a pillow. It was on that evening that Aurora thought she first caught a glimpse of the young dancer slipping through the bellflowers that clung to the bars on the kitchen window. Barely a shadow, a fleeting reflection, evanescent form of the past. She had stretched forward and stared wide-eyed, without getting up because of her injury. It was surely just two fireflies flitting about in the balmy night air . . . Through the open window, she caught the heady scent of magnolia, and drifting through the dark, voices of youth passing by. Aurora absorbed it all: the perfume aroused in her forgotten dreams and yearnings, while her throbbing leg rooted her in her flesh. For one moment, as the fragrance she was breathing in merged with her pain, Aurora felt intensely alive.

II

But for all that, Aurora was still very conscious of her appearance, even though, or perhaps precisely because passion was unknown to her. Being beautiful meant preserving her dignity, escaping the faceless existence to which women like her were condemned. A neighbourhood seamstress, gifted for copying originals, turned yards and yards of black fabric into elegant fashions for Aurora: skirts flaring into waves of material that brushed against her calves; waisted jackets with padded shoulders; silk scarves that she wrapped loosely around her neck to catch a breath of wind. On those rare occasions when she went to town, Aurora stepped into the unknown. She felt drawn to it, but she was careful not to venture too far and kept her distance by bearing herself like a queen in black silk and high-heeled shoes. She never stopped anywhere longer than necessary, never allowed herself the luxury of a stroll. She held her head up high and moved along with a quick, determined step, looking sternly at all the people milling about in the streets. In her own neighbourhood, with a shopping net full of groceries, she tasted the humiliation that everyday life invariably brings, but in the heart of the city, Aurora was a beautiful stranger just passing through. She walked proudly down the streets flooded with sunlight, a tall dark figure, as though the city were her own private domain, and in her wake hovered an uneasy silence with a faint scent of eau de Cologne.

She spent her evenings at home; the night might lead to untimely encounters. Why hurry things? She retired early, wondering if she would still be beautiful in the morning. And so time went by. And each year, her skilful hands traced marvellously intricate designs in her garden which overflowed with blossoms in the spring.

III

One day, the long-awaited news arrived. It was neither a misfortune nor a great joy, more of a questioning, a possibility one hardly dares to contemplate, so out of the ordinary it seems, and it came in the guise of a peculiar visitor they would long remember. A minor official serving in the Government of Quebec turned up as the obsequious spokesman for the supreme authority who watched over poor, helpless Aurora from across the sea, five thousand kilometres away. Her well-meaning brother had decreed that her status as a penniless widow doomed her little clan of women to a far from brilliant future. And so he was proposing that Aurora send her elder daughters to Canada, chaperoned by an aging cousin who was about to emigrate herself to join her family. The girls could register at a Montreal university where they would learn French and English, and that would surely set them apart from the common run of people upon their return to Italy. It was planned as a sort of year abroad, but who could tell? It might also open doors for them, in which case Aurora herself would consider emigrating.

Presented in such terms, the suggested trip did not frighten Aurora in the least, since for the moment it entailed no thorny decisions on her part. She listened to the Canadian emissary, served him coffee and asked all kinds of practical questions, but all the while she was engrossed in a pleasant reverie. Could this be the seed of adventure? She felt again the well-known yet enigmatic premonitions of another life that would spring up within her whenever she dwelt on the unbroken monotony of her existence. The messenger's words reached her through the smoke that curled out of his mouth, as from the cave of an oracle sensed by a crowd of truth-seekers. With her sense of ritual and her belief in omens, Aurora would have preferred a more dignified messenger of the gods: the civil servant from Quebec was short-legged and long-winded. During the entire meal to which Aurora had graciously invited him, he kept repeating with affectation: "I hope you won't take offence, Madam, if I should be so bold as to tell you that your chicken is exquisite."

He worked like a fiend to open a bottle of sparkling wine, so that when the cork finally popped, it shot up like a rocket and nicked the dining-room ceiling. Aurora followed it with her eyes: maybe that was the sign she was waiting for, not to mention the fact that this odd individual was wearing an oversize burgundy-red jacket. Such an unusual attire had to mean something on the cosmic plane where she stubbornly searched for the significance of his visit.

Aurora knew that in its honeyed tones the voice from overseas concealed the wrenching yet to come: the exchange of a sunny, fragrant homeland, where even death's most striking faces reminded one to treasure life, for a land of ice and snow; the erosion of daily certainties never questioned before, of a lifestyle that, for better or for worse, had proven itself and of a language that offered all of its resources, without fail, even in the privacy of one's thoughts; the loss of that reassuring feeling of living in a place one could call home, no matter how limited it might be. But over there, people were less concerned with certainties, and besides, it was a big country, kept repeating the oracle, a land of opportunities. Big enough to get lost in, worried Aurora. In any case, even if she decided to refuse its invitation, the voice had spoken; it had wormed its way into her brain and was spreading its golden promises like a poison. Nothing could ever silence it.

The decision was made. Her elder daughters would leave in the summer. They sailed in July, in the full blush of youth, leaving behind a few broken hearts, but nevertheless delighted at the prospect of a fantastic journey. Aurora stayed on the quay a long time, and like in a silver screen romance, she waved her handkerchief at the ship that was imperceptibly drawing away. She probed her heart at the same time as she scanned the faces in the crowd of passengers on deck. She found nothing but weariness. She had spent so many years trying hard to think up reasons for living, and now her daughters had left her for a country that, until recently, she knew only by name. But it was to be expected. As people had told her often enough, together with many other ancient truths that women use to hide their sadness, children grow up and leave. Like all mothers before her, Aurora had merely abided by the rules, and her life had become all the more pointless. The great white liner, gleaming on the horizon, seemed about to capsize in an uncertain future, and as she watched it growing smaller, it imprinted itself as an indelible image of her own futility.

Soon her youngest's cheering presence drew her out of her thoughts. Through her, Aurora would be granted a few more years of joy, a reprieve of genuine gaiety. She embedded her mother at the very core of life, like a stone in the pulp of a fruit. At those special moments of their perfect understanding, Aurora found herself believing that the child would provide her with the key to that other existence she sensed beyond her shadowy present. She listened intently for the mysterious voices that never ceased to whisper. But every time, a diffuse feeling of anguish welled up inside her, as though she were being pushed into a journey she wasn't quite ready for. Beyond the happiness emerging in the distance, her lifelong enemy was lying in wait. She would be safe as long as she remained within the cycle of life, immutable for all beings; choosing to live intensely, for herself, meant accepting to suffer, Aurora was sure of it. And this time, she would know pain without ritual, unadulterated and sharp, the kind that kills.

Back home, she examined the dining-room ceiling in disbelief. The tiny scar left by the stubborn cork was still there. But no further news had come to confirm the extraordinary nature of that dinner in April, when an absurd little man in a burgundy jacket had eaten chicken at her table.

Translated from the French by the author

George Amabile

Sammy's in Love

The first truly religious event I ever witnessed . . . well, maybe not the first, but the most impressive, was disguised as a fist fight.

It happened on the first day of school in grade five.

Sister Margaret really looked like somebody's sister. She was a blue-eyed, pug-nosed nineteen-year-old with frizzy blonde hair that kept working out from the tight edge of the wimple that framed her face. I remember thinking how much it reminded me of pubic hair peeking out from the hem of a bathing suit, and of one bathing suit in particular, a black one-piece that had obsessed my imagination through the dog days of July and August.

I guess I'd better explain.

It was hot that summer. So hot that if you wanted to you could stamp your footprint into the soft tar of the street. In weather like that we all went a little crazy, but the bigger kids, the ones who used the corner candy store as a clubhouse, drinking *R.C. Colas* and smoking *Chesterfields* while they played cards on the concrete stoop, had a way of calming us down. One of the boys, it was usually Mickey Levine, would sneak a Stillson wrench from his father's toolshed. Then, while we stood on the corners watching for cop cars, he'd unscrew the cap from the fire hydrant in the middle of the block, and open the tap. The sound of rushing water was like a signal that transformed the dusty, oppressive street to a festive pavillion. Dozens of kids appeared in shorts or bathing suits or even their underwear.

The bigger, stronger ones took turns pressing their backsides against the powerful stream until a sparkling rooster tail arched up into the hot sky and came down like a cataract hammering huge drops on the pavement. Everyone pushed and yelled and fought their way into the ice-cold spray, dancing around in circles and gasping for breath until the pressure of the water tumbled the spray-maker into the street. Then another would take over and the jumping and shoving and yelling would begin again. After an hour or so, the police would drive up in their green and white chevy coupe, and we'd all run, shouting, "Two Worms In A Green Apple," as we scattered and then disappeared into the hiding places we'd discovered playing *Kick the Can* for years in broad daylight.

The first symptoms of my breathless obsession with Anita Levine and her black one-piece occurred during one of these pagan celebrations. I was standing under the huge, glittering water-fan that poured icy rivulets down through my flattened hair and over my eyes when she appeared, shorn of her baggy jeans and plaid shirt, like some earthy angel drenching herself at the edge of a waterfall. Droplets caught in my eyelashes and surrounded her with tiny rainbows. As her thin fingers combed back ash blonde hair, a soft light seemed to glow from her skin. Wet through, the black one-piece clung to her stomach revealing the faint outline of a belly button, and the prickly cushion of her pubic hair. I felt a tightness in my chest. My head seemed to float above my shoulders; my heartbeat skipped and raced and fluttered until I thought I was going to burst, or dissolve in a stream of cold water. After that, every time I saw Anita Levine, my face got hot, and I felt like I was going to suffocate.

Anyway, that first day in grade five, I was surprised and confused by the sudden onset of what I had come to think of as Anita Levine Fever. I couldn't take my eyes off Sister Margaret who swaggered demurely across the front of the classroom, picked up a blackboard pointer, and lashed it a few times over the desk, scattering paperbacks and pencils. I guess she wanted us to know she was a tamer. I was ready to jump through rings of fire, just for a shot of light from those blue eyes. But Sammy Ferretti was not impressed.

He was the round faced, left handed hit-man-to-be we all revered and admired. He'd already beaten up the bullies in grade eight. So, after the whisssh and slap and the pages fluttering and the blue gleam of power under those thick blond eyelashes, after the slummy accent we recognized as railroad avenue, our little, victimized souls began to collect around Sammy's inevitable rebellion.

We weren't disappointed. He called her a slut and a wet nurse, in impeccable Sicilian. Some of us looked down at our desks and snickered. But the blue eyed baby sister of God had languages too, even though she was Irish, and pretty, and slender as a boy. She answered, in waspy Sardinian. Something about a seedling penis in Sammy's pants. Well, that broke it. Sam the Man came out of his seat real cool and headed for the open floor at the front of the room. Say that again in English, he said. His hands came up into that relaxed southpaw roll we knew could explode in a flurry of staccato combinations. But sister Margaret smiled and laid her pointer down. Then she walked across the open space between them, hands at her side, and licked her lips.

"You want some action, fellah?"

Sammy's face remained obscure in a kind of handsome gloom. She laughed and turned away, then sucker punched from the left and the undefeated warrior of Holy Rosary School started falling. His eyes filled up with shock, and before his butt hit the floor he was hers.

He sat there, pulled his legs up, held them to his body with locked fingers, and stared. To our great surprise, she didn't order him back to his seat. She just swirled her habit and strode, her slim hips swinging perhaps a little too freely for a nun, back to her desk, and began to instruct us on the major exports of Brazil.

Even after the minute hand on the big round clock at the front of the room stuttered home at three and freed us, he remained seated in the aisle. We tip-toed around him, careful not to acknowledge his ignominious condition, but I noticed, as I passed, that his dangerous body gave off the most peaceful emanations, and I wondered if something had broken inside him.

I was wrong, of course.

The very next day, at recess, Alexander the Giant — a big stupid seventh grader who had never really admitted that Sammy was a better fighter, though Sammy's quick hands had hammered the arrogance out of him more than once and made it less and less possible for him to indulge his oafish compulsion to beat up on us little guys — began to act up. News of Sammy's miraculous conversion had brought the habitual sneer to his big slack face. Now he lumbered around for a while, then waded into our box-ball game and cuffed Skinhead so hard the baseball cap flew off his head. Alexander looked around. Sure enough, there was Sammy, standing against the school wall, one foot back against the bricks, smoking a *Spuds* menthol. He didn't seem to be in the same world as the rest of us. Alexander mumbled, in that sullen, mashed potato voice we had long ago recognized as a signal of danger, "Hey, youse guys, lookit that: Sammy's In Love."

We all woke up, and our hearts broke into overtime. Even Skinhead, lying on the ground nursing a scraped elbow, looked as though he was ready for a significant event, but gathered his feet under his fallen body for flight, just in case the rumours about Sammy's apparent illness turned out to be true.

And for a while it looked like our noble protector had nothing at all on his mind, apart from the memory of intimate contact with Sister Margaret's knuckles. It made Alexander reckless. He actually walked over to where Sammy was lounging against the wall, looking up at the sky and enjoying, as it seemed, the popcorn clouds that floated airily above the trivial politics of the schoolyard. We had never seen Sammy in such a condition and we were worried. He looked, well . . . beautiful. His round face and onyx eyes perfectly relaxed in the soft spring light. He was like a fallen angel who had come out of the flames to the good blue of god's eternal spa. That look rankled Alexander. His big work boot kicked the standing leg from under our roosting hero. But Sammy didn't fall. He just brought his other foot down real fast and flicked his cigarette with middle finger and thumb, all the way over the chain link fence. Then he looked at Alexander. Alexander looked back, smirking. Sammy shook his head.

"You really want to do this crap again?" he asked, his voice polite as tapioca.

"I hear you lost yer balls, nigger," Alexander said.

Some of the bigger kids called Sammy that because, being Sicilian, he had a complexion many shades darker than your average Italian. It usually put him in a fighting mood, but now he just came languidly forward like he was going to kiss something hovering out there just above Zander's head. Then he reached up to pat The Giant on the side of his face, and the big lummox lifted his boot toward Sammy's crotch.

We expected some fast fistwork, but Sammy's hips did a little girlish drift and he caught the Giant's boot in both hands. Then he just walked him back across the schoolyard. Alexander kept trying to hit Sammy but he was always off balance, and he looked more and more stupid. Sammy kept holding his leg up in the air and pushing him toward the fence, smiling. A shadow blotted the April sun for a moment, and Sister Margaret came busting across the schoolyard.

"Stop that, Samuel," she yelled. "Don't you know better than to pick on someone twice your size?

Alexander made a face that looked appropriately put upon. My heart was fluttering and jumping around like a shot squirrel inside me, and the words came out in a silly rush.

"It's not Sammy, Sister, It's Alex, he beat up Skinhead and kicked Samuel's foot and Sammy didn't even hit him." I took a gulp of air. "Yet," I finished, hopeful that we might still get to see a pint sized version of Primo Carnera and the Brown Bomber re-enacted on almost holy ground.

Sister Margaret surveyed the schoolyard and when she saw all those little heads nodding in agreement, she said, "Oh, Zander. Big Bully rides again, eh? I heard about you, boy. What do you have to say for yourself?"

Alexander was pinned to the fence. He decided to roar.

"He's the bully. He won't fight fair."

Sammy laughed. Pushed the leg a little higher.

"Apologize like a nice moron, Alex." he said. "Tell Skinhead how sorry you are."

Alexander kicked hard, his face all twisted and then he glowered at Sister Margaret and made a big mistake. A litany of obscene street talk jumped out between loose lips. We all stood there with our mouths open. Sammy, however, took Zander's words as a personal insult. He dropped the giant's boot and stepped back, his legendary left arm coiled, his fist so tight you could see the white knuckles under his dusky skin. When Sister Margaret put her hand on Sammy's shoulder he looked up at her with a kind of confused adoration.

"It's not your fight, Samuel," she said.

Sammy smiled and stepped aside. Alexander didn't know what was about to happen, so he indulged himself in some more bad language. Something about how nuns have to have their tits cut off cause Jesus is too faggoty to marry a real broad. Sister got that look in her eyes. And she was smiling her Railroad Avenue leather-jacketed smile. Then she slapped the Giant. Not hard, just like a kind of introduction. He looked insulted, like he was going to go home and tell his Mommy. Then he lunged at her and she clipped him a good short right. It rocked him, no lie, but he kept coming. He took a left hook on the ear and grabbed the rope of holy beads around her waist, ripping them apart and kicking her feet out from under her. As she fell, the Giant fell with her, driving his knee into where her private parts would be if nuns had such things. And I guess they do, because she let out a yelp, and clapped her palms against his large doughy ears. It stunned him, but he kept pushing his body against hers.

Most of us were convinced that she had already vanquished the Giant and reduced him to a helpless twitching heap even though he was still on top of her. But Sammy couldn't stand it any more. He teed off and hit Alexander a shot to the left side of his head, then started an uppercut from his ankles and snapped the Giant's head back, rolling him off of Sister Margaret and onto his back in the sun. We all cheered.

Sister Margaret looked a little worse for wear as she pulled her ironed pleats from under the Giant and regained her feet. She dusted herself off, then started to say something to Sammy. I figured she was going to tell him she had it covered and didn't need his help, but she rearranged what was left of her broken rosaries, then looked up again. Her lips were tight for a moment then they relaxed into a grin. All she said was, "I owe you one."

It was different between them after that. Sometimes she had to *ask* him to stay after school to clean the blackboards or empty the wastepaper baskets. And sometimes there was a look that passed between them, a smile of the eyes, an acknowledgement of their new equality. But Sammy won the spelling bee that year, and even though he was no longer delirious about Sister M, if you tried to get him on your side about some of her bitchy behaviour, he'd bristle and warn you off with those big black eyes.

Mary Melfi

Wanting a Baby

Reduced to being less philosophical than a cat asleep on a porch. Reduced to one wish: the wish to conceive, to get pregnant. To create new flesh and mercy.

Would that a child fall into my life, re-activate my energy supply and inspire: tenderness may not be the ruling force in our day-to-day life, but it is one of the reasons for our continued participation in it. Gentle does it. Aren't we all VIPs stranded on earth yearning for charitable souls to recognize, promote and mother us if need be?

My ambition has been spent. Bye-Bye, unwilling surrenders to big corporations and to the profit-motive. Hello to the new and magical. Let the animal within me escape and be jolly, and *not think*. Be thought for.

I will make what does not exist, exist. I will do it and appease my greed to acquire more of life, more of what vanishes, more of my own (im)mortality; will remember what I cannot remember with Kodak pictures. I will win this game of clocks, fair and square. I have more life in me (we) than you think.

My wanting a baby, oddly enough, has little to do with my spouse, an intellectual, who consequently believes himself to be in control of his reproductive impulses. While Daniel appreciates and supports my ambition to excel in my career (the plastic arts) — having the same greed for success, material and, otherwise, the same longing to belong to this world (all we may have) — he simply cannot understand why I, having once vowed motherhood was out of place in my life, now want to experience it. Daniel has become a bit of a stranger to me because of his reluctance to be a parent. What is not strange is my own animal body, impregnated with the ancient directive to reproduce its own kind. From fish to fowl, from fowl to foul. The problems begin to take shape.

"Why can't we have a baby?" I ask the fine arts professor for the *n*th time this year. An aggressive twenty-eight-year-old responding to her biological clock.

"Three years ago when you thought you were pregnant, you considered having an abortion. You blamed me for doing it to you."

"I remember."

Remembering: I was then only too ready to dismiss the so-called joys of motherhood. Children were reserved for uneducated women with no great aims in life, but my career in the arts was to launch me to the stars. Fame and fortune were to come and take care of me, pamper me with all the godly niceties life had to offer. I was the lady with a vocation, the mistress and master of her own. There was no other God, except that of the working woman: me-me-and-only-me.

Actually, the childless couple (ever so fashionable) did not end up having an unwanted pregnancy on their hands at the time. Our shared sense of destiny continued undisturbed.

"It's a woman's prerogative to change her mind. I've changed it," I state, automatically knowing his response.

"We can't afford to have a baby. We have a large mortgage to pay off; most of my income goes toward it. May I remind you that for the past five years of our marriage I've been supporting you. I'm well aware that you're a talented artist so I haven't complained much about it. But don't expect me now to support a third member of this family. I can't. I won't."

"You know I couldn't hold a full-time job and expect to paint too," I reply in my defense, all too aware my husband pays the bills in our household. The only things I pay for are my art supplies (and they cost an arm and a leg) and my clothes (direct from second-hand shops).

"Either you're a feminist who can deliver the goods on an equal footing with me or you're not. Unless you contribute to our household expenses, I will not participate in your new fantasy. Take your friend, Maria . . . Mary, the lawyer. She makes as much as her husband."

"Leave Mary out of it," I plead. But nothing doing. Mary is ever-present in my life: the successful career woman I ought to have been to have pleased my mother, my husband, society, myself.

"When we married you wanted reassurances from me that I wouldn't expect you to behave like a traditional Wop — have babies and keep house for me," the blond North American reminds the first generation Italian immigrant who ought to have taken to her bed a male chauvinist — like the great hero of our television ads, Mr. Clean — to have had her maternal needs fulfilled. Now there was a fellow who would have expected the self-fulfilling prophecy to come true: pregnant, barefoot and *one husband away from welfare*.

"You're being unfair," I complain, simply hating the idea of becoming yet another damsel in distress who has to rely on machismo to come to her (financial) rescue. My residency in the new land ought to have guaranteed I could become a North American heroine with my own version of happily-ever-after (rich by my own efforts).

"Really the problem with you is that you're a Wop. No other woman would be so obsessed with having a baby, certainly not in this day and age."

"It's normal to want one. It's a primeval need. Every living species reproduces. Such basic biological functions are not defined by one's country of origin. I am no different from a Swedish woman, a Mexican, or anybody else."

"From what I read on the subject Italian culture still adheres to *motherolotry*, venerating mothers for their nurturing capacities. It sanctifies their role, giving them special status because of it, endowing them with a "clear sense of purpose." Yet most Italians dismiss women's other roles in society, downright restricting them to the home. It seemed to me that you married me precisely because I offered you an alternative."

"I understand . . . " But my body insists I am the heroine, and he, the villain, in this argument.

"Have you ever considered what I want?" the forty year old inquires, hurt. "I want to travel. Next year I want to go to Africa. I teach a course in African art. I've never even been there. It's inexcusable. Do you want to come with me?"

"We can't afford it."

"I'll take a loan."

"You'll take a loan to hunt down bushmen, but you won't have a baby with me because it's too expensive. Talk about priorities."

Upset, I start to cry. Daniel thinks I am doing so because of his opposition to having a child. But I know the truth of the matter. Ms Nina DiFiore — the independent woman who had kept her maiden name because of her feminist aspirations — has become a geisha girl to earn her keep when she ought to have become a doctor or a lawyer or something of the (executive) sort. She allows her (malevolent?) client to pay her off (partly in insults). He gives her food and shelter and she, in return, gives him the opportunity to brag about it. She wonders if she should serve him with an ultimatum next time he begs special services from her. She knows her client is as dependent on her services as she is on his pay check.

"Nina," Daniel pronounces my name with affection. "If and when I get tenure I'll reconsider."

It is an offer of reconciliation.

"It's impossible to get tenure. The university is cutting back on staff. You know it."

"If I can manage to finish my book and get it published, then I might have a better chance at it. *Sì?*"

The geisha girl smiles, calculating just how much her benevolent master-in-training has sacrificed to please her.

I see no evidence that Daniel will pick up his pen and write his book. He does everything else except dig out his old Ph.D. thesis on the Group of Seven and begin his personal contribution to Canadian art history. The good-looking prof claims he has too many papers to correct, too many lectures to prepare, too many students to pamper with his concern. But he does find time to read spy novels, see horror movies, and play the games usually reserved for members of private clubs.

"When are you going to write your book?"

"If you're in such a hurry for me to write it, why don't you spend less time painting and more time doing my household chores? You could paint the bathroom just as well as I can. You only need to use a different kind of brush than the one you're used to."

He laughs. For some inexplicable reason the gap between his front teeth reminds me of a doll I once owned. I threw it off my balcony one day after Mother had caught me drawing pictures of male genitals. She had made the sign of the cross and declared someone had given me *malocchio* — the evil eye. She attempted to remove the curse by using a primitive pagan-christian ritual. She poured water into a bowl, added oil and then said a prayer. It had no effect. I continued drawing the obscene.

"If I paint the bathroom for you, will you start your book? And if you start your book can we start our family in the not too far distant future?"

He shrugs his shoulders, waving a heating bill.

One of my aunts had asked me at my wedding (as Italian peasant tradition seemed to stipulate): "When are you going to *buy* your baby?"

At the time the use of the word *buy* had irritated me, as much as the question itself. Now, I realize just what a sage she was.

How ironic — when I was a teenager, I had vowed to my mother that I would never have children, that I would remain single. I used to believe that I was perfectly equipped to deal with the world by myself. I felt contemptuous of those who could not. It seemed a mark of weakness to want a mate. To be strong and free, one could not be fooled by love, give in to sentiment, or to social pressure.

I was prepared to be a revolutionary, a modern woman . . . wonderfully single. And I was not going to be lonely because I was destined to become a great artist with an array of lovers, someone who was not going to engage in a middle-class existence or flirt with psychological suicide: the humdrum.

Something happened to this *zingara* (gypsy) or, worse yet, the *putana* (whore) — mother's interpretation of the North American in me. While the lovers proved themselves adequate in college, later the change in bodies irritated me, as did the change in scenery: Montreal, Winnipeg, Vancouver.

I mellowed. True love and time will do it to almost everyone. I rationalized it by believing that the world was meaner than I had expected. I needed an army. I would enrol my husband in my services, in my unit. We were both out to win the best life had to offer: each other, comfort, art, freedom. I even came to like the word *husband*. It sounded better than any other word I knew. It was more familiar, more intoxicating than the name of a wild animal or flower — if only because almost a quarter of a century had passed me by.

Circa the fifth wedding anniversary — the present — we seem to have exhausted each other's stories, our pasts, our idiosyncrasies. We know everything: what to say, what not to say, and how to say the former to avoid a "real" fight. We are both creative — we like to avoid pain. We are mature — not old, mind you — just out of place with youngsters (at discos).

I need to add something new to my life now — an adventure. An exhausting trip out of the country will not do. Jet lag. Nor will sex do the trick. Orgasms are easy.

I suppose wanting to conceive has nothing particularly adventurous or spectacular about it. It may even be less spectacular than a near suicide who fantasizes about jumping off a bridge, in tails, and then does it. But pregnancy has nothing to do with such madness. Or has it?

I can smell my own death approaching and do nothing to stop it. Except I can re-create (a self, myself, unselfish). A baby will build up my self-confidence; my emotional data bank. Keep me sane.

Frankly, I need this baby much more than it will ever need me. Widowers re-marry, employers re-employ and taxes are paid by somebody else. It alone can provide me with the convincing illusion that I am irreplaceable in this life. My husband's love, once all-encompassing, cannot do it any more. I need a baby to improve our marriage, to emphasize the fact that he and I are bound in some very physical way and not just by the mystical force of love and law.

There have been enough discussions about the pros and cons of having a baby: cons, his; pros, mine. On/off fights. Yes. No. Please. I have had more than a year of it. No more, thank you. I have had my IUD removed.

Like someone who aspires to create a new country out of an old one, I need to use illicit methods for my dream to come true. Daniel is unaware my being made pregnant is more important to me than physical pleasure; he is unaware of my willingness to be invaded by something I know nothing about, and I am glad of it — for my baby, the peacemaker.

Each time I wonder: Suppose I were to conceive, would it break us apart? Would it be born a devilish-looking little thing . . . ? Nina, you are too old to worry about devils. Guilt.

Daniel is my best friend, the man who sometimes looks through the same telescope I do and remarks on how the heavens are ready for our conquest. We have had a history of war and peace, zooming in and out of emotional black holes, battling our own personal demons at times, other times battling each other. But more often than not, we have combined our forces to ensure that the peace our country now experiences can be used to our advantage. I believe my co-pilot will stand by me. He knows I appreciate the magic of his presence and not only of his currency.

For my journey to continue I need a family to make a fuss over me, instill me with the courage to accept life, to help me forget that one's minuscule space on earth may be no more important in the long run than the space inside a satellite that has ceased to function, ceased to be monitored or cared about — a piece of junk in an area without wind, water or fire. Love, after all, need not be so easily scrapped. It can update its physical apparatus. It can leap out and capture a new generation . . .

Hoping that in due course our son or daughter can look through any window or telescope and exclaim Wow, in praise for what the universe offers to those who take chances, who reach out to the final frontier — God, of course.

Marino Tuzi

Writing the Minority Subject

Fictional texts by Italian-Canadian writers enter the discourse on ethnicity by exploring the dilemmas of identity formation in a complex cultural topography. In these texts, the subject usually is situated precariously at the interstice of a new and evolving, urban-centred social order and an agrarian-based, albeit altered ethnic community. Italian Canadian identity is shaped by a given social context and is not represented as a unitary concept or cohesive reality. Beset by an array of adverse and often irreconcilable viewpoints, the ethnic protagonist fashions a self-image in relation to several competing belief systems.

The dramatization of the ethnic condition involves a persistent maneuvering among partial and incongruous cultural perspectives. The ethnic subject must constantly rethink his/her social positioning. The volatility of Italian-Canadianness is manifested in stares of anxiety, estrangement, and irresolution.

Such provisionality is compounded by the internal instability of both mainstream and Italian culture, since each cultural context is itself heterogeneous and mutable, and therefore not reducible to a discrete assortment of traits, values, and beliefs. The many connections between the two cultures are tentative because the Italian-Canadian subject continues to reposition himself/herself in a dynamic and pluralistic urban environment. There is a reluctance to commit oneself to values and assumptions that may circumscribe the various social contexts and which, ironically, provide a basis for self-definition.

Cultural dissonance, the presence of contradictory and transitory social stimuli, and the experience of alienation are manifested in the Italian-Canadian text in the form of a fragmented, multilayered, and largely undefinable ethnic identity. Attitudes associated with the social, class, and gender position of the protagonist in the minority group and in the mainstream community become part of the enactment of ethnic subjectivity. These positionings, as ways of making sense of the world, are brought into the text's characterization of the Italian-Canadian subject. Men and women are depicted as being formed by diverse cultural contexts which provide the "raw material" for self-development. The interactions between the Italian community and English-Canadian society imply that sometimes it is possible for the protagonist to negotiate some kind of provisional cultural identity; however, there often is no final resolution, because the content, shape, and direction of this new identity are mutable.

[. . .]

The social ground of the Italian-Canadian experience involves a process of transformation and contradiction. William Boelhower contends that in minority writing ethnicity in the host country "seems to generate the language of identity in the form of an endless production of questions." The questioning of dominant and ethnic group beliefs thwarts the development of a unitary ethnic identity: "the ethnic sign is not socially fixed or predictable because its very position within the culture of the national map makes it peremptorily unstable." Overtaken by such indeterminacy, the ethnic subject participates in a continual process of resignification: "the ethnic subject must inevitably define ethnicity as a means and not an end ... in the place of the real world [of the original culture] there is now only a global strategy of possible worlds."

Achievement of a stable sense of self remains a hypothetical enterprise since the Italian-Canadian is constantly choosing from and being shaped by an array of infinite and changeable subject positions. What is constituted as an identity is prone to dissolution.

The ethnic subject's interpretation of the relationship of the two cultural systems – which are alternately approachable, intangible, and remote – is based on the contingencies of the moment. The ethnic subject constructs a self-image in order to cope with the disorienting effects of cultural multiplicity. William Boelhower argues that "as a pluralized and multiform self, the ethnic's very instability as well as his access to an open series of possible worlds make him unpredictable and aleatory ... Because he [/she] is both inside and outside the dominant culture, his [/her] ethnic framing activity often becomes what surely must seem a contradictory strategy for producing ethnic discontinuity out of the very cultural continuum of the national map." The incompatibility of perspectives results in social discontinuity and makes evident the relativity and internal disjunctions of each cultural context.

What remains constant is that ethnicity, in reaction to the assimilative pressures of the new society, reforms itself without severing its ties to cultural history and genealogy. Ethnicity is always there in the life of the protagonist, however displaced, incongruent, and indeterminate it is. The salience of ethnicity in mainstream society is characterized by what Sneja Gunew refers to as "an insistence on the nontranslatability or incommensurability of cultural difference."

Italian-Canadian writing does not just address marginalization or cultural disjunction. Such a reading of ethnic literature is limiting. Ethnicity is perpetually unfolding, and it encompasses numerous discrepant and frequently overlaying cultural perspectives. Myrna Kostash notes that ethnicity abounds in contradiction and avoids any kind of fixity: "For my generation, however, the question has been posed again, and it has been posed not as a polarized conflict between the either/or assimilation and ghettoization but as the postmodern realization that we ethnic *arrivistes* live in both conditions at once. The point, suddenly, is not [Gabrielle] Roy's dream of the reconciliation of opposites but the acceptance, even cultivation, of what [Eli] Mandel has called the 'interface' of cultures . . . where tension at the point of contact, ambivalence, ambiguity, porousness, is the point, not resolution — the transcendence of paradox, stasis — as has been implied in the older dream." The reorganization of identities and the criss-crossing of dissimilar cultural signifiers announce a "process of becoming" in which a consolidation of perspective is perennially forestalled.

According to Frank Paci, the development of a new consciousness can be uncertain because it issues out of a "dialectic of historical change." Antonio D'Alfonso promotes a view of ethnicity which speaks of continuous effort and multiplicity: "Struggle is the force behind the process of identity which manifests itself in different ways." Citing the poetry of Filippo Salvatore, D'Alfonso observes a "never-ending search betweenthe natural and the cultural, the Old and New World, between the past and present." Italian-Canadianness is many-sided because it interlocks various perspectives in the host country, and because the place of origin is itself composed of various regions and localities which resist cultural homogenization: "Italy is not a unity but a mosaic. Italians are seen not as a group but as individuals with distinct identities."

For William Boelhower, ethnic writing is founded on the idea that identity is engaged in a constant play of subject-positions: "Given the copresence of cultural models and the principle of reversibility deriving from it, the ethnic subject is able to carry out his/her jeu of ambivalence, [to] break out of the unidirectionality of official cultural discourse ... Such a practice of ethnic interrogation as this, and one finds it operating throughout the collection of *Roman Candles*, refuses to reduce the order of discourse to a single meaning, a single code or cultural model, and prefers instead a strategy of perspectival ambiguity."

[. . .]

The Italian-Canadian woman's experience in the Italian family and Canadian society has been one of friction and disjunction. This situation is manifested in various forms in Maria Ardizzi's *Made in Italy*, Caterina Edwards' *The Lion's Mouth*, and Darlene Madott's *Bottled Roses*. In *Made in Italy*, the female protagonist fashions a gender identity from two patriarchal frameworks — Italian and Canadian — which are in themselves inconsistent and precarious. Interaction with mainstream society, primarily through work, provides her with a degree of financial and social autonomy which frustrates her husband's attempts to regulate her behaviour. The moment of emancipation is countered by her socioeconomic disenfranchisement in the host country as a woman and as an ethnic person. Inequality strengthens the bond with her family and reaffirms traditional attitudes about the woman's role in the immigrant community. Intergenerational discord, resulting from her children's assumption of mainstream values, subverts her role in the home. In *The Lion's Mouth* and *Bottled Roses*, this ambivalence is manifested, respectively, by second and third generation protagonists who have a deeper connection to the mainstream. Commitment to one cultural position is not possible without limiting available options and without denying critical parts of a multiple gender/ethnic identity. The female subject inhabits, is distanced from, and is suspended between contentious and intertwining cultural contexts.

The Italian community and Canadian society provide various models of femininity which reinforce or undermine each other: the common valorizing of being a wife and motherhood, and urban society's promotion of social and economic independence to the detriment of a group identity.

Feminine Italian-Canadian identity is many-sided and disjunctive since it is affected by different social and cultural variables. Italian-Canadian femininity is socially produced and continually revising itself in unstable circumstances. On the level of fictional representation, Italian-Canadian women writers, as is the case with their American counterparts (according to Mary Jo Bona) "have recreated their ethnicity to accommodate the changing needs of women."

Italian-Canadian texts by women and men also suggest that traditional Italian masculinity is devalued in an urban-technological environment where the man experiences a loss of status. Likewise, the male must to some degree share power with his female counterpart in order to anchor himself in the host country. Despite this, the male maintains a privileged position in the household, while the patriarchal mindset of the dominant culture reinforces his masculine identity.

Like fictional texts which focus on the male protagonist, the narrative of the Italian-Canadian woman, nevertheless, is characterized by a conflict of allegiances and points to a multiple gender/ethnic identity. Helen Barolini's view of Italian-American women's writing is equally applicable to this study. She asserts that this kind of feminine narrative "exposes the signs and symbols, the auguries and directions of lives which were – and are – subject to great ambivalence, to . . . opposing cultural influence."

Works Cited

Maria Ardizzi, *Made in Italy,* 1982.
Helen Barolini, *The Dream Book,* 1985.
William Boelhower, *Through a Glass Darkly*, 1984.
Mary Jo Bona, *The Voices We Carry,* 1994.
Antonio D'Alfonso, *In Italics,* 1996.
Caterina Edwards, *The Lion's Mouth*, 1993.
Sneja Gunew, *Framing Marginality*, 1994.
Myrna Kostash, "Pens of Many Colours," *The Canadian Forum* (June, 1990).
Darlene Madott, *Bottled Roses, 1985.*
Frank Paci, "Interview with C.D. Minni," *Canadian Literature* 106 (1985).

BIOGRAPHIES

George Amabile was born in Jersey City, U.S.A. of Italian parents and has lived much of his life in Winnipeg, where he is as a professor at the University of Manitoba. His books of poetry include *Blood Ties* (1972), *Open Country* (1976), *Flower and Song* (1977), *Ideas of Shelter* (1981), *Presence of Fire* (1982) and *Rumours of Paradise, Rumours of War* (1995).

Alexandre L. Amprimoz was born in Rome and attended universities in France and Canada earning a Ph.D. at the University of Western Ontario. He has taught French literature at the University of Manitoba and Brock University. In addition to literary studies he has published many books of French and English poetry including: *Chant solaire suivi de Vers de logocentre* (1978), *Selected Poems* (1979), *Changements de ton* (1981), *Fragments of Dreams* (1982), *Conseils au suicides* (1983) and *Bouquet de signes* (1986), and collections of short stories: *In Rome* (1980), *Hard Confessions* (1987) and *Too Many Popes* (1993).

Maria J. De Domenicis Ardizzi was born in Leognano (Teramo), Italy. After she finished her studies in Rome she moved to Toronto, Canada, in 1954. Her first novel, *Made in Italy* (1982), won the Ontario Arts Prize and was published in English with the same title. Ardizzi's second Italian novel, *Il Sapore Agro della Mia Terra* (1984) was followed by *La Buona America* (1987). This cycle of immigration novels was completed with *Tra le colline e di la dal mare* (1990) from which the above sketch is taken. In 1985 she brought out *Coversazione col figlio*, a bilingual collection of her poems dedicated to her son, Paolo, who died of Leukemia at twenty years of age.

Rosanna Battigelli was born in Camini (Reggio Calabria), Italy, and emigrated to Canada when she was three. She graduated with a double B.A. in Italian and French from Laurentian University in Sudbury, Ontario, a B.Ed. from Nipissing University in North Bay, Ontario, and has taught children in Kindergarten to Grade 8. She has published a children's book called *The Enchanted Christmas* and is currently working on adult novel entitled *Crossroads*. She lives in Lively, Ontario, with her husband Nic and children Sarah, Jordan and Nathan.

Tiziana Beccarelli Saad was born in Como, Italy, and emigrated to Canada after some years in France. She grew up in Montreal and has a French education with degrees from the University of Montreal. Her French fiction include: *Les Passantes* (1986), *Les Mensonges blancs* (1992) and *Vers l'Amerique* (1988). In 1991 she published a novella for young readers, *Portraits de Famille.* The above excerpt comes from *Vers l'Amerique*.

Anthony M. Buzzelli was born in Gagliano Aterno, Abruzzi, Italy, and came to Canada when he was six. He grew up in Hamilton, Ontario, where he earned his B.A. and M.A. from McMaster University. He is currently Head of the English Department at Aquinas Secondary School in Oakville, west of Toronto. He has published stories in a variety of journals and has two books in print: *The Immigrant's Prayer/La Preghiera dell'Immigrante* (1994) and *Evil Eye and Other Short Stories* (1995).

Born in Rome in 1612, Francesco Giuseppe Bressani eventually joined the Jesuit Order and spent the years 1642 to 1650 as a missionary in New France. He was captured and tortured by an Iroquois band which sold him to Dutch settlers in New York who helped him get back to Europe. In Macerata, Italy, Fr. Bressani wrote and published his *Breve Relatione* in Italian. This document became part of volumes 38, 39 and 40 of the *Jesuit Relations*, the only part of this great chronicle that is in Italian. In the brief passages translated here Bressani explains why he decided to write his account in Italian and then describes the land and First people of Canada. We notice that his terms of reference are European and that his comparisons are sometimes with Italy. These are Fr. Bressani's words from 1653, the first Italian words published about Canada.

Fulvio Caccia was born in Florence, Italy, and moved to Canada in 1959. He attended French college and university in Montreal and went on to work as a writer, editor and journalist for a number of periodicals: *Vice Versa, Moebius, Le Devoir, La Presse, Le Monde diplomatique, Liberation* and *Glebehebdo.* He edited *Sous le signe de Phenix* (1985); with Antonio D'Alfonso he co-edited *Quêtes:Textes d'auteurs italo-québécois*(1983); with J-M Lacroix he co-edited *Métamorphoses d'une utopie* (1992), and edited *Atlantis: Poètes du Québec et d'Irlande* (1994). This own books of poetry include: *Irpinia* (1983), *Scirocco* (1985) and *Aknos* (1994) which won the Governor General's Award for

French poetry. The narrative "1989" comes from his collection of French short stories, *Golden Eighties* (Editions Balzac, 1994). He has published literary essays in *Canadian Literature* 106 (1985), *Writers in Transition* (1990), and the important statement, "The Italian Writer and Language," in *Contrasts: Comparative Essays on Italian-Canadian Writing* (1985 and 1991).

Caro Cantasano is the pen-name for Francis Macri and appeared as one of the original seventeen poets in Di Cicco's *Roman Candles* (1978). He was born in Toronto of Calabrian parents and lived for many years in Edmonton, Alberta, where he earned a Ph.D. in Comparative Literature and Law degrees at the U. of A. He has published studies in Canadian and Quebec literatures.

Carmine Coppola was born in Pompeii, Italy, in 1953 and has lived in Winnipeg, Manitoba, since 1991. He studied Geology at the University of Napoli and is now a producer at CKJS radio in Winnipeg. The above poem comes from his bilingual collection of poems, *Poesie per Giulia* (1996).

Giovanni Costa was born in Vizzini, Sicily, the same area as Giovanni Verga, and now teaches Italian language and literature at Laval University, Quebec City. Costa's first collection of poems, *Impressioni di terre amiche* (1989), is in Italian only, while his second volume, *Parlami di stelle, Fammi sognare* (1994), is bilingual with English translations by poet, Robert McBryde.

Antonio D'Alfonso was born in Montreal of parents from Guglionesi (Molise), Italy. He studied in both English and French schools and earned an M.A. from the Université de Montréal. In 1979 he founded Guernica Editions. His first book was published in 1973, *La Chanson du Shaman à Sedna.* He has edited several anthologies including: *Quêtes* (1983) and *Voix Off* (1985). His own books include work in French and English: *Queror* (1979), *Black Tongue* (1983), *The Other Shore* (1986), *L'autre rivage* (1987), *Avril ou l'anti-passion* (1990), *Fabrizio's Passion* (1995) and *In Italics: In Defense of Ethnicity* (1996). The prose-poems included here are from *The Other Shore.*

Carole David was born in Montreal of an Italian mother (née Fioramore) and a Québécois father. She has taught in the colleges and the universities of Montreal and collaborated on a number of literary journals: *Spirale, Livres et auteurs québécois* and *NBJ*. She has travelled in Italy and written about her background. Her books include: *Terror-*

istes d'amour, poésie (1986), which won her the Émile-Nelligan Award, *Feu vers l'est, poésie* (1992), *L'endroit où se trouve ton âme, récits* (1991) and *Impala* (1994). The above excerpt is from the English version of *Impala* published in 1997.

Marisa De Franceschi was born in Muris di Ragogna (Udine), Italy, and came to Canada in 1948. She grew up in Windsor, Ontario, has degrees from the University of Windsor and has taught school for a number of years. Her short stories have twice won the Okanagan Short Story Award and have appeared in *Ricordi* (1989), *Pure Fiction* (1986), and *Investigating Women* (1995). She has published a novel, *Surface Tension* (1994) and edited an anthology of women's writing entitled, *Pillars of Satin: The Anthology of Italian-Canadian Women Writers* (1998).

Fiorella De Luca Calce was born in Caserta (near Naples), Italy, in 1963, and emigrated to Montreal with her family at age four. She published her first story in *Ricordi* (1989) ed. C.D. Minni and has produced two novels, *Toni* (1990), and *Vinnie and Me* (1996). Toni was published by Women's Press in the U.K. under the title *It's a Bloody Girl* (1991). Both novels have sold very well and have been published in French translations.

Anna Pia De Luca was born in Italy and as a child emigrated to Canada with her family. After finishing degrees at the University of Toronto she met and married an Italian and returned to live in Friuli. She now teaches English and Canadian literature a the University of Udine and has supervised theses on Italian-Canadian writers. Anna has produced an important translation, Leicht's *A History of Friuli* (1988), and has published articles on Canadian literature in North American and European journals.

Delia De Santis was born in Italy and came to Canada as a child in 1957. She lives in Brights Grove near Sarnia, Ontario. Her short stories have won awards and have appeared in literary magazines in Canada, the U.K. and the U.S. including *Green's Magazine*, *Zymergy*, *The First Person, The Pink Chameleon, Pleiades, Nutshell Quarterly*, *The Prairie Journal,* and the anthology, *Sands of Huron* (1990).

Pier Giorgio Di Cicco was born in Arezzo, Italy, in 1949, and raised in Montreal, Baltimore, Toronto. In 1978 he edited *Roman Candles* an anthology of Italian-Canadian poets which marked the beginning of the recognition of this ethnic minority writing as a body of literature. As a prolific poet in his own right Pier Giorgio produced more that twelve books of poems including: *We Are the Light Turning* (1976), *A Burning Patience* (1978), *Flying Deeper into the Century* (1982), *Post-Sixties Nocturne* (1985) and *Virgin Science* (1986). The four poems reprinted here are from his most popular collection, *The Tough Romance* (1979) which was also translated into French as *Les amours difficiles* (1990). In 1993 Giorgio became a Roman Catholic priest in Toronto.

Mary di Michele was born in Lanciano (Abruzzi), Italy, and grew up in Toronto. She has earned degrees from the University of Toronto and the University of Windsor, and now teaches at Concordia University in Montreal. The subject of several critical studies her poem collections include: *Mimosa and Other Poems* (1981), *Necessary Sugar* (1984), *Immune to Gravity* (1986), *Luminous Emergencies* (1990), and the novel, *Under My Skin* (1994). The Rilke poem and "Life Is Theatre" can be found in *Stranger in You* (Oxford U.P.,1995).

Journalist and writer Mario Duliani came to Canada in 1936 to work for *La Presse,* the Montreal newspaper. Duliani's plays were performed in Italy, France and later Canada. When the Second World War began Duliani was arrested and interned along with hundreds of other Italians. Italy was an ally of Germany until the collapse of the Fascist government in Rome in 1943. At this point Duliani and most other Italian internees were released. During his internment Duliani began to write an account of his experiences which was published in 1945 as *La ville sans femmes.* The Montreal publisher was Editions Pascal, the same press which released another novel of the war period in 1945, Gabrielle Roy's *Bonheur d'occasion* (*The Tin Flute*). Roy's first novel was advertised on the back cover of Duliani's book. In 1946 Duliani brought out *Città senza Donne,* the Italian version of his book. This book remained almost forgotten until Italian-Canadian writers began uncovering old copies of either the French or Italian editions. In 1994 Antonino Mazza published his English translation of Duliani's Italian edition as *The City Without Women.* Included here are the closing paragraphs from Mazza's translation.

Caterina Edwards was born in England to an English father and an Italian mother but grew up in Alberta. She has degrees from the University of Alberta where she has also taught creative writing. Her books include a novel, *The Lion's Mouth* (1982 and 1993), a play,

Homeground (1990), novellas, *A Whiter Shade of Pale, Becoming Emma* (1992) and an anthology of women's stories, *Eating Apples* (1994), which she co-edited with Kay Stewart. Her short stories have appeared in many literary magazines and anthologies including: *Ricordi* (1989), *Alberta ReBound* (1990) and *Boundless Alberta* (1993).

Joe Fiorito was born in Thunder Bay, Ontario, and now works as a journalist and freelance writer in Montreal. His columns for *The Montreal Gazette* and *Hour Magazine* have won awards. This collection of food essays, *Comfort Me With Apples* (1994) was followed by the equally successful book on working people, *Tango on the Main* (1996). "My Old Man" is from *Tango on the Main,* NuAge Editions.

Anna Foschi Ciampolini was born in Florence and moved to Canada in 1981. As the Coordinator of Cultural Activities at the Italian Cultural Centre in Vancouver she organized the first national conference of Italian-Canadian writers in 1986 with Dino Minni and Genni Donati Gunn. She has been editor of *L'Eco d'Italia*, and still contributes articles, reviews and interviews on Italian-Canadian writers and artists to this Vancouver Italian paper. She has co-edited *Emigrante* (1985), a collection of Italian pioneer biographies, and edited with Dino Minni *Writers in Transition* (1990).

Marco Fraticelli is a poet living in Montreal who has published his Haiku poems all over the world. He is editor and publisher of the literary magazine, *The Alchemist*. His books include *Instants* (1979), *Night Coach* (1983) and *Voyeur* (1992).

One of the early writers from the 1950s period was Gianni Grohovaz, a journalist and poet who came to Canada as a displaced person and began to work on railway construction in northern Ontario. Grohovaz was from Fiume, a city in Istria, a north eastern region of Italy which became part of the Yugoslavian Republic of Croatia after the end of the Second World War. Grohovaz and many other Italians of Istria were left without a country. His early experiences in Canada are captured in his posthumously published autobiographical narrative, *Strada Bianca* (1989). In the Toronto area Grohovaz is best known as a journalist who wrote for many Italian language papers. In 1953 he participated in the founding of *Corriere Canadese*, the major Italian paper in Canada. He was also active as a broadcaster and his social and political commentary are collected in his book, *E con rispetto parlando e al microfono Gianni Grohovaz* (1983). For Italian-Canadian writers

Gianni Grohovaz is best known for his Italian poetry collected in two slim volumes. In his first collection, *Per ricordar le cose che ricordo* (1974) we find the above poem in Fiuman dialect expressing the reasons why he is compelled to write.

Linda Hutcheon was born in Toronto the daughter and granddaughter of Italian immigrants. She earned a Ph. D. in Comparative Literature from the University of Toronto where she is teaching. She is the author of many studies on literary theory and a major cultural critic in North America. Her books include: *Narcissistic Narrative* (1980), *A Theory of Parody* (1985), *The Canadian Postmodern* (1988), *The Politics of Postmodernism* (1989), *Irony's Edge: The Theory and Politics of Irony* (1994) and *Opera: Desire, Disease, Death* (1996) written with Michael Hutcheon. In 1990 she edited, with Marion Richmond, *Other Solitudes: Canadian Multicultural Fictions*, an important anthology of ethnic minority writing. A different version of the above piece was given at the MLA meeting in December, 1995 and published in *Profession 96*.

Liborio Lattoni was born in Urbisaglia (Macerata) Italy in 1874. He studied at the universities of Florence, Bologna, Neufchatel, Macerata and Montreal. He married Ada Lombardi of Florence and emigrated to Canada in 1908. For many years he was a United Church minister in Montreal where he wrote a good deal of Italian poetry which appeared in Italian language papers. In 1935 three of his poems, in English translation, were included in the multicultural anthology, *Canadian Overtones*, edited by Watson Kirkconnell in Winnipeg. Lattoni has poems dedicated to Mount Royal and to Timagami as well as to Garibaldi and Italian church bells.

Carmen Laurenza Ziolkowski was born in Italy as Carmen Laurenza. In the early 1950s she lived in England where she worked as a registered nurse. After she came to Canada she studied journalism at Wayne State University, Detroit, and became an active writer in Sarnia, Ontario. Her prose, poetry and drama have been published in magazines in Canada, Italy, the U.S.A. and England and in anthologies including: *Flare-Up* (1983), *Sands of Huron* (1990) and *Voices of the Rapids*. Her books include poetry, *Roses Bloom at Dusk* (1976), *World of Dreams* (1995), and a novel, *House of the Four Winds* (1987). The above fable captures very well the Italian folklore which lies behind many of the narratives by Italian-Canadian authors and filmmakers. This is also illustrated in Paul Tana's film *Sarrasine*.

Darlene Madott was born in Toronto. After her first university degree she worked as an editor with *Saturday Night* magazine, and later for *Toronto Life* magazine. She published short stories in periodicals across Canada and brought out her first novel, *Song of Silence*, in 1978. She then studied law. Her collection of short stories, *Bottled Roses* (Oberon, 1985), includes narratives which reflect the oral story telling traditions of her Italian grandparents. She practices law and continues to write having finished a screen play for a film, *Mazilli Shoes*.

Joseph Maviglia is a Toronto poet and song writer. His books include *Movie Town* (1989) and *A God Hangs Upside Down* (Guernica, 1994).

Antonino Mazza was born in Reggio (Calabria), Italy, and grew up in Ottawa. He has studied at Carleton University, Scuola Normale Superiore in Pisa and the University of Toronto and has taught at the University of Ottawa and at Queen's University, Kingston. His poems, essays and literary translations have appeared in magazines like *Anthos, Vice Versa* and *Gamut International.* In addition to his poetry book, *The Way I Remember It* (Guernica, 1992), he has published translations of Pier Paolo Pasolini which won the 1992 Italo Calvino Prize from Columbia University, and translations of Eugenio Montale and his English version of Mario Duliani's *The City Without Women* (1994). "Echoes in the Garden" first appeared in *AirWave Dreamscapes,* edited by Tim McLaughlin and Robin, London: Egro Productions, 1990.

Mary Melfi was born in Campobasso, Italy, and came to Canada in 1956. After completing her studies in universities in Montreal she began writing and has published many books in a variety of genres: *A Queen is Holding a Mummified Cat* (Guernica, 1982), *A Bride in Three Acts* (Guernica, 1983), *A Dialogue with Masks* (1985), *Ubu, The Witch Who Would Be Rich*, juvenile (Doubleday, 1994), *Infertility Rites* (Guernica, 1991), and *Stages: Selected Poems* (Guernica, 1998). "Wanting a Baby" is from *Infertility Rites*.

Dôre Michelut is the Friulan name for Dorina Michelutti who was born in Italy, grew up in Ontario and in 1972 returned to Italy to study. Dôre Michelut has also lived for many years in Southern Alberta and says the mountains remind her of Friuli. Her books include *Loyalty to the Hunt* (Guernica, 1986), *Ouroboros: The Book That Ate*

Me (Trois, 1990), *Linked Alive* (Trois, 1990), a series of renga poems with Anne-Marie Alonzo and friends, and *A Furlan Harvest* (Trois, 1993), which she edited. Her essay, "Coming to Terms with the Mother Tongue," appeared in *Tessera*, 6 (1989). The above prose poems which use words from the Friulan language are from *Loyalty to the Hunt*.

Marco Micone was born in Montelongo, Italy, and emigrated to Canada with his family in 1958. His education includes an M.A. in French theatre from the Université de Montréal. His plays include: *Gens du silence* (1982; Guernica, 1991), *Voiceless People* (Guernica, 1984), *Addolorata* (French, Guernica, 1984), *Addolorata* (English, Guernica, 1988), *Déjà l'agonie* (L'Hexagone, 1988), trans. *Beyond the Ruins* (Guernica, 1995). His book of essays and narratives, *Le figuier enchanté,* appeared in 1992. The success of Micone's original plays has been matched by his award-winning French translations of plays by Goldoni and Pirandello for Montreal theatres. In 1980 the first French play to deal with Italian immigrants in Montreal, *Gens du silence,* was staged by Marco Micone. It was published in English as *Voiceless People.* In this scene, Nancy, the daughter in the immigrant family explains to her brother, Gino, her frustration with their situation and her decision to finally leave home and the isolation of the immigrant ghetto, Chiuso.After the critical and popular success of *Gens du silence* Marco Micone produced a play which examined the condition of women in the Italian community. Micone called it, *Addolorata,* using the Italian name of the main character who has changed it to Lolita.

C. Dino Minni was born in 1942 in Bagnoli del Tigno, Isernia, Italy, and grew up in British Columbia where he worked as a writer, critic and editor for a number of periodicals such as *The Vancouver Sun* and *The Canadian Author & Bookman.* His own collection of short stories, *Other Selves* (Guernica, 1985), was followed by the fiction anthology, *Ricordi: Things Remembered* (Guernica, 1989) which he edited. In 1986, with the help of Anna Foschi and Genni Donati Gunn, he organized the first national conference of Italian-Canadian writers in Vancouver, and co-edited the proceedings with Anna Foschi, *Writers in Transition* (Guernica, 1990). Dino died in 1989 of Muscular Dystrophy, a disease with had confined him to a wheel chair since he was sixteen years old. The above story comes from *Other Selves.*

Michael Mirolla was born in the village of Ielsi, near Campobasso, Molise, Italy and came to Canada when he was five. He grew up in Montreal and earned a B.A. from McGill University and a Master's degree in Creative Writing from the University of British Columbia. His poems and short stories have been published in many journals in Canada, the U.S. and the U.K. including the *1992 Journey Prize Anthology* and *Tesseracts II*. He produced two plays: *Gargoyles*, performed in Vancouver and St. Catharines, and *Snails*, staged in Toronto and Vancouver. His collection of short stories, *The Formal Logic of Emotion* appeared in 1991.

Frank Paci was born near Pesaro in the Marche region of central Italy. He grew up in Sault St. Marie in Northern Ontario and went on to earn degrees from the University of Toronto and Carleton University in Ottawa. His first novel, *The Italians* (1978), was a Canadian bestseller and was also published in French, *La Famille Gaetano* (Guernica, 1990). The second novel, *Black Madonna* (1982), was a critical success and is still read in literature courses. His other novels include: *The Father* (1984), *Black Blood* (1991), *Under the Bridge* (1992), *Sex and Character* (1993) and *The Rooming-House* (1996). His work has been included in many anthologies and his critical essay, "Tasks of the Canadian Novelist Writing on Immigrant Themes," appeared in *Contrasts* (Guernica, 1985 and 1991). The above excerpt is an early version of a scene from *Black Blood,* Oberon Press.

Gianna Patriarca was born in Ceprano (Frosinone), Italy, and came to Canada in 1960 with her mother and sister to join her father who had emigrated in 1956. For the past thirty years she has lived in Toronto and teaches for the Metro Separate School Board. She earned a B.A. and B.Ed. from York University. Her book of poetry, *Italian Women and Other Tragedies* (Guernica, 1994), was a critical and popular success, and the above poems are from this volume. The story comes from her second book, *Daughters for Sale* (Guernica, 1997).

Romano Perticarini was born in Fermo, Italy, and emigrated to Vancouver in 1967. His first book of poems, *Quelli della fionda / The Sling-Shot Kids* (1981), was bilingual as was the second volume, *Il mio quaderno di Novembre / From My November Record Book* (1983). The above poem comes from his third book, *Via Diaz* (Guernica, 1989). He has published his poems in Italian periodicals and won awards in Italy.

Penny Petrone was born Serafina Petrone in Thunder Bay in Northern Ontario where she grew up and eventually taught school for many years. She later earned a Ph.D. in English from the University of Alberta and then taught at Lakehead University. She is a pioneer in the academic study of Native literature in Canada with the books she edited: *First People, First Voices* (1983), *Northern Voices: Inuit Writing in English* (1988) and *Native Literature in Canada: From the Oral Tradition to the Present* (1990). The sketch, "Mamma," comes from her memoir of growing up in an Italian-Canadian home, *Breaking the Mould* (Guernica, 1995).

Concetta Principe is a Toronto writer. Her novel, *Stained Glass,* was published by Guernica in 1997.

Bruno Ramirez was born in Asmara, Eritrea, of Italian parents. After moving to Canada he earned university degrees and now teaches history at the Université de Montréal. He has published several books on the history of Italian settlement in Canada including *The Italians of Montreal* (1980) with M. Del Balso, *Les permiers Italiens de Montréal* (1983) and *On the Move: French-Canadian and Italian Migration in the North Atlantic Economy* (1991).

Joseph Ranallo was born in Vinchiaturo (Molise), Italy, and moved to Canada in 1952. He earned a B.A. from the University of Victoria and an M.A. from Washington State University. He is one of the original seventeen poets from *Roman Candles* (1978), edited by Pier Giorgio Di Cicco. His poems have been included in literary magazines and anthologies. In recent years he has been teaching in the University of British Columbia West Kootenay Teacher Education Program based at Selkirk College in Castlegar, B.C. He has also taught English and Creative Writing for Selkirk College.

The first woman writer of Italian origin in Canada was Elena Randaccio who came from near Bologna, Italy. Using the pen-name Elena Albani she published *Canada mia seconda patria* in 1958. Under the name E. MacRan she brought out *Diario di una emigrante* in 1979 from which the brief scene above is translated. The narrator, Climene recalls the night on their farm near Montreal when the police came to arrest her husband, Beppe, at the beginning of the Second World War.

Nino Ricci was born in Lemington, Ontario, to parents from Molise, Italy. After earning a B.A. from York University he taught school in Nigeria for two years. He spent a year studying in Italy and earned an M.A. in Creative Writing from Concordia University. His articles and short stories have appeared in many magazines including: *Saturday Night*, *Alphabet City*, *Vice Versa*, and the *Eyetalian*. His novel, *Lives of the Saints* (1990) won the Governor General's Award for English Fiction, a number of other prizes and has been published in the U.K., the U.S.A. and translated into several languages. His second novel of this trilogy, *In a Glass House* (1993), is also a bestseller and is followed by *Where She Has Gone* (1997). The above story is from *Ricordi*, ed. C.D. Minni.

Filippo Salvatore was born in Guglionesi (Molise), Italy, in 1948 and emigrated to Canada in 1964. He has degrees from McGill University and Harvard, and now teaches Italian literature at Concordia University in Montreal. Filippo Salvatore is a trilingual writer as evidenced by his many books in Italian, French and English: *Tufo e Gramigna* (1977), *Suns of Darkness* (1980), *La Fresque de Mussolini* (1985), *Le Fascisme et les Italiens à Montreal* (1995), *Fascism and the Italians of Montreal* (1998), and *Scienza ed umanità* (1996). His famous literary essay, "The Italian Writer of Quebec: Language, Culture and Politics," was first printed in *Contrasts: Comparative Essays on Italian-Canadian Writing* (1985 and 1991). The poems included here are from *Suns of Darkness*.

Paul Tana was born in Ancona, Italy, and came to Canada in 1958. After studying a College Ste Marie and at UQAM be began working as a filmmaker and produced several films including *Les grandes enfants* (1979), *Deux contes de la rue Berri* (1975), *Caffè Italia, Montréal* (1985), a film on the Italians of Montreal, and *La Sarrasine* (1992).This film was both a critical and popular success and is now in video. Paul Tana and Bruno Ramirez wrote the screenplay for *La Sarrasine*, a film which Tana directed in 1992. Giuseppe Moschella, a tailor from Sicily, accidentally kills a French-Canadian during a fight in the street. After the trial he is sentenced to death. The scene is Montréal at the turn of this century. *Sarrasine* was translated into English by Robert Gray and published by Guernica in 1996.

Marino Tuzi was born in Italy, grew up in Toronto and earned a Ph.D. from York University with a thesis on Italian-Canadian novelists, the first Canadian doctoral thesis devoted entirely to this body of literature. He has given conference papers and published articles on ethnic minority writing. He has taught Canadian Literature at Seneca

College in Toronto. The essay, "Writing the Minority Subject" is made up of excerpts from his book, *The Power of Allegiances: Identity, Culture and Representational Strategies*, which appeared in 1997.

Pasquale Verdicchio was born in Naples, Italy, and came to Canada as a teenager. He has degrees from the University of Victoria, B.C., the University of Alberta and a Ph.D. from UCLA. His publications include literary studies of Italian and Italian-Canadian literature as well as translations of Antonio Porta, Giorgio Caproni, Alda Merini and Pasolini. His own books of poetry include: *Moving Landscape* (1985), *A Critical Geography* (1989), *Nomadic Trajectory* (1990), *Approaches to Absence* (1994), *Devils in Paradise,* essays on literature and film (1997), as well as two books on philosopher Antonio Gramsci.

Sante Arcangelo Viselli was born in Strangolagalli (Frosinone), Italy and came to Canada in 1969. He has studied in Canada and has a Doctorate in French literature from l'Université Paul Valéry in Montpellier, France. He has taught university in Newfoundland and is now a professor at the University of Winnipeg. He has published many studies on French literature and on Italian-Canadian writing in English and French. The poem, "Montpel(l)ier," is from his collection of French poems, *Le Pendule* (Rediscovery, 1993). Sante Viselli explains that the verse, "Sans L" is meant to suggest the wings of the bird and to symbolize those of the poet.

Liliane Welch was born and grew up in Luxembourg, and at nineteen emigrated to North America. She earned a B.A. and M.A. from the University of Montana, a Ph.D. from Pennsylvania State University and now teaches at Mount Allison University in New Brunswick. She has produced many books of poetry and prose including *October Winds* (1980), *Manstorna: Life on the Mountains* (1986), *Seismographs* (1988), *Life in Another Language* (1992), *Dream Museum* (1995). In the summers Liliane and her husband Cyril are in Italy mountain-climbing. These poems from *Word-House of a Grandchild* (1987) deal with her Italian grandfather.

Bianca Zagolin was born in Ampezzo (Friuli), Italy, spent her early childhood in Udine before emigrating to Canada when she was nine. She grew up in Montreal and went to French schools. After completing a B.A. in English, she earned a Ph.D. in French literature from McGill University. She teaches language, literature and translation at Vanier College in Montreal. She has published short stories, articles and a critical essay on novelist Marie-Clair Blais. The above excerpt is from her novel, *Une femme à la fenêtre* (Paris: Ed. Robert Laffont, 1988), which has been translated into English and Italian, *Una donna alla finestra,* Edizionzi del Noe Padova, 1998, The narrative cycle is completed in a second novel.

Selected Bibliography

For futher reading in the area of ethnic minority writing you can choose from among the books listed below. Many book titles are also listed in the biography of each writer.

Amabile, George. *Presence of Fire,* Toronto: McClelland and Stewart, 1982.

Amprimoz, Alexandre. *Hard Confessions*, Winnipeg: Turnstone Press, 1987.

Ardizzi, Maria. *Made in Italy,* Toronto: Toma Publishing, 1982.

Bagnell, Kenneth. *Canadese: A Portrait of the Italian Canadians,* Toronto: Macmillan, 1989.

Beccarelli Saad, Tiziana. *Vers l'Amerique,* Montreal: Triptyque, 1988.

Begamudre, Ven & J. Krause, eds. *Out of Place: Stories and Poems,* Regina: Coteau Books, 1991.

Birbalsingh, Frank, ed. *Jabaji Bhai: An Anthology of Indo-Caribean Literature.* Toronto: TSAR, 1987.

Black, Ayanna. Ed. *Fiery Spirits: Canadian Writers of African Descent*, Toronto: HarperCollins, 1994.

Borovilos, John, ed. *Breaking Through: A Canadian Literary Mosaic.* Toronto: Prenice-Hall, 1990.

Caccia, Fulvio. *Aknos and Other Poems.* Toronto: Guernica Editions, 1998.

Caccia, Fulvio. *Interviews with the Phoenix*, Toronto: Guernica, 1998.

Castrucci, Anello. *I miei lontani pascoli.* Montreal: Riviera,1984.

Clarke, George Elliott, ed. *Eyeing the North Star: Directions in African-Canadian Literature,Toronto:* McClelland and Stewart, 1997.

Costa, Giovanni. *Parlami di, Stelle Fammi sognare / Speak to me of stars, Let me dream*, 1994.

D'Alfonso, Antonio. *The Other Shore,* Montreal: Guernica, 1985.

D'Alfonso, Antonio. *Fabrizio's Passion*, Toronto: Guernica, 1995.

D'Alfonso, Antonio. *In Italics: In Defense of Ethnicity,* Toronto: Guernica, 1996.

D'Alfonso, Antonio, *L'apostrophe qui me scinde.* Montreal: Éditions du Noroît, 1998.

David, Carole. *Impala,* Toronto: Guernica, 1997.

De Franceschi, Marisa. *Surface Tension,* Toronto: Guernica, 1994.

De Luca Calce, Fiorella. *Toni,* Montreal: Guernica, 1990.

De Luca Calce, Fiorella. *Vinnie and Me*, Toronto: Guernica, 1996.

Di Cicco, Pier Giorgio, ed. *Roman Candles*, Toronto: Hounslow Press, 1978.

Di Cicco, Pier Giorgio. *The Tough Romance,* 2nd. edition. Toronto: Guernica, 1990.

Di Cicco, Pier Giorgio. *Virgin Science,* Toronto: McClelland & Stewart, 1986.

Di Giovanni, Caroline, ed. *Italian Canadian Voices: An Anthology of Poetry and Prose.* Oakville: Mosaic Press, 1984.

Di Michele, Mary. *Debriefing the Rose.* Toronto: Anansi, 1998.

Di Michele, Mary. *Mimosa and other poems,* Oakville: Mosaic Press, 1981.

Di Michele, Mary. *Stranger in You,* Toronto: Oxford U. P., 1995.

Di Michele, Mary. *Under My Skin,* Kingston: Quarry Press, 1994.

Edwards, Caterina. *The Lion's Mouth,* 2nd. edition. Toronto: Guernica, 1993.

Edwards, Caterina. *Homeground*, Montreal: Guernica, 1990.

Edwards, Caterina. *Whiter Shade of Pale, Becoming Emma,* Edmonton: NeWest Press, 1992.

Fiorito, Joe. *Tango on the Main,* Montreal: NuAge, 1996.

Fraticelli, Marco. *Voyeur,* Montreal: Guernica, 1992.

Gasparini. Len. *Ink from an Octopus*, Toronto: Hounslow Press, 1989.

Gunew, Sneja. *Framing Marginality: Multicultural Literary Studies,* Melbourne: Melbourne University Press, 1994.

Gunn, Genni. *Mating in Captivity,* Kingston: Quarry Press, 1993.

Harney, Robert F. Ed. *Gathering Place: Peoples and Neighbourhoods of Toronto,* Toronto: MHSO, 1985.

Hutcheon, Linda. *The Canadian Postmodern*, Toronto: Oxford U. P. 1988.

Hutcheon, Linda. *Irony's Edge: The Theory and Politics of Irony,* New York: Routledge, 1995.

Hutcheon, Linda and M. Richmond, eds. *Other Solitudes: Canadian Multicultural Fiction.* Toronto: Oxford U. P., 1990.

Iacovetta, Franca. *Such Hardworking People: Italian Immigrants in Postwar Toronto.* Montreal : McGill-Queen's U. P., 1992.

Kamboureli, Smaro, ed. *Making a Difference: Canadian Multicultural Literature,* Toronto: Oxford U. P., 1996.
Karpinski, Eva and I. Lea, ed. *Pens of Many Colours.* Toronto: Harcourt Brace, 1996.
King, Thomas, ed. *All My Relations: An Anthology of Contemporary Canadian Native Fiction,*Toronto: McClelland & Stewart, 1990.
Loriggio, Francesco, ed. *Social Pluralism and Literary History*, Toronto: Guernica, 1996.
Madott, Darlene. *Bottled Roses,* Ottawa: Oberon Press, 1985.
Mazza, Antonino. *The Way I Remember It,* Toronto: Guernica, 1992.
Melfi, Mary. *A Bride in Three Acts*, Montreal: Guernica, 1983.
Melfi, Mary. *Infertiltiy Rites*, Toronto: Guernica, 1991.
Melfi, Mary. *Stages: Selected Poems,* Toronto: Guernica, 1997.
Michelut, Dôre. *Loyalty to the Hunt*, Montreal: Guernica, 1986.
Michelut, Dôre. *Ouroboros: The Book that Ate Me,* Montreal: Éditions Trois, 1990.
Micone, Marco. *Two Plays,* Montreal: Guernica, 1988.
Micone, Marco. *Beyond the Ruins,* Toronto: Guernica, 1995.
Minni, C.D. *Other Selves,* Montreal: Guernica, 1985.
Minni, C.D., ed. *Ricordi: Things Remembered*, Montreal: Guernica, 1989.
Mirolla, Michael. *The Formal Logic of Emotion*, Montreal: NuAge Editions, 1991.
Norris, Ken. *Whirlwinds,* Montreal: Guernica, 1988.
Oliva, Peter. *Drowning in Darkness,* Dunvegan: Cormorant Books, 1993.
Paci, F.G. *Black Madonna,* Ottawa: Oberon Press, 1982.
Paci, F.G. *Under the Bridge*, Ottawa: Oberon Press, 1992.
Paci, F.G. *The Roming-House,* Ottawa: Oberon Press, 1996.
Patriarca, Gianna. *Italian Women and Other Tragedies*, Toronto: Guernica, 1994.
Patriarca, Gianna. *Daughters for Sale,* Toronto: Guernica, 1997.
Perin, Roberto and F. Sturino, eds. *Arrangiarsi: The Italian Immigration Experience in Canada,* Montreal: Guernica, 1989.
Perticarini, Romano. *Via Diaz*, Montreal: Guernica, 1989.
Petrone, Penny. *Breaking the Mould*, Toronto: Guernica, 1995.
Pivato, Joseph. *Echo: Essays on Other Literatures,* Toronto: Guernica, 1994.
Principe, Concetta. *Stained Glass,* Toronto: Guernica, 1997.
Ramirez, Bruno. *Les Premiers Italiens de Montréal,* Montreal: Boreal, 1984.

Razzolini, Esperanza Maria. *All Our Fathers: The North Italian Colony in Industrial Cape Breton,* Halifax: St. Mary's University, 1983.
Ricci, Nino. *Lives of the Saints,* Dunvegan: Cormorant Books, 1990.
Ricci, Nino. *In a Glass House,* Toronto: McClelland & Stewart, 1993.
Ricci, Nino. *Where She Has Gone,* Toronto: McClelland and Stewart, 1997.
Rossi, Vittorio. *Two Plays, Little Blood Brothers and Backstreets,* Montreal: NuAge, 1989.
Salvatore, Filippo. *Suns of Darkness,* Montreal: Guernica, 1980.
Salvatore, Filippo. *La Fresque de Mussolini,* Montreal : Guernica, 1985, 1991.
Salvatore, Filippo. *Fascism and the Italians of Montreal,* Toronto: Guernica, 1997.
Salvatore, Filippo & Anna Gural-Migdal. *Le Cinema de Paul Tana,* Montreal: Balzac, 1997.
Sturino, Franc. *Forging the Chain: Southern Italian Migration,* Toronto: MHSO, 1990
Tana, Paul and B. Ramirez. *Sarrasine,* Toronto: Guernica, 1996.
Tuzi, Marino. *The Power of Allegiances,* Toronto: Guernica, 1997.
Verdicchio, Pasquale. *Approaches to Absence*, Toronto: Guernica, 1994.
Verdicchio, Pasquale. *Nomadic Trajectory,* Montreal: Guernica, 1990.
Verdicchio, Pasquale, *Devils in Paradise,* Toronto: Guernica, 1997.
Viselli, Sante. *Le Pendule,* Edmonton: Rediscovery Press, 1993.
Welch, Liliane. *Manstorna: Life on the Mountains,*Charlottetown: Ragweed Press, 1985.
Welch, Liliane. *Word-House of a Grandchild,* Charlottetown: Ragweed Press, 1987.
Welch, Liliane. *Life In Another Language,* Dunvegan: Cormorant, 1992.
Welch, Liliane. *Fidelities, poems,* Ottawa: Borelais Press, 1997.
Zagolin, Bianca. *Une femme a la fenetre,* Paris: Robert Laffont, 1988.
Ziolkoski, Carmen L. *The House of Four Winds,* Sarnia: River City Press, 1987.

ACKNOWLEDGEMENTS

The editor and the publisher would like to thank the writers who contributed to this anthology and made it possible. Many of the texts included here have not been previously published. Some texts first appeared with various publishers. With the list below we wish to thank those publishers for supporting this project.

Liborio Lattoni, "Winter Night," The Columbia Press.

Mario Duliani, Antonino Mazza, Mosaic Press and the Estate of Mario Duliani.

Elena Randaccio, Tamari Editore, Bologna, Italy.

Maria Ardizzi, Toma Publishing and Guernica Editions.

Tiziana Beccarelli Saad, Éditions Triptyque.

Giovanni Costa, privately printed.

Dôre Michelut, "Coming to Terms with the Mother Tongue," *Tessera*.

Carole David, Les Herbes Rouges, Daniel Sloate, and Guernica Editions.

Liliane Welch, "His Last Visit," Ragweed Press.

Joe Fiorito, "My Old Man," NuAge Publishing.

Pasquale Verdicchio, "The Southern Question," Bordighera, Inc.

F. G. Paci, Oberon Press.

Fulvio Caccia, Éditions Balzac and Guernica Editions.

Sante Viselli, "Montpel(l)ier," Rediscovery Press.

Carmine Coppola, "Benevuta, Primavera," Winnipeg.

Alexandre Amprimoz, "Rome Afterwar," Hounslow Press.

Mary di Michele, "Passeggiata di sogno," Oxford U. Press.

Caro Cantasano, "Grandfathers Didn't," Hounslow Press.

Linda Hutcheon, the PMLA.

Bianca Zagolin, Éditions Robert Laffont.

The texts by the following writers were previously published by Guernica Editions: C.D. Minni, Gianna Patriarca, Pier Giorgio Di Cicco, Marisa De Franceschi, Marco Fraticelli, Filippo Salvatore, Antonio D'Alfonso, Pasquale Verdicchio (poems), Nino Ricci, Paul

Tana, Bruno Ramirez, Penny petrone, Concetta Principe, Joseph Maviglia, Marco Micone, Mary Melfi, Dôre Michelut (poems), Romano Perticarini, and Marino Tuzi.

On the Editor

The editor of this anthology, Joseph Pivato, was born near Bassano del Grappa in Italy. He grew up in Toronto and earned a B.A. from York University. His M.A. and Ph.D. from the University of Alberta are in Comparative Literature which he teaches at Athabasca University in Alberta. He has published many articles and given conference papers on ethnic minority writing. He edited *Contrasts: Comparative Essays on Italian-Canadian Writing* (1985 and 1991) and wrote *Echo: Essays on Other Literatures* (1994). His research website is http://www.athabascau.ca/html/depts/langlit/research/ethnic.htm

PRINTED AND BOUND
IN BOUCHERVILLE, QUEBEC, CANADA
BY MARC VEILLEUX IMPRIMEUR INC.
IN OCTOBER, 1998